ENDLESS FLIGHT

BENJAMIN ASHWOOD BOOK 2

AC COBBLE

Cobble Publishing LLC

CONTENTS

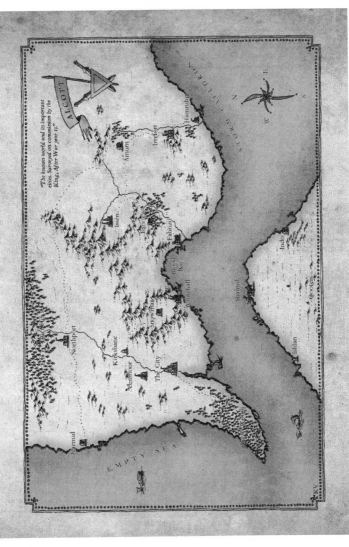

1

BETTER BE RUNNING

BEN WOKE UP. He was shirtless and his pants were damp. He ached from sleeping on a hard floor with no padding. He shifted and the chill autumn air slid over his bare skin, raising goose bumps and sending a shiver through his body.

He was lying in a small gazebo on the late Lord Reinhold's estate. In the madness of the night before, it seemed just as good a hiding spot as anywhere else.

Ben sat up and saw Mathias was also awake. The barkeep was peering over a railing into a foggy, grey morning. Mist drifted by the gazebo. The entire world was silent. The moisture enfolded them in a tight embrace.

Ben didn't like fog. He didn't like the lack of visibility. After the past year, he preferred to see where he was going.

Mathias was relaxed, though. Watching him, the tension drained from Ben's body. Mathias wouldn't be sitting so calmly if he felt there was a threat lurking out of sight.

Rolling to his feet, Ben wrapped his arms around his bare skin. He had been lying back to back with Amelie on the floor of the gazebo and the warmth from her quickly vanished.

Mathias turned when Ben rose and nodded a good morning.

Ben settled down next to the veteran. Stretching and rubbing his hands over his arms and shoulders to loosen up and keep warm, Ben nodded back.

"You think she's going to be ready to move this morning?" Mathias whispered, glancing at Amelie's sleeping form.

Ben shrugged. "She has to be."

Together, they stared out into the gloom.

A bell later, Amelie began to stir underneath Mathias' fleece-lined lambskin coat. She rolled over and saw Ben occupying the same position Mathias had when Ben woke.

"What's happening?" she called in a low voice.

Ben smiled down at her. "Good morning to you too."

She rolled her eyes and sat up.

"Mathias went back to the City," Ben explained quietly.

Amelie's eyes shot open.

"I don't know if that is a good idea," she protested. "The Sanctuary is going to be looking for us, looking hard. And if they find us, well, suffice to say I think we need to get away from the City as quickly as possible. If they catch him..." She left the rest unsaid.

Ben nodded. "He knows. We talked it over before he left. What else can we do? We threw half of our clothes into the river last night, and we have no food and no supplies. We need information before we start running in any direction."

Ben stood and began to pace across the small space in the gazebo. "They won't know Mathias was involved yet, we hope. He has the row boat and can tie up at one of the smaller docks, one where they won't have guards. He can slip in, gather supplies, contact our friends, and be back out before the mages even hear his name."

"They'll know more than you think and quicker," challenged Amelie. "We can't stay here long." She paused and then continued with a sigh, "But you're right. We have to get supplies and learn what we are up against."

"What do you think..." Ben swallowed nervously. "What do you think Meghan told them?"

Amelie sighed. "I don't know. Everything?"

She shifted around on the wooden floor. "Meghan was growing distant over the last several months. The only thing she thought about was studying, learning faster, and progressing to the next step. Anything they'd ask, she would do. Anything they told her, she would believe."

Ben frowned. "What kind of things?"

"Our instructors say the Sanctuary exists to serve the greater good," responded Amelie. "It's a compelling message, that we are part of something larger, something that is important. They suggest the more complicated history of the Sanctuary is because the mages were pursuing a worthwhile end, and it justified some questionable means. Maybe they really believe that, maybe they don't. I can say for sure though, Meghan believed it. She really thought she would do great things. Not just for the Sanctuary, but for all of Alcott."

Ben sat on the railing and kept listening.

"I think that is how the mages are able to accumulate so much power and never get challenged," continued Amelie. "They say it's to help everyone. It's easier to believe that they want to help than it is to challenge them. They have a lot of power, more than any individual lord does."

Amelie took a deep breath. "It's intoxicating, the first taste of power, and Meghan is on track to become one of the most powerful women in Alcott. That is something I don't think she ever imagined before. There are a lot of things people will over-look to achieve that. There are a lot of compromises along the way."

"It's just..." Ben struggled to find the words. "It's just that the girl I grew up with, my sister, wouldn't do something like that. She betrayed us! Meghan is kind, she is loyal. I wouldn't have thought anything would make her turn her back on me."

Amelie smiled sadly. "You are right, Ben. She is loyal, just not to us anymore."

Early morning turned to mid-morning and the fog lifted. Ben and Amelie stayed huddled down in the gazebo, waiting. They were about two hundred long strides up from the river. The gazebo was perched under a rise in the manicured lawn. The rise blocked their view of Reinhold's estate and their hope was that no one would be wandering the grounds on such a foggy, unpleasant morning. Also, before long, word of what happened outside of Arrath would get to Reinhold's estate and the place would be in utter chaos.

Based on Ben's description, Mathias surmised that the Coalition forces blockaded Arrath to prevent anyone spoiling the ambush. Once the battle was over, Lord Jason would let the people out, and they would find the bodies. The word would spread like wildfire. The disruption outside of the Sanctuary would be assumed to be part of it. Amelie thought the Sanctuary would encourage that guess, it made things nice and tidy for them.

Any confusion would help Ben and his friends. The bodies at Arrath and the events outside the Sanctuary would be the only thing anyone talked about within one hundred leagues of there. They hoped the distraction would allow them to slip away unnoticed.

Still, waiting wasn't easy. They knew the Sanctuary and the Coalition would be out there looking for them.

"The Sanctuary will not stop until they find us," Amelie explained in a hushed tone. "What I know about their magic would be enough. With what we know about their politics, they cannot let us go free. If we get to Whitehall and tell Argren they betrayed him, I-I don't know what will happen, but it won't be good. The ships last night were just a taste of what they are capable of. They would do anything to stop us. The guards, hunters, and mages...they will all be on our trail."

Ben rubbed a hand through his hair and stared down at the river where he hoped Mathias would return soon.

"What do we do?" he asked. "Do we make for Whitehall? Issen?"

Amelie thought and answered slowly, "Issen is months away. By the time we made it, we could be too late to warn the Alliance. If they can't find us soon, the Sanctuary and the Coalition will react long before I could make it home. I think Whitehall is the only option. My father and I joined Argren's Alliance. We have to trust he will be faithful and help us."

Ben nodded and placed a reassuring hand on Amelie's shoulder.

Whitehall. Why not? He couldn't think of anything better.

They settled down to wait, but by midday, they were getting impatient. They knew Mathias would be gone several bells, but sitting in the small gazebo was driving them mad. They decided to have a look around.

Ben and Amelie crept up the short grass of the lawn and wiggled to the top of the rise where they could see Reinhold's massive estate spread out in the distance. It was quiet. Tendrils of smoke drifted out of a forest of chimneys thrusting up from the slate roof. There were no signs of people.

"It's almost noon," muttered Amelie. "I cannot believe there would be no activity at an estate this size. Is the staff sleeping in with their lord away?"

Ben nudged her arm and pointed to a dark shape by the side of Reinhold's gate, at least a quarter league from where they lay.

"I think that's a tipped over wagon," he guessed. "They aren't sleeping in. They've left. Look over at the stables. All of the doors are open but no one is moving about. Reinhold's staff must have taken all of the horses and fled. Judging by that wagon, they took a lot of other stuff too."

Amelie peered down at the silent estate. "What should we do?"

Ben glanced behind them at the river then back ahead. "I think we go in. Let's leave a mark for Mathias to let him know we're still around, and then see what we can find. It won't be long before someone else comes along. The Sanctuary, another lord, looters...someone will be here soon. Now is our only chance."

The massive silver-studded oak doors of Reinhold's estate stood open. They rose twice Ben's height and led into a large open chamber braced by two sweeping marble staircases. Below the staircases, hallways led deeper into the building.

One hundred strides across, the foyer was covered in marble and little else. The walls were studded with places where rich sconces, tapestries, and paintings may have once hung, but now, everything of value had been stripped away. The vast empty chamber echoed with their voices.

Amelie glanced to Ben. "Are you sure we should be doing this? If we get caught in here, there will be nowhere to run."

Ben nodded. "Let's be quick. They took the candlesticks but may have left something we can use."

They moved quickly through the front part of the estate. It contained offices, reception areas, and meeting rooms. It appeared to be where Reinhold ran his merchant banking business. Everything portable and of value had been taken. Some fine furnishing and carpets remained, but neither had any interest for Ben and Amelie. They noticed open drawers and cabinets that looked to have been looted as well. Scatters of loose paper lay around the floors and doors hung open with irregular shelves of documents missing.

"Reinhold's business advisors," muttered Amelie. "They would have taken any documents describing Reinhold's business. They'll sell it or use it to barter for employment with his competitors."

After ducking into several of the offices, they gave up on that wing and moved deeper into the estate. They needed food, clothes, and supplies for traveling.

The building was massive and there wasn't time to explore every room. Ben thought the place could house every resident of Farview with room to spare. The silence in a building that size was unnerving. They could hear only the soft slap of their bare feet on the cool marble floor. Shoes were definitely an item Ben wanted to find.

Deeper into the building, they found grand ball rooms and open verandas for strolling. It was built for entertaining large numbers of guests. Ben realized they would find nothing useful here. Just like the foyer, the valuables had been taken. Only large, heavy items remained. It gave them hope though. If looters focused on the valuables, maybe they had left more common goods like clothes behind.

Past the entertaining spaces, they finally found something useful. The kitchens. There, the looting had been minimal. Long pantries containing a wide variety of delicacies and basic foods items lined the narrow hallways off the main kitchen. Ben found sacks full of potatoes which they emptied out and began stuffing with food they could easily travel with.

Amelie eyed a shelf of marmalades, passed them over for a sack of dried beans, and sighed. "That is one thing I will miss about the Sanctuary. The food."

Ben grinned. "You don't like my cooking?"

She snorted. "I don't like *my* cooking."

They collected a few more useful items like a frying pan and cutlery then left the pantry to continue exploring. They didn't get far before finding something completely different.

Behind the kitchen, in a large room which must have been the staff mess hall, they opened the door and paused in shock. The floor was painted in blood. Bodies were scattered about, the results of a violent confrontation. At least two score of them by Ben's quick count.

Ben looked at Amelie before tentatively stepping into the room. The lifeless corpses were dressed in Reinhold's livery.

Most appeared to be servants, but there were three guards also. Ben edged around the pools of still tacky blood and realized he knew one of the guards.

"I recognize this one," he told Amelie, pointing at the dead man. "He was at Arrath and fled when I hid. He must have come straight here after the attack."

She glanced around the room thoughtfully. "That explains the looting. He would have brought news of what happened. If he arrived yesterday like you did, there would have been plenty of time for knowledgeable servants to strip the place."

"Yes, but what happened in here?" asked Ben, waving a hand at the surrounding carnage.

"A disagreement, perhaps," answered Amelie. "It looks like it was internal, whatever it was. Maybe some of the staff resisted the looters?"

She was right. All of the bodies were wearing Reinhold's livery and were either servants or guards. Ben eyed a few of the guard's weapons and thought about taking them. He had managed to hold onto his Venmoor steel longsword and the hunting knife Serrot had given him. He didn't need any of the guard's weapons and they looked to be too heavy for Amelie's use, so they passed out of the bloodstained mess hall and kept searching.

In a distant wing of the estate, they finally found what they were looking for, the servant's and guard's quarters. Reinhold had hundreds of employees on staff and the rooms spread out across several hallways and floors. It felt more like a huge inn than an estate. Most of the rooms showed signs of a quick exit. People had hastily packed their things before fleeing.

The majority of Reinhold's guards had been with him in Arrath, though, so those rooms were intact. Ben was able to find wardrobes full of clothing and boots. He searched until he found some that fit and breathed a sigh of relief as he dressed. He left behind his still damp pants and changed into a simple set of britches, tunic, and cloak. A worn pair of marching boots completed the outfit. He strapped on his longsword and knife before grabbing two more changes of clothing and stuffing those in his potato sack.

Back in the hall, Amelie had also changed. She carried a backpack with her and held it up. It looked to be packed for a trip. "Flint, steel, twine, and a few other useful things."

"Good find," Ben replied appreciatively. "We'll need that. Now, let's get out of here."

It was afternoon by the time they made it back over the small rise in Reinhold's lawn and saw the gazebo. From a distance, Ben could tell Mathias had returned and was hunkered down behind the railing.

When they drew close, he stood and waved.

"All clear at the estate?" called the gruff barkeep.

"Nothing left but bodies," Ben answered.

Mathias raised an eyebrow.

Ben explained, "We think an argument broke out between what was left of Reinhold's staff and what was left of the guards. It turned ugly."

"Aye, not surprising. You cut off the head of the snake and the body doesn't know what to do." Mathias gestured toward the pack and potato sacks. "It looks like you found some supplies. You were more successful than I was."

"How was it?" inquired Amelie. "Any sign of a search for us in the City?"

"Nothing overt," replied Mathias. "But enough that I wasn't going to stick around long. There were disguised guards at all of the bridges, and watchers stationed around key intersections. I spotted one outside the Flying Swan. After that, I didn't even bother with the Issen Consulate or the brewery. But I did track down one of my employees, someone we can trust, and told him to get word to Renfro, Saala, and the others. We can't wait on that, though. There's already plenty of heat in town and my man said that the army is being assembled."

"The army?" asked Ben. "I didn't think the Sanctuary had much of an army."

"They don't have a standing one, aside from the guards, of course," Mathias answered. "But they do have a reserve they call in times of need. Supposedly, it's to investigate and protect against what happened in Arrath. They're spinning it like it was an attack on the City. I think it's safe to assume, the real reason is us. If the full force of the army is looking for us, we need to move fast. Any thoughts on where you want to go?"

"We're thinking Whitehall," answered Ben. "And I agree, we should leave today." Ben paused, then asked, "Mathias, are you sure you want to come with us?"

Mathias sighed. "I don't think I have much choice. If they're watching the Flying Swan, then they must suspect I was involved last night. There's no way I can risk being taken in for questioning. That'll be the last anyone sees of me."

The barkeep rubbed at the stubble on his chin. "Whitehall. That makes sense. Try to get help from Argren. Let him get word to Lord Gregor. The problem is, that will make sense to the mages, too. They'll be waiting for us."

"Like you said though," replied Amelie grimly, "we don't have much choice. Where else can we go?"

They all looked at each other. No one had an answer to that.

"Whitehall it is then," declared Mathias after a long pause. "Following the Venmoor River north is the obvious route. We can't do that. The main roads are just as bad, with the army involved they're sure to have that covered. There are some back roads through the mountain towns we can try, or maybe go off the map and rough our way up to Kirksbane. We might be able to do it. The Sanctuary doesn't have much of an army, and they aren't professionally trained. They'll be spread thin the further out we get."

"I'm comfortable in the woods," remarked Ben. "We'll be okay there, but I'm not sure the army is what we need to worry about. The mages, what are they capable of? Can they track us somehow?"

"I don't think so," answered Amelie. "To track us, they would need to mark us to create an affinity. I think I'd know if they did that to me, and they had no reason to do it with you before last night. There are other ways they could find us, far-seeing for example, but those are rather random if they don't know where to start looking. The further we get from the City, the more difficult it will be for them."

"If they could easily find us," agreed Mathias, "then we'd already be found."

"That's it then," declared Ben. "Let's go."

They quickly distributed the supplies into the backpack Amelie found in Reinhold's estate and one Mathias had collected in the City. Ben fashioned a strap on a potato sack and swung it over his shoulder. Not ideal, but better than carrying it in his arms.

They didn't have much, but it would be sufficient for a few days. If they survived that long, they would worry about more supplies then.

Instead of taking the road which would carry them north through the other estates and eventually to Kirksbane, they decided to traverse across the estates and stick close to the river. The risk of running into a lord's guard was a lot easier to handle than seeing the Sanctuary's troops on the road.

In half a bell of brisk walking, they made it to the border of Reinhold's property and found a head- high stone wall.

"I know we need to keep moving, but let's wait here for dark," suggested Ben. "From what I recall when we came down the river, most of these main houses have views looking all the way down. We'll almost certainly be seen if we cross in daylight."

"Good thinking." Mathias nodded. "Let's get some rest now. I advise we travel all night while we have the cover of darkness. Then we find a place to hole up during the day tomorrow. It's going to be a long night. But…" He glanced toward the river. Around the bend, the City was still uncomfortably close. "I want to put as much distance between us and that place as we can."

The three of them sprawled out in the autumn sun and tried to get some sleep. Mathias quickly dozed off, but Ben and Amelie lay awake.

After several minutes of silence, Ben asked, "Do you think we'll make it?"

"I don't know," answered Amelie somberly.

2

THE ROAD

WHEN NIGHT FELL, they had a quick meal of cold provisions, scaled the wall, and dropped easily to the other side.

The property was much like Reinhold's, wide open lawns with a scattering of trees. The moon rose and they trotted across smooth grass.

The main building was well lit. The rest of the estate was dark. They were worried about guards patrolling the grounds but in half a bell made it through without seeing anyone.

The night was cool but the quick pace kept them warm. A gentle breeze rustled the leaves of a nearby tree and the scent of flowers wafted up from an unseen garden. It should have been a pleasant evening, thought Ben.

At the border to the next estate, they found a wall similar to Reinhold's, head high and easy to scale. Five more walls, five more hurried trots across open lawns. They squatted down to catch their breath.

In a soft whisper, Ben remarked, "I don't know if we're getting lucky or if they just don't have guards, but this is easier than I expected. I thought we'd have to be watching and hiding as we moved."

Mathias grunted. "Don't get cocky now. Just because these were easy doesn't mean the next one will be. I've been thinking, though. It's taking us nearly half a bell to cross each property. Unless they keep an entire army to do patrols, they can't have enough men to watch all of the walls. They must keep the guards close in at night. As long as the buildings are guarded, there's nothing out here anyone would be interested in sneaking to."

"It's not the lord's guards we need to worry about," muttered Amelie.

"Do you think the Sanctuary would have people out here on the estates?" Ben worried.

"I'm not sure," she replied. "That's what scares me. We know they have resources, but how quickly can they deploy them? How long before they realize we're not moving on any major roadways?"

Ben frowned. It wasn't such a pleasant night any longer.

"They are either out here or they are not," declared Mathias. "If they've already locked down cross-country routes, then we're cooked no matter what we do. The one thing we can affect now is time. The quicker we go, the further they will have to expand the net, and the better our chances."

Ben stood and settled his makeshift pack. "Shall we?"

The next two estates passed smoothly like the ones before them. The manicured lawns were just as easy to travel across as a well-paved road. The high moon provided plenty of light. It gave Ben a little concern that they would be visible to anyone really looking, but so far, the only sign of life was in well-lit buildings they easily avoided.

The next wall proved to be a bigger challenge. It stood nearly twice the height as the others and the top was studded with sharp glass shards.

"This fellow is a bit more worried about security I guess," grumbled Mathias.

Luckily, despite the increased height, the wall was roughly mortared field stones and had plenty of finger and toe holds. Ben gripped a stone and pulled himself up. At the top, he swung his cloak off and folded it before draping it across the glass shards. They were worn from exposure to the weather, but still felt uncomfortably sharp. He pressed a hand down on the cloak to test then called to his companions, "Mathias, I wouldn't recommend straddling the wall and sitting down, but this should hold for us to swing over quickly."

The barkeep snorted derisively in the darkness below.

Ben hung a leg over, found footing, and moved to the other side. Amelie came up next. Ben stayed near the top to help her get across. Mathias brought up the rear and the three of them descended into the grounds of the new estate.

"Not bad," whispered Mathias as they all scanned ahead. It looked just like the other properties they'd traversed. Open lawns, stands of trees, and a small wooden structure in the distance that appeared unoccupied.

"Whoever lives here," Ben responded, "they may be worried more about security, but like you say, no one can afford to pay enough guards to patrol all of this. Let's move."

At a quick jog, they made good time with only a little delay when they came across a small stream. In the darkness, Amelie almost ran straight into it. Ben caught her arm at the last second before she plunged in.

She gave him a thankful look and they moved upstream until they found a short bridge to cross and stay dry.

"Two or three more of these estates and we should start looking for a good place to hole up and rest." Mathias panted.

"I'm with you on that," replied Ben.

Amelie only nodded in agreement. It was an easy pace for Ben, but he was used to training with Saala for several bells at a time. Amelie and Mathias weren't adjusted to this much physical activity.

Ben was considering running ahead to scout their path when he thought he heard something.

"Hold on," he said, gesturing for everyone to stop.

Over the heavy breathing of his companions, he strained to hear what it was.

"A guard? Should we run?" Amelie gasped.

"I don't think it was a guard," he answered.

Then they all heard it—the sharp bark of a dog followed quickly by more. It was a pack of them, and it sounded like they were on the trail of something.

"Oh damn," groaned Ben. "We run."

If this estate was the same size as the others, they were only halfway across, a quarter bell at the pace they had been maintaining. The dogs would be on them before that. They started at a flat run but slowed when they realized they couldn't keep that up for long.

The barking drew closer and Ben got nervous. He and Mathias were both armed with swords, so even against a large pack, they might be able to defend themselves, but the dogs would bring guards. Even if they were able to fight off the guards, just being seen could ruin their chances of escape. A word in the wrong ear and the Sanctuary would suspect it was them. They would blanket the area with troops, hunters, or even mages.

He glanced over his shoulder but couldn't see anything yet. He couldn't see the wall in front of them either.

"Come on," he urged, pulling ahead of the others. "We can't get caught."

A look of determination painted Amelie's face and she increased her speed. Mathias grimaced and kept up as well. Ben could tell it was taking a lot out of both of them.

Before they saw the exterior wall, he spotted the first of the hounds behind them. It crested a hill almost a thousand strides back. It was coming fast. Ben estimated it was moving at least twice as quickly as they were.

The hound accelerated when it caught sight of them.

They poured on more speed and were back at nearly a full run. Packs and weapons bounced uncomfortably as they ran.

The calls of the dogs rose and Ben knew the rest of the pack had seen them. He looked back again and saw the hounds were a large breed of short-haired hunting dog. It was difficult to be sure at the distance, but they might be half his weight and there were close to a dozen of them. If it came to it, the fight could go either way.

Suddenly, Amelie shouted, "There! The wall."

Five hundred strides back, the hounds were closing quickly.

Ben reached behind his back and pushed his pack to the side to free the hilt of his sword. They might make it. If they didn't, he would have to be ready. He could fall back and protect the rear while Amelie climbed.

Another look at the dogs and his heart sank. At the far hill, where he first saw them, he could now see pinpoints of light from lanterns or torches. The guards heard the dogs and were coming to investigate.

"Move, move, move!" he extolled Amelie and Mathias.

The wall was just one hundred strides away, but the dogs had pulled within two hundred strides. They were howling with excitement.

At a full run, Ben's companions made it to the wall. He swept his sword out and spun to face the approaching pack. One hundred strides back, they seemed to be flying toward him. Amelie and Mathias both hit the wall and started to climb. Amelie glanced back and yelled at Ben, "Don't be stupid. Climb!"

Ben grunted and turned to the wall. The dogs were within fifty strides now. He tossed his sword over the stone barrier then jumped to cling to the rough rock.

Before he was halfway up, the first dog reached him and hurled itself into the air. Ben was able to swing his legs to the side and the poor creature smashed face first into the rock. It fell to the ground whimpering. The rest of the pack was just behind it.

Mathias and Amelie were above him and had reached the top. They were struggling to hold a cloak over the glass shards before they climbed over.

Ben gained another two footholds before he felt a hard tug on his pants leg that jerked his foot loose. He nearly went crashing down into the snarling pack, but was able to kick his leg free and haul himself up another arms-length.

It wasn't high enough. He felt a set of jaws clamp down on his tough leather boot before slowly sliding off when they couldn't keep a grip.

Mathias and Amelie swung over the wall and were hanging on the other side, ready to help Ben across.

"Hurry Ben," growled Mathias. "Lights are coming fast. They must know the dogs have something."

Finally, Ben reached the top of the wall, but his legs were still hanging halfway down and he felt his pant leg get caught again. In a flash of desperation, he surged upward, swung an arm over the top of the wall, and immediately regretted it. The glass shards dug into his forearm and sliced his skin as he continued the motion, hauling himself up and over. Another scrape cut into his side when he dragged his body across. He ignored the pain and scrambled over. Sharp glass was better than snarling teeth.

On the other side, he dangled briefly before losing his grip and crashing down to the ground. He felt his ankle turn when he landed and he fell heavily on his side.

Mathias and Amelie dropped down next to him. Mathias collected Ben's sword and Amelie bent to help him up.

"Can you move?" demanded Mathias. "Those guards will be at the wall in less than two minutes. They know someone was here. If they spot us…"

Ben groaned and rose unsteadily to his feet. His eyes teared up when he put weight on his ankle, but it wasn't broken, he could move on it. His arm and side were steadily leaking blood. There was no time to properly care for it. Amelie quickly pulled out a spare shirt and wrapped it around the bleeding arm.

"We can't leave a blood trail," she murmured.

"Hurry!" implored Mathias. "The first thing they'll do is look over that wall and the second thing is alert whoever owns this estate. We have to get going, now!"

Ben lurched forward and began a shuffling run across the grass. He clutched his wounded arm to his cut-up side to put pressure on both. A sharp jolt of pain ran up his leg every time he put down his twisted ankle, but Mathias was right—stopping now and getting caught meant being turned over to the Sanctuary and certain death.

The night descended into a blur of pain and exhaustion. There was no thought of stopping or resting now. The guards they avoided may raise the alarm at all of the neighboring estates and everyone would turn out their barracks. Getting distance between them and where the disruption took place was their only hope.

Each time they climbed another wall and dropped down, they were worried there might be another pack of dogs or worse waiting for them, but there was no other option. Moving forward was risky, but staying was inevitable capture. Bells later, Ben had lost track of time and was stunned when he saw the sun's predawn glow lighten the sky. He paused, panting.

Mathias and Amelie both came to an exhausted halt, looking around wildly.

"We have to stop." Ben wheezed. "If they're searching for us or not, we can't move through here in daylight."

"Behind us," said Amelie, gasping for air. "There was a stand of trees behind us."

Mathias scanned the grounds around them. Much like the other estates, it was open grass lawn, areas of gardens, and small wooden structures. In full daylight, if there was a search, none of it offered anything close to sufficient cover.

"The trees it is," he rumbled.

The three of them ran back then pushed their way into the thick stand of short trees. They wiggled into the tight undergrowth. Too tired to eat or think about the trail they were leaving behind them, they huddled close and quickly fell into a deep sleep.

A SHARP BRANCH digging into his side edged Ben into wakefulness. He rolled over. The herbal scent of the undergrowth surrounded him. Underneath his body, a carpet of fallen leaves was as comfortable as a fine feather bed. For a pleasant moment, he drifted, half-awake. Quickly though, the dull pain in his arm and side dragged him awake.

In the quiet, he surveyed his surroundings. It was afternoon. He lay beneath a close canopy of ferns and low bushes. Mathias and Amelie lay near him. Both were still resting. A now ragged and blood-soaked shirt was wrapped around his arm where the glass from the wall had cut him. He could feel his shirt stuck to his side near a shallow cut on his rib cage. All in all, it could have been worse. They were alive.

His stomach growled. Ben realized he hadn't eaten since the middle of the previous night, before they encountered the dogs and had to run. His pack was within reach and he dug out a crust of bread and hard wedge of cheese. He sloshed a drink from a half-empty water skin and thought they would need to find fresh water today. It was likely the least of their problems.

His gnawing hunger sated, he sat up. Brushing vegetation aside, he wiggled to a clearer area in the thicket. With a pained grimace, he unwrapped the ruined shirt from his arm, yanking it free from where dried blood glued it to his skin.

He had several cuts along his forearm including two deep ones that oozed blood with the release of pressure from the shirt. A thorough washing and a few stitches of thread and he would be okay. If he was going to bleed out from the cuts, it would have already happened the night before.

Checking these injuries earlier probably would have been prudent. He rewrapped it as best he could and decided to wait for help before he tried to stitch the gashes with one hand.

He bent his ankle to test it and winced at a spike of pain. A light sprain. It wouldn't be pleasant, but he thought he could walk on it. He searched through his pack for an extra pair of britches and used his hunting knife to cut strips to bind the ankle. The extra support would be worth having only one change of clothes left.

Before long, Amelie and Mathias woke and they all crawled into the small open space Ben found in the middle of the thicket.

Silently, using only gestures, they also ate. Amelie tended to Ben's arm. Despite him trying to wave her off, she used a third of their water to wash it then pulled some thread from his shirt and a needle from her pack. He cringed and tried not to jerk his arm away when she threaded six quick loops into his skin. Her apologetic look said she knew it was messy, but on the run and with nowhere to turn to, they didn't have a better option.

She ran a hand over his arm and he felt a slight tingle. A look of concentration grew on her face and she stared down at the cuts. A warm sensation spread across his skin. He clamped a hand down on hers. Magic. She was trying to use magic to heal him.

He leaned close and whispered in her ear, "It hurts, but I'll survive. I can walk with this. I can run if we have to. Don't waste your energy. You'll need it tonight."

She wrapped her arms around him and pulled him tight. He could feel tremors in her body but her arms felt strong. She was scared and determined.

Over Amelie's shoulder, Ben saw Mathias give him a nod. Last night was just the beginning. If they were going to make White-hall, they needed to be mentally prepared. The mages, the most powerful force on Alcott, wanted them dead. Nothing about this was going to be easy.

Twilight fell and they felt confident enough to venture out to the edge of the thicket. Nothing was there besides open grass and flower gardens in the distance, just like they'd seen at other estates the night before.

With no one in sight, they risked speaking.

"I hate to say it, but I'm not sure this is going to work," started Mathias. "There's too much risk. If one place had them, then other estates might also have dogs. We stirred them up last night, so it's possible there could be guards on patrol as well. If they're on alert, then they'll see us. There is no cover through here."

Amelie frowned. "What do you suggest? We sank the boat before we left Reinhold's. Even if we stole a boat, they'll be watching that way. It's crazy to try the river. The road is even worse, it's wide open."

"East," answered Mathias. "We cross the road and head east away from the river."

"There are mountains to the east and not much else," complained Ben. "That's rough going. It will slow us down. We'd make a third of the distance each night. We'd have nowhere to get food and supplies."

Mathias cracked his knuckles. "You are right. It will be tough going, and we may run short of food, but we can't stop for food and supplies anyway. The road and river aren't worth consider-ing, and the estates are too dangerous, so what else does that leave us? If we get in the mountains, there is no way the Sanc-tuary can cover all routes. We can come back to the river at Kirksbane and figure out a way to go through the Sineook Valley. It's the only thing I think may work."

Ben and Amelie contemplated silently. Neither liked the idea of going into the mountains, but Mathias was right. Starvation was a possibility, but the mountains gave them a chance.

They waited until nightfall then started moving again.

Exiting the estate was nerve wracking. After the night before, they proceeded cautiously. They imagined a legion of guards over every hill. Each bird call or insect noise brought back memories of the howling dogs.

Whether it was luck or not, they made it to the exterior wall of the grounds with no encounters. The wall followed the north road that started in the City and extended through all of the grand estates. West of the road was the river and the lord's palaces. East of the road was also property of the lords, but it was rougher. It was typically used for hunting or vineyards, whatever passion the lord tasked his servants with pursuing.

At the wall, Ben grimaced at a twinge of pain in his arm but fought through it to pull himself to the top. He peeked his head over. The well-maintained road extended both ways in the moonlight. Across the empty road, a similar wall passed north and south as far as he could see.

"Looks clear," he called down to his companions, and then rolled over the top. The cut on his side tugged. He worried it broke open again. Luckily, there were no glass shards sticking out along the top of this wall.

He realized he probably should have checked that before rolling on it.

Cursing himself, he clambered down the other side. Amelie and Mathias followed behind him.

They crossed the road without seeing a soul, quickly scaled the opposite wall, and dropped down behind it. Rows and rows of grape vines climbed away from the wall, up a hill, and out of sight in the pale moonlight.

Bell after bell, they hiked through narrow dirt rows, ripe grapes hanging on either side. Ben limped along on his tender ankle, but the pace they set was slower than the previous night.

They were still eager to get distance between them and the City, but the chances of being spotted in the vineyard were low. They risked quiet conversation as they walked.

"Do you think they'll try to find us?" asked Ben. "Saala, Rhys, Renfro...our friends."

"I don't know," answered Amelie. "Saala would try to find us if he could. He's loyal to me and my family, but what will the Sanctuary tell him? If he thinks we're dead, he'll have no reason to look. Renfro, I don't think he'll come looking. As for Rhys, well, Rhys is one of them, isn't he? I know he doesn't always agree with what they are doing, but he's part of the Sanctuary."

"No," growled Mathias, shaking his head. "He is not part of them. He has no loyalty to that place. I can't say Rhys has always been a good man, but he is a loyal man, to his friends at least. He'll leave the Sanctuary and not look back. If he has reason to suspect we're alive, that is, and if he knows where to look for us."

"You've known him a long time, haven't you?" asked Ben, brushing a fragrant grape vine out of his way as they walked.

"Many, many years," affirmed Mathias. "We served together when I was a greenhorn recruit and fresh off the farm. We were part of an expeditionary force up north. He took me under his wing and taught me just about everything I know about fighting and staying alive. It's rough and dangerous country up there. Half of us didn't make it back from that first expedition. I owe him my life more times than I can count."

"How is that possible?" wondered Ben. "Rhys is at least ten years your junior, isn't he? He looks like it at least. Is there some secret to youth in all of that ale?"

Mathias smirked. "Rhys looks the same age today as he did back then."

"He's a long-lived!" exclaimed Amelie.

Ben blinked in confusion. Long-lived were a myth.

"Aye, that he is," answered Mathias. "He doesn't like to talk about it much, and he's never told me everything, but he's been around a long, long time."

"What does that mean?" queried Ben, curiosity fighting through disbelief. "I thought the long-lived was just a story. Is it magic? Is he some sort of creature?"

"Not exactly magic," replied Amelie. "From what I understand, the long-lived start out as normal people, just like you and me, but over time, they have gained expertise and achieve a level of control that is beyond us—control over themselves, control over their surroundings. That control, it allows them to regulate their bodies in ways that begin to seem like magic. It takes enormous will, certainly, and that is a lot like magic. The long-lived can arrest the natural aging process. I don't understand how it's done exactly, but mastery in a skill is the key."

"That sounds right with what I've heard," agreed Mathias. "It's typically something like mastering the blade or, of course, actual magic."

"Of course." Amelie nodded. "The most famous long-lived, and one of the few who is public about it, is the Veil. The current Veil has been ruling the Sanctuary for three hundred years."

Ben stopped walking. "Three hundred years! She has been alive for three hundred years?"

Amelie paused beside him. "Longer than that, I would think. That's as long as she's had the job. Getting the necessary respect of the other mages must have taken at least that long, if not longer. Her age is something the Sanctuary uses to show their power, but they don't exactly share the details."

Ben looked to Mathias. "How old is Rhys, then?"

Mathias shrugged. "He never told me. Come on. Let's keep moving. They don't have the dogs on us tonight, but I'd like to make it out of these vines before daybreak when the workers start showing up."

"Wait," urged Ben, starting after Mathias. "The control—how is it achieved?"

Mathias grinned and rubbed a hand over his bald head. "I haven't figured that out yet. I'll let you know when I do."

They shuffled along silently after that, everyone lost in their own thoughts.

Long-lived. Not only did they exist, but Ben knew one. The world was a strange place.

A bell before daybreak, they made it to the edge of the vineyard. There was no wall there, just an unceremonious end to the vines and the start of a forest. It wasn't the pine forest Ben was used to from home, but it felt good to walk into the concealment of the trees and out of the open vineyard.

"What do you think?" asked Mathias, huffing and puffing with his hands on his hips. "Travel another half bell then rest? In here, I think it's safer to move during the day." He gestured to the leaf cover above that was blocking the moonlight. "Without light, we'll be tripping over every unseen branch and rock. It'll make a racket and one of us could break a leg."

Ben and Amelie shared a look then shrugged.

"Makes sense to me," replied Ben.

They rested late into the morning and spent two more days gaining elevation and putting distance between them and the City. There were no signs of other people and they began to feel comfortable. On the third day, they sat around a cold camp, getting ready for another hard day of travel. Their pace in the forest wasn't quick. It had been uphill the entire way.

"Should we break for a day and restock our supplies?" suggested Ben. "Hunt, fish, and gather what we can?"

"Aye, I think we should," answered Mathias. "We have maybe two days left of what you got from Reinhold's pantry. While I'd like to keep moving, it won't do us any good if we run out of food."

"If we stop," added Amelie, "I'd like to practice."

"Practice?" inquired Ben.

"The sword," she replied. "Hopefully we get through this with stealth and speed, but if we don't, I need to learn to defend myself."

"Why not," agreed Mathias. "I could use a bit of practice myself. I got rusty tending bar the last several years," he finished with a grin.

Amelie smiled. "You two help me with the sword, and I'll teach you a few things I learned at the Sanctuary that might come in handy if we meet a mage."

Ben's eyes lit up. "You can teach us to fight with magic?"

She snorted. "I can't teach you to fight with magic, but there are things I learned that can negate someone else's magic, at least when it comes to affecting you. As you know, it's all about willpower. If someone tries to impose their will on you, it's possible to resist that with your own will."

"Did they teach you to fight at all?" asked Ben. He was thinking the lightning bolts that Lady Towaal called in Snowmar could come in handy.

"No, unfortunately they don't teach that to initiates," she answered. "That's too much power too soon. It's dangerous to learn that kind of talent. They teach us defense only, in case we were to encounter another mage. Someone who learned on their own or outside of Alcott, I suppose. If we get into a mage fight, our best bet is to run."

"Too bad," muttered Ben.

"Actually, there is one advantage we have." Amelie pulled a small carved wooden disk from a pocket in her dress. "This."

Ben remembered seeing the disc before. Amelie had taken it from the glass building they fought Eldred in. "What is that?" he asked.

"It's a repository," she explained. "It's infused with energy. It takes weeks for a skilled Mage to create one, constantly drawing energy from the air or their body and transferring it into the disc. The energy is captured in these runes you see inscribed along the edge. I knew it was there because our instructor was demonstrating its use the previous day. She used it to draw energy off of the living plants in the laboratory then applied it back into them. It's not full, but she showed us how to charge it. It's not difficult. I think once I establish the link, I can do it while we walk."

"Is it a weapon?" Ben asked, fascinated.

"Not exactly," answered Amelie. "They are used to cast great spells more powerful than the mage or the environment could support. It can be any spell, really. So it may be helpful because I am not very strong. When it's used properly, the mage channels the extra energy into whatever they are trying to do. When used improperly, the energy could be released explosively."

"Explosively?" wondered Ben.

"That means run."

THE DAY PASSED QUICKLY but productively. Right after breakfast, Ben set a couple of small game snares and managed to catch a rabbit by afternoon. He also collected a pouch full of nuts and a few other things to supplement their supplies. The rabbit was lean and gamey, and the nuts carried a slightly bitter taste, but they would need both if they wanted to keep up their energy during the hike.

After Ben showed Mathias and Amelie how to set the traps, they spent the afternoon practicing the sword. Ben didn't participate. He wanted to take the opportunity to rest his sprained ankle. Mathias proved a capable teacher for Amelie, though.

They didn't have the proper sparring equipment they used back in the City, so they practiced with their real blades. It was a careful and slow dance. Practice was best when it seemed realistic, but none of them wanted to risk an injury.

They had Ben's Venmoor steel longsword, a sturdy, well-used broadsword Mathias brought, and a curved saber Amelie had pulled off the wall in one of Reinhold's office rooms. It wasn't the best quality, which is likely why it was overlooked, but it was better than nothing.

Mathias was a steady and efficient fighter. He didn't have near the grace of Saala, or even what Ben was starting to achieve, but unlike many swordsmen, he stayed away from the flourishes and complicated sequences that were common in sparring. It left him with short and economical strokes. He got the job done with minimal wasted effort.

Amelie showed a great deal of improvement from when she first started training with Saala. She was still nowhere near the skill of Ben or even Mathias. She kept at it though with a determined look on her face.

After a bell of sparring, both Mathias and Amelie were exhausted.

"It's been a few years," huffed Mathias.

Amelie nodded breathlessly. "Not a few years for me, but this is more tiring than sitting bell after bell in a lecture hall hearing about vegetal growth patterns." She paused. "Actually, maybe it's not more tiring than that."

Ben chuckled. "Don't go too hard. It's the first day and we have a lot of travel to do. It won't do any good if you're so tired you can't hike. Maybe we can try doing the Ohms. That's not as strenuous."

They started at the beginning and Ben instructed Mathias and Amelie how to move through the forms. Amelie had seen them before when they were on the road going to the City, but she hadn't practiced them since then. She quickly caught up and before long was cycling through the first set of movements.

Mathias struggled with the challenging flexibility positions. At one point, he glanced over at Amelie who was twisting around with no difficultly and he muttered under his breath, "Nice to be young."

"You'll get there," encouraged Ben. "It will just take some more work, that's all."

"I don't think so," grumbled Mathias in response. "Some things are lost in time. Me bending down and touching my toes is one of them."

He straightened up and stretched, cracking his back and joints in the process. "It does feel good though. Even if I can't do it like you kids, I can get better. You can always get a little better."

The next morning, they started early and well rested. For three days, they hadn't seen any signs of pursuit. Now they were well off the established roads and pathways. They knew the Sanctuary had soldiers and likely hunters searching for them, but this far away, they were gaining confidence that it was possible they could get out of the mages' noose.

The terrain grew difficult throughout the day as they progressed deeper into the foothills of the mountains. Rocky outcroppings began to appear and they decided they would turn north after stopping that evening. Gaining elevation put them further from civilization and reduced the chance of running into someone, but if they went too far, they would lose some of the plant cover. The trees were already noticeably smaller and the undergrowth was thinning out.

"Just like home?" Amelie asked Ben.

"No, not quite," he responded. "It's pine forest back home. These are sycamore, beech, and maple. Farview is a little higher up too, so the air is different."

Looking around, he added, "The pine is also evergreen. Before long, these trees will start to lose their leaves. By the end of this month, the color of the leaves will change. In two months, it will be nothing but bare branches."

"You know a lot about trees," Amelie said with a grin.

"I come from a family of wood cutters." Ben smirked. "Everyone knows about something."

That evening, they made camp and started a fire. They had

been keeping cold camps, but they figured they were far enough from civilization it was safe now. It was autumn, and this deep in the mountains, the night air was brisk. Ben was glad of the cloak he'd found at Reinhold's estate. He pulled it close and huddled near the fire.

Mathias had dinner duty that evening, which both Ben and Amelie appreciated. The former soldier and tavern owner was easily the most skilled at mixing the motley supplies they'd brought and coming up with something resembling a decent meal.

Mopping up a hearty stew with a crust of hard bread, Ben had to ask, "Mathias, this is delicious. How did you learn to cook like this?"

"Years of practice and experimenting," the gruff veteran answered with a smile. "Soldiering is mostly about sitting around and waiting. Occasionally, there is some marching. Very rarely, there is a fight. It feels like you are almost always waiting. You've got to find something to do or you'll go mad. Some take up wood carving. Some learn an instrument. I cooked. I realized early on that the most popular man in the camp is the one who can make dinner. Unless of course," he continued with a yawn, "you've got a man who can brew ale. You brew good ale, and someone will always watch your back. A good brewer has more protection on a battlefield than the lord does."

"Glad to know I'll be welcomed then." Ben smirked.

"Aye. If you ever join an army, make sure they know what you can do." Another yawn and a stretch. "I think it's time for me to get some shut eye," mumbled the veteran.

Mathias rose to his feet, started toward his pack, and then froze.

A whisper of steel against leather. Ben's senses spiked with fear. Ben couldn't see around Mathias in the dark, but he could sense the alarm in his friend's stance.

Suddenly, Mathias dove toward his pack and the broadsword

he had tucked under it. He shouted back to Ben and Amelie, "Run!"

A shadowy figure was revealed standing at the edge of the firelight. All Ben could see was a dark silhouette of a man. The light reflected along the edges of two blades. A long, slender rapier and a dagger. Before Ben could react, the figure charged toward Mathias.

Ben sprang up and yanked his own sword out of its battered leather sheath. Amelie was struggling to draw her saber.

The dark figure was on Mathias in a blink and stabbed down with the rapier.

Mathias, instead of pulling his sword free or scrambling away, surged forward and caught the assailant in the midsection with his shoulder. He propelled them both back onto the ground. The hilt of the rapier bounced harmlessly off Mathias' back.

Mathias landed on top of the figure but the attacker continued the momentum and kept rolling, kicking with his feet and flipping Mathias up and over. The veteran somersaulted in the air before landing hard on the ground.

Ben charged forward, ignoring the twinge of pain in his still tender ankle. He tried to catch their attacker while he was still down, but the man sprung to his feet before Ben could get there.

Ben swung his longsword but his wild swing was expertly turned aside by the man's dagger. The attacker's rapier lashed forward and Ben scrambled back, narrowly avoiding being gutted. A thin burning cut blossomed across his stomach where the point nicked him.

Mathias clambered to his feet and drew his broadsword. He stood squarely behind their assailant. Ben and Amelie were in front. All three spread out to encircle the man.

"I don't know why you are doing this or who you are..." started Ben.

"Enough, boy," interrupted the man with a snarl. "You may

not know me, but I know you, and your heads are the same price, dead or alive."

The rapier flicked toward Amelie and she scrambled backward out of reach. Mathias and Ben both saw an opportunity and charged forward. The attacker responded by lunging toward Ben.

Ben stopped and set into a defensive posture while Mathias continued his charge at the man's back. Instead of the expected attack at Ben though, the man spun around and crashed his rapier against Mathias' broadsword. The heavy weapon was shunted aside and Mathias crashed inside the guard of the rapier. The grizzled veteran was startled by the attacker's pivot and didn't react in time to the dagger, which whipped around and slashed him.

Mathias yelled a strangled cry and flailed backward, clutching at his neck. A spray of blood arced out from a wound as he flopped onto his back.

Ben's stomach churned with concern for his friend. He was also concerned for himself. The assailant was too quick and his fighting style was completely foreign. He used the two blades like they were extensions of his arms. There was no defense against both of them when he was able to block with one and counterattack with the other.

With Mathias out of the fight, the man slowly turned to face Ben. The firelight cast frightening shadows across his face. His wicked smirk gave him a nasty, demonic look.

Ben backed up to give himself room and time to think. Amelie circled behind the man's back. She was hesitant to attack after what happened to Mathias.

"Amelie," called Ben, thinking quickly. "See to Mathias. I will deal with this."

The man smiled. "You're awfully confident boy. You sure you don't want help from the girl?"

"I don't need it," growled Ben.

The man cackled and stalked forward.

Ben stepped back and circled to what he hoped was the man's offhand–if there was one. While the man slowly advanced, Ben kept backing up. He stayed in the circle of light from their fire and didn't engage the man.

"Too scared to fight me, boy?" taunted the attacker.

Ben remained silent and continued to stay just out of reach.

"Very well," snarled the man.

He surged forward and lashed out with his rapier. Ben parried and stepped back again. A momentary flash of frustration crossed the man's face, giving Ben hope.

Again the rapier whipped out and Ben easily parried and continued his slow retreat. The man swung forward again, following it with a weak slash from his dagger. Ben kept out of reach of both.

The man started a series of ferocious swings and jabs, but Ben refused to engage. He kept meeting the attacks with minimal force and stepping away when he could. The thrusting attacks from the rapier became faster and wilder as the man grew angry.

"Fight me!" he yelled. Recklessly, he leapt forward, trying to catch up to Ben's withdrawal.

It was what Ben had been waiting for. With both of the man's blades extended and the man jumping in the air, Ben burst forward, ducking the sharp steel and thrusting his longsword deep into the man's chest. The impact of their bodies colliding drove the longsword clean through the man. He collapsed lifeless into Ben.

Ben shoved the body off his weapon, panting heavily. He looked down at the dead man, still uncertain about whom he was.

"Ben!" cried Amelie.

She had been watching the fight, looking for an opportunity to assist, but now that it was over, she knelt next to Mathias.

Ben dropped his longsword and ran to Mathias.

The barkeep was lying on his back, his breath was coming in

strained, wet gurgles. The flickering fire lit his blood slick hands. They were clasped around his neck and Ben could see in his eyes that it was over. When Ben drew close, Mathias tried to whisper something. Only blood bubbled out of his mouth. Crimson streaks leaked down his cheek.

Ben rocked back on his heels, struggling in vain to think of something they could do.

Amelie sobbed and gripped Mathias' arm tightly. "Hold on," she begged. "I can heal you."

Mathias tried one more attempt at speaking, but couldn't get out the words. He met Ben's eye and withdrew his hands from his neck.

A splash of blood shot out with the release of pressure and Ben saw the gaping wound that went from just below Mathias' ear to the front of his neck. He knew Amelie didn't have the skill to heal that.

With each heartbeat, a progressively weaker spurt of blood pumped out. Within the space of a dozen breaths, Mathias was still.

They spent half the night burying their friend. Ben dug out a shallow grave using his hands and the veteran's broadsword. Amelie kept watch, jumping at every little sound in the surrounding woods.

Ben said a few short words. Then they moved camp one hundred paces further up the side of the mountain. They tried to lie down and rest, but neither of them could sleep.

After a half bell, staring up at the stars, Ben broke the silence. "Who was that?"

"A hunter," answered Amelie morosely. "Someone the Sanctuary sent after us. He said there was a price on our heads."

"Do you think he was working alone?" asked Ben.

"I hope so. It's not unusual for men like that to work alone."

"If he wasn't alone, he would have waited." Ben sighed. "At

least I think he would have waited. But if he could find us, then others might also find us."

"You're right," said Amelie. "But what does it matter? What else can we do but keep moving? If we stay still or we try to hide, it will just make discovery quicker. If they capture us, we may as well be dead."

3

PICK UP THE PIECES

THE NEXT MORNING came early and both Ben and Amelie woke groggy.

Ben walked back to their previous campsite and used the daylight to quickly search their attacker. His body was cold to the touch and unpleasantly stiff, though, fortunately, it had not begun to smell.

The man must have dropped his supplies before attacking them because he didn't have much on him. He had a belt pouch with a handful of coins, a bloodstained handkerchief, a strange tiny copper bowl inscribed with miniature runes around the rim, and a set of flint and steel. He had a utilitarian knife on his belt, the rapier, and the dagger. Other than that, Ben found nothing worthwhile. Ben tried to remember what Rhys looked for when he searched bodies. The only thing Ben could recall was being disgusted by the concept. That hadn't changed.

He took the bowl to show Amelie, and on a whim, he picked up and wiped off the man's weapons.

He brought them back to where Amelie was preparing a quick breakfast they could eat on the move. Despite being exhausted from almost no sleep the night before, neither of them was interested in hanging around the area for long.

Amelie looked up. "Find anything?" She frowned at the two blades. "What are you doing with those?"

"They're good quality and light weight. I thought..." Ben shrugged. "Well, I thought maybe you could use them. That man was pretty effective with them last night. If you can learn that, I think they'd be a better fit for you than the saber."

She frowned. "Saala has been teaching me to use weapons like the saber. I don't know how to use a stabbing weapon like that, much less two of them."

"You'll learn," assured Ben. "We can start with the rapier. If you like it, we can see about adding the dagger. I don't know much about fighting with two blades either, but after seeing what that man was able to do, I think it's worth trying. He was able to keep three of us at bay. Anytime we struck at him, he could use one blade to defend and one to counterattack. That style relies on quickness and not strength." Ben shrugged. "Maybe..."

He trailed off without completing his sentence. He was going to say maybe she wouldn't end up like Mathias.

"I understand," she finished for him.

He showed her the copper bowl the attacker had. "He was carrying this."

She kept making breakfast and then looked at it. "It does look like a magical device, but I have no idea what its purpose could be. Did he have anything else strange?"

"Everything else was normal," answered Ben.

Amelie stood up and handed Ben a chunk of bread stuffed with cheese. "Let's walk and eat."

They headed north toward Kirksbane. They stayed just below the tree line, in the light cover of the forest. This far into the mountains, the travel was quicker than they experienced below. Speed was their friend now. Ben opted to stay high and make use of the clearer ground instead of heading deeper into the thicker growth which would provide better concealment.

It was a hard day, but neither complained. They kept moving through lunch and only paused long enough to refill their water skins at a small stream. Barely speaking, they communicated by hand gestures and in whispers when necessary. Silence was wise if someone was nearby, but also, they just didn't feel like talking.

By evening, they covered several leagues and felt comfortable stopping to rest. They slung their packs down on the ground. Amelie started digging through to find something they could eat. Earlier, they decided to forgo a fire that night. They weren't sure how the hunter had tracked them, but a campfire was too obvious a giveaway to anyone nearby looking for them.

Ben sat, staring blankly while Amelie worked. Before long, she paused and glanced at him.

"I understand what it's like, Ben."

"What do you mean?" he responded.

"Losing a friend," she answered solemnly. "It wasn't that long ago I lost Meredith. I'd known her my entire life. When she died at Snowmar, for a while there, I didn't know how I could continue."

Ben sighed.

"I didn't know him like you did," she continued, "but when you needed help with an insane plan to break into the Sanctuary and sneak someone out, he's the one you went to, and he actually did it. Friends like that don't come along very often."

Ben picked up a rock off the ground and rubbed his thumb over its rough surface. "You're right. He was a good friend. Better than I deserved, and I got him killed. If I hadn't gone to him, if I hadn't asked him to help with that insane plan, then he would still be alive and tending bar at the Flying Swan."

"Ben, you can't think like that," protested Amelie.

"But it's true, Amelie," replied Ben harshly. "I know you're going to say that he knew the risks and he came along anyway.

You'd be right, he did know, but it doesn't absolve me of asking him in the first place."

She rummaged in the pack and pulled out a paper wrapped packet of dried beef. She didn't answer for several minutes.

Finally, she said, "I've realized since I left Issen that the world is a hard place. Meredith died. Reinhold died. Mathias died. I don't know what the hell happened with Meghan, but as far as I'm concerned, we lost her too. To me, she may as well be dead. I'm going to be pretty damn tempted to make it official if I see her again."

Unwrapping the package of dried meat, she continued talking, "Ferguson would have died if it wasn't for Towaal. We've both gotten cut up, you were captured by thieves, we've been banged around, and barely escaped death ourselves a couple of times, but here is the thing Ben, it's only going to get harder."

Ben blinked at her, unsure of how to respond.

Amelie kept going, "If one hunter found us, then others will too. We've got a long way to Whitehall and it's only the two of us now. We don't have a mage, a blademaster, and whatever exactly Rhys is to protect us. It's all on us, and if we do somehow make it to Whitehall, we still won't be safe. Lord Jason slaughtered a hundred men and was going to come after me at the Sanctuary. We killed at least one man and maybe a mage when we escaped. King Argren and his tall walls won't stop them. Ben, we may never stop running."

Ben frowned at her. "Are you trying to cheer me up? It's not working."

"I'm trying to be realistic," she replied. "If we lose focus, if we stop trying, if we stop moving, then we are as good as dead. If we're not committed to doing anything necessary to get through this, then we might as well march back to the Sanctuary and give ourselves up. The easy part, if there ever was one, is over."

Ben tossed the rock he was holding into the woods. "So what do we do?"

"We stay alive, we get to Whitehall, and we tell Argren what happened with Coalition and the Sanctuary. We warn the Alliance so they have time to prepare for what the Coalition is planning. Unless you want to go into hiding somewhere deep in these mountains and ignore what's going on in the world, what else can we do?"

"I don't know," he answered morosely. "When you put it like that, there isn't anything else."

4

FREE STATE

THEY SLEPT hard and fast and were back on their feet at day break. Amelie was right. Losing Mathias left a hole in Ben's heart, but what else was there but to push on? It's what the veteran and barkeep would have wanted.

That didn't mean they had to be foolish about it though.

"We can't just keep running without thinking," said Ben as they crested a low ridge and descended into a shallow ravine.

"What do you mean? We have to keep moving, right?" countered Amelie.

"Yeah," agreed Ben, "but we can't be stupid. That hunter found us somehow. It's too big of a coincidence that he happened to be in such a random area of the mountains at the same time as us at night. How did he do it?"

Amelie shifted her pack and grimaced.

"I've been thinking about it, and I think it must be magical," suggested Ben.

"He was a man," muttered Amelie. "He couldn't have any magic."

Ben smiled for the first time since Mathias passed. "I think you mean he shouldn't have any magic."

Amelie stopped walking and looked at Ben.

"Think about it," said Ben. "We were three days from the road. We've been in the middle of nowhere and recently moving across pretty rocky ground that wouldn't leave much of a track. I find it hard to believe that man just happened to be lurking way out here with no clue we'd be nearby. What other explanation is there? He somehow used magic to find us. That little copper bowl had runes on it, just like the wooden disc you're carrying."

Ben motioned ahead. "Let's keep walking. You know magic better than I do. Is there any way someone could use it to track us?"

Amelie knitted her brows and thought. "I don't know anything about that bowl. In theory, it could be possible to track someone if you have a strong enough attachment to them. A very strong attachment. If they're family or you've had a sexual relationship with them, maybe."

"I didn't have sex with that guy, if that's what you're implying," joked Ben.

"A strong and knowledgeable mage might be able to replicate that attachment," continued Amelie, ignoring Ben's comment. "I don't know of it being done by anyone in the Sanctuary, but it's conceivable. Blood or other bodily fluids could contain enough matter for someone to use. There is a force called cohesion where like particles attempt to stay united."

"I don't understand," said Ben.

"If someone had fresh blood or another bodily fluid," she supposed, "they might be able to amplify the cohesive force enough to draw the sample toward a person."

Ben blanched. "My blood was all over the walls we climbed. It was probably scattered through the vineyard and the woods too."

Amelie shook her head. "I've only studied cohesion in regards to simple things like drops of water. I'm not sure it's even a possibility." She shrugged in frustration. "It's probably not possible with dried blood because the chemical change would disrupt the cohesive property. I don't know enough about these things, but I can't think of anything else."

"I have no idea what you just said," muttered Ben. "What I followed though, is that as long as we don't leave fresh blood where a mage can find it, we should be okay?"

"You've got it." She smiled, then stopped and frowned.

Ben walked ahead before realizing she had stopped. He turned to wait. "Amelie, even if they can't track us, we really should keep moving."

She'd gone pale and was barely breathing.

"Amelie, are you okay?" asked Ben.

"Ben," she whispered, "Mistress Eldred had my blood."

"Your blood!" he exclaimed.

"For our training on healing, we extracted some of our blood. The mages preserved it. We studied the different properties individuals had and how to screen for disease. Mistress Eldred kept samples for further training. It's preserved. It's fresh..." Amelie trailed off.

The somber pair kept moving and quickly covered ground over the rocky terrain. They didn't know if Mistress Eldred even survived the confrontation in the Sanctuary. If she did survive, did she know how to use that blood to track them? Amelie had never heard of it being done, but if someone at the Sanctuary did have the skill, it would be Eldred.

Her role at the Sanctuary was the head of the laboratory, which was the half glass building Ben and Amelie fled through on the night of the escape. The laboratory was where many of the early initiate classes were held, but also where advanced research took place. Knowledge was critical to performing magic, so the initiates went to the lab to learn the fundamentals of science. Experienced mages ran experiments there to uncover new ways of manipulating the physical world. Mistress Eldred, as head of the facility, was familiar with all of the experiments. If someone developed a way to use blood to track a person, she would know of it.

"Do you think she survived?" asked Ben. "What was that stuff you hit her with anyway? It looked like her face was melting or something." He cringed at the memory.

Amelie shrugged. "I don't know what it was. I just saw the beaker and thought it looked heavy enough to do some damage. Whatever was in there though, I'm glad it didn't get on me."

"Shouldn't they store that kind of thing somewhere safe?"

Amelie laughed. "Apparently they didn't imagine anyone would want to break in. The whole building is full of stuff like that. They spend almost the entire first week telling us how we could get killed in the lab or the other training buildings."

"Mages are crazy," sputtered Ben.

"You don't know the half of it," quipped Amelie.

That evening, they stopped early. Traveling hard to gain distance made sense, but if someone could track them, there was no sense pushing to their limits. If they could be tracked, they needed to be alert and prepared to fight.

They began sword practice again but avoided sparring. They only had real blades and didn't trust that they wouldn't injure each other. Instead, they focused on footing, grips, and some basic forms. Amelie's rapier had a guarded hilt, which was different from the practice swords she used in the City. It was awkward at first, but she quickly realized the benefit of the new weapon over the saber she was carrying. The rapier was light and fast, ideal for her natural speed. She became determined to adjust.

Ben also showed her some thrusting attacks she had not learned yet. The rapier would be next to worthless as a slashing weapon. Many of the forms she learned with Saala would have to be discarded.

After two bells, they settled down and laid out what remaining food they had on top of their packs. It wasn't much.

"We should hunt and forage again," proposed Ben.

"I think we have enough for another two days if we're careful," replied Amelie. "Maybe we should go a little longer before stopping. You're right, we can't risk running out of food, but I'd be more comfortable if we get a little further from where we were attacked."

"Fair enough," agreed Ben. He picked up a few items from the food pile. "How does tough jerky and hard biscuit sound for dinner? It's highly recommended. At least, compared to the dry beans and rice. Without a fire to boil water and cook them, I'd prefer to save those for later."

Amelie rolled her eyes at him. "The food on this trip isn't nearly the quality I've come to expect on the road," she joked.

Ben uncorked his water skin and took a drink to wash down a dry bite of biscuit. He eyed the water skin. "One thing I miss is all of the drinks Rhys brought along. I like water as much as the next guy, but right now, I'd kill for an ale or skin of wine."

Two DAYS LATER, they started downhill and into the forest around the base of the mountain range. They were looking for a suitable spot to stop and forage for food. Ben hoped they would find a nice stream to fish and find trails where animals came to drink. They were far enough away from where the hunter attacked that he was willing to risk a campfire if he had something to cook over it.

As they moved deeper into the woods, dappled light played on the floor of the forest. High above them, the leaves rustled in a light breeze. Ben noted that amongst the bright green were splashes of yellow and orange. The season was changing. Soon, these woods would be a riot of color.

He steered them into a hollow between two ridgelines. He

hoped to find a stream trickling its way down from the mountain heights. In addition to food, they needed fresh water.

Just as he suspected, at the base of a shallow ravine was a small stream, maybe three strides across—not large enough for fish, but a sufficient source of drinking water. Hopefully the local rabbits and deer used it as well.

"How are you going to take down a deer?" asked Amelie skeptically. "Don't get me wrong, I'm sure you are a master huntsman, in addition to being a master brewer, but you don't exactly have the right tools for the job."

"I'll make a spear," answered Ben more confidently than he felt. "If we find a fresh game trail, I can make a spear out of a straight, solid branch. I'll hide close to the water until the deer gets near. If it's close enough, I can spear it. Back in Farview, people talked about it all of the time."

He didn't mention that talk was always at the Buckhorn Tavern and after a few pints of ale.

Amelie bent down to the stream and dunked her water skin beneath the surface. "If you say so."

Ben also moved to fill his skin then stopped and stood.

"Do you smell that?" he asked.

She also stood and looked around. "I didn't until you mentioned it. Is that smoke?"

They both peered around the creek bed but there was nothing to see.

Ben stooped back down and filled his skin, thinking.

"It is smoke," he affirmed. "This ravine could be acting as a chimney and is pulling it up. We may be nowhere near the source."

"So, should we keep moving?" asked Amelie.

"I don't think so," reflected Ben. "That smoke may be someone after us or it may have nothing to do with us at all. If it's someone after us, we need to find out who they are and understand how we can avoid them. If it has nothing to do with us, then it won't hurt to find out for sure. Either way, we benefit from knowing who else is out here."

Amelie hesitated. "What if it is someone who is after us and they catch us?"

Ben shrugged. "Let's not get caught."

They stalked quietly through the forest and Ben was grateful it was not yet autumn. There were few leaves on the ground to crunch and give them away. They followed the stream down the ravine, working on Ben's theory that it was acting as a chimney and the source of the smoke would be somewhere below.

The further downhill they got, the stronger the smell.

"It makes sense they would camp near the water," he whispered to Amelie.

She nodded in response.

Ben had spent years hunting game around Farview with his friend Serrot, so he was comfortable moving silently, but Amelie was not. She tried to follow in Ben's footsteps and winced every time she stepped on a fallen branch or inadvertently brushed against low-hanging foliage.

Ben glanced back at her and smiled encouragement. He hoped the trickle of water over rocks in the stream would mask any sounds they made.

Near the bottom of the ravine, the ridgeline tapered off, and the smoke smell grew stronger. Ben frowned. They were not smelling a temporary campsite. This was a serious encampment, or possibly a small village.

Again, he looked back at Amelie and saw her raise her eyebrows questioningly. She was no outdoorswoman, but even she could tell there were likely more people ahead than they wanted to fight.

"A little further," whispered Ben.

Together, they moved past the end of the ridgeline and saw another narrow creek meeting the one they had been following. They walked until they were on the end of the spit of land between the two creeks. They looked downstream but could see nothing.

Thick trees and undergrowth around the water obscured anything further than thirty paces away. Ben was certain the source of the smoke was nearby. Like he had speculated, it seemed to be located near the stream.

A distant clang of metal on metal jolted both of them. It continued at a regular interval.

"Men at arms training?" whispered Amelie nervously.

"No," answered Ben, listening closely. He smiled. "That's a blacksmith."

Once he identified it, it was clear. Ben could almost picture the blacksmith's hammer coming down over and over again.

"What do we do?" she asked in a low tone. "If it's a blacksmith with a forge, it can't be anything related to us."

Ben nodded. "I think you're right. Let's head back up the other creek and find a place to cross. We can keep going north. Whoever is down there, they are not interested in us."

One hundred paces upstream, they saw a small foot bridge connecting the two banks.

They looked at each other then back at the bridge.

"Let's cross," Ben suggested. "That's easier than finding a shallow point somewhere else, right?"

On close inspection, the bridge was solidly built but with crude tools. The walkway was made of split logs instead of milled planks and the handrails were affixed with wooden pegs instead of nails. Despite that, it didn't shake or even move when Ben stepped onto it.

Amelie followed quickly behind. She tried to shake the handrail but it didn't budge. Next, she hopped up and down, causing thumping sounds through the pleasantly solid logs. She grinned at Ben then they started walking across.

"Myland!" called a firm voice. "Is that you?"

Ben and Amelie froze. They were paused halfway across the bridge, trying to determine which way the voice came from.

"Aye," answered a call from behind. "Come help me. I've got your dinner!"

Panicked eyes met. Ben and Amelie started forward but stopped short at the foot of the bridge when a man stepped into view. He appeared almost as shocked as they did.

"Ho now," he blurted. "You don't look like Myland."

The man stood a good hand taller than Ben. He was dressed in a rough tunic and britches and carried a huge longbow. He had a hunting knife on his belt and a quiver full of arrows over his shoulder. He was otherwise unarmed.

"I'm, uh, I'm not Myland," replied Ben.

"I think he knows that." A man behind them laughed.

Myland, as the newcomer must be, was a shorter, stouter version of the first man. He was a hand shorter than Ben but made up for it with a bulky frame. It wasn't fat though, as evidenced by the deer slung over his shoulder. He balanced it with one hand and clutched a longbow similar to the first man's.

The newcomer continued, "Since we've established that your name is not, in fact, Myland, would you be so kind as to share it?"

"Ben." Ben cursed himself for not thinking to give a fake name. "And this is my friend Meghan."

"Well, pleased to meet you, Ben and Meghan. Now, if you'd care to take a step off the bridge, I'd like to keep moving. This deer weighs at least five stone and I'm ready to put the damn thing down."

Ben and Amelie sheepishly stepped off the bridge and Myland strode confidently across with the deer hanging over his shoulder.

"You folks are obviously not from around here," stated the woodsman. "You in a hurry or do you have time to stop over for the night? My friends and I don't get to hear a lot of news from the rest of the world. We're always willing to share a bite to eat and a few drinks for an update on what is happening."

Ben and Amelie looked at each other nervously.

The man sighed. "We don't much care what you're running from. Most of us in Free State, we've been on the run before, too. As long as you don't have a dispute with one of us, which I highly doubt you do, then you are welcome around our fire."

The man started off again then turned back to them. "You look like you need a rest. Come on!"

Free State turned out to be a humble village with about forty log and mud structures. It was set on the bank of the stream they'd been following and it was filled with people moving about their daily tasks.

A gaggle of small, yelling children came running up when the party walked into the village. The children swarmed around them, which drew a smile from Amelie, but Myland shooed them off.

He glanced apologetically at Ben and Amelie and explained, "They don't see outsiders very often."

He turned to his companion and instructed, "Athor, tell everyone we'll have a gathering at the common house this evening. I'm sure they'll all want to hear any news."

The man nodded and headed to one of the low buildings where a woman poked her head out to see what the commotion was.

"You two can come with me to my house," Myland offered to Ben and Amelie. "Later, everyone will want to hear all about whatever you can tell us. First, I suggest you rest."

Myland's house was fashioned of rough logs and mud like the rest of the village. He dropped his deer on the ground near the back then they went inside. The low ceiling barely cleared Ben's head.

"Sorry about that." The man grinned. He patted his own

lower-to-the-ground head and chuckled. "Plenty of room for me."

"Thank you for offering to put us up," said Ben. "Is there anything we can do for you? We don't have much in the way of coin."

Myland shook his head. "It's my pleasure."

The man rushed about, tidying up. After a minute, he added, "Honestly, I talk to the same folks around here every day. A man gets tired of it. It's worth sharing this hut for a night to get some fresh conversation."

Ben nodded and looked around the small structure.

It was split into a kitchen and sitting area in one room and a separate bedroom in another. Myland gestured toward the bedroom and suggested, "I'll sleep on the floor tonight if you two want to share the bed. You are together, right?"

Amelie blushed.

Ben started to answer but she interrupted him. "Yes, we can share the bed."

Ben looked at her. Her eyes darted toward the window carved in the back of the bedroom wall. The only opening in the main room was the door. If something happened and they needed to escape, that window would be a useful exit. Ben nodded to her in understanding.

They deposited their packs in the bedroom while Myland filled a pair of large buckets from the stream. He dumped one of them into a washbasin.

"You look like you've been traveling hard," he remarked. "Feel free to wash up and change. If you need any medicine or first aid, we have some people who could make do." Myland glanced at Ben's bound arm and torn shirt but didn't comment further.

"I've got to go settle a dispute. It's about a goat." Myland sighed. Shaking his head, he continued, "Some people... Anyway, I should be back in half a bell. We'll head to the gathering at twilight, if you're still up for it."

Ben smiled at him and the man left.

"Do you think we can trust them?" asked Amelie before walking over to the washbasin.

"Maybe," replied Ben. "They're too far away from any roads or real towns to be bandits, and we don't have anything worth stealing anyway. I doubt they have ties to the Sanctuary. Could be they would turn us in for a bounty, but we're going to have to take that risk sooner or later. When we get to Kirksbane, it will be a bigger problem than here I think."

Amelie agreed. "You're probably right."

She then paused before the washbasin and looked back at Ben coyly. "Don't get any ideas just because we're sharing a bed tonight, Master Ashwood, and whether in the woods or her manor house, a lady prefers to bathe privately."

He blushed and stepped outside of the small hut.

Life in the village was going on just like it was before they arrived. It was rougher, but it reminded him of Farview. Aside from a few long, curious glances at him, men and women went about the same domestic tasks they did back home. Children played amongst the buildings and a few chickens pecked fruitlessly nearby.

A young man with a nasty scar across the left half of his face and one missing eye stopped by Ben. "Stranger, you'll be at the gathering tonight?" he inquired.

Ben nodded.

The man walked on, calling behind him, "The name is Bartholomew. I'll see you there."

The man had the light gait and wariness of someone used to combat, but Ben didn't sense any threat from him.

On further observation of the village, Ben decided they could trust these people. He saw plenty of curiosity in the faces around him, but no one seemed to be hiding anything.

Before long, Amelie poked her head out of the door and told him he could wash and change now.

Ben ducked inside and saw she'd laid out a change of clothes for him, his only one.

"Sorry," she said. "I had to go through both packs to find everything I needed. I figured you would want to change too." She was wearing a different outfit and looked like she had been bathed and dressed by her handmaids. Her hair fell loosely around her shoulders and her cheeks had a rosy glow.

He looked down at the washbasin then back at her.

"Um, are you going to give me some privacy?" he asked.

"I'm not going to go wandering around outside by myself, if that's what you're suggesting," she responded curtly. "You say we can trust these people but we don't really know."

"B-But…" he stuttered.

"Ben, hurry up and wash," she insisted. "You think too much."

That evening, as the sun began to set, Myland took them to the common house. It wasn't any more than an open dirt space with a high, thatch roof.

"We have community meetings here, the occasional feast, and anything else that requires a lot of room," he explained.

Earlier, he told them that the village was called Free State and it was a community of people who were sick of living under the thumbs of lords and ladies, so they found their own place. There was no government and no leadership, he said, but as they arrived at the common house, it was apparent Myland was at least an informal leader.

With quick commands and gestures, he organized the few early arrivers.

Soon, there were long tables in place and people placing a disorganized jumble of food on them. It was simple stuff, game that could be caught in the surrounding woods, rich-smelling stews, rough grained breads, and piles of vegetables that Ben recognized would be easy to grow with minimal cultivation. A bored looking boy was turning a whole hog on a spit over a fire in the hearth.

"It's not fancy," Myland said with a grin, "but it will fill you up."

"It's better than we've been eating recently," muttered Amelie.

"You haven't seen the best part." Myland beamed. "My own contribution."

He took them to one side of the pavilion and showed off two large jugs containing a clear liquid. He unplugged one and lifted it up to them. "Smell," he encouraged.

Ben inhaled deeply then stepped back, coughing. His eyes watered and he felt a tingle at the back of his throat. Amelie looked suspiciously at Myland, who held the jug toward her, a broad smile plastered across his face.

She sniffed delicately at the jug then frowned dubiously at Myland. "What is that?"

"It's made from corn. Want to try some?" he asked.

"No thank you," she answered abruptly.

"Come on. It's good for you!" insisted Myland.

His enthusiasm for the brew was infectious. Eventually, Ben and Amelie gave in and let him pour some of the concoction into three battered tin cups. He clinked his against theirs and they took a tentative sip. The solution tasted just like it smelled, like liquid fire scorching its way through the mouth and down the throat. Ben got nervous about what it would do when it hit his stomach.

He coughed and spluttered. "That is awfully strong."

"Have a few more and you'll start to like it," defended Myland. "I tell everyone it's the third cup that tastes the best."

Eyes watering, Amelie choked, "Do you have any water?"

Myland sighed. "I think we can find some water. Let's go over and I'll introduce you around."

The common house began to fill up as the sun dropped below the trees and darkness fell across the village. The hearth on one end of the open structure and a roaring fire in the middle provided the light.

Myland's brew set a warm tingle in Ben's body. He found himself famished when scents of the food drifted to him. They gathered a flagon of water and piled heaping plates with the simple but hearty fare the villagers were carrying in. Myland led them to a table and bench. Before long, people crowded around, tentatively asking questions. Ben tried to answer between mouthfuls of food, but as soon as he answered the first question, more people pressed close.

"Let them eat. Let them eat!" barked their stout host. He stood up and shooed people away so Ben and Amelie could finish their dinner.

"He wasn't kidding about them wanting news," whispered Amelie.

"I don't mind telling them a few things in exchange for this," answered Ben before tearing into a steaming shank of venison. Juices dripping down his chin, he added, "Of course, we can't tell them anything about our situation or who you are."

"Of course," she agreed.

As soon as Ben mopped up the last of a puddle of gravy from his plate with a slice of bread, Myland reappeared with his jug of spirits and refilled the tin mug.

"If you don't mind obliging us, some of them are desperate for news," he said with a smile.

Ben turned on the bench to face a crowd of people who were shuffling closer.

The young man with the scar and missing eye who spoke to Ben earlier that day was the first to draw close.

"You remember me from earlier?" he asked quickly.

"Yes. Bartholomew, right?" answered Ben.

The man nodded eagerly and blurted, "Can you tell us about Argren's Conclave and the Alliance?"

Ben and Amelie exchanged a worried glance.

"It's okay if you don't know anything about it," continued the man apologetically. "The last visitors we had said it was happening soon. A great force was to be raised to meet the threat of the Coalition in the east. We've been hearing about the Coalition for years now. How it's growing, taking more territory."

"Ah," said Ben, relaxing and leaning back against the wooden table. "Yes, we do know a little bit about that."

"Just what has been told on the streets," added Amelie quickly. "You tell them, Ben. You're better with stories."

Bartholomew sat down on a nearby bench to listen. Several other villagers drew close.

Ben took a sip from his tin cup and winced at the burn. He thought about what to say while the fiery liquor leaked down his throat.

"Well," he started, "what you heard is correct. There was a Conclave in Whitehall and King Argren did form an Alliance. As you say, they plan to oppose the Coalition. Most of the cities on the Blood Bay and along the Venmoor River joined. Northport, Venmoor, Fabrizo, and of course the Sineook Valley. I'm probably forgetting a few..." he trailed off.

"What about the City?" blurted a young woman. She looked down sheepishly when the group turned toward her. "My sister lives there."

"I heard the Sanctuary had a representative at the Conclave," said Ben slowly. "They didn't sign the agreement though. From what I understand, the mages try to stay out of these kinds of things. I couldn't tell you what their intentions are." He looked at Amelie who shrugged. "Who knows if they really support the Alliance, or if it was just an act," he finished, a bitter note creeping into his voice.

Myland snorted from the back of the crowd.

"Will it be war then?" asked Bartholomew.

"It may come to that." Ben nodded. He was certain it would be war if he and Amelie made it to Whitehall and informed Argren what the Coalition and the Sanctuary had attempted, but they couldn't tell these people that. "I would say it is a strong possibility."

"Of course it will be war," growled Myland, glaring around the group. "It's always that way. That's why we live out here. Why I live here at least."

After that, the villagers asked less dangerous questions and ones frequently Ben and Amelie couldn't answer. They wanted to know what was happening wherever they came from or had family. Most of the places they asked about, Ben had never heard of. He certainly had no details on whether long lost loves ended up getting married or what people's parents were doing.

Before long, the questions tapered off and Ben was able to ask a few of his own.

"So, what exactly is this place?" he asked. "I think you called it Free State?"

Myland turned up his tin cup and gulped the liquor. He splashed another measure into his cup and offered to refill Ben's. Ben nodded. Once he was topped off, Myland answered, "We don't call it Free State because we're a bunch of creative geniuses, I'll tell you that. When I first arrived, they were already saying Free State. When I suggested they change it, well, people around here are stubborn. They call it Free State because we are free here. We are free from the influence of any lord, lady, mage, or whoever else tries to tell us how to live our lives."

"That's not so different from how I grew up," responded Ben.

"Is that so?" asked Myland. "It's not common these days, being able to tend to yourself and make your own decisions. Where are you from, if I may ask?"

"A little mountain town called Farview. It's a long way from here," responded Ben. "I guess technically, we were part of Issen, but I never knew it until I left."

"You're lucky then," replied Myland. "Growing up truly free is a gift, one that is getting too rare. I'm told it was different years ago, but now, you can't find many places that don't have some lord trying to put a boot on your neck."

"Not all lords are like that," objected Amelie. Ben shot her a warning glance but she continued. "If it wasn't for lords, then who would build the roads? Who would supply irrigation for crops?"

Myland spread his hands wide and replied, "We seem to be getting by okay here without some lord building our roads. And for irrigation, that is subservient thinking. Why does some lord have more of a right to water than I do? Who are they to decide which field grows and which withers and dies? Every man has equal right to nature's bounty, including water. The stuff falls from the sky!"

Amelie flushed. "What about protection then? King Argren, for example, is forming his Alliance. Don't you want protection against enemies like the Coalition?"

"Girl," snorted Myland. "Why do you think the Coalition is my enemy?"

Amelie blinked in confusion. "You support the Coalition?" she gasped.

"Of course not," explained Myland. "I'm just saying, why should I consider them my enemy? Are they trying to do something in Whitehall that Argren himself doesn't already do? I hear he rules that place with an iron fist. A lord is a lord. Doesn't much matter to me which one you're talking about."

"I-I..." she stuttered.

"Think about it," argued Myland. "The Coalition wants to control resources. They want power. How is that different from what is already happening? How is that different from this Alliance? As you said earlier, lords already feel like they have a natural right to something as basic as water!"

Myland downed another cup of spirits and sat back. "In my mind, it's not whether you should support the Alliance or the Coalition. It's why you'd want to support either one of them?"

Amelie frowned and remained silent.

Ben spoke up for her. "There are good people in the Alliance. Lords and ladies who want to do right by their people. When it comes to it, when there is a war, you have to take a side. From what I know, the Alliance is the side I want to be on."

Myland took another swig of spirits, swished it around then spat into the dwindling fire. It flared momentarily. "That's the thing people get wrong. You don't have to take a side. You don't have to play in their system and serve as a pawn in their games. You can leave. That's what we did here. Earlier, you asked what Free State was. That is Free State. It's a group of people who decided to say fuck it and left."

Myland refilled his tin cup, looked around the common house, and groused, "This is getting depressing. I don't live out here so I can be sad and serious all the time. Let's pick it up a little."

He stood up and called out, "Harold, get that flute of yours. Pica, let's hear some drums."

Free Staters scrambled around the common house, clearing space for dancing. The assigned residents brought out their instruments. Myland's jugs of spirits started making their way around the crowd, though Ben noticed several people turned up their noses at the potent brew.

The flute and the drums started sounding a steady beat and the familiar laughs and squeals of revelry filled the air, just like home on a festival night, or at any of the taverns they'd stopped at on their first journey. It was comforting to Ben, whenever he saw people having a good time and enjoying themselves.

Both he and Amelie sat out the dancing though. They'd been traveling hard and his injuries still bothered him. They were content to watch the action from the comfort of a rough-hewn wooden bench.

Myland sat beside them, also comfortable just watching. He

kept silent, neither asking them questions nor making any further attempt to recruit them into his small community.

Several more cups of the powerful clear spirit and Ben's head was swimming. The dancers flashed by in a low lit blur. The fire burned behind their silhouetted forms.

Ben and Amelie stumbled back to Myland's dark hut as the fire was dying down in the common house. The dancing had not stopped. In the dim corners of the common space, he saw some of the residents pairing up and practicing their freedom. They might think they are different, he thought drunkenly, but that happened at Argren's gala too.

Outside in the dark, Ben felt like a baby colt walking for the first time. He and Amelie bumped into each other and stumbled over unseen obstacles. They finally made it back and collapsed in the blackness of Myland's hut. The world swayed back and forth, rocking him like the gentle waves of the ocean.

5

PLOWMAN'S REST

THE NEXT MORNING, Ben woke to find himself pressed against Amelie. His head ached something awful, but he quickly realized he had a bigger problem. They were packed close together in Myland's small bed. The man assumed they were a couple, which wouldn't have been a problem, but since that wasn't actually the case, Ben was in an awkward position.

The night before, Myland's fiery spirits had put both Ben and Amelie quickly to sleep. Now, with the dim morning light peeking through the cracks in Myland's walls, Ben's arms were wrapped tightly around her still-sleeping form. On the other side of him was the rough log and mud wall. Her body was pleasantly warm against him. His front was in firm contact with her backside.

Parts of his body started reacting against his will to her comfortable softness. He knew if she woke up and felt him like that, the opposite of soft, he would never be able to explain it. He needed to move.

To extricate himself from the bed, he would have to pull his arms out from under her then somehow crawl over her. Slowly, he thought. He could get himself out of this and into a less compromising position if he moved slowly.

He started by barely moving his right arm, which was trapped underneath her. A finger's width at a time, he slid his arm out from under her, slow and steady.

Her eyes popped open and she was instantly awake. A lance of panic shot through his body. He shifted, trying to move before she felt his uncomfortable situation pressing against her.

"What are you doing?" she mumbled.

"Uh, trying to get up," he answered honestly.

She looked around the room and then back at him, her face a hand's length from his. "Did we sleep like this?"

"I think we did," he answered. "I just woke up."

"Oh." She stretched and yawned, which caused her to wiggle pleasantly against him. He froze, certain she'd notice.

"It's nice to wake up in a bed again, isn't it? But we'd better get up. It's going to get harder the longer we wait," she said with a wink.

Ben swallowed uncomfortably. He didn't have anything to say to that.

Myland served them a simple breakfast of hot porridge and they bartered Amelie's saber for another week of food.

"Where are you two headed, if you don't mind me asking?" he inquired.

"We're headed north," evaded Ben.

"I understand ya'll are running from something." The man chuckled. "This isn't the place you need to hide it. Like I said yesterday, most of us have been running at some point. If you need help finding your way north, I suggest you talk to Bart."

"Bart? You mean Bartholomew? The one with the eye?" asked Ben.

"Aye," answered Myland. "Bart knows these hills better than anyone except me and Athor, and neither of us is leaving. You want someone who can guide you along the quickest path to where you are going, then Bart is your man."

"Thank you," said Amelie. She looked at Ben and shrugged.

"Where is Bart's house?" asked Ben. It wouldn't hurt to talk to the man. Worst case, they would leave without him.

"East edge of the village about a stone's throw from the stream," directed Myland. "Bart is a good man these days and he has a good head for direction. One word of caution though, he wasn't always a good man. They called him Black Bart a few years back. It wasn't for the color of his hair. That's his story though, and I'll let him tell it. I thought you should know. When he lost his eye, it woke him up, I think. He's been living a different life since then."

Ben reached out a hand and took Myland's to shake it firmly. "Thank you for all of your help. It was good to have some hot food and a bed to sleep in. We've been camping rough the last few days."

"And thank you for the news," replied Myland. "We say we live apart from the world out here, but that doesn't mean we don't like hearing what's going on. Always nice to meet some potential recruits too," he added with a wink. "Remember what I said—just because some lord says 'these are the rules' doesn't mean you have to stick around and follow them. You get tired of that life, you come on back here."

"Understood," agreed Ben.

Later that morning, Bart led them along a barely visible game trail that wound up and away from the stream. It was clear of the undergrowth and fallen branches they had been fighting through previously. Ben realized they were making much better time. Enlisting Bart might be the best decision they'd made since leaving the City.

"I been out here about five years now, I reckon," the man drawled. "I'm not much use hunting with a bow since I lost my eye, but I can set a snare and do a bit of fishing. It doesn't take much to keep yourself alive if you live simply. I catch enough game to barter with the rest of the folks and try to keep social, but if I'm honest, I prefer to spend time by myself. That's why Myland sent you to me, I suspect. I spend a lot of time wandering these hills for the peace and quiet."

For someone who likes peace and quiet, thought Ben, Bart loved to talk.

Their guide was dressed in a rough brown tunic and faded black cloak. He carried a half-full pack and had a hand axe strapped on one side of him and a well-used cutlass on the other. The cutlass was an odd choice for a woodsman, but they knew Bart wasn't always a woodsman.

The pack was half full, Bart explained, because he intended to fill it up on the way back. He agreed to guide Ben and Amelie as far as Kirksbane in exchange for eight heavy gold coins.

"No one in Free State bothers with coin," remarked Bart. "It's all barter. But they like coin in town just fine. I'll pick up a few things which I can trade back here. Get me some decent hooch, too. That swill Myland distills isn't fit for my goat."

Eight gold coins was a significant portion of what they'd managed to keep after fleeing the City and raiding Reinhold's estate. If it got them to Kirksbane safely though, it would be worth it. Ben didn't like the idea of stealing, but if it came down to it, they could survive in the fertile Sineook Valley for a long time without coin. It was farm after farm. No one bothered placing a guard over cabbages in the field.

"Bart," asked Amelie, "How long is it to Kirksbane?"

The man scratched unceremoniously at his behind and answered, "Should take us about four weeks. It's faster on the river road of course, but I'm guessing you don't want to go that way."

Amelie cringed. They hadn't told Bart much, but it wasn't hard to surmise they were running from something. Why else would they be out in the middle of nowhere?

"Don't worry, lady," assured the Free Stater. "No one is going to find you out here."

That night, Ben and Amelie huddled together and decided to keep at the sword practice. In the past, they avoided practicing around strangers, but that was while they were trying to hide Saala's true skill and keep a low profile. Out here, they didn't have much skill to hide, and there was no avoiding Bart.

As it turned out, Bart was happy to help them. He disparagingly eyed the forms Ben was instructing Amelie on then interrupted.

"No, no, no!" he griped. "You try and swing a rapier like that, you're going to get chopped up in heartbeats."

He drew his cutlass and stomped over to where they were practicing. "What you are doing is just fine with that longsword, but using a lighter blade is different. Let me show you a few things."

After that, every evening involved at least a bell of sword practice. Bart was proficient with the cutlass and was even able to help Amelie handle both of her blades at once. Like Ben found when they were attacked, Bart explained the trick was using the offhand for defense.

"Think of it as a shield with an edge," he instructed. "If you try to attack with both blades, it's awkward and weak. Always use one to defend and the other to counterattack. Then you've got a deadly fighting style."

He unslung his axe and demonstrated some maneuvers. "Back in my day, before I lost the eye and my depth perception, I used a dagger in my offhand. Helps turn aside a blow, and if someone gets close, well, it's easy to turn to offense and stick 'em. Overall, the style is defensive though. If you want to get aggressive and attack, you might be better off ignoring your dagger hand and just using the rapier. You can't effectively swing both at once. I can show you some attack postures if you like."

Amelie, breathless from the practice, panted. "Defense and

counterattack is good for now. I don't intend to go around attacking people."

Bart grinned, twisting the scar around his missing eye. "You never intend to attack someone, until you do."

Two weeks into the trip from Free State to Kirksbane, Ben was starting to feel confident. The cuts and scrapes he'd gotten fleeing the City were healed and they hadn't seen a soul since departing the village. For the first time since the attack on him and Renfro by Gulli's men, he felt like he didn't need to look over his shoulder.

Early one morning, he was up just before dawn and settled on a moss-covered log to watch the sunlight break through the canopy of leaves above them. A bright array of colors was on display. Soon, the leaves would fall to the ground. The air was crisp and promised the chill of winter was just around the corner. We need to get some warmer clothing in Kirksbane, he thought.

A muted scuff of boots on dirt caught his attention. He turned to see Amelie picking her way over to join him.

"It's getting hard to sneak up on you," she whispered.

Ben smiled. "I feel like I'm at home in the woods. It feels right. It feels good. Anything that is not in place seems to jump out."

"Is that like the blademaster sense Saala spoke about?" she asked, wide eyed.

Ben shrugged. "I don't know. I just feel more connected out here."

"You know we can't stay out here, right?" inquired Amelie.

Ben sighed. "I know. We have to get to Whitehall and warn Argren about what the Coalition and the Sanctuary are doing."

"These Free Staters," Amelie added, "they ran away from the world. Maybe that was easier for them, but that doesn't mean it's the right thing to do. People need us and we can't turn our backs on them."

Two weeks later, they were in the last stretch of woods

outside of Kirksbane and stopped early.

"From here, we'll start to see people," explained Bart. "You haven't told me what you're running from, but I think it's time you told me a little. What are we up against? Is there anything I need to know about before I walk into that town with you?"

Ben frowned. "Maybe it's best for you if you don't walk in with us."

Bart fingered the hilt of his cutlass. "Ya'll came from the City, right? You think someone's going to be looking for you all the way up in Kirksbane?"

"I don't know. Hopefully not." Ben sighed. "You got us all of the way here. There's no use for you to take any additional risk. Tell us which way to go and we can make it on our own. You've earned your pay as far as I'm concerned."

Bart smirked and gestured to his half empty pack. "Remember, I gotta get into town too. I'm not spending two months walking out here and back just to keep drinking Myland's swill. How about this? Ya'll camp here tonight and I keep moving. That will put me into town a few bells earlier than you two and no one will suspect we traveled together. I wish you the best of luck, I really do, but if someone's looking for you, I don't want to be seen together."

"I understand," agreed Ben.

Ben clapped Bart on the back then watched as the man disappeared into the trees without further word, stuffing his new shiny gold coins into his belt pouch.

"He was nice," said Amelie. "Once you get past the fact that he won't shut up."

THE OUTSKIRTS of Kirksbane posed an intimidating obstacle. It was nearly five weeks since they were attacked and lost Mathias. They hadn't seen any sign of Sanctuary pursuit since then. That didn't mean the mages had given up. Kirksbane was a major intersection of both river and road traffic, so it made sense someone could be watching it. Despite the risk, Ben and Amelie felt they had to stop.

Away from civilization, they had no idea what they were up against. They needed news and supplies. They needed to know what was happening with Issen and Whitehall. A busy town was the only place they could get that information.

That didn't mean they would be stupid and just walk right in, though. They spent the entire morning slowly circling the sprawl and looking for anything out of place.

The wagon and barge traffic was heavy this time of year. It was harvest time in Sineook Valley. Wagons covered the road going into Kirksbane and barges clogged the river heading south toward Venmoor and the City.

"If we can attach ourselves to an empty wagon train, that may help us move through the Valley unnoticed," muttered Ben. "Maybe we can pose as guards."

"Yeah, but empty wagons don't need guards," remarked Amelie.

"Hmm. Then maybe we could be lovers eloping a step ahead of your angry father?" joked Ben.

Amelie rolled her eyes. "You had better stay a step ahead of my father if you want to be my lover," quipped Amelie.

Want to be her...

"Come on," continued Amelie. "Let's go. We haven't seen anything suspicious out here. They are either watching the roads or they are not. It's been five weeks since we escaped. Not even the Sanctuary can have men guarding every road in every town between the City and Whitehall. We need information and this is the only way to get it."

Ben hitched his pack higher on his shoulders and loosened his longsword in the scabbard. "As you command, my lady."

Minutes later, Ben thought they'd made a horrible mistake. A pair of guards stopped them at the entrance to town. Both were dressed in long chainmail jerkins and carried sturdy-looking pikes with a short sword on their belts for good measure.

"Hold up there," barked one of the guards.

Ben tensed, prepared to fight. He thought they might be able to take the two guards if they acted fast and surprised them, but they would have to flee quickly. If any of the guards in this town were mounted, they would have no chance of escape.

"It's harvest time and the inns are almost full. Meaning, they're all charging full fare," growled the guard. "There's no room in town for vagrants. We don't need any wagon men and the barge jobs go to locals."

"Vagrants?" mumbled Ben, confused.

"Son, you look like you've been living in the forest for a month." The guard snorted mirthlessly. "If you don't have two coins to rub together, then you're best off turning around and going back to whatever hole you crawled out from."

"Sir," broke in Amelie, "we do have coin for an inn."

The first guard eyed her up and down skeptically.

His companion took another look at her and licked his lips. "Lass, you look like you might clean up pretty. How about you come on back to my apartment? I'll see you're taken care of. You can share my bed as long as you like."

Amelie blushed furiously. "That won't be necessary." She shook her belt pouch. The clink of coins was unmistakable.

The second guard continued to stare lasciviously, but the first eyed the pouch and allowed, "Very well. You two can come in, but be warned, we clear the streets every night. If you can't find a bed, then out you go. And I'll be very disappointed and not nearly so friendly if I've got to turn you out later."

The man finished with a stone-faced stare. Ben and Amelie quickly scurried past the pair.

"I thought..." started Amelie.

"Me too," groaned Ben. "I think we made a mistake coming

here. We need information, but anyone here could be working for the Sanctuary. My heart is going to be in my throat until we can get back out and away from people."

"Maybe you're right." Amelie sighed. "But we're here now. Let's find out what we can and leave quickly. If we finish before dark, we can fit in with the vagrants getting tossed out at night. You have to admit, that is good cover. People won't expect me to be traveling so rough."

Ben nodded. "We have half a day then. In the stories, people are always able to get information from talkative barkeeps. Should we try a tavern?"

"Yes," she agreed, "but in the stories they always know the barkeep. Do you know anyone running a tavern here?"

"There's the Curve..." started Ben before he realized that bringing up that particular tavern was probably a bad idea.

Amelie glared at him. "We are not going to the Curve."

"Right, of course," he said, red-faced. Stupid, he told himself. "There is another place I remember from last time. It was by the barge moorings. I remember it because it was separated down the middle. Half was river men and half was wagon drivers. Rhys said they kept them apart to prevent fights. If the Sanctuary has people here, they are probably watching the river, but we only need to know what is going on in Sineook Valley. If we stay on the wagon driver side, we could learn what we need and keep relatively safe. What do you think?"

"That's a better idea," Amelie said with a scowl, "but it doesn't entirely make up for your first one."

The incongruously named Plowman's Rest was packed full of river men on one side and wagon drivers on the other, just as Ben recalled. Autumn, when they transported the bulk of Sineook Valley's harvest, was the busy season for both groups, but no sane merchant was going to ask the men to skip a little bit of fun at the end of each haul.

The place was near overflowing. A wall of noise washed over

Ben and Amelie as they walked inside. Rough benches and tables stretched the length of the room. Untouched platters heaped with stew and loaves of bread were surrounded by empty tankards of ale.

"I guess we just find a place to sit?" inquired Amelie.

She was used to classier places, realized Ben. The rough tradesmen filling the room weren't too different than what Ben was used to back home or the taverns the guards favored in Whitehall. In the City, he'd usually sold his ale to nicer places than this, but he'd been in his fair share of dives.

"We order up there," he said, nodding toward a busy bar. "Then find a place to sit."

"There are no serving women?" asked Amelie, peevishly. She was eyeing the long line at the bar.

Ben gestured to the roaring and carousing crowd around them. "How many girls could you find willing to brave this pack? Imagine after night fall when it gets really wild."

Amelie looped an arm around Ben's and groused, "I'll stay close to you then, tough guy. Let's get something at the bar, so we fit in, and then try to find someone who has been through the valley recently." She added after a pause, "And isn't too drunk yet."

They pushed and jostled their way through the crowd to the bar where Ben ordered two ales and two bowls of stew.

A harried serving man sloshed stew into the bowls and passed over two large tankards with foam spilling down the sides. Ben's mouth watered.

In the back of the room, Ben found space on a bench that they were able to squeeze into side by side. Next to Amelie was a man lying face down on the table snoring. His companions were laughing uproariously around him. At a point earlier, someone had stacked a pile of upside down bowls on the man's head. Gravy from the stew and globs of congealed fat dripped into his face and hair.

"I don't think we'll get much out of him," whispered Amelie.

On Ben's side sat a small, dark man who was involved in a contentious argument with a fellow across the table from him. Ben picked up that they were discussing where in the Sineook Valley they should go next. He gestured to Amelie that they should listen in.

Apparently, the men had assured a particular farmer they would return for his goods, but one of the men thought they could earn a better margin elsewhere.

Ben listened while he dug into his stew. It was lumpy and certainly not fresh, but after the four weeks in the woods since Free State, he devoured it. Stale ale washed it down. He glanced at Amelie to see if she was also following the conversation next to him.

Instead, he noticed she was leaning back, focused on a discussion behind them. He looked to see who she was listening to and saw a foppish man, likely a courtier in a minor court, who was expounding loudly to a merchant across from him.

"I tell you, Barnes, it's the opportunity of a generation!" exclaimed the foppish man.

Barnes, the merchant, responded calmly in a voice that Ben could not pick up over the noise of the crowd.

"Argren doesn't give a damn about them. He's shown that," insisted the courtier.

Ben's ears perked up.

"You can't get there anyway, so there are only two sides to play," continued the courtier emphatically. "Northport or the Coalition."

The merchant grunted a garbled response. Only one word was audible to Ben and Amelie—Issen. They glanced at each other.

"Your loyalty is admirable," appeased the courtier. "But it gets you nowhere. Lord Gregor of Issen is in no position to pay you and Argren apparently doesn't share your sense of honor. If you insist you are still Gregor's vassal, then Northport is an option, of course. Rhymer has more gold than he knows what to do with and he has a small shred of decency. He knows what Coalition rule will do to him. He might make you whole just to keep it out of the Coalition's hands, but why take that long journey and risk it?"

The courtier paused for effect. "You let me broker the deal now, and you've got your profit without having to travel to Northport. Don't be foolish."

The merchant was starting to raise his voice. Finally, his half of the conversation was loud enough to hear. "My deal was with Gregor. If he's unavailable, I will rely on his liege to make me whole. I won't go running to Northport to beg on that slob Rhymer's doorstep, and I sure as shit won't deal with a toad like you!" snarled the merchant.

"You're making a mistake," debated the courtier. His tone took on a snake-like smoothness. "Argren doesn't believe the mages should be as big a source of power in Alcott as they are. He's not going to funnel gold into their pockets no matter what is promised about the efficiency of the devices. Besides..." The man's voice dripped with venom. "You'll soon find the mages aren't as supportive of Argren and his Alliance as you imagine they are."

"What do you mean?" demanded the merchant. "The mages were at the signing of the Alliance. I have it on the best authority that they support Argren still. Lord Gregor's daughter is one of them for goodness sakes! It's well known all over Alcott."

The courtier raised his hands in a defensive posture and tried to placate the merchant. "You're right, that is known. I shouldn't have said what I did. My point is valid though. You know Argren doesn't believe in the mages like the rest of the lords do, and you can see by the way he is treating Issen what his honor is worth."

"I don't give a damn about his honor!" thundered the merchant. "It's my honor I'm concerned about."

"Hold on. Hold on. This isn't a discussion to be had in public," chided a new voice.

Ben risked a glance behind them and saw a soldier had arrived. The man was wearing a knee-length chainmail coat and had a heavy broadsword hanging from his belt. His linen tunic displayed a generic-looking coat of arms Ben did not recognize.

"Who are you?" challenged the merchant. "Another Coalition stooge?"

"I'm just trying to make my way in the world like everyone else," snapped the soldier. "Let's continue this elsewhere. There are too many ears in this place."

The merchant stood from his bench and slapped his hands down on the table. "I won't be told what to do by any Coalition bootlicker. I'm loyal to Lord Gregor and King Argren."

"Your lord's city is under siege, fool. No help is coming!" cried the courtier. "Lord Gregor will be licking our boots by next summer."

Ben's blood ran cold. He felt Amelie tightly grip his arm.

"Shut your mouth," ordered the soldier. "This is not the time or the place. We have other concerns and this situation can be dealt with later," he finished ominously.

"I don't report to you," retorted the courtier. "And I'll decide when it's the time or place."

The dandy man leaned toward the merchant. "How about this offer. You sell me the devices right now, or I will take them! You and the rest of the sheep supporting Argren and his Alliance are finished. Issen is surrounded and no reinforcements are coming from Whitehall or anywhere else. Argren has abandoned Gregor. Everyone sees it. You think they will stick together after that? Change sides or I'll be dancing on your grave a year from now!" howled the courtier.

The shouting was drawing the interest of the rest of the room. People were turning to see what the commotion was about.

"What did you say about the Coalition?" called a voice from

two benches down.

The soldier realized they'd made a mistake and placed a hand on the courtier's shoulder to warn him. The man was too excited to listen to reason though. Practically foaming at the mouth, he shouted, "What is it to you?"

The soldier looked to the door of the tavern and gestured frantically to someone out of view.

The merchant took the opportunity to garner support from the room. "These two are Coalition lackeys and they just threatened to rob me!"

Drunken men shifted in their seats. Several of them stood, facing the confrontation. Ben nudged Amelie and tried to subtlety push her toward the back of the room. She resisted and hissed, "We have to hear this. He's talking about my father!"

Four more armed men entered the tavern. The merchant pointed and shrieked. "There, Coalition forces coming to rob and kill us all!"

The place exploded in violence.

The first soldier, standing by the courtier and merchant, was prepared, but his companions didn't realize what they'd walked into. He managed to pull his broadsword. His men were swarmed before they knew what was happening. Drunken wagon drivers crowded around, swinging balled fists and kicking with booted feet.

A drunken man grabbed the arm of the original soldier. The drunk paid the price for being first. The soldier swept him aside and his heavy blade followed. The drunk screamed in pain and collapsed into a tangle of his table mates, blood splashing across the room.

The soldier leapt onto the table and slashed wildly around him, trying to clear space. Chunks of body parts from unprepared patrons rained across the room.

Men scrambled fiercely to get away from his blade.

The courtier was too slow and the broadsword caught him

square in the head, creating a gruesome display of brain matter as his body flew backward, crashing into Ben and Amelie. Shocked, they pushed the corpse away. Ben met the eyes of the soldier.

For a brief moment, the soldier paused with a stunned look, staring at Ben then Amelie. It was the beginning of his end. A bench smashed into his legs and Ben heard the sharp crack of broken bone. The soldier fell hard onto the table and a wagon driver jumped on top of him, fists flashing down into the fallen man's face. The soldier wasn't done yet though, and the wagon driver was thrown off, the bloody broadsword sticking into him.

The merchant, seeing his opportunity, yanked his belt knife out and charged the soldier. The military man drew his own dagger but was too late to prevent the merchant stabbing down into his unprotected neck. In his last breaths, the soldier pulled the merchant close and punched his short blade into the other man's stomach. The merchant smacked the soldier's blade away, strings of blood flying behind it as it clattered to the ground.

Again and again, the merchant thrust his knife into the soldier's neck. It was clear the fallen soldier wouldn't be moving again. The merchant slumped back, falling off the table crashing against a nearby bench, clutching his profusely bleeding stomach.

The fight near the door had already finished. Ben could see the bodies of the other armed guards lying prostate on the floor. Bloody-fisted wagon drivers mingled around them, almost unbelieving at how quickly their afternoon had been consumed by vicious violence.

From across the room, the barge men looked over a chest-high wall in confusion.

A shout of, "City watch!" got everyone moving again. The wagon drivers started rapidly disappearing. Even serving staff seemed to vanish behind the bar.

Amelie surged forward and scrambled across the table to get to the fallen merchant. Ben jumped across behind her and they knelt next to the injured man.

He was staring down at his crimson hand and the pool of blood forming around him.

"I think I'm finished," he muttered to no one in particular.

"You work for Lord Gregor?" Amelie asked him.

The merchant stared back at her with glazed over eyes.

She shook his shoulder and tried again. "You work for Lord Gregor?"

"I used to." The merchant coughed wetly, a trickle of blood leaking down his chin.

"We can help you, but first, you must tell me what you know about Issen. It is under siege? What is the status?" she urged.

"Issen is done. It's just a matter of time now," the man answered sorrowfully. "Banath was right. It is surrounded. The Coalition got there sooner than Gregor or Argren anticipated and with twice the men."

"What is Argren doing about it?" implored Amelie, pain evident in her eyes.

"He's fortifying what he can. He thinks it's a trap and won't send reinforcements to Issen." The merchant's voice was fading. One, maybe two minutes was all he had left, thought Ben. The clang of a bell out in the streets told him that they might not have more time than that before the city watch arrived. They couldn't risk getting caught here standing over a pile of dead men.

"Amelie," he said.

"No, I have to know more." She met the merchant's eyes. "Please, tell me anything else you know. Has the Coalition attacked yet? How much time is left?"

"They haven't attacked, just cut off entry and exit from the city," gurgled the man. Blood flowed freely down his chin now. "They're waiting on something. A peaceful solution they say. Lord Jason is on a secret mission to do something to persuade Lord Gregor to surrender…"

Ben and Amelie looked at each other.

The merchant continued, unaware of the world around him.

"That's what Banath told me. He told me that as soon as word came back from Lord Jason, Issen would surrender, or the siege would begin. Everyone will be killed…"

"If they haven't attacked yet, there is still hope," Amelie said to Ben. More to convince herself than him, he thought.

"How—" started Ben. The dying merchant interrupted him.

"Rhymer," the man groaned. "He's seen this coming for a long time. He's been building up his army for years. He's the only one who's got the men to do something. He knows he can't live with the Coalition. He might…" the man finished with a wet cough. A fountain of blood poured out of his mouth.

The clanging was intensifying outside. Ben realized the watch was heartbeats away from arriving. He grabbed Amelie and hauled her to her feet.

"We have to leave now, or we may not be leaving at all," he demanded.

He tugged her toward the bar where he'd seen the staff fleeing through a doorway. The front was where the watch would arrive first. He hoped they could still slip out the back unnoticed.

The streets around the Plowman's Rest were chaotic and Ben blinked in the bright sunlight. In the dimly lit bar, he'd forgotten it was still early afternoon.

People were running in all directions, mostly away. It was clear many of them didn't know what they were running from. Shouts about attacks on Kirksbane mixed with more exotic conclusions.

Heavily armed city watch swarmed the area, many of them just as confused as the citizens. Ben spied the pair of guards who stopped them earlier that morning. They were calling out to their fellows asking where to go.

They wouldn't get a better opportunity to escape unnoticed, realized Ben. Whether it was the city watch or Coalition flunkies, it would be hard for anyone to keep track of all of these people running around in confusion.

6

ENDLESS FLIGHT

THE SUN SET behind the trees before Ben and Amelie stopped, comfortably back within the forest southeast of Kirksbane.

"That escalated quickly," remarked Ben dryly. He wasn't sure how to address the information they learned and what it would mean for Amelie. "What do we do now?"

"The Coalition attacked Issen. It's war now," she replied abruptly. "I'm shocked those men admitted they were Coalition in public. At least they got what they deserved," she finished darkly.

Ben sighed and thought about how to comfort her. Her childhood home was under siege, and as far as they knew, her entire family was trapped in Issen. He had tried to talk to her while they were walking and she said to wait, that they needed to focus on getting away from Kirksbane. Now that they were away, he didn't know where to start.

"It's okay, Ben," she said. "I'm worried. I'm scared for my family, but I can't focus on that right now. You are right. We have to think about what to do next."

"You don't think we should go to Whitehall anymore?" asked Ben.

"If everything they said was true, then there's no point in going there."

"But, we have to tell Argren about the Sanctuary's betrayal, right?" he insisted.

Amelie frowned and shook her head. "If Argren is reluctant to send help for Issen now, he will be even less likely to do so when he hears what we know. I think we were making a mistake, believing he would help once we told him about the Sanctuary. A man like Argren, when he has reason to believe the Sanctuary is poised to plunge a knife in his back, will never send his army elsewhere. What we heard proves it. He will keep his men close to home. We have to look elsewhere."

"Northport then?" guessed Ben.

Amelie nodded. "It's the only thing I can think of. Outside of Whitehall, Lord Rhymer is the only one with the power to stand up to the Coalition and the Sanctuary. I'm not sure he'll do it, but I have to try something."

Ben dropped his pack and began to look around the small clearing they occupied. "We might as well make camp here," he suggested. "It's a long way to Northport. We can get started at first light."

Amelie slowly lowered her pack then stepped toward Ben. "Ben, we've gotten away from the Sanctuary. I will be eternally grateful that you risked your life and rescued me. If it wasn't for you, I would be in Lord Jason's custody or dead right now. I can't thank you enough for that."

Ben blushed and shrugged uncomfortably.

She placed a hand on his arm. "That was enough, Ben. You don't have to do this. It's too much for me to ask. You could go back to Farview or find somewhere else quiet and let all of this blow over."

Ben frowned. "I've been thinking about that a lot since we left Free State. That is what they are doing, the Free Staters. They found somewhere quiet and are letting it all blow over. I don't think I can do that. If I can help, then I have to. I can't let these things happen if there is something I can do about it."

"Northport is a long shot, Ben," warned Amelie. "I've met Lord Rhymer. He thinks of only himself. If we convince him there is something in it for him, then maybe he'll help. He won't do it out of the goodness of his heart."

"Then we'll have to convince him," declared Ben. "I know it will be hard, I know it will be dangerous, but I have to do this. I'll go to Northport with you and I'll help however I can. We are in this together, Amelie. Until it is over."

Amelie let out a sob and wrapped her arms around Ben. They stood there in the quiet clearing, her sobbing into his shoulder and him holding her.

THE NEXT MORNING as they were preparing a quick bite to eat before getting back on the road, Ben recalled something from the day before.

"Amelie, do you remember the Coalition soldier? Right before they knocked him down and jumped on him, did you see what he was doing?"

She shrugged. "I don't remember much about the fight. It was a bloody blur to me."

"I think he looked at me. Right into my eyes. He paused like he knew me."

Amelie swallowed hard and grimaced.

"If he knew me..." continued Ben.

"Then others will know you too," finished Amelie.

"They'll know both of you," called a new voice.

Ben jumped back, startled. Bartholomew was standing at the edge of the clearing. The man was positioned defensively with his hand on the hilt of his cutlass.

"You scared me!" exclaimed Ben, looking curiously at their former guide. "What are you doing here?"

Relaxing, Bartholomew chuckled and stepped forward. "Sorry about that. I heard about a ruckus in town yesterday. It sounded like something you two might be involved in. I checked around and found out you weren't in the pile of bodies afterward. I'd done my errands and thought there was no sense in hanging around that place. Figured you might be hiding out in the woods, so I came looking."

"Thanks," said Ben uncertainly. "That is very kind of you, but we are okay."

"No problem," answered the one-eyed man. "Spent a few weeks with you folks. I guess I grew attached. I didn't want something bad to happen to you."

Ben edged closer to his pack and his longsword. Something wasn't right here.

Bartholomew stepped forward again and slung his own pack down. "I left before I had breakfast this morning. I don't suppose you have enough to share?"

Amelie nodded and glanced nervously at Ben. He stared ahead at Bartholomew. Then his gaze dipped down to the man's pack. The pack was half full.

Ben lunged toward his longsword in the same heartbeat Bartholomew swept out his cutlass.

Ben rolled to his feet, and Amelie scrambled behind him. Her rapier and dagger were on the other side of the clearing.

"No breakfast to share?" remarked Bartholomew with a smirk.

"Why are you really here?" demanded Ben.

The man's cutlass held steady in front of him as he looked over the clearing with his one good eye.

"This could have been easier and a lot less painful if you'd let me take you after you fell asleep tonight," snarled Bartholomew.

"Sorry about that," responded Ben. "You can walk away. That would be easy to do."

He was studying Bartholomew and his movements. In the woods, the man had proven to be a competent and experienced swordsman, but he was hampered by his missing eye. It affected his depth perception and he had difficulty adjusting to quick movements. Ben's biggest concern was that the man was waiting for someone else to arrive. With Amelie unarmed, Ben did not want to face more than one attacker.

"Walk away? I don't think so. I would have preferred the easy way, but this works too," said Bartholomew with an evil smirk.

"You can't beat me," stated Ben coolly, fishing to see if Bartholomew would mention help on the way. "I've sparred with you. You don't have the skill."

"Boy, I've fought and killed more men than you have even known," retorted Bartholomew confidently.

"Was that before or after they poked out your eye?" taunted Ben.

Bartholomew sneered. "A whore cut out my eye. And now she's as dead as anyone else who ever came at me. I had a lot of fun with her before she died, though. I don't think she enjoyed it." He leered over Ben's shoulder at Amelie. "It took days before she finally died."

"A great slayer of unarmed whores? Pardon me if I'm not scared." Ben stalled for time. It didn't appear that Bartholomew was waiting for help. The longer he kept talking, the more Ben would find out about his motives. "I'm surprised you managed to defeat her and only lost one eye."

"You don't know me!" shouted Bartholomew. "You think because I was in Free State that I'm some peace lover like Myland? I wasn't there because I'm frightened of my shadow like him. I was there because if I step foot in any port city on the Blood Bay, I'll be hanged. I'm Black Bart, boy. I spent ten long years raping and pillaging my way from one side of that bay to the other. I had a pile of gold coins higher than you are tall. You could fill a house with the blood I spilled taking it."

"You don't have any of that gold left, I'm guessing?" chided Ben.

Bartholomew was getting emotional, something Saala taught Ben to avoid and something Rhys encouraged him to instigate in his opponents.

"I will, once I take your heads," crowed Bartholomew. "That soldier offered me ten gold coins just for word of where you were going. He's dead now, but there will be others. If news about you is worth ten, then I'll ask a hundred for your head. Each," he finished triumphantly.

"You have to take it first," Ben challenged.

Bartholomew growled and charged forward. Ben was waiting. Instead of settling in a defensive stance, he charged as well. Momentarily, Bartholomew was confused, his lone eye adjusting to the rapid movement. It gave Ben time to smash aside the man's cutlass and stick his longsword deep into the former pirate's chest.

Bartholomew's eye popped open wide in shock. Ben witnessed the life drain out of it before the man slumped backward, sliding off the sharp blade of Ben's longsword.

"You're getting good at that," announced Amelie in a shaky voice.

"Maybe," replied Ben. "He was over confident, and I used that. Thinking you are good doesn't help you in a sword fight."

"Do you think he really did what he said, killed scores of people?" asked Amelie. "He acted like he was a famous pirate."

"I don't know," replied Ben with a shrug. "I've never heard of him."

They quickly packed the rest of their gear, rifled through Bartholomew's pack, then left the clearing. The dead pirate lay on his back in the pale morning sun.

7

BLOOD AND ASHES

GETTING AROUND KIRKSBANE PROVED EASY. The terrain was flat, and there were enough people about that the two of them did not stand out. Ben was worried there would be Sanctuary watchers, but they passed unmolested.

North of Kirksbane, they found a small track that steered away from the river. It continued north as far as they could tell. Thinking that was less likely to be watched than the river road, they started down it.

"This journey isn't going as smoothly as I hoped it would," muttered Amelie as they walked.

"I know," agreed Ben. "Including the soldier at the Plowman's Rest, that is three times now we've run into people who recognized us and were trying to capture or kill us. We lost Mathias already. It's only a matter of time before someone else sees us and we aren't able to defend ourselves."

"I wish we had Mathias with us now," said Amelie. "I didn't know him well, but from what I saw, he was a practical man. There has to be a practical solution to this. Stumbling around and hoping for the best isn't working."

"I miss him too." Ben sighed. His friend always had a way of cutting to the heart of a problem and finding an elegant, easy solution.

"Let's think about it like he would," Ben started. "Let's lay out the facts. We need to get to Northport, time is a factor, we don't know the way, we're almost out of food, and we don't have much money. There could be watchers from the Sanctuary or the Coalition ready to kill us at any turn."

"That's pretty depressing." Amelie frowned. She plucked a tall blade of grass from the side of the track and swished it at low-hanging braches they passed. Slapping grass against branches didn't do much to alleviate her frustration, but it was better than nothing.

Despite the somber topic, Ben grinned. "It is. Instead of thinking about all of it, let's focus which of those problems we can solve and which ones we can't solve."

Amelie shrugged. "Worth a try, I guess. I don't have anything better to do." She hit a branch and broke her grass blade in two. She grunted then threw the grass into the woods.

"We've decided Northport is the only answer already, so let's not change that. We can't change the time factor because the Coalition isn't going to wait on us, and we can't change the fact that both them and the Sanctuary want to kill us. That leaves direction, food, and money," summarized Ben.

"Are you planning to apply for a job?" asked Amelie mirthlessly.

"Direction and food then," he answered. "I think we can agree those are problems that need to be solved."

Amelie was down, but as she said weeks ago, they only had one choice now. That was to continue. He had to keep her spirits up. He thought a plan was the first step.

"I'll give you that," she answered. "Direction and food. What do you suggest?"

"Well, I said we don't know the way to Northport, but we do

know a little. The Venmoor River originates near there. I remember last time we talked about it being used for trade."

Amelie nodded. "You are right about that."

"Then the first thing we need to do is stop following this track and head back to the river," he decided. "If that is the only way we know for sure gets us to Northport, then that is the way we need to go."

"But there's more risk of being found by the river," argued Amelie.

"Remember," suggested Ben, "we solve only the problems we can. We can't stop them looking for us, but we can stop ourselves from going the wrong way. We don't know where this track goes or how far out of the way it will lead us. For all we know, they could have a troop of guards and a mage waiting around the next bend."

Amelie stayed silent. She didn't have an answer for that.

"As for food," declared Ben. "We can solve that once we get to the river."

THEY SAT and watched the water flow by silently. The crackle and pop of a small campfire was the only sound. Around them, a curtain of willow branches hung motionlessly in the still night air.

The fire was an indulgence after many nights of cold camps, but Ben figured the risk was mitigated now because there would be plenty of other travelers on the river road. A campfire wouldn't draw any extra scrutiny.

The campsite he'd chosen was secluded. They were tucked away in a small willow grove on the land side of the road. It would be difficult for anyone to get a good look at them without stepping beneath the trees.

In the morning, they would take the broad flat road beside the river and hope for the best, but already, Ben doubted his plan. They would be incredibly exposed on the road. He realized it was almost certain watchers would be placed between Kirksbane and Northport. He didn't want to tell Amelie that.

She had agreed to his plan simply because she didn't have a better one. Amelie was determined to make Northport and try to help her family. She would risk anything to do it. He couldn't let her do that. Getting captured would only make it worse.

In the still air, Ben detected a low sound and peered around curiously. In minutes, the sound grew clearer. He realized it was coming from up river and headed toward them.

In the distance, he spotted a dim light bobbing closer and he could detect faint words drifting across the water. The sound was a man singing on one of the river barges. He had a deep, sonorous voice. He filled the night with a humble melody. Ben saw the man reclining at the rear of the empty barge, leaning sleepily against the tiller. He must be singing to keep himself awake, thought Ben.

While the barge floated past, they listened to the singing, and Ben had an idea.

When the first shards of daylight sliced through the curtain of willow branches, Ben sat up. Today, they would find a river barge to ride north on.

Much like to the south of Kirksbane, the barges were floated downstream but were pulled upstream by a team of horses. The difference was, north of Kirksbane, the loaded barges headed up river and empty barges floating downriver—the opposite of what happened south of the town. The river traffic was primarily agricultural goods coming from the Sineook Valley and going to Northport, Venmoor, or even the City.

Pulling a loaded barge up river was hard work. A team of horses would walk along the bank with a stout rope tied to the barge. Men were needed to tend to the horses and also man the tiller. Occasionally, they used long poles to push off from the river bank.

Ben guessed it was difficult to get manpower to work the barges up river. It was seasonal work, and it looked hard. More men were needed going up than coming down.

"We don't have coin to pay for passage," argued a still sleepy Amelie when Ben told her the plan.

"That's the thing, we don't offer to pay. We offer to work," explained Ben.

"To work?" she asked, confused.

"These men don't own the barges. They are just paid to move them," he responded. "To them, an offer to help just makes their lives easier."

"Won't they be suspicious?" rejoined Amelie.

"Not if we spin it right. We have two problems, direction and food, right? We can be honest and tell them it's about solving our problems. For food, we'll work the barge and take it to Northport."

"Who would really do something like that?" wondered Amelie.

"People who look like us," Ben smiled. He gestured to their road-worn clothing. They hadn't had a proper bath since Free State and they looked like they were living on the ragged edge. "We say we have friends in Northport who can help us, but we've run out of food and money to get there. They get help piloting their barge, and we get food and transportation. It should be safer, too. People are less likely to look for us actually working our way north. It is win-win."

"It's worth a try," conceded Amelie.

They hurried along the river road, looking for a suitable barge while the sun was still low in the sky.

The barges generally tied up on the bank at night because it was too difficult to pilot them in the darkness. At first light, they would push off from the bank and start pulling up stream with the horses. This time of year, every few hundred paces, a barge was tied up. The men were stirring around the campfires making breakfast or pouring steaming black liquid out of tin kettles. Ben recalled Rhys' favorite hangover beverage, kaf, was popular in the north.

"Why don't they just keep the produce in wagons and carry it all the way," asked Amelie as she skeptically eyed one barge which the crew was struggling to push off the bank. It was embedded deep in thick river mud.

"These barges are twenty times the size of a wagon," answered Ben, "and they use the same number of horses. It's cost efficient."

"That seems like something a lady should know." Amelie sighed. "That kind of thing used to be important to me. I'm not sure it matters now. If Issen falls, then what is left for me? Am I even a lady if I have no city?"

"You're still a lady to me, no matter what happens," consoled Ben. "Rhys once told me it's the perception that is reality. If our actions show the world we are noble, isn't that more important than a birthright?"

Amelie laughed. "For someone who is a completely unapologetic rogue, Rhys certainly gets philosophical from time to time."

"I think it's the old age," joked Ben. "Old folks have a lot of time to sit around and think about things."

Her mood brightened, Amelie tapped Ben's arm and pointed to a barge ahead of them. "Want to try that one?" she asked.

Ben shrugged. "Why not?"

It did look promising. They were searching for a small crew that needed help. There were only three men clustered around the morning campfire and their barge was piled high with cabbages, beans, potatoes, and carrots. Friendly faces didn't hurt either.

"Ho the barge," called Ben.

The men looked up and one of them stood and put his hands on his hips. "What can I help you folks with?"

Ben told him honestly, "We want to work our way up river."

"We can't pay you," blurted the man.

"Understood," replied Ben. "All we ask is to be fed during the trip."

The man glanced back at his companions. One of them laughed and remarked, "Food is something we have more than enough of."

The first man turned back to Ben. "Our master wouldn't like us taking on strangers, but if you work hard, we can feed you." Before Ben could answer, he continued, "And it will be hard work. Half my crew quit a few days back when they saw how high this barge is loaded. Damn Hoff tries to squeeze every copper out of these trips."

Ben stuck out his hand for the man to shake and replied, "I'm not afraid of hard work. I've never been on a barge before, but if you tell us what to do, you won't be sorry."

The man took Ben's hand firmly. "Welcome aboard. The name is Harry."

Ben hoped Harry wouldn't regret it. They solved their direction and food problems, but the Sanctuary and Coalition were still out there. These men didn't know what they were getting themselves into.

There wasn't another way, though. If they couldn't reach Northport, then Amelie's family wouldn't get help, the members of the Alliance would never hear about the betrayal by the Sanctuary, and countless lives could be lost before Argren, Rhymer, and the other lords were able to react.

Harry was a quiet and efficient man. Because they were unfamiliar with the large work horses the crew used, he directed Ben and Amelie to barge duty. They climbed aboard and took turns with another crew member to hold the tiller in place and constantly steer away from the bank. Periodically, when they approached a shallow part of the river or debris caught on the bank, they would grab long poles and push themselves out into deeper water.

They were part of a steady stream of barges using the same tactics. All were bringing goods north to Northport and other towns.

Jonas, the other crew member who was stationed on the barge with them, was also quiet and introspective. He took time to instruct them on proper barge handling, but it was not a difficult activity, and the discussion was quick. After the brief tutorial, he let them take the first shifts and climbed over the mountain of produce to settle down at the front of the barge. Ben and Amelie were left at the rear, manning the tiller. Jonas said he would be watching to make sure they didn't get too close to the river bank, but Ben suspected the man would be napping before long.

Harry and the third man, Lawrence, were on the bank, guiding the slow-moving draft horses. Simple and efficient, thought Ben. They were pulled effortlessly upriver.

The first night, they found a pair of ancient tree stumps and tied wrist thick ropes to them. The river bank was regularly cleared of trees now for the barge lines, but years before, they must have grown tall. The stumps were almost a man height across.

From the barge, Jonas picked out a handful of potatoes, carrots, and onions then tossed them to his companions on shore.

"How was your first day as a barge man?" asked Harry when Ben and Amelie hopped off onto solid ground.

"Not too bad," replied Ben happily. "Once you get the hang of it, there's really nothing to manning that tiller."

Harry cracked his knuckles absentmindedly and began tending to the horses while Lawrence started a fire.

"It gets a bit more difficult," admitted Harry while brushing down the big animals.

"Slow part of the river," grunted Jonas, who dropped down next to Ben and Amelie on the bank.

"There are some rapids further up," explained Harry. "It's calm enough down here that you could fall asleep and we probably wouldn't notice for a bell or two. You'll earn your keep when we get to the rapids."

"We'll do what we need to do," answered Ben. Rapids or no rapids, it was better than walking.

The next few days, they traveled along the glass smooth river with no issues. Occasionally, they would see armed men along the banks but they were able to duck down in the back of the barge and avoid anyone spotting them. After the first time it happened, Ben volunteered that he and Amelie would take all of the tiller shifts and Jonas could relax. Ben said they wanted to get practice for the rapids. The barge man had no complaints. He scampered up front and was quickly dozing.

One time, a squad of twenty soldiers marched past, heading down river. Ben and Amelie were lying low and out of sight. They tried to be subtle so the barge crew didn't notice they were hiding. It wasn't difficult. Jonas was content to watch the world from the front and Harry and Lawrence were busy keeping the horses calm while the armored men clanked by.

"Do you think they're looking for us?" asked Amelie.

"I don't think so," replied Ben. "That many armed men around here must be Alliance forces. Otherwise, they would draw too much attention."

"Then why are we hiding?" groused Amelie.

"Better safe than sorry," Ben smirked. "Really, I'm more worried about watchers we don't notice, individuals or small groups. The Coalition uses soldiers, but the Sanctuary will send hunters or even mages. Those will be tougher to spot. They are more dangerous than soldiers too."

"If we can't hide..." she started.

"Then we just have to hope they aren't paying close attention to the barges," responded Ben. "There are hundreds of them on this river. Hopefully, we float by unnoticed."

Harry and his crew worked long days, but they indulged at night with hearty meals. They had an entire barge loaded with vegetables. For meat, they packed some salted cuts that would keep for weeks. They also traded with people who set up stands by the road.

At one stand, Ben saw the proprietor had a large keg rolled up next to his rack of meats. Ben looked at Amelie imploringly. She rolled her eyes and dug out a handful of coppers.

Ben jumped into the shallow water by the riverbank and strode up to the stand. Harry looked back and nodded appreciatively when he saw what Ben was doing. The barge crew kept moving, but Ben would easily catch them with a few minutes of brisk walking.

"Good day, sir. Is the ale any good?" inquired Ben.

"Best you'll find within a day of here." The man grinned. "You pull the tap and I start counting. One copper for every number I reach."

"Do you have a skin or a jug I can use?" asked Ben. He cursed himself for not thinking to bring one before he jumped off the barge.

"Ten coppers for a skin," offered the man.

Ben grimaced at the price.

"It's a big one."

"Let me see it." Ben sighed.

Later, Amelie looked on in only slight disapproval while Ben and the barge crew enjoyed the purchase. It wasn't the same quality of ale Ben brewed, but the man was probably right, it was better than anything else they were going to find on the roadside. They were lying sprawled around the campfire and the barge crew was particularly mellow.

"We get to the first rapid tomorrow," mentioned Harry.

"Is it dangerous?" asked Amelie.

"Not really, just a lot of work," answered the barge captain before taking another swig of the ale skin and passing it to the next man. "It's a bit worse this time of year because you have so many other crews out here, but nothing terrible. The only dangerous part is a barge ahead of us getting loose. If that happens, they'll float downstream. They could get some speed because the current is faster. You've got to be quick with the poles to push them off if they're headed for you."

"Does that happen often?" asked Ben.

"Nah," answered Harry. "An experienced crew won't lose their craft. But like I said, it's worse this time of year because there's more traffic and inexperienced hands working the barges."

"That doesn't sound too bad," remarked Ben.

"See how you feel after the first long run." Jonas yawned. The man slept nearly all day. Ben couldn't fathom how he slept at night.

"First long run?" queried Amelie.

"Aye, you can't tie up in the rapids. The current is too fast," explained Jonas. "We call it a long run. There's a few of them that will take us almost two days to pull through. Gotta watch out for other barges, boulders, and keep a strong hand on the tiller. It's a long shift. With a crew this small, we won't get much sleep. Not sure we could have made it without you two."

Amelie looked nervous.

Ben reassured her. "Remember, they do this because it's easier than hauling in wagons. It can't be that bad."

AT THE BOTTOM of the first rapid, a line of barges was waiting to start up the turbulent waters.

They weren't as violent as the rapids Ben remembered from around Farview, but he'd never tried to pull twenty wagon loads of goods up those.

"Now what is this?" Ben heard faintly from the front of the barge. He rose up on his tiptoes and saw Jonas clambering back toward him.

"What's going on?" asked Ben.

"Not sure," muttered the barge man. He ducked down below the tiller and came up with a short-bow and quiver. He then climbed onto the potato pile, which was the best vantage point on the barge.

Ben looked worriedly at Amelie. They both collected their weapons as well.

Jonas called from his perch, "Harry, what is it?"

The barge captain looked back and raised his hands uncertainly.

Ben saw it now. Beside the river road, there was a military-style encampment, one large tent like a commander might use with a scattering of pup tents around it. A few armored men were visible milling around the area.

Lawrence, the third barge crew member, darted ahead of Harry and the horse team to see what the commotion was.

While they waited, the barge crept closer. Amelie whispered to Ben, "Do you think we could slip over the side and swim across the river?"

"Remember what happened when we tried to swim away from the Sanctuary?" he replied ruefully. "Also, Harry and his crew would probably tell them where we went. They have no reason to protect us."

She gripped the hilts of her weapons grimly. If the arms men wanted to search the barge, there was no where they could hide. Flight seemed futile. Not that fighting would be any better, thought Ben.

Shortly, Lawrence returned and briefed Harry on what he learned. The captain shrugged and they kept moving forward. Jonas, seeing the exchange, relaxed as well and slid off the potatoes.

Ben shouted to the shore and asked what it was.

"Nothing involving us," yelled back Harry. "They're looking for some highborn lady."

Ben met Amelie's eyes.

Slowly, they approached the line and certain discovery. Ben's mind worked frantically. If they tried to escape, Harry and the crew were certain to give them away, but on the other hand, if they didn't run, what chance did they have? Fighting a company of soldiers was suicide.

"Come on," he urged Amelie. "We have to go."

Resolutely, she followed him to the side of the barge. They both stood tall, preparing to jump down into the water, wade to shore, and then run. If they got enough of a head start, maybe they could keep ahead of the men in heavy armor.

Standing on the gunwale, Ben tensed for the leap. He paused when one of the arms men appeared from around their horse team. The man paused momentarily then shouted, "Lady Amelie!"

Ben's hand dropped to his longsword, but Amelie placed her hand on his arm. "Those are Issen's colors."

Ben noticed the pale blue tunic the man was wearing.

"Lady, I can't believe we found you!" exclaimed the arms man.

"That's an Issen accent," breathed Amelie. "I think we're safe."

Ignoring Jonas' stunned look, Amelie tossed her travel pack and weapons to shore then plunged into the waist-deep water. Ben followed right behind and thrashed after her to the bank where the arms man was offering Amelie a helping hand.

The man led them directly to the large military tent. The nearby soldiers bowed in respect when they saw the dripping wet and shivering Amelie. Ben was nervous, but at least so far, they weren't being clapped in irons or dodging razor sharp blades.

Inside the tent, Ben instantly felt relief and irritation. Seneschal Tomas was reclining on a comfortable-looking camp chair and reading a thick book. A half-empty decanter of wine sat on a table next to him, and an empty crystal wineglass dangled from one hand.

A sly smile split his face when he looked up and saw them.

"Tomas!" cried Amelie.

"You," answered the seneschal, eyeing her up and down, "have looked better, my lady."

She blushed furiously. "We've been having a bit of a rough time. What are you doing here?"

"I can imagine," the small ferret-like man responded dryly, not answering her question. He stood up. "First things first, let's get you bathed and into some dry clothes. After that…" He raised his glass. "Some wine and a good meal."

"That sounds wonderful," murmured Amelie. "We've been stuck on a barge the last week, and before that, well, I can tell you the rest after we get cleaned up. I must know though, what news do you have of Issen? We heard there was a siege."

"A barge, you say?" He glanced at the original soldier, who nodded. "Hmm, maybe I shouldn't oversell the meal then. We will still have one, but not as fine. We can discuss the situation at Issen then. I'm afraid it will be a long discussion, and there's no sense getting started until we can finish." The man set his hands on his hips. "Frankly, I do not have good news, but there is nothing to be done about it this evening."

Amelie pursed her lips and nodded in agreement.

"As for supper," continued Tomas, "Raphael normally does my cooking, but he may need to sort out this barge crew. You." He pointed at the soldier. "Take Raphael to see the barge and anyone else who saw Lady Amelie. Then tell your friends outside to get some hot water for bathing started."

Raphael detached himself from a back corner of the tent. Ben jumped. He hadn't seen the hulking man standing there.

"How many?" asked the swordsman.

Ben and Amelie stared back at him.

"How many men were on the barge?" he asked again, patiently.

"Oh. There were three of them," answered Amelie. "I really worry they may have trouble without us. I'm not sure that is enough men to make the rapids."

Flat-faced, Raphael replied, "I will make sure it isn't a problem."

Silent as a cat, the big man brushed out of the tent, the soldier that brought them in trailing behind.

Tomas smiled sweetly at Amelie. "My tent is yours, my lady. Take your time getting ready, and I'm eager to hear your story. I will tell you all I know about your father." He walked to one side of the tent and flipped back the lid of a glossy mahogany chest. "We don't have any suitable clothing for you, but you are near my size, and it is clean. Take whatever you like."

The seneschal swept toward the tent flap to exit, gesturing for Ben to follow. "You, boy, come with me. We'll get you cleaned up as well. Maybe the soldiers have something you can wear. I suppose I shouldn't be surprised you're still around." The mousy man sighed dramatically.

Ben followed without comment.

Seneschal Tomas was undeniably rude, but Ben had to admit, the man did know how to run a comfortable campsite.

Washed, changed, and feeling safe for the first time in weeks, they relaxed around a rickety folding table in Tomas' tent. The food was simple military fare, but the wine was excellent.

"Tomas, I'm glad you found us, but what are you doing here?" asked Amelie once they settled.

The small man fidgeted in his seat and then replied smoothly, "After we got back from Akew Woods, we knew something was wrong. You were gone from the Sanctuary, they were cagey about what happened, and then we got the news about Issen. I discussed it with my colleagues at the Consulate. We decided that finding you should be our first priority."

"Akew Woods, of course. I had forgotten you went there," replied Amelie sheepishly.

"You've been through a lot, my lady." Tomas smiled.

"Saala went with you. Where is he now?" she inquired.

"We didn't know where you would go." Tomas reached across to the wine decanter and refilled his glass. "We assumed White-hall and Northport were the strongest possibilities. Once you found out about Issen, I knew you would try for one of them, so we split up. Raphael and I covered the river road to Northport. Saala went to Whitehall."

"What do you know about the siege?" asked Amelie. "We only heard about it a few days ago."

Tomas frowned. "I'm afraid it doesn't sound good. Issen is surrounded and the Coalition's force is larger than anyone expected. Your father was preparing for war, of course, but how ready was he? I've been gone so long that I really don't know."

Amelie laid down her cutlery and looked between Ben and Tomas. "I think it is clear then. We must continue to Northport and do whatever we can to enlist Lord Rhymer's help."

Tomas shook his head slightly. "No, my lady. I do not think that is wise. I believe the best course of action is to go to White-hall and speak to Argren. You will be safe there."

"Argren has not sent reinforcements to Issen yet. Do you think he will just because we ask him?" demanded Amelie.

"We won't know until we do ask," argued Tomas. "Saala is there. He is a military man and has a head for these kinds of situations."

Amelie pursed her lips in frustration.

"I don't know…" she started.

"He is your liege lord," reminded Tomas. "There is an obliga-tion there. You should go to him first. If he does not support you, then you can try Northport. If you ask him in person, I am sure he will agree to send help. The other lords in the Alliance won't stand with him if word gets out that he refused a personal request from a vassal. It wouldn't be much of an Alliance then, would it?"

Reluctantly, Amelie shook her head yes. To Ben, Argren shouldn't need Amelie's request before he sent reinforcements to his banner man, but he didn't understand the world of lords and ladies. They played mysterious games. Ben knew he had to trust the people like Tomas who knew those games best.

The next morning, the camp was a kicked anthill of activity. The soldiers were packing up tents, tables, chairs, and a wide variety of other equipment. They had commandeered a wagon from someone and loaded it high. Ben, who was used to traveling light and camping in the rough, watched on amused.

Beside him, a high-pitched voice remarked, "A bit silly, isn't it."

Ben jumped and glanced over his shoulder to see the hulking bodyguard Raphael standing right next to him. The man moved as silently as the wind.

"My Master Tomas does enjoy his comforts," continued Raphael, nodding toward a heavy barrel of wine the soldiers were rolling to the wagon.

Amelie came over to join them. Raphael bowed shallowly to her with a sly smile.

"That's unnecessary," she told him uncomfortably. "I've gotten used to being treated just like everyone else. Also, I don't think it's wise to give away I'm highborn."

"A good idea, my lady," murmured Raphael.

The heavyset bodyguard padded away.

Amelie remarked, "That man has always made me uncomfortable."

"You know him from Issen?" asked Ben.

"As long as I can remember, he has been with Tomas," she replied. "He stayed mostly in the background at my father's court. I've heard he's a deadly fighter. The guards there said he was a blademaster, though he doesn't claim the sigil. I'm not sure why. He is a very strange man."

"I agree. He's creepy," grumbled Ben. "He keeps sneaking up on me."

"Better to have men like that by your side than behind you," concluded Amelie.

Finally, the soldiers got all of the equipment loaded onto the wagon and they were ready to begin. Tomas and Raphael took the lead. Ben and Amelie walked together in the middle of a ring of steel. Twenty armored soldiers of Issen walked around them.

As they started walking, a plainly dressed woman appeared and kept pace with Tomas.

Ben frowned and nodded ahead. "Who is that?"

"I'm not sure," answered Amelie. She turned to one of the soldiers. "Excuse me. Who is that with Tomas?"

The man shrugged, causing a sharp scrape of metal on metal from his armor, "I'm not sure, my lady. I believe she is from the Consulate, a diplomat, though I don't recognize her. She's been with us since the City."

"That's strange," said Ben. "I was in the Consulate many times visiting Saala. I don't recognize her."

Amelie breathed deep. "We'll have to ask Tomas about her when we stop." She stretched her arms above her head and swung them loosely. "I've gotten so used to hiking with a pack on that I don't know what to do with my arms without one. It's nice to be walking without all of that extra weight."

Ben grinned. "I feel the same." He was carrying only the Venmoor steel longsword Rhys had given him after Snowmar and the hunting knife Serrot gave him right before Ben left Farview. His and Amelie's packs were lying in the back of the wagon.

"We can find some extra armor if you want to try walking in that all day," grumbled the nearby soldier good naturedly.

The travel with Tomas and the armed guards was vastly

different than the mad scramble away from the City or even the initial journey with Lady Towaal.

Each evening, they sat around a fire and sipped wine while the soldiers set up Tomas' tent. Raphael did most of the cooking for them and he was an expert chef. The meals he created over an open fire were just as good as any of the ones Ben had at nice taverns in the City.

Early in the mornings, while the soldiers were still packing everything away, Raphael offered to practice the sword with Ben. At their request, Raphael added Amelie to the exercises also.

The man moved with a lazy sort of grace that belied how quick and strong he was. Ben found he had just as much trouble landing a strike on Raphael as he did Saala. Raphael's style was similar to Saala though, so Ben didn't completely embarrass himself.

With Amelie, Raphael was patient and instructive. He slowly walked her through handling her two blades at once, and while she wasn't adept at it yet, she started to get a feel for what was possible. Just like Black Bart, Raphael advised using the weapons for defense and counterattack. He showed her a few attack sequences but was keen to point out their weaknesses.

In all, Ben started to relax and enjoy the odd man's company. He was a quiet and kind counterpoint to Tomas, who loved to hear himself talk and was constantly rude to Ben. Despite Tomas' demeanor though, Ben became comfortable with him as well. He didn't like the man, but it was so obvious the man didn't like him either that Ben felt he knew where he stood with the seneschal. It was refreshing in a way, to drop the pretense of false friendship.

The soldiers were also nice to Ben and very courteous to Amelie. The advantages of being a highborn, Ben supposed. Anything she needed, they were quick to do it for her.

The outlier was the strange woman who stayed near Tomas' side while they were on the move then frequently disappeared when they stopped. She rarely spoke. She claimed she was employed at the Issen Consulate in the City but neither Ben nor Amelie could recall ever seeing her. For a career diplomat, she was strangely uninterested in Amelie.

Ben and Amelie speculated over what secrets the woman was hiding but eventually shrugged it off. The mystery and sense of danger around one odd woman was nothing compared to the fear they felt over the last two months. The ring of Issen steel around them did a lot to dispel fears of the Coalition finding them.

Ben mentioned their concern about mages, but Tomas brushed it off. "Mages don't go out into the world for manhunts, boy. They have soldiers and hunters for that kind of thing, and we are well prepared for whatever attack those types throw at us."

Ben wasn't so sure, but Raphael, who constantly loitered around Tomas, smiled serenely. Ben felt a little better. The bodyguard was a force to be reckoned with.

THEY APPROACHED KIRKSBANE AGAIN, this time from the north. Ben couldn't help but feel a tingle of trepidation. It felt like he was being watched or like he had a constant itch in the middle of his back that no amount of scratching would soothe.

Amelie felt it as well. They both stayed close and cleared the hilts of their weapons.

The soldiers around them continued on like they had the entire trip, coarsely joking and laughing with each other. Their homeland was under attack, but near Kirksbane, deep in the heart of the Alliance, they felt no fear.

Raphael noticed Ben and Amelie's tension and hung back to walk with the young people.

"Feeling a little jumpy today?" he asked in his soft voice.

Ben shrugged uncomfortably. "Last time we were here we got

involved in a deadly fight in a tavern. Then we were attacked again right outside of town. It was a bad two days. The time before that, an assassin tried to murder us in the middle of the street in broad daylight. I'm starting to not like this place."

"Don't worry. You have Tomas and me with you this time. Tomas has a plan," assured the swordsman.

"A plan?" asked Amelie.

Raphael looked at her silently.

"A different plan than we know about?" she insisted.

"No, of course not." The swordsman smiled.

"Maybe I should talk to Tomas," she stated.

"Sorry if I have concerned you," rumbled the swordsman. "Yes, talk to Tomas, but not now. We should pay attention."

As they spoke, they reached the outskirts of Kirksbane. The small trading town that seemed so friendly the first time they passed through was a maze of hidden threats now. Ben couldn't help but search every face they saw, looking to see if anyone recognized him. Despite Tomas' assurances they would be safe, Ben was convinced Coalition and Sanctuary watchers would be nearby. Maybe they didn't have enough force to attack, but they could alert their masters to where Amelie was located.

Tomas steered them toward the Curve Inn. Amelie abruptly put a stop to that. Without explaining why, she demanded they stay somewhere else.

Ben stayed out of that discussion and avoided Amelie's side-long glares.

Finally, Tomas agreed with a dramatic sigh and they found another place to stay.

The oddly named Angry Badger sat near the outskirts of town and looked to be an inn catering toward the wealthier merchants and lords coming from Sineook Valley. It had an unusually large stable yard and plenty of room to tie up wagons. It had a separate bathing facility and offered a comfortable- looking common room. It wasn't nearly as raucous as the Curve, which was fine with Ben.

On initial inspection, they had plenty of ale kegs stacked behind a long bar.

"Tomas," called Amelie. He'd just finished with the innkeeper, and the rotund man was counting a fistful of silver, enough silver to pay for twenty-five new guests.

"Yes, my lady?" replied Tomas.

"We need to talk," she declared.

Tomas met Raphael's eyes and hesitated before answering. "Certainly. Right after we get freshened up."

"Now, Tomas," she complained.

"My lady, we've been on the road for days. Let us get cleaned up, have some refreshments brought, and we can spend the entire evening speaking." The seneschal wasn't outright defying Amelie's wishes, but Ben noticed even some of the soldiers looked over with curious expressions.

Amelie glared at Tomas then agreed. "Fine. Immediately after we've bathed."

The inn keep, who had been nervously standing back, bustled forward, describing the amenities his inn had to offer. Ben let the man's hurried voice wash over him and he surveyed the room. Nothing seemed out of place that he could see, but the tingle of concern had not left him.

He drew close to Amelie and whispered to her, "Keep your weapons close."

She stared ahead hard-eyed, then nodded.

Both the women's and the men's bathing chambers were located across the wagon yard in a back building that spilled steam every time a door was opened. Tomas insisted the women's room be cleared before Amelie entered then he posted a handful of guards outside of the door. He instructed the other guards to make a patrol of the inn's premises and report anything out of the ordinary. He gave Amelie a cheeky smile as if to say, 'see, I told you so'. She disappeared inside without smiling back.

The men's side was empty as well when Ben, Tomas, and Raphael entered.

The swordsman quickly stripped down and circled the room, picking up towels and soap. There was a large tank of heated water which he happily scooped up in buckets and filled three tin tubs.

Tomas ducked back outside and returned with a large earthenware pitcher of wine and three tankards.

"I hope you don't mind I got red," apologized the mousy seneschal. "I prefer white for bathing, but it isn't chilled here," he remarked with a petulant frown. "I just can't stand that. Red will have to do."

The naked Raphael strode over to Tomas and poured three full tankards. Tomas placed a hand on the big man's back before accepting his and retreating to a corner where he also stripped.

Ben took his tankard then plunged into the steaming bath.

The room was filled with sounds of soft splashing from the men washing. None of them spoke. Ben's head was ringing with unfocused concern. The other two seemed entirely focused on enjoying the hot water and wine.

Before long, a soldier poked in his head and called, "Lady Amelie is finishing up, sir. You wanted me to let you know."

Tomas waved a hand at the man then stood. "We shouldn't keep a lady waiting," he acknowledged.

They quickly dressed and Ben strapped on his longsword and hunting knife. It felt odd being armed in a bathing chamber but he saw Raphael and Tomas kept their weapons as well. Raphael had a long scimitar and Tomas an unusual thick-bladed rapier, almost a broadsword, but with a basket hilt. Ben wasn't sure if the seneschal knew how to use the sword. He never practiced with them on the road.

Out in the courtyard, they waited briefly for Amelie to appear.

When she came out, she saw Tomas and informed him, "We will meet now. I want to be clear on what our next move is."

"As you wish, let us be clear. I think now is the time we all put our cards on the table," replied the seneschal in a condescending tone.

Amelie peered at him quizzically, and then looked around in alarm as the telltale jangle of armed men running filled the air. In heartbeats, the courtyard was filled with crossbow-carrying men decked in chainmail and nondescript tunics. They were led by the mysterious woman who had traveled with them. She was still wearing the plainly made dress she wore on the road, but had gained an air of superiority that Ben hadn't noticed previously.

The pale blue-clad Issen soldiers drew their swords and formed a loose circle around Amelie, Ben, Tomas, and Raphael. They were outnumbered three to one and at a disadvantage to the crossbows.

"What is going on?" shouted Amelie.

"I'm putting my cards on the table," replied Tomas coolly. "Issen is surrounded. Argren was too stupid to see it coming. His Alliance is facing an unbeatable Coalition to the east and an unfriendly Sanctuary at their backs. I'm afraid there is just no reliable future in your father's employ. I've decided to go freelance and sell my services to the highest bidder."

"You're working for the Coalition now! How could you?" cried Amelie.

"Not the Coalition." Tomas smirked.

The woman demanded in a commanding tone, "Initiate Amelie, your presence is requested back at the Sanctuary."

Amelie glared at the woman and demanded, "Who are you?"

"Lady Ingrid," she responded with no emotion. "The Veil assigned me to secure your return."

"My return?" asked Amelie incredulously.

"Return. That has a better ring to it than captured, dead or alive, doesn't it?" asked the woman. A sinister smile spread across her face.

Ice ran through Ben's veins and he cursed himself. The woman was a mage. Why hadn't they seen it!

Amelie took an aggressive fighting stance. She didn't have her weapons, though. Ben wasn't sure what kind of magic she could call against a full mage. The Issen soldiers saw their lady preparing to fight and grips tightened on their swords. They nervously eyed the crossbowmen, but didn't back down.

Tomas held an amused look.

"Don't be foolish, Initiate," said the woman. "The only thing resisting will do is get you and your men killed. I'm quite happy to take you alive, but I do not need to."

Amelie glared at the woman.

"Initiate, these men have families back home. You are a brave girl, I am certain you are willing to throw your own life away fighting a hopeless battle. Are you willing to do the same for them? Will you deprive their children of fathers? Look around you. You will be killed in heartbeats."

The soldiers glanced around anxiously. They were loyal, but with three times their number pointing crossbow bolts at their chests, they knew it was a fight they couldn't win.

Amelie weighed the odds then visibly deflated.

"That is better," said Lady Ingrid. "Now..." The woman stopped talking and turned as a new pair entered the courtyard.

Ben blinked in surprise. Lady Towaal and Rhys were standing behind the line of crossbowmen.

Lady Ingrid snarled, "What are you doing here? I thought the Veil told you to stay close to the Sanctuary and leave this to me."

"You are correct. The Veil did ask me to do that," answered Lady Towaal. "I declined."

The courtyard burst into chaos as Lady Ingrid swept her hand toward Towaal. A brilliant jet of red and blue flame shot out.

Three crossbowmen erupted like dry kindling when the blast touched them. Lady Towaal raised one hand and the inferno parted around her.

Before anyone else could react, Rhys' longsword leapt from his scabbard and he cleaved into the line of crossbowmen. He felled two of them almost instantly with two sweeping slashes.

Raphael was next to move. He charged toward Rhys but was blocked by a stumbling wall of his own men scrambling to escape the burning heat of Lady Ingrid's fire.

Another man exploded in flame and three more fell to Rhys' longsword by the time Ben drew his own weapon. He moved to protect Amelie but didn't know where to turn. The Issen soldiers and crossbowmen fell on each other in a panicked crash of violence and screams.

Ben turned to Lady Ingrid but quickly decided to leave that one for Towaal. The woman's face was a locked in a rictus of mad energy. She directed her twenty-pace long funnel of flame across the courtyard, torching everything in its path.

Ben glanced back at the warring soldiers, looking for an opportunity. He nearly lost his head when Tomas swung his thick-bladed rapier at Ben. Out of the corner of his eye, Ben saw it and ducked a heartbeat before the steel would have chopped into his skull.

"I will enjoy this," growled the seneschal before dancing forward and jabbing at Ben.

Ben jumped to the side and yelled at Amelie to stay behind him. She was unarmed and would only be a distraction if she got within Tomas' reach. It was clear now, Tomas would have no compunctions about killing her.

His longsword held steady in front of him, Ben faced off against the seneschal. Blood and fire framed the man's haughty, wicked grin.

Tomas charged, swinging a tight figure-eight attack. Ben parried then barely avoided being skewered when the seneschal finished his attack with a powerful thrust toward Ben's chest. Almost too late, Ben realized the man knew what he was doing.

Behind them, Ingrid continued to lay fire indiscriminately across the courtyard, torching her own men and the Issen men alike. A grim-faced Towaal calmly advanced through the fire, parting it harmlessly around her. Ben saw Raphael had fought his way to Rhys now, but he didn't have time to see what happened as Tomas advanced again.

The mousy man was surprisingly strong and quick as a mongoose. Ben gained a shallow gash on one thigh and a deep cut on his shoulder during the next volley of attacks. He preferred to fight defensively, but waiting for the smaller man to make a mistake was not working.

Ben attacked in a complicated sequence which Saala taught him in the City. Tomas merely swept it aside and flicked his blade at Ben's face, slicing a neat cut beneath one eye. Laughing, the seneschal darted toward Amelie, who had been exposed when Ben dodged the last attack. She was ready and ran behind Ben again before Tomas reached her.

Ben pivoted to face the man and saw Rhys battling Raphael out of the corner of his eye. Inspired, he yelled back to Amelie, "Watch out for the fire. Duck!"

Surprised, Amelie dropped down and Ben started to crouch. Tomas froze too, unsure if Lady Ingrid was really about to torch his back. It was the break Ben needed. He charged and slung his weapon at the seneschal's face.

Tomas evaded Ben's thrown longsword and started to bring his own blade up. He was too late. Ben was inside his guard.

Ben crashed into the smaller man, sending them both flailing into the dirt. Using his weight to hold Tomas down, Ben slammed one knee on the man's sword arm and jerked his hunting knife from his belt.

Panicked, the little man pounded his fist into Ben's side. From his back, he couldn't get enough leverage to do damage. Ben absorbed the blows then plunged his hunting knife down into the seneschal's chest and ripped it out. A gush of blood followed. Almost immediately, the small man stopped fighting and gurgled his last breaths.

Ben looked up to see Rhys engaged in a furious battle with Raphael, Lady Towaal still advancing on the flame throwing Lady Ingrid, and the battle between the crossbowmen and Issen soldiers was nearly finished. Half of both parties lay in charred heaps where Ingrid burned them.

One crossbowman was unengaged though and came running at Ben. Ben lurched to his feet but he had only his knife. The man was covered in chainmail and came waving a short sword. Ben staggered back, trying to think of what he could do. The soldier, seeing Ben's panic, redoubled his speed and was in a full sprint toward Ben.

Suddenly, Amelie slid in between them and snatched Ben's sword off the ground. The soldier slowed at the unexpected obstacle but not in enough time to prevent Amelie from swinging with all her might at his unprotected knees. The man went down hard, crashing into and over Amelie. He let out a howl of pain, clutching at his ruined legs. Ben reacted quickly and jumped onto the man, drawing his knife across the fallen soldier's throat.

Amelie rolled clear and stood, still holding Ben's longsword. Together, they turned and faced the battle.

Ben saw Rhys risk pointing toward Tomas' fallen body. Raphael's face drained of color and his sword trembled in his grip. The swordsman cried in anguish and his eyes watered, right before Rhys elegantly swept his blade around and into the swordsman's neck. Raphael's scarred, bald head thumped onto the packed dirt of the courtyard. A heartbeat later, his body crashed down next to it.

The silver sigils inscribed on Rhys' dark steel longsword blazed brilliantly.

On the other side of the courtyard, Towaal was a half-dozen

paces from Lady Ingrid when she finally displayed her own magic. Her adversary was chanting now and had both her hands raised, concentrating her fire on Towaal directly in front of her.

Towaal simply waved her hand and a blast of narrow, jagged shards of ice materialized out of thin air. They imploded into Lady Ingrid, skewering her from all directions. Ingrid collapsed in a crunch of broken ice, water, and blood.

The fight between the soldiers was almost finished, with only two standing crossbowmen drawing in on a lone Issen man. Rhys casually walked up behind one of the crossbowmen and punched his longsword through the man's back. Stunned, the man's companion looked over in time to catch Rhys' long-knife in his eye.

The last remaining Issen soldier looked around the absolute wreckage of the courtyard and fell to his knees. "Flaming hell," was all he could muster.

Ben agreed.

Flames licked all of the building surrounding the courtyard. Half of the bodies were merely charred and smoking piles of ash. The rest had the ghastly injuries of men who died in violent, close combat.

Ben and Amelie faced Lady Towaal and Rhys. The pop and crackle of the burning buildings filled the courtyard with sound.

Rhys met their eyes then gestured with a thumb toward the courtyard exit. "We should probably get going," he suggested.

"We're not going with you," Amelie quaked.

"Don't be silly, girl," retorted Lady Towaal, stepping over the blood-drenched corpse of Ingrid. "We're leaving together."

Amelie held up Ben's longsword and assumed a fighting stance.

Rhys chuckled, but it was Towaal who answered. "Amelie, if we meant you harm, we would just kill you now. Lady Ingrid was quite clear what her intentions were. We saved you. You saw that, right?"

Amelie scowled, unsure of what to do. Ben decided for them.

"She's right," he said. "If they hadn't come in, Ingrid would have us. We can talk about it later, but right now, we need to leave."

As if to make his point, the familiar clanging of the Kirksbane watchmen's bells started ringing.

"You too," muttered Rhys as he dragged the stunned remaining soldier to his feet and propelled the man toward the exit. "We can't leave you behind to flap your gums to the sheriff."

8

HOW TO LIVE FOREVER

THE PARTY STUMBLED from the smoldering Angry Badger. A steady flow of people were streaming away from the area, some progressing orderly, and some running flat out. Unlike when they fled the Plowman's Rest, the city watch was not rushing toward this conflagration.

"I suppose there is no way to hide that magic was involved," groaned Lady Towaal.

"You did stab a woman to death with a dozen shards of ice that materialized out of nowhere, right after she torched three or four buildings using only her mind. Also, there is the score of men who look to have spontaneously combusted," Rhys replied dryly. "Yeah, I think they may suspect magic was involved."

"The ice will have melted by the time anyone risks getting close," snapped Towaal.

Rhys just laughed.

The lone soldier that Rhys had pulled along with them suddenly broke out sobbing.

"I'm sorry, Lady Amelie. I can't do this," he managed to say through choking shudders. He undid his sword belt, dropped it, and started running. The heavy jingle of his chainmail preceded him down the road.

The four companions stopped and watched him run.

"How long do you think he can run in that chainmail?" asked Rhys.

"It looks like he can go pretty far, though not very quickly," answered Ben.

They watched the man run, fascinated at his slow progress.

The man was near one hundred paces down the road and approaching a bend. He was still going at a steady pace. His rasping and wheezing breath was getting more difficult to hear as he got further away.

Rhys looked to Towaal. "Should we stop him?"

She shook her head. "Amelie's presence was well known in Kirksbane. The outcome of the battle is obvious. There is little the man can tell the Sanctuary that they won't be able to find out on their own."

"They will probably ruthlessly torture and kill him," mentioned Rhys.

She stared at the rogue. "Do you want to run after him?"

Lady Towaal pushed them to keep moving long into the night. After the battle, no one complained. Besides, fleeing Kirksbane was becoming a bit of a habit.

On the walk, Ben and Amelie decided it was time to get answers. After the experience with Tomas, they weren't going to wait.

"Lady Towaal," started Amelie, "Can you explain why we should be walking with you right now?"

"Girl," replied the mage. She paused and frowned. "I suppose I shouldn't call you that anymore. Of course you are right to question us. Let me think about the best way to explain."

Amelie looked at Ben and he nodded encouragement.

"We quit the Sanctuary," blurted Rhys helpfully.

Towaal stared at him.

He shrugged. "That's what they want to know."

"What Rhys said is true," agreed Towaal finally. "We returned to the City shortly after you left and immediately knew something wasn't right. The Veil and her stooges were peddling a story about you attempting to kill your roommate, Meghan."

"That's not true!" interjected Ben.

"Obviously," snorted Towaal. "I knew it wasn't true the second I heard it. When I was refused access to the poor girl, I decided I must do something. With the help of Rhys, I was able to sneak in and see Meghan. I was wasting my time. She is Sanctuary heart and soul now. Meghan told her jailors I saw her and the Veil called me in. I have known the Veil for a long time, but luckily, I was able to hide much of my true intent. That woman personifies arrogance. She demanded I stay within the Sanctuary grounds until this matter was settled. Rhys and I left later that day."

"Why?" asked Amelie. "You're a mage. How can you quit?"

"I'm not quitting being a mage, girl." Towaal sighed distractedly. "Sorry, I mean Amelie. I am not quitting being a mage. What I quit doing is following the orders of the Veil. For decades now, I have been unhappy with where she is steering us. This, well, it was too much for me. I could not be a part of it any longer."

"Then you know?" asked Amelie. "You know how they were going to sell me to the Coalition? How Reinhold and his men were killed? What happened the night we escaped?"

Towaal grimaced. "I know a lot, but not all. We were able to find out or guess all of what you just said. Is there more we don't know?" The mage shrugged. "Probably."

"Why, though," asked Ben, "why is the Veil doing this?"

A cool autumn breeze rustled the leaves around them and Ben pulled his cloak close. Lady Towaal paused before answering. They gave her time to think.

"It's both simple and complicated, I think. King Argren has no respect for mages, which of course, is offensive to my former brethren. He didn't invite a Sanctuary representative to his

Conclave, for example. Keeping the respect of Alcott's lords is something the Veil considers very important. She could not let a slight like that sit unanswered. Also, with his Alliance, King Argren created a formidable force. Whitehall, Issen, Venmoor, and Northport. These are four of the six most powerful cities in Alcott, the City and Irrefort being the other two. Add in Fabrizo and the others, and Argren could field significantly more swords and better trained soldiers than the Coalition. The balance of power shifted, and the Veil acted to even it out."

"I-I don't understand," stuttered Amelie.

"The Sanctuary claims to be above the fray, above the silly political games of lords climbing over other lords to be at the top of the pile. The truth is, the Sanctuary considers itself already on top of that pile. King Argren's Alliance was gaining enough power that it might actually overshadow the Sanctuary. For the Sanctuary to maintain its position, they can't allow that to happen."

"So," extrapolated Ben, "they will help the Coalition finish the Alliance?"

"No." Lady Towaal shook her head sadly. "They will give the Coalition just enough support to make it an even fight."

Ben and Amelie frowned.

"If neither side can gain a decisive victory," explained Towaal, "then it will be a bloody war of attrition. In the end, the Sanctuary is the only winner."

"Like the Blood Bay!" exclaimed Ben.

"I am glad you remember that story." Towaal smiled wanly. "That war was four hundred years ago, but it is still fresh in my mind. Countless men died, and for what?"

"I can't accept that!" growled Amelie. "We can't just sit by and let this happen. My home is under siege!"

Towaal placed a comforting hand on Amelie's shoulder while they walked. It was one of the only signs of human emotion Ben had seen her give.

"We won't just sit by and let it happen," agreed Towaal. "We may not be able to prevent war, but maybe we can mitigate the carnage. Maybe we can save a few souls. First things first, we try to get your father some help."

They rested that night. In the morning, they started again toward Northport.

"I'm getting pretty familiar with this road," grumbled Ben.

Amelie gave him a playful shove. "At least this time we have a mage, and, uh, Rhys, what is it you do?"

The rogue ignored her.

"That's true," agreed Ben. "We have a real plan now. We're not just running out of fear."

Rhys coughed and Lady Towaal looked back at them.

"What?" demanded Ben.

"We just fought and publicly killed a mage," explained Rhys. "You don't think we should be afraid?"

Ben looked at Rhys apprehensively.

"Remember the discussion last night?" reminded Rhys. "The one where the Sanctuary wouldn't let slights sit unanswered, how the Veil would do anything to maintain the respect of Alcott's lords?"

"Oh," groaned Ben.

"That fight just ensured we have the Veil's full attention," said Rhys grimly.

"What does that mean?" asked Amelie. "An army of mages?"

"There will be a bounty placed on our heads," declared Towaal. "A significantly larger one than was already on yours. That will draw hunters from all over the continent, if we live long enough. Worse though, much worse, my brethren will hunt us. The Veil will send anyone she thinks is capable of defeating me. There are several. We must be suspicious of any woman who looks out of place. Staying hidden is the safest course, but in case we are found, we should always be prepared to raise our defenses."

"Our defenses?" queried Ben.

"Hardening your will to defend against a mage's attack," explained Towaal.

Ben looked at her blankly.

"Damn it, girl," Towaal barked at Amelie in frustration. "You are being hunted by mages and you didn't teach him to defend himself?"

"We, um, I was learning to use the sword," mumbled Amelie in embarrassment. "I meant to teach him. I said I would."

"Oh my." Towaal sighed. "We have a lot to do."

They kept walking another hundred paces then Towaal continued, "Rhys, we need somewhere close by where we can hide out for a few weeks. We need to instruct the young ones. Can you go ahead of us and find a place?"

Rhys groaned but took off at a brisk jog without objecting.

"Hide for a few weeks!" complained Amelie. "We must reach Northport and help raise forces to save Issen."

"Girl, I am certain you two will not survive this if you are unable to protect yourselves. The siege of Issen will take months, there is some time. We have a bigger, immediate problem. I cannot extend protection to you both and hope to defeat one of my colleagues. Remember your training. The only sure defense against an attack is an individual's own hardened will."

THREE DAYS LATER, they settled into an abandoned farm house north of Kirksbane. It was set well off the road and in a sorry state of disrepair. Rhys speculated there must have been an elderly occupant who couldn't care for the place any longer. Whether the occupant passed away or moved on, they did not know. Nearby fields lay fallow. It had been at least a season since anyone tended to them.

The first day, Ben and Rhys cleaned up what they could and

tried to make the place more comfortable. For people used to living on the road over the last two months, four walls and a leaky roof seemed like luxury.

They cleaned out the hearth, kicked out a relatively debris free area for sleeping, and even found a sturdy table with usable chairs.

Behind the farmhouse, they found a narrow creek sufficient for gathering water. It looked too small to contain fish, but they would look anyway.

Ben scouted the area for signs of game. In the field, he found markings he thought belonged to wild pigs. He made a note to check for additional signs. Maybe they could stock up on ham and bacon for the rest of the journey.

Also that day, Towaal sat down with Amelie and interrogated her about her training. Towaal had occasionally visited Initiate Amelie, but she was usually in the field. She was never assigned to training new mages.

Ben overheard snippets of the conversation as he worked.

"I understand the concept of hardening your will," stated Amelie. "If you have hardened your will, and maintain the space around you, then another mage cannot manipulate matter within the sphere of your influence, right?"

Towaal murmured assent.

"And that is how you were able to push aside Lady Ingrid's fire?" surmised Amelie.

"Yes," affirmed Lady Towaal. "It requires less willpower to control your body and the immediate area around you, hence, it's easier to play defense than offense in battle. It is the property of inertia. Instead of trying to effect change in the world, you are trying to maintain stasis. Simply put, the physical world is inclined to keep doing what it is doing."

"Then how did you defeat Lady Ingrid? Was she not protecting herself?" questioned Amelie.

"She was trying," remarked Towaal dryly. "It is easier to maintain stasis, but a stronger will can still overpower a weaker will. A strong enough will can even manipulate matter within your body, despite you trying to stop it. They say the Veil can stop a person's heart from beating using only her will, though I'm not sure how anyone would know that since the woman hasn't been outside her residence in a century."

Amelie frowned at the reference to the Veil, but questions about the fight with Ingrid were more pressing. "So, are you that much stronger than Ingrid that you were able to overpower her? What kind of defense can Ben and I put up then if we are facing experienced mages?"

"It's important to understand that against a strong enough mage, you may not be able to put up any defense," advised Towaal, "but that doesn't mean you shouldn't try. Lady Ingrid, I believe she was near my strength. She was also a field mage and had experience in combat. She forgot one important lesson though, which we teach all initiates. Magic involves two core capabilities, will and knowledge. Ingrid was pouring all of her willpower into the attack. She pulled heat from the courtyard and from her own body to generate the fire she was using."

Lady Towaal paused and sipped from a water skin before continuing. "By drawing in the heat, she created an abundance of its opposite in the atmosphere, cold. I understood that, but she may not have. In a sense, she helped me by creating the necessary conditions to use the drop in temperature to freeze the moisture in the air. After that, I formed the frozen water into icicles and directed it toward her at a high rate of speed."

Amelie sat back pensively. Ben hurried out of the door before he was caught eavesdropping.

That afternoon, Rhys found Ben collecting firewood and bent down to assist. While they were working, Rhys simply asked, "Mathias?"

Ben cringed. He hadn't exactly forgotten about his friend, but so much had been happening that he hadn't told Rhys yet.

"He," Ben paused, shifting the stack of wood in his arms. "He didn't make it."

"How did it happen?" asked Rhys softly.

"About a week outside of the City, a hunter found us. We fought and Mathias…"

"It's okay," said Rhys.

"Rhys," Ben added, "if it wasn't for Mathias, Amelie and I would both be dead now. He saved us outside the Sanctuary and he saved us in the woods that night. He didn't have to help me. He knew what he was going against and he did it anyway, without a second thought. He was a good man."

"He was a good man." Rhys agreed. "Tonight, we'll toast to his memory."

"Mathias would like that," agreed Ben.

AMELIE WAS eager to get back on the road and reach Northport with minimal delay, but after Lady Towaal and Rhys fully explained the capabilities of the Sanctuary, even she agreed they needed time to prepare. Mages, hunters, assassins, and soldiers would all be set onto their trail. Speed and stealth were two important factors, but they could not count on avoiding all conflicts. Already on the journey they had been attacked numerous times. It didn't take much to imagine it happening again. They had to be ready to fight.

So began two weeks of intensive training. Each morning, Rhys started with sword practice. In the afternoon, Lady Towaal taught them how to bolster their magical defenses, and in the evening, they practiced the Ohms, which relaxed their bodies and minds.

Rhys' sword training was different from Saala's. Where Saala taught a variety of forms and spoke about how to react to an opponent and use them, Rhys emphasized creativity and getting your opponent to react to you.

"Lead them into a mistake and never let them see what is coming," he barked. "Remember, we are fighting, not dueling!"

"We are practicing," grumbled Ben.

"I don't practice, remember?" Rhys snorted. "Once I'm done with you, you won't practice either. When you draw your longsword, you need to plan on using it."

Another difference was that Saala fought with a clean and elegant style. He favored observing an opponent and molding his attacks and defense to what they were doing. Rhys was quick, efficient, relentless, and brutal. He didn't care what you were doing because he acted before you did it. Sparring with Saala was like dancing. Sparring with Rhys was like a no holds barred tavern brawl.

It was exhausting for Ben and Amelie.

On the first day, Rhys fashioned practice swords from materials he found in the woods around the farmhouse. He expected them to be used several bells each day.

Ben quickly realized that while hiking through the woods kept him active during their travel, it didn't have the same intensity as sword practice. He'd gotten out of shape compared to when he sparred regularly with Saala. Rhys was determined to get him back in shape.

Amelie had it worse. She had never spent a significant amount of time practicing the sword. Several bells of handling two wooden practice blades were difficult for her. Rhys was able to motivate her easily, though.

"How are you going to help your people if you can't lift a sword," chided Rhys.

Amelie's face contorted in a determined scowl and she charged forward, vigorously swinging her weapons. Rhys laughed and jumped out of the way.

During the second week, Ben felt he was beginning to regain

some of his conditioning. While he was less successful sparring with Rhys than he had been Saala, he did manage to strike the rogue a few times.

That was until Lady Towaal got involved.

Ben was balanced on the balls of his feet, circling Rhys while the man described tactics for facing more than one opponent. He had been demonstrating it earlier against both Ben and Amelie, but she was lying on the ground, completely worn down. Ben was tired too. He kept going though, hoping that Rhys would finally get distracted by something and he could get a strike in.

Instead, Ben was distracted.

A steady, cool breeze was blowing through, portending a storm later that evening. All of a sudden, the breeze turned into a gale.

Rhys' clothing flapped violently around him and Ben was blown off his feet and tumbled across the clear space they used for practice.

As quickly as the gale started, it stopped.

Amelie sat up, startled. She had only been ruffled by the burst of wind. Its effects nearby were apparent though. A cloud of dust was settling around Ben and a pile of loose objects were strewn around behind him.

"What the…" he started. Then he saw Lady Towaal, calmly observing from twenty paces away. He stopped speaking. He knew what happened.

"If a mage attacks you, she is unlikely to give you warning beforehand," instructed the stern-faced woman. "You must be prepared at all times."

"How is that possible to be prepared for that?" complained Ben.

"I didn't get knocked over, did I?" remarked Rhys.

That was the start of the second phase of Lady Towaal's training.

Earlier in the previous week, she began by teaching meditation exercises to calm and center them.

"It's not so different from the Ohms Rhys has been teaching you, if that helps," she said, "but where the Ohms require concentration to achieve physical balance, this requires a mental balance. Eventually, either with the Ohms or holding your will, it should become second nature. Balance is a habit that you do without thinking."

Ben frowned, not understanding.

"When you walk," explained Lady Towaal, "do you have to think about every step?"

Ben shook his head no.

"That is because your body and mind unconsciously adjust as you move. You've done it enough that you no longer think about it. If you start up a hill, your center of gravity changes, and your body responds before you fall over."

"What is center of gravity?" asked Ben.

Towaal sighed and rubbed the back of her neck. "Never mind. Just understand that physical balance and mental balance are similar. The goal is to maintain both at all times and always be prepared to adjust to your surroundings."

Well, that part made sense at least, thought Ben.

To teach them defense, Lady Towaal instructed them to focus on every tiny detail about what was happening in their bodies and around them. When they concentrated, they could feel their hearts beat and feel the air filling their lungs. They could sense small movements around them, like a bird flying between two trees or an ant crawling across their legs.

While they concentrated, Lady Towaal would use her will to affect a small change around them. At first, the goal was just to sense the change.

After several days, they both were able to do this the majority of the time. Amelie picked it up easily and she was able to help Ben by explaining things in different terms than Towaal used.

Between the two women, at least one of them could usually describe it in a way he understood.

Once they were able to sense the changes, Towaal showed them how to prevent them. It was easiest when it was something within their bodies or touching them. Outside of their immediate space, it grew difficult. The further the change was from their physical presence, the more difficult it was to hold. Amelie was able to hold objects static that were a dozen paces away from her. Ben struggled with anything that wasn't touching him.

Ben was getting frustrated, but Towaal assured him he was doing well. "Remember, she's had months of training in the Sanctuary. You haven't. Many of these concepts are familiar to her."

"If she's been there for months," Ben glanced at Amelie apologetically before continuing. "Then shouldn't she know how to do this?"

Towaal broke a tiny smile. "Many in the Sanctuary consider this to be a combat skill. That is not something taught early to initiates. Besides, what I am teaching you is an infinitesimally small part of becoming a mage. You are learning to impose your will on your own body. That is natural. You do it unconsciously all of the time. Extending that will beyond yourself and gaining knowledge to understand what you are doing is the difficult part of being a mage."

Holding their will and keeping their surroundings static was, as she said, the easiest part of Towaal's training. They would sit in a quiet space and wait for her to create a disturbance. Then they would try to stop it. It was fairly entertaining, like a game, and Ben found it pleasant.

The surprise attacks she began conducting during the second week were unpleasant. Whether it was during sword practice, dinner, or even one time when Ben was leaning over the creek to get water, she was remorseless in showing Ben just how little attention he was paying to his surroundings.

After the water incident, while Ben was returning soaking

wet to the farmhouse, he decided Towaal might be enjoying this a little more than was necessary.

Late in the evening, after long days of sword, will, and Ohms practice, they would relax around a fire in the farmhouse hearth or outside in the open. The leaves on the trees had turned and the evening air carried a distinct chill. After so many nights on the road, it felt good to Ben to be in one place. Huddling close to the fire became his favorite part of the day.

One night during the second week, Rhys produced a silver flask and shared its contents with Ben. It went down with a warm tingle, unlike the harsh burn of the rough spirits he drank in Free State. Someone had put a lot of time and care in distilling this liquor.

They were sprawled out in the open beside a fire pit Ben had dug the prior week. It reminded him of previous times he'd camped with his friend Rhys. It reminded him of Renfro too.

"Before you left the City, did you see any of our friends?" inquired Ben. "I worry about Renfro."

Rhys nodded. "I did some poking around as soon as we realized something was amiss. That little thief has a second sense for these things. He was already in hiding. I managed to track him down and I told him to leave town. I don't think he'll do it, but when I found him, it scared him. At the very least, he'll dig in deeper. The Sanctuary will be inclined to think he fled the City. I worked for them, and I know, they won't be able to imagine someone not running. If he stays out of sight, he'll be all right."

"And the brewery?" Ben asked, relieved. Renfro could do foolish things sometimes, but if he wasn't caught on the initial sweep, then he had a chance. Whatever wrongs Renfro had done in the past, he didn't deserve what the Sanctuary would do if they caught him.

"It's been dismantled." Rhys shrugged. "The warehouse was empty. To be honest, I didn't look into it much. With you, Reinhold, and Renfro gone, well, what can you expect?"

"You're right," agreed Ben with a sigh. "I would have liked to see it continue on without me. I suppose that was never going to happen. I put a lot of effort into that place."

Rhys took a drink from his flask and passed it to Ben. "A toast. To what you built and what you'll build in the future."

Ben sipped the liquor then handed it back. "I can't believe through all of this you hung onto a flask."

Rhys winked at him. "You have to know your priorities."

Towaal shook her head ruefully from across the fire.

"We'll have to think about resupply soon," continued Rhys, ignoring Towaal's disapproval. "After this flask, and the other one I brought, we'll be completely dry. Unacceptable."

Towaal snorted and claimed, "Enough for me tonight. I think I'll turn in."

Rhys waved to her goodnight, took another pull on his flask, and let out a content sigh. Ben wondered how much of Rhys' incorrigible rogue persona was an act to keep their spirits up. In an extremely stressful situation, the man's humor was welcome. Or maybe it was there to plaster over a deeper pain beneath the surface.

Early the next morning, before the women woke up, Rhys took Ben up the small creek behind the farmhouse to see if they could find a place to fish.

Ben decided to broach a topic he'd been wondering about.

"Rhys," he started tentatively. "A while ago, Mathias mentioned something about you. He said you are, ah, rather..."

"Old?" Rhys finished for him with a grin.

Ben blinked. "Yeah, something like that."

"I was wondering when you would ask about that," replied Rhys. "I never bring it up, but I figured we have gotten to know each other well enough that you had to be curious. Particularly after you spent time with Mathias. He liked to gossip more than a village milk maid."

"What…" Ben wasn't sure how to continue. "How old are you?"

"That's a rude question, isn't it?" asked Rhys with a raised eyebrow.

"It's only rude when you ask a woman," retorted Ben.

Rhys paused, shook his head, and snorted. He looked at Ben then started walking along the creek bed again without answering.

"It's true though, isn't it? You are a long-lived?" inquired Ben.

Rhys sighed. "Yes, it is true."

Ben followed the rogue through the low bush and kept his eyes on the narrow waterway. It was unlikely they'd find fish in there, he thought.

"How?" asked Ben.

Rhys scratched an arm, eyes on the water. "It just happens. There is no ceremony, no official acknowledgement. One day, I just stopped getting older. I'm not even sure when it happened. I certainly didn't feel any different. I was traveling a lot then and not spending much time around the same people. I came home one year, back to where I was born and spent my childhood. I realized everyone looked different, older, but not me."

Rhys continued walking. "It was…uncomfortable. People noticed and thought it was strange. Folks I'd grown up around suddenly treated me like I was a monster or, even worse, like I was some sort of god."

"Can you stop it?" asked Ben.

Rhys nodded. "Of course. Anyone can stop living if they want to. All you have to do is give up. Being a long-lived, it's not much different in that respect. You let go of your control and nature's course will take back over."

They walked together in silence until Ben found the courage to risk another question.

"Can…Can you teach me," he stuttered. "Can you teach me how to be long-lived?"

Rhys smiled. "What do you think I'm doing?"

Ben blinked in surprise.

"The sword practice, the Ohms, even what Towaal is teaching you," explained Rhys. "That is skill. That is control. You gain enough skill, you become better than anyone else at your chosen vocation, and then you can live forever."

9

BY THE MOONLIGHT

AFTER TWO WEEKS of training and conditioning at the farmhouse, they got back on the road. It was three weeks travel to Northport, and they all sensed that if they didn't leave now, it could be too late for Issen. Towaal grumbled about how they weren't ready. They would have to be, thought Ben.

They were well provisioned now with smoked ham from a wild pig and fruit from an overgrown orchard at the back of the farm. Simple fare, but it was all they needed.

Instead of the river road, which Ben thought they would take, they took several winding paths and ended up on a narrow track only wide enough for a handcart. Trees and abundant mountain laurel bushes pressed in close. The breeze barely stirred the air in the dense forest, and when it did, it carried the thick scent of vegetation.

"Are you sure this is the right way?" Amelie called to Rhys, who was leading them.

"The river road is certain to be watched," answered Rhys. "That's how Tomas caught you, right? This route isn't exactly a secret, but if they have limited resources, they may not be watching it."

"And if they have unlimited resources?" rejoined Amelie.

"Then remember what Towaal showed you and be ready to draw your sword," drawled Rhys.

Amelie stumped further down the road, brushing a low-hanging branch aside. "This doesn't look like the right way," she grumbled.

Rhys smiled and tapped the side of his head. "All up here, my lady."

Three days down the narrow, tree lined path and they reached a small village.

"What is this place called?" asked Amelie.

"Not sure," responded Rhys.

She stared at him. "I thought it was all," she tapped the side of her head. "Up here."

"A lot, I should have said," he answered impishly. "A lot is up there. All might be an exaggeration."

She rolled her eyes and they started toward the village. Ben was expecting Towaal to steer them through the town and keep going like she did on their earlier journey, but instead, she directed them to a quiet-looking inn. It was a bit smaller than the Buckhorn Tavern back in Farview. The town itself was smaller.

Inside, early afternoon sunlight streamed through open windows at the front of the building. A fire was sputtering in the hearth. It had been bells since anyone tended to it. With the open windows, the fire did little to fight the chill autumn air in the room.

"Are you sure we should stop here?" protested Amelie, waving a hand toward the empty room. "We'll stand out like sore thumbs in this place."

"If any watchers are in this town, they already saw us as soon as we turned the bend in the road," argued Towaal. "For a small town like this, any stranger is noteworthy, even more so if they pass through without stopping. Correct, Ben?"

He affirmed, "People saw us as soon as we saw them. In a place like this, word will have already spread."

A small tin bell sat on a table near the doorway. Towaal gave it a sharp ring. Heartbeats later, a portly, red faced man bustled out of the back calling, "Welcome, welcome. Please, take a seat. I am Master Perrod. What can I help you with? Food, drink, lodging?"

"Let's start with a drink," suggested Rhys.

The inn didn't have a name that Ben could determine, but Master Perrod and his wife made them feel right at home. They bustled in and out of the kitchen, describing what they had to offer and making extra efforts to please their guests. After the first round of ales, they found out why.

"Three silvers for the four of us!" Rhys coughed, ale splattered the table. He wiped at his mouth and stared incredulously at the innkeeper.

Master Perrod bowed slightly and raised his hands apologetically. "We don't get many travelers this way, sir. For us to make ends meet, we must charge a steep price."

Rhys mumbled something about finding another inn under his breath.

"Sir, the next inn is in Weimer," remarked the innkeeper flatly. "It's a four-day journey, if you're walking quickly."

"Shush, Rhys," placated Lady Towaal. "Master Perrod, we'll pay the silver gladly for a fine inn like this. I wonder if there is something you can do for me though."

The man nodded eagerly.

"I have a small list of items we could use. Is there a general goods store in town?" she asked. "Maybe you could send someone over with the list and collect some items for us?"

"Absolutely!" Perrod smiled, obviously happy to please his guests and collect his coin. "I will go myself and ensure you get what you need at the very best prices! Master Reynold, he adds an ungentlemanly mark up for foreigners."

"I'm sure he does." Lady Towaal smiled. "If you have a scrap of paper, I can jot down what we need."

The man scurried off.

Towaal turned to the group. She primly stated, "When negotiating, there is always more than one way to win."

"I see your point," agreed Rhys nodding. "Very deftly handed."

Towaal gave him a suspicious look but didn't comment.

When the innkeeper returned with a small sheet of parchment, Rhys tipped up his ale and asked for another.

Perrod returned and Rhys casually inquired, "Master Perrod, as you can tell, I am a thirsty man. I hate to bother your wife in the kitchen while you are a way at the general goods store. Do you have other staff we can call on for a refill?"

Perrod glanced back at the kitchen and grimaced. His wife was likely in the midst of starting dinner for the evening crowd and couldn't be bothered every few minutes to refill a mug of ale.

The innkeeper appeared distraught and finally answered, "Sir, you appear to be a trustworthy type." Ben almost laughed out loud but managed to hold it in while the poor man continued, "Please feel free to refill your own ale. I am confident you'll leave me the correct amount of coins."

A broad catlike smile broke out across Rhys' face. The rogue didn't even bother to hide it. "Certainly. Two coppers a mug, right?"

The innkeeper nodded then accepted the scrap of paper from Towaal. He barely glanced down at it before rushing out the front door. The sooner he got their goods, the sooner he'd be back to keep watch on his ale keg.

Rhys dug two coppers out from his belt pouch and took his time moseying over to the keg.

"Really, Rhys?" called Lady Towaal.

Grinning, he filled up his mug, pausing toward the end for the foam to settle down then opening the tap again to fill to the very rim.

Lady Towaal stared at him disapprovingly.

Meeting her eyes, he ducked down, took a big gulp, and topped it off again at the tap.

Towaal threw up her arms and exclaimed, "Oh please! That is just ridiculous and petty."

Ben and Amelie burst out laughing. Rhys sauntered back to the table, two copper coins sitting on the bar behind him.

That evening, Rhys stacked the pile of coppers high.

Ben contributed his fair share as well, but when he started feeling lightheaded and caught himself loudly, and unnecessarily, debating a topic with Rhys, he slowed down and only had one more ale. When he passed on the next round, Lady Towaal flashed a small smile then stood.

"I think I shall get some rest," she stated. "Amelie, are you coming as well?"

Amelie nodded, standing up from the table.

Rhys frowned. "Everyone is abandoning me?" he asked pitifully.

Amelie sighed and returned to her chair. "I'll stay while Rhys finishes this ale. I don't believe that sad look for a second, but I'm not very tired yet. I'll be quiet when I come up."

Towaal nodded and swept down the hallway toward her and Amelie's room. Ben and Rhys were sharing a room also. Ben figured he may as well stay with Rhys and Amelie while Rhys finished the ale.

It didn't take long. Rhys gulped it down quickly then declared, "If none of you are going to be any fun, I will turn in too."

"I'll get some fresh air first, and then I'll be right after you," said Ben.

"Mind if I join you?" asked Amelie.

"Don't go far," advised Rhys. "This town seems quiet, but you never know."

Ben nodded. He and Amelie stepped out the front door and Rhys went to bed.

The street outside was lit silver from a three-quarters moon hanging low in the sky. The town was quiet this late in the evening. Two locals and Master Perrod remained inside the inn, but other than them, it looked like everyone else had already found their beds.

Ben glanced around then led Amelie to the side of the inn. There was a long bench against the wall that looked out past the edge of town into the woods. The stars were starting to poke through and join the moon in the black blanket of the night sky.

They settled on the bench and Amelie scooted close to Ben.

"It's getting cold now," she whispered.

Ben wrapped an arm around her and draped his cloak across her back. A draft of cool air chilled him, but her warm body felt good against his side.

"We'll have to find warmer clothes in Northport," he replied back in a low voice.

She shivered and burrowed deeper in his cloak.

They sat like that silently for several minutes, watching the stars twinkle to life. They huddled next to each other. Together they stayed warm.

A silver streak shot silently across the sky. They both tracked the shooting star until it disappeared behind the branches of a great oak tree.

Ben breathed deep of the cool air then looked down at Amelie. She was looking back up at him. Moonlight painted her face like a beautiful doll that he saw at a shop in Fabrizo. Her lips were parted slightly and her eyes twinkled like the stars.

He leaned toward her and she gasped and scooted away. A wedge of cold slid between them.

"I…" Ben started.

She silenced him with a finger on his lips.

"It's not that," she said.

He met her eyes and waited for her to continue.

"This is not the right time," she finally said.

He nodded. "I understand," he whispered, afraid to speak too loudly and betray the lump in his throat. He didn't understand.

"I hope you do," she breathed. "Coming for me in the Sanctuary, risking your life, and sticking with me through whatever happens next. Ben, I couldn't possibly ask for more than that. You've been more loyal to me than I deserve. I've been thinking about that, a lot."

He stayed still, letting her speak.

"Then we were in Kirksbane again, and we saw the Curve," she added.

Ben swallowed uncomfortably. That night at the inn with the barmaid hadn't been his most honorable moment.

"No." She sighed. "I am saying this all wrong. Ben, when we saw that place and I thought about that whore being with you..."

He wondered how to unwrap his arm from her shoulder without being too obvious.

"Ben, I was jealous. I still am," she whispered.

"I'm sorry, Amelie," he responded painfully. "I know it's not an excuse, but I was drunk. I didn't mean to hurt you."

"I know that. I was mad then, but I am not mad anymore...as mad at least," she said with a sigh. "Ben, I mean I was jealous because I care about you. I wanted what she had. Ben, I still want what she had. That morning after, I told myself I'd been stupid. I was a lady and I was going to be an initiate at the Sanctuary. That kind of thing wasn't an option for me, I had other plans. It was foolish then, but, that's not me anymore. That life is over."

He wasn't sure what to do. That sounded like someone who wanted a kiss.

"Amelie..." he started, yearning creeping into his voice.

"But now is not the time," she continued. "We have too much happening right now and too much danger to be distracted. We have to think about what we are doing and not...what we want to be doing. This town seems safe, but Rhys is right, we never know.

We could be attacked here, we could be attacked anywhere. We have to stay alert."

"You're right," he replied, understanding finally but not wanting to. If they let their guard down, it could be fatal. They couldn't afford distractions.

Then she kissed him.

Her soft lips, cold at first in the night air, warmed quickly when pressed against his. Before he could respond, she pulled away.

"We should go to bed," she said, breathing quickly. "Towaal and Rhys will be ready to get on the road at first light."

Ben stood with her and walked slowly back to the inn. He didn't trust himself to speak.

The door to his room creaked shut noisily. Rhys stirred under his blankets while Ben stripped off his boots and his outer clothes.

A window was open and their room was cold. Ben buried himself under the rough blankets and tried to still his swirling thoughts. The meditation Lady Towaal taught them back at the farmhouse wasn't helping at all now.

"Hands above the blankets," mumbled a sleepy Rhys.

"What?" whispered Ben.

"Keep your hands above the blanket." His friend yawned.

"What are you talking about?" Ben hissed in reply.

"You just went for a moonlight stroll with Amelie but you weren't gone long enough to really enjoy it. I hear you breathing over there like a farm boy who just saw his first naked woman. Well, you are a farm boy, but you know what I mean. Keep your hands out," barked Rhys. Then he rolled over and started to snore softly.

Ben stared at the dark ceiling.

SPARKLES OF SILVER frosted the thatch roofs of the town. They crunched through the frozen morning dew on the way to the narrow road that led back into the woods. Ben's breath puffed out in a cloud in front of him. He rubbed his hands together to warm them up.

"Are you sure we needed to leave this early?" he complained from deep within the hood of his cloak. "It's cold."

Towaal answered, "The sooner we reach Northport, the sooner Lord Rhymer can send troops to aid Issen." Before Amelie could speak up, she raised one hand. "You had to learn to defend yourselves against magic. If you can't defend yourselves, then there is no point in continuing. Stopping was necessary. Sitting over a hot bowl of porridge by the fire and sipping a steaming mug of kaf is not necessary."

"Aren't you from the mountains?" Rhys asked Ben. "Surely it gets colder than this in Farview. You should be used to it."

"It does get cold in the winter," objected Ben, "but I'm smart enough to stay inside then!"

"Well, I hate to ruin your morning, but we're going to Northport, and it's about to be winter. It's going to get a lot colder."

Ben trudged on.

The narrow path wound deeper into the woods and started climbing in elevation. Northport wasn't in the mountains, but it was a significantly higher elevation than the City. They would continue at a steady climb along a low rise for another two weeks until they got there.

On the path, they saw hardly anyone.

"Who uses this road?" groused Amelie one morning after running into a low-hanging branch. It was heavy with rain water from the night before. The cold water showered down on her when she tried to duck underneath it.

"There are some mining towns further up," answered Rhys. "That's what Northport is known for—mining. Down here, it's mostly fur trappers and the occasional farming community. It's rough scratching out a field in these woods though."

Shaking off the water from the branch, Amelie stepped over a fallen tree trunk and kicked it in frustration. "Who maintains the path then? They are doing a terrible job."

"The people who use it," Rhys grinned. "We can move that tree trunk if you like. Make this road nice and smooth for the next travelers. I don't suppose you brought an axe or a saw?"

Amelie glared at him.

"Sooner or later," added Rhys, "someone is going to come this way with heavy carts of iron ingots from one of the mines. They'll clear the way as they pass through. After that, the vegetation will start the slow process of growing back."

"No lord claims this land?" asked Ben curiously. Aside from his hometown of Farview and Free State, everywhere they went seemed to be claimed by someone.

Rhys shrugged. "Not that I know of. It's been a few years since I last passed through this way. They seemed pretty independent then. It could be part of Northport, I suppose."

"Those Free Staters aren't as unique as they think," declared Amelie.

Something else occurred to Ben. "Rhys, why do they carry the iron ingots in carts? Couldn't they make their way over to the Venmoor River and barge it down? I assume they are going to Venmoor with it?"

"Good question," acknowledged Rhys. "I imagine they would have to cut a new road to get over to the river, and that is no easy task. And if they got there, they would have to locate a barge that would be willing to load heavy cargo off the side of the riverbank and not at a mooring. All of that is assuming they could find a barge at all. They might spend a significant amount of time waiting."

"There are plenty of barges," argued Ben. "We had no problem finding one before Tomas found us."

"There are plenty now because it's harvest," responded Rhys.

Ben was about to ask another question when Towaal held up a hand and demanded, "Everyone, stop!"

They all halted and put hands on their weapons, looking around on high alert. The forest seemed peaceful.

Lady Towaal was peering around intensely.

"Do you feel it?" she asked.

Ben frowned. All seemed normal to him.

Rhys whistled in appreciation. "Subtle. I would have walked right into that."

Lady Towaal glanced at Amelie, who was staring ahead pensively.

Ben looked in the same direction. The trail continued on like it had been doing for days. Thick mountain laurel edged into the path, backed by tall oak and elm trees. Nothing stirred that he could see.

"I..." mumbled Amelie. "I feel something. I'm not sure what it is."

Towaal beckoned her closer. "Come. We'll approach it from the side and I will show you."

The two women pushed into the forest. In a rustle and crash of branches, they vanished from sight.

"I guess they aren't worried about being overheard?" remarked Ben.

"I don't think anyone is nearby," replied Rhys, standing relaxed in the center of the path.

Ben raised an eyebrow.

"Wait and see," said Rhys.

Minutes later, Towaal and Amelie reappeared.

"Let's go," said Towaal, waving to the men. "We can pass it undisturbed."

Amelie, seeing Ben's look of incomprehension, explained, "A ward."

"A magical ward?" asked Ben.

She nodded. "It's a little wooden device wedged in the nook of a tree branch. Towaal says there will be another one on the other side of the path. They are connected somehow. Anything that passes between will trigger an alarm."

"There are magical wards?" asked Ben again.

"Of course there are," replied Lady Towaal, looking at him curiously.

"Are there," Ben swallowed, thinking furiously. "Are there any magical wards on the north river bank of the Sanctuary? Ones that could be tripped if someone snuck in there?"

"No," denied Towaal. "The Sanctuary doesn't need wards. Who would be so foolish as to...oh, right." Towaal shook her head, turned from Ben, and pushed her way back into the undergrowth.

In the brush, Ben heard Towaal muttering under her breath, "How they managed to avoid being caught before I found them, I will never know."

Rhys clapped Ben on the back and said, "You learn something useful every day, don't you?"

They all shoved their way through the mountain laurel after Towaal. She steered them through the undergrowth until they were behind a nondescript tree. From where they were standing, Ben could see the side of a palm-sized wooden disc, similar to the one Amelie carried, which she said was a repository of power. This close, Ben felt the disturbance the thing created, like a buzzing at the edge of his consciousness. It felt like a bee was flying around just outside of where he could see it.

"What you feel," described Towaal, "Is a disruption in will."

Amelie and Ben stared at her blankly.

"This device and its partner on the other side of the path are creating a field within which a minor suggestion is being made. It's probably something very simple. Scratch your arm or sneeze. It's a light suggestion, so someone of strong will could easily resist it without knowing. An animal, or someone of weak will, would likely comply. If the suggestion is resisted, that would trigger an alert to whoever set this field up and tell them that a person or persons of reasonably strong will passed through."

Ben studied what he could see of the disc. It was covered in intricate carvings but seemed simply made. Any artisan that worked in wood could replicate it.

"What do those etchings mean?" asked Ben.

"I am not entirely sure," replied Towaal. "Generally, they help focus the creator's will into the device and retain whatever activity it is meant to do." She shrugged. "I am not very knowledgeable about these things other than an awareness that they exist."

"But you're a full mage!" exclaimed Amelie.

Towaal ruefully shook her head. "Girl, the more you learn, the more you will realize what you don't know. Creating something like this requires extensive knowledge in an area which I have not studied. No one person, even the Veil, knows everything there is to know."

They edged around the mysterious device and returned to the path.

"So, does that mean a mage is nearby?" wondered Ben nervously.

"They are not likely on this path, or they would just watch for us instead of setting the device," answered Towaal. "I don't think we need to be concerned about running into someone immediately, but it does mean someone thought we might travel this direction. It could have been Lady Ingrid, or it could be someone else. When we get to Northport, we'll have to be cautious. At least one mage thought we might travel this way."

Ben groaned.

10

CORINNE AND GRUNT

TWO WEEKS LATER, they peered from behind a thicket of brambles at the city of Northport. Sturdy walls rose the height of ten grown men and spread out for half a league in each direction. Around the walls, all growth had been cleared for at least five hundred paces. It gave the guards on the wall an ample killing ground for anything that approached. No buildings or even vendor's stalls stood outside of the walls.

On top of the wall, Ben could see the tiny figures of guards on patrol. There weren't many of them, but it was clear Northport was prepared for battle. Catapults and ballista stood at regular intervals.

"Are they expecting an attack?" worried Ben.

Rhys replied, "They're always expecting an attack up here and there are always guards on the walls. It's demon country. This appears a little unusual though." Rhys pointed down the wall in the distance where a handful of men were standing at the base. As they watched, a huge pile of rock rose into the air, lifted by a pulley system atop the wall. Another group of men stood on top to unload the rock.

"Ammunition for the catapults," explained Rhys.

"What do you think they're getting ready for?" asked Ben.

Rhys shrugged.

"Maybe we shouldn't go in until we know more," suggested Ben, shifting nervously around the bramble bush to get a better look.

"We have to go in!" exclaimed Amelie. "We are so close now."

Lady Towaal put a placating hand on Amelie's shoulder. "It likely has nothing to do with us. Whatever they are preparing for, we need to go inside and find out more."

The companions moved out from the cover of the forest and started toward the arched gates of Northport. Two huge iron doors marked the entrance, but only one of them stood open. It was still wide enough for two wagons to pass abreast, but Ben took it as another sign Northport was preparing for something.

They joined a short line of wagons waiting at the gate for inspection by a heavily armored team of guards. Unlike all of the other cities they passed into, these men were actually inspecting the goods in the wagons before letting them pass. This wasn't a simple glance to determine a customs tariff, this was a security measure.

When they got to the front, a brutish man with a wild, bushy beard asked, "Purpose of your visit?" He was eyeing their weapons closely.

"We're looking for employment," replied Rhys. "A few years back, I heard there is a rich bounty for demon horns. What is the problem here? Is that not the case anymore?"

The guard grunted. "Aye, there is a bounty. Though there ain't too many going into the Wilds these days." He waved for them to pass and turned his attention to the next wagon.

Once inside the gate, Amelie whispered, "Well, that was easier than I expected."

"They are used to hunters up here. It's the one place looking menacing and going armed actually helps you fit in. Getting inside Rhymer's keep might be a little trickier."

"I can just announce myself," offered Amelie. "Lord Rhymer knows me. I am sure he will grant us an audience."

Rhys shook his head but Towaal was the one who responded. "You can't announce yourself. We know a mage was watching for us to travel this way. Remember the ward? If you are declaring yourself at Rhymer's gates, we might as well hang a big sign for her pointing to where we'll be sleeping. We must be subtle and get to Rhymer without alerting his entire staff to our presence."

"That sounds like my area of expertise," chimed in Rhys with a grin.

Curious, they followed Rhys deeper into the city. The streets were teeming with people, and at first glance, it didn't seem so different from the other big cities Ben visited. After a while though, he noticed that nearly everyone here was armed. From the plate-and-chain encrusted guards at the gate to a woman selling soup out of a cart, no one was walking the streets without some type of weapon.

The soup seller carried a long knife at her belt. It was close in size to a short sword. She had a separate hand-length blade she used to carve a bowl out of a loaf of bread then ladled a steaming heap of soup into it. A man nodded thanks to her and passed a few coins before making his way down the street, sipping from the bread bowl. A longsword hung on his belt and a crossbow was strapped to his back.

"Everyone here is armed," observed Ben to his companions.

Rhys sarcastically replied, "The bar fights must be epic."

Rhys was trying to make light of it, but Ben could sense the tension in his friend. The rogue lived in Northport years before. It was obvious that this level of militarization was not normal.

In half a bell, they made it to the hulking stack of stone that was Rhymer's keep. There was none of the elegance of buildings in the City. Not even the brutal artistry of Argren's fortress. This was simply a huge pile of stone built to resist whatever the elements and enemies could throw against it. The stone was stained black from generations of smoke and weather.

"Not the most attractive place," noted Amelie.

"It's been here for a long time," remarked Rhys. "This keep stood here before the rest of the current city. That outer wall is over six hundred years old. It's new compared to the keep."

"How will we get inside?" asked Ben.

"Well, normally I would find a chambermaid. The lustiest one that's available..." Towaal cut Rhys off.

"Be serious, we don't have time for this," she warned.

He sighed. "We need to find the gate where they take the slops out."

"What did you say?" asked Amelie. She hadn't been paying close attention. She was peering intensely at the people who passed them. Looking for mages, Ben guessed.

"The gate where they take the slops out," expanded Rhys. "They'll have the laziest, most junior guards working at that one. We talk our way in there."

"We just talk our way in?" asked Amelie skeptically.

"Yeah. We're not trying to get into Rhymer's changing room. There are thousands of people in that keep and most of them will be guards. The fellows at the gate, they don't care if we go in as long as it doesn't come back on them. They just want to finish their shift then go have a drink and a twirl."

Amelie crossed her arms but kept silent. Her view of the way a lord's men should behave and Rhys' view of how they actually behaved didn't always match.

The slop gate was a narrow door set at the base of the keep in the back. It was barely wide enough for a hand cart to be pulled down. There was a small window the size of Ben's two hands put together. No one was outside.

"Where are the guards?" inquired Ben.

"Inside," answered Rhys. "They're probably asleep. You can't keep them outside or it would be too easy to jump them and get in. Plus, it just makes you look bad when people see sleeping guards in front of entrances to your keep."

They walked up to the gate and it turned out the guards weren't actually asleep, although they were caught by surprise when Rhys pounded on the iron-bound oak door.

Startled, two young men who looked in danger of being swallowed by their oversized armor jumped to attention.

"Step away from the door!" demanded one of them when they saw Rhys peering through the tiny window. "All business must go through the front gate."

"Well, here's the thing," drawled Rhys. "I don't have any official business. I'm here to surprise my girl."

"You still have to go to the front gate," declared the guard.

"Come on. Help a guy out!" pleaded Rhys. "It's our anniversary and I've got a plan to sneak into her room. I'll put some flowers and the like around. She'll love it."

"There is no sneaking in this gate," whined the guard.

"You're right. That was a poor choice of words," admitted Rhys. "It's not sneaking, really. Some of my girl's friends are in on it. I was told to come this way so there is no chance she'd see me. Her friends are supposed to meet me at the Queen's Garden. They'll take me to my girl's room."

"She has a room here. Who is she?" asked the guard.

"She's, ah, Karina. A chambermaid. A lusty one," he added helpfully. "You may know her. She has a lot of friends in the guards." He glanced at his companions and winked. They were standing back where the guards couldn't see them through the window.

Towaal rolled her eyes and crossed her arms.

"I don't, uh, I don't know her," replied the guard.

"That's your loss," consoled Rhys, "but, hey, I realize you guys would be doing me a favor, so let me make it up to you. It's worth a silver coin for each of you if you let me in. It would really mean a lot to me and my girl. Maybe I could introduce you to some of her friends later? They work all of the time and don't get out a lot. They're always looking for some kids, some men, I mean, like you, to show 'em a good time."

"I'm not sure…" wavered the guard.

Rhys flashed two silver coins outside of the window and smiled his friendliest smile.

The voice of the second guard broke in. "I could use that silver. You sure you'll introduce us to your girl's friends? Chambermaids, you said?"

"Yeah, of course I will," replied Rhys. "If you let me in, I'll talk to her tonight. She'll be in a good mood after my surprise. We can see about setting up a party or something."

The guards broke and two bolts noisily slid out of the door frame.

Rhys gestured to his companions and pushed his way inside as soon as the door started to move. He pressed the coins into the guard's hands and pulled Amelie along after him, before the guards realized more people were coming in.

"Hey!" shouted one of them, trying to block their path. The guard had seen maybe fifteen summers. His head barely cleared Ben's shoulder. Ben gently nudged him out of the way and kept walking.

"Who are these people!" exclaimed the red-face guard.

Rhys swept down the narrow hallway, not pausing. "You had better close that door," he called back. "You don't want anyone sneaking in here."

The hallway from the slop gate was narrow and long. It passed deep into the keep before emerging again in a small courtyard ringed by nondescript doors. Rhys paused briefly before selecting one and steering them into another hallway. They passed by a series of doors then began ascending a set of stairs.

"Does he know where he's going?" whispered Ben.

"Probably not," responded Towaal tartly, "but neither do I. So, we may as well follow him."

Occasionally, they would pass other people, but no one stopped them. Ben couldn't help but notice even the chambermaids carried belt knives. These people were ready for something.

Before long, the hallways widened and Rhys started moving slower. Under his breath, he muttered something about real guards.

Ben and Amelie exchanged nervous glances, but then Ben thought, they weren't actually sneaking, they were just trying to be found by the right person.

Next, tapestries and standing suits of armor appeared along the walls. The tapestries largely depicted scenes of battle with the occasional portrait of one of Northport's previous lords. The armor wasn't merely decorative, the stuff had seen use. Ben guessed that it also belonged to previous lords of Northport. Possibly it had been worn in famous battles of old.

Strangely, there were no signs of wealth like he had seen in other keeps. Argren's hallways were practically paved in silver and gold.

"I thought Northport was wealthy?" questioned Ben, looking at a battered and tarnished set of plate armor.

"Don't whisper," replied Rhys. "It makes it look like we're sneaking."

"Okay," responded Ben, a little too loudly. He cringed as his voice filled the empty hallway.

Rhys rolled his eyes and muttered, "Where is a good thief when you need one? Too bad Renfro didn't make this trip." He paused. "Well, maybe not Renfro either."

Ben snorted.

Rhys finally answered, "Northport doesn't display luxury items because they don't need to. The other lords are showing off and trying to impress their guests. Northport though, everyone already knows they have wealth. This is where gold, silver, and gemstones actually come from. They are too commercially minded here to waste resources by setting it on a table in some hallway only the maids walk down."

They turned another corner and Rhys gestured everyone to silence. Ahead of them were three slender courtiers dressed for a ball. The group was one of the few Ben had seen who weren't armed. Rhys led their party to follow closely behind the trio.

Around several more turns and down a set of stairs, suddenly they walked into a wide-open foyer. The ceiling soared four floors above Ben's head. Banners hung from it, both ancient and new. Circling the space was an army of empty suits of armor, standing like silent sentinels. Like the ones in the hallways, these had all seen use.

Voices echoed around the room, bouncing off the hard rock walls. The three courtiers moved to join more like them and Ben's group paused to observe the room. It was near three hundred paces across and was teeming with courtiers, soldiers, and others moving about.

"Is there a party?" wondered Ben.

"No." Amelie shook her head. "This looks just like the foyer in Issen. These people are all waiting to see Lord Rhymer or are doing business with those who are waiting. Places like this in the lord's keep are always busy."

Rhys nodded. "We found the right area."

People were in constant motion. Groups would form for discussions then break apart minutes later. Young boys darted across the floor, delivering messages or fetching items and documents. On one side, there was a desk set up with a harried-looking clerk frantically jotting down names. A long line of disgruntled people stretched out in front of him. Many of them were dressed plainly compared to the rest of the room.

"Petitioners to Lord Rhymer," explained Amelie. "He may see one or two of them each day to seem a benevolent lord, but most of them won't get in. If they're lucky, some minor functionary will deal with them. Otherwise, they'll be left in another room to wait all day before getting kicked out in the evening."

"How do you know all of that?" asked Ben.

"I grew up in a place just like this," answered Amelie with a smile. "What I described is exactly what my father did."

Ben frowned. "If these people have a complaint, shouldn't the lord try to see them?"

"Look at all of these people." Amelie gestured to include the entire room. "There is not enough time in the day to see all of them. My father's theory was that the serious folk would come back again and again. He would have his clerk note how often they came back and those are the ones he would see. My father thought that most of the petitioners knew the solution to their own problems and just wanted validation, so he turned them away and hoped they would figure it out themselves."

Ben shifted his feet and looked around again. That made some sense. There were hundreds of people, and Amelie was right—no lord had time to see all of them.

"That leaves us with a problem though. If he doesn't see everyone, how do we get Rhymer to see us?" queried Amelie.

"Working on it," said Rhys to his companions. He moved to stand next to Lady Towaal, looped his arm around hers, and walked her several paces forward. "You may not like this," he apologized.

She knit her brows and was about to respond. Rhys acted before she could.

He snuck out a foot and hooked it under a passing woman's ankle, sweeping her legs out from under her.

The woman, a young girl Ben saw, went crashing to the stone floor in a pile of embroidered silk and sparkling jewels.

Rhys jumped back from Lady Towaal, pointing at her.

"Why did you do that?" he demanded.

Towaal glared back at him. "I didn't do anything!"

Courtiers appeared as if out of thin air to help the bejeweled woman back to her feet. Red-faced, her eyes darted between Rhys and Lady Towaal. Rhys was quicker than Towaal. He rushed to bend one knee in front of the woman.

"I am so sorry, my lady. My sister is a jealous bitch! I told her to just ignore you, but, oh my, I am just so sorry! Please forgive her," pleaded Rhys.

Towaal scowled down at him in vexation.

"Jealous?" the girl asked.

"She just can't stand seeing another woman with the lord," claimed Rhys. "It's been years, but she still yearns for his bed."

"The lord? His bed?" choked the girl. Her tone was accentuated by her bright red lips, which were painted into a sulky pout. Her eyebrows were elegantly arched to perfection. Young men were speeding across the floor, all clambering to assist her.

"Oh, yes. For many years my sister shared Lord Rhymer's bed," claimed Rhys. "When he called her to the keep today, when he begged to see her, she thought the old spark had been rekindled. She just isn't ready to move on."

The girl's face went from a red flush to a deep crimson, fringing on purple. In a heartbeat, she went from pouty to icy. Ben realized she wasn't much older than him, maybe younger.

"He begged to see her, did he? We shall see about this. Come with me," she demanded.

Courtiers scattered as she spun around and stormed toward a set of tall doors at the far side of the room.

An elderly gentleman, who was decked out in Northport's colors and had a silver badge pinned to his doublet, caught up to her side, trying to calm her down. "Issabelle, he is in a meeting now. This must wait."

"This slut says he called for her, Franklin. Called for her today!" snarled the girl. "He told me he was done with this kind of foolishness. I will not wait. If you try to stop me, I will have you flogged."

The elderly man wrung his hands and gave Ben's party an angry look. He did nothing further to slow the enraged Issabelle.

"Who is that?" Ben whispered to Amelie.

"She looks like a strumpet." His friend sniffed. Her eyes widened and she glanced at Rhys appreciatively. "She is a strumpet! Lord Rhymer's little play thing."

The group rushed across the stone floor toward the doors, the small girl leading the way. A pair of guards at the door looked to the elderly man then quickly pushed the doors open when he waved frantically at them.

Towaal shot Rhys a bemused look as they breezed into Rhymer's reception hall.

The lord was sitting at the far end of the hall behind a massive mahogany table. He had ink, paper, and a half empty decanter of bright red wine on the table. A delegation of what looked like merchants stood in front of him. All of them turned at the interruption.

Rhymer stood and Ben saw the man was a good three or four stone lighter than he remembered from Whitehall. Rhymer had gained a sallow, sickly visage as well. His eyes had the look of a man whose troubles outweighed any joy in his life.

"Seneschal Franklin," he called. "What is the meaning of this? As you can see, I am entertaining the diamond miner's guild."

The elderly man, who must be the seneschal, raised his hands apologetically.

Issabelle strode forward. "Do not ignore me!" she shouted.

Rhymer looked at the small girl and sighed. "What is it, Issabelle?"

"This slut attacked me!" she screamed, pointing at Towaal. "Worse, she says you called for her today and that you begged for her to come. Hoping to give one of your old flames another roll in the bed, were you? Am I not satisfying you, my lord? Do you need someone with more, ah, experience?"

The girl was nearly to Rhymer's desk now. The contingent

from the diamond miner's guild backed away, giving her room. They looked amused as the petite Issabelle cowed the powerful Lord Rhymer.

Rhymer tried to pacify her. "Now, now, Issabelle. I don't even know who this…"

He met Towaal's eyes and paused. Towaal smiled back at him.

Witnessing the exchange, Issabelle shrieked, "I thought she might be lying, but you do know her!" She turned from Rhymer and set her hands on her hips, glaring at Towaal. "I'd have you flogged just for showing up here. You should know better than that, but you tripped me, bitch. For that, I'll have your head."

"I don't think so," replied Towaal in a patronizing tone. "Why don't you go run and play so the adults can talk?"

Pretty Issabelle's mouth dropped open and her eyes flared. She demanded to Franklin, "Call the headsman. Now!"

Towaal ignored Issabelle and looked at Rhymer. "Some privacy might be best," she suggested.

Rhymer nodded contritely and asked the diamond miner's guild if they could wait. The guild leaders agreed and exited the room. They were delighted to have witnessed such juicy gossip.

As soon as the doors boomed shut, Rhymer groaned. "You are causing me quite a bit of grief, Lady…"

Towaal held up a hand to stop him. "No names. I wasn't sure you would recognize me. You were rather, ah, intoxicated last time we spoke at Whitehall."

"Drunk at Whitehall? I knew you had a reason for keeping me here," screamed Issabelle. She snagged a sharp letter opener off of Rhymer's desk. "I won't wait for the headsman. I can do this myself."

Issabelle stalked toward Towaal. The mage just raised an eyebrow and said to Rhymer, "This one is feisty. I like her. She has a lot more spunk than your wife."

"Issabelle!" shouted the lord, stopping his mistress in her

tracks. "This isn't what you think. This woman is not some former lover of mine. Wait for me in my chambers."

Issabelle scowled at Towaal and fingered the point of the letter opener.

"Now, Issabelle, or I will be upset with you," he added ominously.

She petulantly threw the letter opener down on the thick rug and hissed at Towaal, "I will be seeing you later. No matter what he says, you will pay for tripping me!"

She darted out a small door in the back of the reception hall and slammed it shut with more strength than Ben thought she had in that little body.

"This better be worth it," moaned Rhymer. "Did you really trip her? I will pay for that."

"I've come to ask for your help," replied Towaal. "But first," She looked to Franklin. "I need to know we have absolute trust. No one can know who I am or why I am here."

"Franklin hears what I hear," grumbled Rhymer. "He has been with me for years. I trust him as much as I would my own blood. After the mess you caused with Issabelle, don't push me any further."

Towaal nodded curtly.

Amelie stepped forward.

"You may recognize me as well, from when we signed the Alliance agreement in Whitehall. Or maybe earlier when I was just a girl, at my father's keep in Issen."

Lord Rhymer's eyes opened wide and Franklin scurried around to look at Amelie's face.

"You are not dead..." murmured Rhymer.

"Not yet," replied Amelie tartly.

"The Sanctuary," Franklin said, sparing a quick glance at Towaal. "They said you were dead. A mage was here in person. She left just a week ago. She told us you were killed, in training I believe it was."

"I see we have a lot to discuss." Rhymer grimaced. "Franklin, call for food, some glasses, and a lot more wine."

Ben was unsure how much they should trust Lord Rhymer, given the last time he saw the man, he was assaulting a young girl at Argren's Fireworks Spectacular. Lady Towaal and Amelie seemed to trust him completely though. Over the course of the next two bells, they unfolded their story for him.

The news weighed heavily on the lord. As they spoke, he shared concerned looks with his seneschal Franklin. He also emptied several decanters of high-quality wine, rivalling even Rhys on the rogue's best nights.

Rhymer kept a clear head though and he asked pointed questions throughout the tale. By the end of it, his head was bobbing with the new information. Ben could tell the wheels of thought were turning.

At the end of the story, Amelie made her impassioned pitch to the northern lord.

"I do not know how things are going in Issen right now, but I do know how they will go in Issen if my father does not get help. You have known him for years, even decades. You have always been allies. Now, you are officially committed with the signing of the Alliance. Please, honor your commitments and send help for Issen."

Rhymer drank deep of his wine and remained silent. Frustration and concern was evident in his every movement.

Amelie waited then asked, "Do you know something more of what is happening in Issen?"

Rhymer shook his head then gestured to his seneschal.

Franklin said, "We do not know much more than you do. Issen has been surrounded by a force that is both larger and better prepared than any of us expected. We thought it would be at least another year before the Coalition could raise such an army, maybe two. If we in the Alliance were prepared, it would be a small threat. Combined, we possess far more able bodies and swords than the Coalition, but we were not prepared. As far as the situation on the ground, there have been skirmishes reported, but that is it. So far, they appear content to cut off Issen and wait it out. Our concern is that the Coalition forces are merely waiting for their leader. They have built siege equipment and reports say they have a sufficient force. What else do they need? The missing piece, Lord Jason, has not been there to lead the army. With what you told us, my concern is that he is on his way to Issen now, and when he arrives, they will attack. I believe your father will be able to hold out for months. Issen is well fortified and he knew this was coming eventually, so they are well provisioned, but once the attack begins, entry and exit from Issen will be impossible."

Amelie shifted in her seat.

Rhys cleared his throat and stated, "That sounds right to me as well. If the initial plan was to capture Amelie and cutoff the weapons supply, they could barter with Gregor from a position of strength. Everyone knows he would do anything for his daughter."

Amelie's face tightened but she remained silent.

Rhys continued, "Without Amelie, the next option would be an all-out assault. That fits the narrative the Sanctuary is spreading—that Amelie was killed. If he thought she was alive, Lord Gregor would continue fighting until the end."

"Once the fighting starts," said Franklin. "It will be a matter of time. Gregor will hold out as long as he can, maybe a very long time, but he does not have the resources to break the siege."

"Are you saying you will not send troops to support my father?" asked Amelie bluntly, turning to Rhymer.

Lord Rhymer shook his head. "It's not whether I want to or not. Regardless of anything you say to me, I simply do not have the men to send."

"Sir," retorted Amelie, "it's readily apparent that you have raised an army within this city. Even the maids are armed! With the Coalition engaged at Issen, there is no threat to Northport. I respectfully disagree that you cannot send help. I ask again, please honor your commitment to my father and Issen. Send your men!"

Rhymer stared down at his near empty wineglass. "I am not worried about threats from the Coalition, or even the Sanctuary for that matter. We have bigger problems to deal with."

Amelie blinked and looked to her companions in confusion.

"Demons," muttered Franklin.

"Demons are always a problem in Northport!" interjected Rhys. "What is different now that your help is needed elsewhere?"

Rhymer held up a hand and replied to Rhys. "You are traveling in high company and you speak like you know Northport, so I will give you the benefit of the doubt and assume you do have some experience with my city, but things have changed. The threat has changed."

Rhys sat back and frowned.

"What was once an annoyance," Rhymer continued, "is now a serious risk to both Northport and I believe all of Alcott."

Ben drank the rest of the wine in his glass.

"In the Wilds, the demons are massing like we have never seen before. There is nothing like it in the records. Swarms of them are ranging freely and have completely overrun several of the small towns north of here. I am arming every able-bodied man, woman, and child. The few reliable reports we've gotten have described packs with four dozen demons. One man, likely crazy, said he counted near two hundred of them together. That he survived to tell about it gives the lie to his story, but, the fact remains, there are too many reliable reports to ignore. The butchery we've found at overrun towns is self-evident. The threat is like nothing we have faced before, even in the histories. Hunters no longer risk the Wilds. The population of demons is now growing unchecked."

Lady Towaal's face had gone completely white. The rest of the table sat stunned.

"Hundreds of demons in one swarm!" exclaimed the lord, slapping his hand on the table. "That is why I cannot risk even a single armed man leaving the defense of this city. If I send troops away, the people will panic, and they will flee. A mass exodus could draw the attention of the swarms. I may not have the forces to stop them. On the road and away from my protection, the people would be butchered."

"There must be something that can be done!" protested Amelie.

"Just three weeks ago," Rhymer replied, "two companies of one hundred veterans each was lost completely. Not a single man made it back. We only discovered their fate through use of a far-seeing device. The bodies..." Rhymer slumped back in his chair.

The man's pallid look made perfect sense now. He wasn't suffering from alcohol-induced illness, a sickness of the body, or even stress caused by his young and energetic concubine. Lord Rhymer was contemplating the destruction of his city, the loss of everything.

Ben's companions all looked at each other across the table. If what Rhymer said was true, it was clear Northport could offer no help to Issen.

Lady Towaal leaned forward, both elbows on the table. She looked hard at Lord Rhymer.

"Has anyone determined the cause of this influx of demons?" she asked.

It was Franklin who answered. "No, we haven't been able to get reliable information back from the Wilds. Without the hunters venturing deep enough to learn anything, we are blind and guessing. We sent the two companies thinking it would be sufficient but," he shrugged. "They are gone now. We're talking about sending ten companies. One thousand men. Maybe that is enough to face down the swarms."

Rhys coughed politely. When Franklin looked at him, he suggested, "Too large a force will just draw the demons to them. The creatures are attracted to life forces. A large group like that is impossible for a demon to ignore. Individually, they have enough survival instinct to avoid that confrontation, which is why they don't attack towns, but with a swarm of hundreds, it will be like setting out a fresh roast on a buffet table. They are going to come and feast."

Franklin grimaced. "We have no other choice."

"If you have the men and you are able to get there, is your intention to close the Rift?" asked Towaal quietly.

Rhymer moaned and wouldn't meet Towaal's eyes.

"I thought so," she said.

The room was eerily silent until Ben couldn't take it anymore. "What is the Rift?" he blurted.

Towaal, still looking at Rhymer, answered. "It is a rumor, something that very few have knowledge of and no one really understands, at least, no one I've spoken to."

Rhymer stood, stomped over to a side table. He poured himself another wine, filling the cup all of the way to the brim.

"We know less than you and your Sanctuary brethren think we do," muttered the lord.

"Tell us what you do know," encouraged Towaal.

The lord gulped down half his wine glass and refilled it before walking back to his chair and settling down.

"My librarian can tell it better than I, but I will try," he started. "The Rift, in short, is where demons come from."

Ben sat forward on the edge of his seat, fully focused on Rhymer.

"According to our scholars, the demons and us live in two different worlds. Our world is full of life. The demonic world is full of, I guess you could say, the absence of life. From time to time, the fabric between these worlds tears and the demons, attracted to the life force in our world, are able to cross over.

Like all living things, our world has the capacity to heal. These tears are only temporary. The fabric of the world repairs itself, and demons cannot cross over in that space until there is a new tear."

Ben noticed Lady Towaal was listening just as intently as he was. Despite her vast knowledge about many subjects, this was new to her.

Rhymer ran his hands over his face. "The Rift is a permanent tear in the fabric, though maybe it's better described as a hole, an intentionally created hole. Ages ago, long before Northport existed in its current state, a group of mages created the Rift. As I understand it, the intent was to relieve tension elsewhere in the space between our two worlds. By leaving one small opening, it acts like the spout on a tea kettle. When pressure builds enough, there is a mechanism to release it."

Ben watched Towaal as closely as he did Rhymer. He saw her nodding slightly to this new development.

"Here in Northport, we are prepared to deal with the inevitable consequence of that release mechanism, meaning the arrival of demons. Thousands of years ago, the system of hunters was instituted here. As you know, these men and women are highly skilled and make a vocation of hunting down demons and other prey. By paying a bounty on horns, we attract enough hunters to keep the demon population manageable. Every few decades, a large swarm may develop and we send the army to deal with it. It has worked for a very long time."

"What changed recently?" questioned Towaal.

Rhymer shrugged. "That I do not know."

"A few summers ago," added Franklin, "we started noticing the demon population did not drop off as expected. At the end of the summer hunting season, there were reports of just as many sightings as the start of the season. We paid three times the bounties we did just a few years back. It didn't help. Hunters flocked to the Wilds, but the population continued to rise, and many of the hunters didn't come back. Since then, even the boldest hunters have been reluctant to venture far out. We started recruiting for the army, hoping to build a sufficient force, but I worry we acted too late."

"Last winter," Rhymer retook the narrative, "We lost the first of several towns to large swarms. We knew then we had started losing the battle. When I joined the Alliance, I did so in hopes we could blunt the threat of the Coalition and gain assistance from the other lords of Alcott. That is why I cannot help you, Lady Amelie. When I joined the Alliance, it wasn't so I could help your father and the others. It was because I needed their help, help that will not be coming now."

The room fell silent.

"We have a lot to think about," said Towaal after a long pause. She met her companion's eyes. Ben could see concern reflected back at him.

"I'm sorry," said Rhymer. "For Issen and for Northport."

They were given comfortable rooms in the guest wing of the keep. Rhymer said it was the least he could do.

Ben and his companions sat around the comfortable common room, staring morosely into the fire.

"If Rhymer cannot help, who can we turn to?" Ben finally asked.

Towaal shook her head. "I do not know. Venmoor, Fabrizo, the rest of the cities in the Alliance...None of them have large standing armies of their own. They are in the process of building them, but it will be months or maybe a year before they've raised a large enough force to face the Coalition. King Argren is the only other one I'm aware of with the men to break the siege. The betrayal by the Sanctuary, this new threat against Northport," Towaal sighed and clasped her hands tightly. "Everything we learn is another excuse for Argren to keep his men home. Maybe we can try, but I do not believe he will help us."

"We have to do something!" objected Amelie. "I can't just wait while my people die. We have to speak to Argren."

"With the information we have, I would not send men if I was in his position," admitted Towaal. "I am sorry, Amelie, but that is the reality of the situation."

Amelie buried her head in her hands. The companions all looked on. They wanted to comfort her, but what was there to say?

Minutes passed with only the pop and crackle of the fire breaking the silence of the room.

Ben frowned, thinking out loud, "Lady Towaal, what was it you mentioned to Lord Rhymer, something about closing the Rift?"

She nodded. "The Sanctuary knows little of the Rift. It is clear to me Rhymer and the lords of Northport have kept a lot of information from us, though, maybe the Veil and her inner circle know more. What we do know is similar to what Rhymer said. The Rift is a place demons come from. Northport has always dealt with these demons on its own. To my knowledge, Northport has never asked for our help. My question to Rhymer about closing the Rift comes from a discussion I heard years ago. If the Rift was opened, then maybe it could be closed. Some in the Sanctuary have wondered what would happen if the lords of Northport grew tired of being the world's protector. Would they close the Rift to cut off the flow of newly arriving demons?"

Amelie shot to her feet. "We can close it!" she exclaimed. "If no new demons can come through, then maybe Rhymer can take care of the existing ones and help Issen."

Towaal, less enthusiastic, replied. "And then what happens? If Rhymer is correct, then ages ago, a group of mages created it for a very specific purpose—to relieve pressure elsewhere in the world. If we close the Rift here, will it tear the fabric elsewhere?"

Amelie sat down, frowning.

"I understand, Amelie," said Lady Towaal, "but we must know

more before we come to any conclusions. Rhymer mentioned his librarian may know more. Tomorrow, I intend to locate this person and find out."

Amelie nodded, somewhat pacified.

"Also," continued Towaal seriously, "you must understand that dealing with the remaining demons will not be a quick process. Hundreds of demons cannot be dispatched in a few days. No matter what we do, it may be too late to prevent the Coalition from beginning the siege."

Ben watched his friend struggle with what she wanted to be true and what she logically knew to be true. As the emotions warred across her face and grim acceptance finally won out, he realized that was the mark of a truly remarkable person—to separate what you wanted to be true from what was true.

EARLY THE NEXT MORNING, the four of them went to Northport's library. It was housed in a separate structure adjacent to the keep. It was in a quiet building, as one might expect, but the surprising thing to Ben was how nondescript it was. Lord Rhymer and the proprietors of the library did not intend the place to be open to the public. There was no signage, no helpful staff directing people in, and no welcoming looks from the two stern-faced guards standing outside of the door.

"This establishment isn't open," growled one of the men, lowering a heavy hafted pike to bar their path.

"Here," said Lady Towaal, handing him a thick square piece of parchment. "A note from Lord Rhymer granting us access."

The guard snatched the parchment and stared at it intently.

Moments passed.

Finally, Rhys guessed. "You can't read, can you?"

The guard looked up, twisting his lips into a scowl but not answering.

"You are guarding a library, and you can't read," Rhys guffawed. "How about you?" he asked the man's companion.

That guard stared back angrily.

Towaal sighed. "Take it to a librarian. They'll agree to let us in."

Shortly after, one of the guards returned with a tall, gaunt man. He was dressed in unbleached robes and had a wispy fringe of hair circling his head. His gaze bored into the visitors.

"Come with me," he instructed in a thin voice.

As they walked inside the building with the man, Towaal asked him, "Are you a librarian?"

The man smiled. "I am the Librarian. Lord Rhymer isn't a trusting sort when it comes to the knowledge within this place. There is me, and there is my apprentice."

"Maybe that's why the guards can't read," surmised Rhys.

"The guards can't read? I did not know that. How is that possible?" asked the Librarian.

Rhys shrugged. "It's your library."

The Librarian led them into the dark building, which was lit only by piercing beams of sunlight pouring through tall windows. They passed narrow racks of books both ancient and new. There were tens of thousands of them. It was more books than Ben had ever seen before, but the tight confines made it seem far less grand than he was hoping. These books were not being displayed, they were being stored.

What Ben thought might be midway through the building, they turned. Up against one wall, they found a small, windowless room. There was a stone table and uncomfortable-looking metal chairs. The Librarian pulled out flint and steel. By feel, he sparked alight a mirrored lamp, which filled the room with a warm golden glow. "I try to keep fire away from the books. They are quite flammable."

He sat down in one of the chairs and gestured for them to take seats as well. "Rhymer's note referred to 'our most ancient' texts. I believe I know what he means, but it is unusual he would share that knowledge. Just so we are clear, what is it you seek?"

"The Rift," stated Lady Towaal simply.

The man nodded and asked for them to wait in the room. A quarter bell later, he returned with four slim books which he laid out on the table. To Ben's surprise, they appeared fairly new.

The Librarian saw Ben's puzzled expression. "One of my projects is transcribing the older works into new volumes. I'm not sure why some of the famous libraries in this world insist on maintaining their decrepit stacks. It's the knowledge that is important." The man shook his head at the folly of his peers.

"Before you start reading," he offered, "maybe there is something specific I can direct you to?"

Lady Towaal explained what they learned from Rhymer the night before and asked the Librarian what he could add to that.

The man laced his fingers together and thought.

"I should start by warning you that almost everything I can tell you about the Rift is conjecture," he said. "It is based on a few scraps of fact from the time it was created and a large amount of speculation by scholars since then."

They all settled down and waited for him to continue.

"It is, as Rhymer suggested, similar to a tea kettle," explained the man. "When pressure builds, there is a flexing, and the Rift opens for a brief time. Demons come across when that happens. That much, I think we can be comfortably assured is correct. As to where the Rift is, that is less certain. There are maps in the books here, but they were drawn thousands of years ago. You are familiar with erosion and geology, yes, tectonic plates and the movement of the earth?" He raised an eyebrow.

Towaal murmured that she was. "Then you understand the geography is unlikely to be the same it was then."

"We understand that," agreed Towaal.

"And finally, the thing I would classify as utter guesswork is what would happen if the Rift were to be destroyed. We simply do not know. Some writing speculates that the object itself is unimportant and that the thin point of the fabric between the worlds would continue regardless. Others say the object is critical, and if it was destroyed, the location would revert to just like anywhere else in the world. Most scholars who hold that point of view believe if the Rift was destroyed, it would put strain elsewhere. Demons would become prevalent in areas where they are currently rare."

The Librarian nodded, evidently satisfied with his own explanation.

Ben raised his hand then quickly lowered it after an amused look from Amelie. "What do you mean 'the object'?" he asked.

Spinning one of the books around, the Librarian quickly leafed through the pages until he found a sketch of a stone archway covered in runes. To Ben's eye, similar runes to what he had seen on other magical devices.

Towaal leaned forward. Without speaking, she took the book and began flipping pages back and forth around the rendition of the archway.

Rhys asked the Librarian, "What is your opinion of what would happen if the Rift was destroyed?"

The man's mouth twisted into a disapproving scowl. "It is not a scholar's place to give opinions, particularly in this case where there is a great deal of danger hinging on the uncertainty. We should stick to the facts. The fact is, we do not know."

"When the facts are inconsistent or do not tell a full story," argued Rhys, "sometimes it is necessary to extrapolate from available information and give an educated guess."

The Librarian grunted, eyeing Rhys speculatively. "My educated guess, then, is that it is irrelevant what happens elsewhere if the Rift is destroyed. If the reports are correct, which given they are recent and based on eyewitness accounts, we can assume they are correct, then we can calculate what will happen. At the current rate of expansion, the demons will overwhelm

Northport's defenses by next winter–a little over a year from now."

The man looked around, waiting for a response. When none came, he added, "There are approximately half a million souls normally within the walls of Northport. Due to the recent evacuations of the northerly towns, we can estimate there may be six hundred thousand people here now. Demons grow and thrive when they consume life-blood. If a demon swarm were to overtake this city and consume the blood of six hundred thousand individuals, is there a force outside of the Sanctuary that could stop them? Could the Sanctuary stop them?"

"So you think the Rift should be closed?" pressed Rhys. "To protect Northport and prevent what would happen to Alcott if Northport was overrun?"

"I wish it was so simple," answered the thin man. "Deciding something should be done and how it can be done are different decisions. Closing the Rift would be a difficult and dangerous task. It would require a combination of magical ability and a determination to survive for weeks in the Wilds. Even with exceptional skill and preparation, success is not assured. I have thought about this a great deal, and I have decided I must stay here, protecting the knowledge in this library. It is too large a risk if I am insufficient to the task. If the Rift is to be closed, it will not be by me. Finding someone else who does have that capacity and courage to do it," the man finished with a shrug. "That is easier said than done."

Ben leaned forward to ask the Librarian if he knew how to close the Rift. It sounded like the man had considered trying to do it.

"Librarian," interjected Towaal. She was pointing to a passage in the book. "This page is describing the leader of the mages who created the Rift. It says, 'he.'"

The Librarian nodded and explained while Towaal flipped to another page. "Prior to the Sanctuary's founding, it wasn't uncommon for there to be male mages. Men have the same facilities as women to learn the art. The recent ban on male mages is simply a move by the Veil to consolidate power within her walls."

"I am aware that there used to be male mages. I had not heard the Sanctuary's role described in such terms before," remarked Towaal, a drip of acid sneaking into her tone. "I am not sure it should be described as a ban."

The Librarian met Towaal's eyes. "What are your instructions from the Veil should you encounter a man who practices magic? Do you leave him alone?"

Towaal frowned. "We are getting rather far afield from why we came here."

"Yes," agreed the Librarian. "Male mages are a rather uncomfortable topic for those of the Sanctuary. Shall we change the subject back to the Rift?"

Lips pursed, Towaal tapped on a page in the open book. "What I was getting to was this bit. It says Nyerga, who I believe is the leader referred to earlier, the male mage, founded the Order of the Purple to continue his work and protect all the lands from the ancient evil."

The Librarian knitted his brows. "And your question is?"

"This book," explained Lady Towaal, "describes an organization of mages which I was not aware existed, an order founded by a male mage. What happened to them?"

"That," stated the Librarian flatly, "is not answered in any of the books in this library."

Over the objections of the Librarian, they borrowed the four books he provided and pressed him for other resources. Lady Towaal at one point demanded to be shown the racks which contained the texts about the Rift. When she returned, she gestured for the group to leave, satisfied they had everything they were going to get.

They returned to their rooms, split up the books, and quickly began to leaf through. They were looking for anything that might be relevant. When they came across something, they shared it with Lady Towaal, who jotted down notes.

Lord Rhymer sent Franklin with a dinner invitation, but Lady Towaal waved him off. "We need to get through this and understand what is happening," she said. "We came here to ask assistance for Issen, and, well, we have a lot of new information to take in."

The seneschal bowed. "Lady, Lord Rhymer is beside himself with worry about what is going to happen to Northport. He understands Issen's plight, but there is nothing he can do. He is sorry, but our resources are required here."

"What about King Argren?" inquired Towaal. "He has not sent men to Issen, but he knows Lord Rhymer well. Surely Rhymer has asked for aid?"

Franklin shook his head sadly. "King Argren is solely focused on the Coalition. My lord travelled to Whitehall and tried to explain the situation, but left frustrated. Argren kept mentioning the attack at Snowmar, which I believe you are well aware of. Argren refused to acknowledge the difference. It is his belief that he handled Snowmar, and Rhymer should handle the Wilds. He actually asked my lord to send more troops to Whitehall, if you can believe it."

"You said a mage was here before us," remarked Towaal. "Is the Veil willing to offer support?"

Franklin looked back at her. "You tell me."

Towaal grimaced. "I am not on the best terms with the Veil at the moment. Surely, you spoke to the mage about this when she was here?"

"The mage, Lady Anne," grumbled Franklin. "We raised our concerns several times with her and she promised to look into it. Instead, she left abruptly in the middle of the night with no word on where she had gone. We finally found a messenger who arrived shortly before her departure. The man had delivered a sealed envelope he was given in Kirksbane. He didn't know what was in it, but he said there was a terrible incident right before he left. Scores killed and a dozen buildings burned to the ground. A mage battle was the rumor, the messenger said." Franklin shrugged. "We can only assume that is why she left."

Ben met Amelie's eyes.

"Yes, I believe Lady Anne would have left after hearing something like that," murmured Towaal.

"You know her?" asked Franklin. "Will she tell the Veil about our plight? Do you think the Veil will send help?"

Towaal frowned. "Lady Anne could be distracted by...whatever happened in Kirksbane. Even if she is not, it will take her over a month to reach the City and even longer for help to return here. Before that, of course, she would need to gather mages or arms men. Three months would be optimistic."

Franklin paced back and forth in their small sitting room. "We don't know where else to turn!" he exclaimed.

"Give us time," advised Towaal. "We need to think. Maybe there is another solution."

The seneschal nodded curtly and departed.

"Well, this trip got depressing quickly," quipped Rhys, but no one was in the mood for his banter.

Late that night, long after the twelfth chime of the bell and the start of a new day, they finally put the books down and considered what they had learned.

Both the Librarian and Lord Rhymer were correct, there was not much more included in the books that they didn't already know.

"The Rift, I believe, is tied to the physical object of the gateway," said Lady Towaal. "The Librarian would not understand this, but the runes used on the stone are what facilitate the opening between the worlds. It is just like the other magical devices I have seen. Because of that, I believe it can be destroyed. That would likely restore the location to the same risk of demon generation as anywhere else in the world. Stemming the tide of new demons coming into this area would greatly assist Lord Rhymer and Northport but would not guarantee their safety. The demons already in this world still need to be dealt with. That is not going to be to an easy task."

"What would happen elsewhere in the world?" asked Amelie.

Towaal shrugged. "I do not know. There is no factual information in these books about it. My instinct tells me that the frequency of demon generation in random locations would increase, but it's possible that is a safer scenario for the world. Individual demons are dangerous but can always be eradicated. A swarm of hundreds, on the other hand, is an incredible problem."

"What about the Purple?" asked Ben. "If they were created to protect the world from this risk, could they know more?"

"Yes, if we could find them," answered Towaal, "but I do not know where to start. If the organization still exists, then I would think they would have already surfaced here."

"Whether they exist or not," brought up Amelie, "is irrelevant."

"Did you learn that word from the Librarian today?" whispered Ben.

Amelie shot him a dark look then finished her thought. "We don't know where the Purple is or how to look for them. We would likely be wasting our time if we tried. We must proceed as if they no longer exist."

Lady Towaal laid her quill down next to the notes she had been writing and listened.

"If the Purple no longer exists," declared Amelie, "and the Sanctuary is not offering assistance, then we must assume Rhymer and his men are the only force capable of containing the demon threat."

They all nodded, agreeing with Amelie's line of reasoning. She was following a clear, logical path.

"If Lord Rhymer's men are the only force capable of containing this," she continued, "then he will not release his men to help my father and Issen, no matter what we tell him, if we even feel comfortable asking for help after this. It is becoming clear to me that Northport is in just as bad shape as Issen. If Northport falls, then all of Alcott could be in danger."

"I do not believe Rhymer or anyone in Northport has the ability to close the Rift," stated Towaal. "It is a magical device, and it will require magic to destroy it. If the Sanctuary does not have help on the way..." Lady Towaal trailed off. The rest of them could complete her thought.

"What are we saying?" asked Ben. He paused, swallowing a lump in his throat. "Are we saying we will try to close the Rift?"

They all looked at each other. It was crazy, but what other options were there?

Rhys spoke up, "I suppose I will play the other side of this. Isn't it a more realistic choice to go to Whitehall and talk Argren into sending his men to Issen, or to Northport for that matter? I know he has been reluctant to do it, but Gregor and Rhymer are his banner men. He's losing face with the rest of them by not giving support."

Amelie and Towaal both shook their heads.

"As we said before," the mage stated, "he didn't send them before he knew about the Sanctuary's betrayal. With that information, I'm not sure how we could convince him to send men anywhere now. He's a powerful man, but a paranoid one as well. With the Coalition on one side and the Sanctuary on the other, he will keep his forces nearby."

Amelie nodded in agreement.

Rhys shrugged. "It was worth mentioning."

"Let me summarize what we know," said Lady Towaal, ticking items off on her fingers. "First, we believe that destroying the gateway will disrupt the Rift. Second, destroying the Rift, while possible, may be easier said than done—we are not certain of its location. Third, Lord Rhymer will not divert his attention from Northport while the demon threat exists. Fourth, Argren is unlikely to be of any assistance. Fifth, we are not aware of any new options to get assistance to Issen."

Lady Towaal clenched her fist and finished. "Lastly, we do not know what unforeseen consequences disrupting the Rift may have for the rest of the world."

Amelie, stone-faced, raised another point. "By closing the Rift to help Lord Rhymer and Northport, we may be saving a great deal more. The Librarian described a scenario where the demons feasted on over half a million people in Northport. That would be unprecedented, right? Can anyone predict how powerful the demons would be? If we accept the demon threat is real, can we turn our backs on this?"

Ben, feeling left out, asked, "Do we even know how to close the Rift?"

"With this," declared Amelie. She placed the rune carved wooden disc she took from the Sanctuary onto the table. "We don't close the door. We smash it."

Lady Towaal leaned forward and traced a finger over the object. "This is what you took from the laboratory? I believe it will be sufficient."

The next morning, they informed Lord Rhymer and seneschal Franklin of their decision. They would travel into the Wilds, attempt to locate the Rift, and destroy it. It was left unsaid what would happen after. They all knew that even with the Rift closed, the demon threat was substantial. There was a very real risk that Rhymer's forces would be unable to defeat them. They would cross that bridge when they came to it.

Franklin argued for them to wait one more day to gather food, clothing, and other necessary equipment to brave the Wilds. He also suggested sending soldiers with them, but Rhys declined the offer.

"More people will draw more demons to us," explained the rogue. "We'll be better served by stealth. We have sufficient skill to survive an attack by a small number of demons."

Rhymer objected. "Four of you are not enough! And of that four, you have a half-trained boy and a former initiate mage. You need more swords."

Rhys shook his head.

"What about hunters?" offered Franklin. "A few extra bodies shouldn't draw much attention. With their skills, they could make a difference."

Rhys and Lady Towaal shared a look. The rogue shrugged. She asked, "Do you have someone in mind? Someone you trust?"

"This is important. I believe more important than anything else we could devote resources to. I do have someone in mind. Someone I would trust my life with," answered the seneschal. "I will send them to your rooms later today."

The rest of the day they spent packing and organizing their gear. Rhymer suggested they go back to the library and ask for additional insights, but once they got back to the room, Towaal decided not to. The man had not been helpful, she explained, and they needed the time to get prepared.

The Wilds were like any wilderness, with two added risks— the cold and the demons. For the cold, Rhymer sent ample supplies, winter gear, and broad, paddle-like shoes.

"What is this?" asked Ben, holding one of them up.

"Snowshoes," answered Rhys.

"I don't get it," muttered Ben.

"You strap them to the bottom of your boot. The broad surface helps you walk on top of the snow. Trust me. Walking on top of it is better than trying to wade through it. This late in the year, there could be drifts that come above your shoulder. You spend your day trying to break through that, and we'll never find the Rift."

Ben looked the snowshoe over again, then copied Rhys and tied it to the outside of his pack. He also had new fur-lined trousers and tunics, a heavy new cloak, boots that had been treated to be water resistant, and a hat with ridiculous-looking flaps that would cover his ears. Ben intended to let someone else put their hat on first before he risked looking a fool.

One thing Ben realized they did not have was armor. He mentioned it to Rhys. "Should we have some protection? Maybe a helmet or some chainmail?"

Rhys grinned at him. "Just wait until you get out there and see what we're up against. The cold and the weight of that much metal will kill you during winter in the Wilds. We have to stay mobile and stay warm."

Ben frowned and went back to organizing his pack.

At midday, a knock sounded on the door of their shared rooms. Lady Towaal opened it and found two heavily armed individuals on the other side.

"Franklin says you folks could use our assistance," called a sassy-sounding woman.

Towaal nodded and let the pair inside.

The woman had pale, freckle-sprinkled skin and long red hair that was pulled back into a pony tail. She wore tight fitting fur-lined leathers. A bow was slung over one shoulder next to a quiver full of arrows. On her belt hung two hand axes and Ben thought he saw a long dagger poking out from one of her knee-length boots. She swaggered with the confidence of someone who was sure in her abilities.

A man entered behind her. He moved with a similar strut to the woman. It reminded Ben of two dogs showing off for a new pack. The man carried a dagger on one hip, a compact crossbow hung on the other, and across his back, he carried a massive bastard sword. He wore a tunic of leather-covered scales that draped down almost to his knees. His spiky black hair was barely held in place with a cotton headband.

The woman introduced them. "Corinne and Grunt."

"Grunt?" asked Amelie.

"Broke my jaw a few years back," the man explained. "A bunch of assholes started calling me Grunt because the physic wired my mouth shut so it would heal. The only sound I could make was a grunt. It pissed me off, so I broke their jaws too. That was kind of funny, but the name stuck."

Corinne added, "I think 'ironic' is the word you're looking for, Grunt."

The man grunted in response.

"I am called Lady Towaal. This is Rhys, Amelie, and Ben," said Towaal, gesturing to the companions.

"You have a first name, Lady Towaal?" queried Corinne.

"Not one you need to use," answered Towaal.

Corinne frowned.

"Did Franklin inform you of what we intend to do?" asked Towaal, ignoring Corinne's sour expression.

Corinne nodded. "He told us. You're looking for some ancient rock out in the Wilds. He wants us to escort you there and back."

"Yes," agreed Towaal. "You should know our mission before you accept. We are looking for something called the Rift, and we intend to destroy it. We're not certain we know exactly where it lies and there will be numerous dangers in the Wilds."

"Look, lady," responded Corinne. "I was born in Skarston, about twenty leagues north of here. I was raised in the Wilds. I don't know what this Rift is, but you don't need to tell me about the danger. From what I understand, it's you who doesn't know what you're getting into. Franklin said you'd never been past Northport."

Towaal smirked. "That is true. I have not been past Northport."

"Then let me explain some things to you," scowled Corinne. "Because Franklin asked, I'm willing to lead this foolish expedition, but…"

Towaal interrupted her. "If you come with us, you will not be leading. I will."

Corinne frowned back and looked around at the rest of the group. "You've got one swordsman," Rhys mock bowed, "one boy, a girl who doesn't look like she can use that worthless rapier, and yourself, who isn't even armed. What exactly is your plan when you encounter a demon out there?"

Amelie raised her hand toward Corinne and snapped her fingers. A brilliant spark burst into life between the two women. Corinne scrambled backwards, nearly tripping over a chair.

"What was that!" she shouted.

"Party trick," replied Amelie with a smirk.

"Seneschal Franklin was apparently remiss in telling you a few details about us and our mission," said Towaal. "While we are not all swordsmen, or women, we do have a few tricks. Are you sure you want to go with us?"

Grunt snorted. "He wasn't remiss about the pay. We get you back here safely and there are one thousand gold coins for us to split. I don't give a damn about what you're going to do out there. For that much gold, I'll take you out, help you capture a demon, and train it so you can ride it like a pony!"

The man finished in a huff then crossed his arms, waiting.

Corinne stepped forward again, eyeing Amelie out of the side of her eye, and agreed. "As Grunt says, the price is right. Also, my fa...Franklin, didn't exactly ask. I'm going to have a little chat with how he explained this to me, but he's sending Grunt and I because it's dangerous, not in spite of the danger. You go in the Wilds these days, you'll need us."

11

TRACKS IN THE SNOW

THE NEXT MORNING, Ben's booted feet thumped down a set of stone steps, and he walked into an open courtyard. Heavy, steel grey clouds dropped a misty rain and a chill wind whipped it into a frenzy.

The rain blew into Ben's face. He blinked his eyes, trying to get his bearings in the busy cobblestone space.

"Well, this is a pleasant day to start a journey," muttered Rhys, who passed by and waded into the dreary morning.

Corinne and Grunt were already outside, waiting for them.

"Morning starts early in the Wilds," chirped Corinne.

"No need for the bluster, girl," remarked Rhys. "I've been in the Wilds once or twice myself."

Rhys removed one of his ubiquitous silver flasks and took a quick sip. Corinne looked on frowning.

"Keeps me warm," explained Rhys. He offered the flask to Corrine, who waved it away.

"You say you've been in the Wilds?" she challenged. "I know most of the hunters around Northport, but I don't know you."

"Who says I'm a hunter?" Rhys covered a yawn with the back of his hand. "Anyway, what you mean is you know most of the hunters who are active around Northport these days. The world is a big place, and you haven't been at this very long."

"I've been hunting demons for three years now, longer than most," growled Corinne.

Rhys took a final sip from his flask before putting it away. "This is going to be a long trip, isn't it?"

Ben thought it would help if they didn't start the quest at each other's throats, so he sidled up next to Grunt. The man was blunt, but seemed less prickly than Corinne.

"How long have you been hunting demons?" inquired Ben.

Grunt thought about it then answered. "About five years now."

"That's a long time, isn't it?" responded Ben. "Are you from Skarston too, like Corinne?"

"I'm originally from Whitehall," answered the hunter. "Served in the guards there but had a bit of a disagreement about a debt."

"You owed somebody money?" wondered Ben.

"No," Grunt replied. "Someone owed me. Things got a little heated one night and the guy got banged up a little. Well, pretty bad if I'm being honest. Turns out he was some minor lordling. I decided it was best for me to change the scenery."

"You said you were in the guards. Did you know Master Brinn?" asked Ben.

Grunt glanced at Ben in surprise. "You know Brinn?"

Ben nodded. "I passed through Whitehall early this year and spent about a week practicing with the guardsmen. I got to spar with Brinn one morning."

"How'd you do?" asked Grunt curiously.

"I got a couple of strikes in. Then he knocked me down and spent the next bell pounding on me." Ben jokingly rubbed his back side and Grunt chuckled at him.

"Aye," agreed Grunt. "He has a mean swing with that two-hander."

Grunt reached out a hand to Ben and they clasped forearms.

"Good to meet you, Ben."

The single gate of Northport stood open and the six companions made their way through. Ben felt a sense of trepidation as they turned north and started down a worn road. The hard-packed dirt was softened by the light drizzling rain, but it had not yet turned to mud.

We're likely to die out here thought Ben as he stomped through a shallow puddle, but the fear of death strangely held no power over him. He'd committed to this mission and committed fully, meaning that no amount of danger would turn him back. If they were killed attempting to destroy the Rift, it would be worth it. Even though this wasn't necessarily his problem, and not his fight, he refused to be the kind of man who would turn his back on people who needed him. The citizens of Northport and the rest of the world would be protected as best as he was able. As they continued marching, his resolve grew and grim determination spread across his face.

"You're a serious chap, aren't you?" asked Corinne.

Ben jumped when she spoke. He hadn't noticed she was walking beside him.

"A bit jumpy though," she continued. "Let me guess, you were some sort of government functionary before you fell in with this crew? You have the look of someone who thinks deeply about stuff no one else does."

Ben frowned at her, unsure how to take that. "No, I was a brewer when they found me," he finally responded.

The girl blinked, uncertain if he was joking with her. "You were a brewer? You made ale?"

Ben nodded.

Grunt called from behind them, "I knew I'd like you!"

"What about you?" Ben asked Corinne. "How did you end up a hunter?"

Corinne grimaced. "Like a lot of people up here, I just didn't have anything better to do."

"Tell 'em the truth, girl," barked Grunt. "We're gonna be with these folks a long time, hopefully. We may as well be friendly."

Corinne sighed. "It's a long story, but very well. I think I told you yesterday I grew up in Skarston. It's a little town about twenty leagues north of here. We'll pass through it actually."

They kept walking. Ben noticed Amelie had moved closer and was listening.

Corinne continued, "Well, up there, you've got to learn to defend yourself, whether you're a hunter or a baker. It wasn't uncommon for people to get picked off by demons when they were out alone. Every few years, we'd get a swarm attacking the village itself." She shrugged. "You get used to it after a while."

Ben winced. The demon attack in Farview had shaken the entire village for weeks. He couldn't imagine living life with that as a constant threat.

"Anyway," she kept going, "my da is a bit of a nervous type and didn't want his girl going off and getting eaten in the Wilds, so he trained me with this." She tapped the bow hanging on her shoulder. "And he trained me well. By the time I was full grown, I could shoot better than any of the women in town and all but two or three men. That kind of thing makes you a valuable resource in a place like Skarston. I got plenty of attention from the boys, of course," she said with a wink.

Ben played along and replied, "I bet you did." He tried to ignore the feel of Amelie's eyes boring into the back of his head.

"My da was as serious about protecting me from the boys as he was the demons. He was a big man back then, before he got old. He was just as good with a bow as me and no slouch with a broadsword. Most of the boys started paying attention to the other girls once we got old enough for things to get interesting." She sighed. "I felt like I was missing out."

Ben listened intently. It was like talking to one of the older girls back in Farview. He knew plenty whose story would match Corinne's. A girl's father was the same where ever you went.

"As these things go, I started to get a little rebellious." She smirked. "I made some choices that, looking back, I shouldn't have. I ended up falling hard for one of the few boys who was brave enough to sneak around behind my da's back. He convinced me to come with him into the Wilds. We had a big plan, me with my bow and him with his spear and sword. We thought we'd make a perfect team–hunters and lovers. Well, here is where it turns sad. My da was away when I left. He'd been given an important position in Northport and wasn't around in Skarston much anymore. He was still connected enough that he heard about it though. He couldn't come after me, so he sent my brother. My brother was a good man, but he didn't have the skills that Da and I have."

She sighed heavily. "I didn't even know my brother was coming after me. Didn't know until I found him two weeks later. Dead. He didn't get more than a day north of Skarston when a demon surprised him."

Ben cringed. "That is awful."

Corinne nodded. "Aye, it was. Losing my brother hurt too much. I didn't know how to cope."

"I can't imagine," said Ben consolingly.

Walking along the dirt road, she kept talking, "I found out the boy I was with was only interested in what was between my legs, not comforting a girl about her brother's death. He up and left a few days later. I was mad at him, I was mad at my da and brother, but mostly, I was mad at myself. I went pretty hard for a couple of years, not really caring about anything. Drank too much, spent a lot of time with the boys." She shook her head ruefully. "Not my proudest moments. One day, three years ago, I finally woke up," she said with a grim expression. "Skarston got attacked by the biggest swarm we'd seen in decades. I was drunk as a goat, but I ran out into the streets like everyone else and tried to defend the town. I put arrows in half a dozen demons. I think may have killed one or two. It was the first thing that made me feel good in a long time. I realized I was wasting time being mad at everything. It was a demon that killed my brother. I sobered up the next day and I've been killing demons since then."

"Tell them the rest," demanded Grunt.

"Oh, right. He always wants me to mention this part. I put an arrow in him too," she said unapologetically, hooking her thumb to point at Grunt. "I flew one right into his back. I wish I could say it was a great shot, but it was an accident. I felt pretty bad about it at the time, but he's fine now. Tough man. You wouldn't know it though, if you heard how much he bitched about being shot."

"You shot him with an arrow?" exclaimed Amelie incredulously. She looked back at Grunt and the hunter nodded confirmation.

"Like I said," answered Corinne. "I was drunk as a goat."

"If you put an arrow in a man, I think you should take some responsibility for it," claimed Grunt. "Drunk or not. We've been traveling together now for three years. I'm still waiting for an apology."

Corinne shrugged. "I don't lie and I'm not that sorry. I'll buy you an ale."

~

THE FIRST NIGHT on the road, they stayed at a small inn in a town call Kapinpak. The inn wasn't nice, but it was getting cold at night. Not even Towaal was eager to rush into that when they would be facing the Wilds soon.

"Why is it called the Wilds?" asked Ben over a steaming joint of mutton and a mug of poor quality ale.

"It's untamed," answered Rhys. "No one lives there, and for as long as anyone can remember, no one ever has."

"Is it," Ben paused, unsure what he wanted to ask. "Is it different?"

Rhys shook his head.

Grunt spoke up. "It's further north. You start getting up in the mountains, so it's cold, and of course, you've got the demons. Other than that, it's not too different from the forests near Northport. Same trees, same dirt." The big man sipped the slightly sour ale and made a face. "I'm not sure this should count as my free ale."

"You always say that," grumbled Corinne.

"This stuff tastes like horse piss!" complained Grunt.

"Then why have you had four of them?" argued Corinne.

Their banter reminded Ben of the way Rhys acted—always putting up a front and always trying to make a joke out of everything. He supposed that once you'd seen enough hard times, you force yourself to enjoy the good ones.

Ben leaned forward with his elbows on the table and, hiding behind his hands, made a face at Amelie. She stuck her tongue out at him then rolled her eyes at the hunters.

"Brewer," asked Corinne suddenly. "Where did you get those scars?"

She was looking at his arms. Ben followed her gaze down. With his hands held up, his sleeves had fallen to show part of his forearms. On one arm, he had the three parallel cuts from the demon at Snowmar. The other had deep punctures from climbing over the glass-studded wall the first night after fleeing the Sanctuary.

"Which ones?" he replied.

"Either, I guess."

He tapped his right arm and explained, "I got this climbing over a wall one night. I found out too late the owner didn't want people doing that."

Corinne snorted.

Ben continued, ignoring the snort. "And this arm, I got this from a demon."

The red-haired girl suddenly sat forward and looked at him

hard. "You've fought a demon?"

Ben grinned and shrugged casually. "A few times."

Corinne and Grunt shared a look. Ben sensed a growing appreciation on their part for the company they were with. He wasn't sure why, but so far, Lady Towaal and Rhys had been circumspect about their abilities. The lack of trust wasn't healthy for a company embarking on a quest like they were, but it was their story to tell, not his.

Lady Towaal cleared her throat and interrupted.

"Let's talk about where we are going to go," she suggested.

They all leaned forward, scooting empty platters and half full ale mugs aside for Lady Towaal to lay out one of the volumes she had borrowed from the Librarian.

"I think he may charge you if you don't return that," remarked Rhys.

"We needed it more than he did," replied Towaal sharply.

She flipped quickly through to a page showing a rough map which Ben took to be the Wilds. Jagged upside down Vs looked to depict mountains, and there were wavy lines he thought could be rivers. In the center was a small symbol, which Towaal placed her finger on.

"This is the Rift," she explained.

Frowning, Corinne and Grunt leaned in close. They had experience in the Wilds, and were trying to match the squiggles on the map to what they knew of the actual terrain.

"I'll be honest," remarked Grunt. "I don't know where that is."

Towaal nodded. "I suspected it wouldn't look familiar. Since the Rift's creation, it's likely the terrain has changed significantly. Even if it hasn't, the Wilds are a vast territory and this could be anywhere. What we need to do is narrow the search."

"How do we do that?" asked the hunter.

"We know the Rift is where the demons are coming from. Where the demons are thickest is intuitively where we should expect to find the Rift. If we can trace the highest concentration of demons, then we have narrowed our search, and hopefully can make some sense of this map."

"You're saying you want to know where the most demons are, and then actually go there?" demanded Corinne. Everyone ignored her.

After a pause, Ben asked, "How do we know where the highest, uh, concentration of demons is located?"

Rhys answered, "I think I know."

They all turned to him.

"How do you know where all of the fish are in a lake?" he asked, grinning. When no one responded, he answered his own question. "You ask the oldest fisherman."

AFTER RHYS SAID THAT, Corinne and Grunt both immediately thought of the same person. The 'oldest fisherman' when it came to demons was a retired hunter named Long Axe who lived in Corinne's hometown of Skarston.

It was one day north of Kapinpak and the last bastion of civilization before the Wilds began. They left just after dawn and arrived midafternoon.

"That's a bit dramatic and silly, isn't it? Long Axe," remarked Ben derisively.

"I am called Grunt," said Grunt.

"Right," acknowledged Ben. "That is a good point."

The hunter muttered under his breath and they kept walking down the street.

They were restocking their supplies in Skarston while Lady Towaal and Corinne tracked down Long Axe. Corinne knew the man from when she was a girl. They hoped the personal connection would open the door for Towaal to ask what they wanted to know. Like many old people, Long Axe had a reputation for telling a good story, just not always the one you wanted to hear.

"Rice, beans, kaf…what else did we need?" asked Grunt. Ben hoped the man wasn't changing the subject because he was offended about the name thing.

"Rice and beans? Is that a good idea?" inquired Ben. "I wouldn't think a fire in the Wilds is wise."

Grunt shook his head. "Demons don't care much about fire. People do. Trust me, if we're out there long enough and winter hits, we'll want that fire. And if we have fire, we might as well cook some rice and beans."

"Demons aren't attracted to fire?" wondered Ben. "You mean, they can't see it or even smell it?"

"I have no idea what a demon sees or smells," responded Grunt. "I just know that fire doesn't seem to attract them. I've had hundreds of fires in the Wilds and never had a problem with it. Demons are attracted to life-blood, I know that. And they hate water," he finished.

"I knew that about water," agreed Ben. "We should keep that in mind, it's saved me before. I don't think they like daylight either. I've always heard they are more active at night."

Grunt snorted. "Son, there ain't no real water in the Wilds during winter. It's frozen. And daylight, well, we go up north, the days get shorter and shorter. You worry about darkness, and you're going to be doing a lot of worrying before we make it back to Northport."

"Oh," replied Ben. He had a lot to learn.

They ducked into a shop front where Grunt said they would be able to find everything they needed. With a quick look, Ben saw the place carried merchandise geared toward adventurers and hunters. Perfect.

When they exited the store, Ben saw a long plume of dark black smoke rising into the air. He grabbed Grunt's arm and pointed toward it. "What is that? An attack?"

Grunt shook Ben off and replied, "Nah, probably was an attack. That smoke is clean up."

"What do you mean?" asked Ben.

"Burning demon corpses," explained Grunt. "The things are noxious and burning 'em makes that thick black smoke. Worst thing you've ever smelled. That's why they're doing it out of town. You don't want that smoke getting around your house. My advice when you see a burn pile, do not get down wind of it. You'll be sick for a week."

"Why do they burn them if it's so bad?" queried Ben.

"Well, unburned dead demons don't exactly smell good," replied Grunt seriously.

Back at the inn, with supplies in hand, they passed a table of three men who were discussing the burn pile. Ben loitered nearby while Grunt went to speak to the innkeeper.

"'Bout eight or nine of 'em, small ones," muttered one man. "Not good, a swarm that size coming at the town. They're getting run outta somewhere."

"You'd rather it be a bigger swarm?" snorted another man.

"Course not!" said the first, "I'm just saying. Small groups usually aren't active that close to Skarston. If they're coming this way, that means one of two things. Either something's pushing them this way, or they can't find anything to eat out in the Wilds."

"And why do I give a pig's filth about demons not being able to find something to eat?" The second man laughed.

"Because if that swarm couldn't find anything to eat, it's because someone already ate it all," explained the first man patiently. "It means there are bigger swarms, and it's just a matter of time before they come here. I think that's why old Rhymer in Northport is encouraging everyone to leave."

The second man barked, "Rhymer wants us to leave so he can get all the land. I heard the mines are running thin this season and prices are edging up for produce out of Sineook. I'm telling you, it's a ploy to get our farmland."

"I don't think so." The first man paused dramatically. "I'm thinking about moving the family down south."

"What!" shouted the third man, finally joining the conversation. "You can't leave here! Your business will be ruined, for one. And that father-in-law of yours is going to go nuts if you try and take his daughter and grandchildren away. He'll straight up kill you! Didn't he say that at your wedding?"

The first man sighed heavily. "He and I spoke about it. He thinks maybe it's not such a bad idea."

The three men sat back in silence, contemplating the mugs of ale sitting in front of them.

Ben edged quietly away from the table and went to find the rest of his companions.

The next morning, they were back on the road, heading north from Skarston. Ben glanced behind them and watched as men patrolled along the walls. The walls reached three-man heights but had nowhere near the thickness of Northport's.

At one of the corners, workmen were busy adding another story to the watchtower. Ben could see other newly built towers rising behind the walls in town. The signs were obvious, but these people didn't want to see them.

He told Amelie about the conversation the men were having the day before.

She shrugged helplessly.

"Most of these people have never been further than Northport. Skarston is all they know, it's their home," she said.

"They've got families, they've got children. How can they stay and risk the kids?" wondered Ben.

Amelie replied, "I don't know how many fled the Coalition in Issen before it was surrounded, but I'm guessing it's not a lot. How many people left Farview when you had the demon there? If we hadn't arrived, what would have happened?"

Ben frowned.

The demon threat was real. Their leaders knew it, and even if they didn't want to admit it, the people knew it, but no one was taking real action. Building up the walls and carrying around a dagger to buy bread were worthless if what Lord Rhymer believed was true. If hundreds of demons fell on Skarston, the place would be a wasteland of blood-drained bodies. Why weren't they doing more to stop it, or more of them running? In Farview, they had done something. They had called for a hunter.

"I just don't get it," mumbled Ben in response.

"People know something is wrong and they are scared," replied Amelie, "but that doesn't mean they know what to do. Or maybe they do know, but they don't have the courage to do it."

Towaal, overhearing the discussion, added, "It's the madness of crowds. Everyone is sitting around waiting on someone else to act. Everyone can see the problem, and sometimes they even talk amongst themselves about the problem. They always call for someone else to solve it. It takes a special individual to stand up in that crowd and do something." Towaal adjusted her pack then looked Ben in the eye. "Are you a person who will stand up and do something?"

BEN WAS quiet as they settled down to camp in an open field near the road. They started a campfire several strides out from under an ancient oak tree. The flickering light barely lit the bottom branches which rattled eerily in the cold wind.

Grunt volunteered to take the first dinner shift and was busy boiling water for his specialty, rice and beans. Corinne was lingering around Rhys, pestering him with questions. Lady Towaal gazed north into the night sky.

Amelie settled next to Ben and mentioned, "You have been quiet all day. Scared?"

He shook his head. "Not scared for me, no. More scared for what this world is coming to."

"Thinking about what Towaal said earlier?"

"Yeah, I guess so," he answered. "We're going into the Wilds to close some demon rift. We're trying to gather support to help Issen and your father. We're running from the Sanctuary, who it turns out isn't exactly interested in helping their fellow man. It... it's just so much. Lady Towaal acts like I am someone who can do something about all of this. I'm just a brewer from Farview. Who am I to fix all of these problems?"

Amelie answered, "If we, including you, don't do something about all of it, then who will? You have to start somewhere, and you have to start with someone. It might as well be us."

"You know what I think you should do," declared Rhys, who stomped up noisily. "You should lighten up a little bit."

Ben smiled wanly at his friend.

"Seriously, the world's a messed up place and it always has been," said Rhys. "You can't be down on yourself about it all of the time."

Rhys was holding his pipe and stuffing a wad of dried leaves into the bowl. Corinne came up behind him.

"I told you I didn't like pipe smoke," she said.

"I know," Rhys responded with a roll of his eyes. "That's why I'm going to smoke it."

Instead of being offended, Corinne's expression grew determined. Ben smiled to himself. Rhys would have to watch his back with her.

Amelie looked on smugly as Rhys retreated toward his pack. The bow-wielding hunter followed close behind.

Ben reached out and squeezed Amelie's hand. "Whatever happens, we'll do our best," he told her.

THAT NIGHT, they set a watch schedule. Demons were active after dark. They would all be slaughtered if one came across them and no one was awake to alert the others. Ben pulled the last shift.

He spent his two bells walking around the perimeter of the

camp and occasionally moving to lay another log on their fire, trying to avoid looking into it.

He pulled his cloak tight around his shoulders and wished he could sit by the fire. He needed to be on his feet to stay awake and worried that if he was close, he couldn't stop himself from staring into the dancing flames. There was no point in having the light of a fire if he stared at it and ruined his night vision.

It was a cold, late autumn night. Not any worse than winter in Farview, though.

They didn't know how long this journey would take. No one thought it would be quick. By the end, it would be full winter in the north and the chill Ben was facing now would seem comfortable.

He kept circling the camp and peering out into the field around them. They had great visibility at this campsite. Aside from the huge oak tree, they were in a wide-open clearing. It was contrary to all of the other campsites they had chosen since leaving the Sanctuary. Then, they did not want to risk being seen by other people. Now, they wanted plenty of opportunity to spot approaching demons.

Before long, a weak light suffused the air from the pre-dawn sun. Ben could see across the field to a ragged line of trees north of them. Somewhere in the distance, he thought he saw a tendril of smoke rising from within the woods. They would be heading that way later in the morning. He wondered if the smoke was some hard-headed farmer who refused to leave the area or if it was something else.

A stirring behind him drew his attention. He saw Grunt was sitting up, covering an impressive yawn with his hand. The man, despite his size, rolled silently to his feet and rummaged through his pack. He produced a battered metal tea kettle and filled it with his water skin. Ben continued his patrol, watching the hunter out of the corner of his eye.

Soon, Rhys was up as well. He wandered off behind the tree they were camped next to and Ben heard him relieving himself.

Grunt's tea kettle was at a soft boil. He produced another cylindrically shaped kettle which he filled with what looked like a coarse black powder. He then poured the boiling water into the new kettle and fastened the lid.

Rhys moved over to squat beside Grunt, holding a cup eagerly in two hands.

Grunt pushed down on a plunger at the top of the kettle and then filled his and Rhys' cups.

Ben finally noticed the smell and realized the hunter was brewing kaf.

Steam rose from the cups and both men gave it a minute before taking a tentative sip of the hot liquid. Rhys sighed appreciatively and sipped again.

He stood and walked over to Ben, whispering, "It's nice to travel with a man who knows his priorities."

"I thought your priority was alcohol?" joked Ben.

Rhys grinned. "At daybreak, outside, during winter in the north, I am willing to make an exception and enjoy a mug of kaf before I start on the serious beverages."

Ben smiled and thought about getting his own cup. When he looked back at Rhys, his gaze was drawn over the man's shoulder, and he frowned.

Two hundred paces away, bouncing in and out of the knee-high morning mist, was a black shape.

"Look," he hissed in a low voice, pointing at the figure.

Rhys and Grunt both turned and observed.

Grunt took another sip of his kaf then remarked, "Piece of advice, Ben, and I mean this in the most friendly way possible."

The man sat down his cup then picked up his crossbow. "When you see a demon out here, don't whisper about it," he said. Then he shouted, "You yell!"

The rest of the party bolted upright in their bedrolls and saw

Grunt stride forward to the edge of the camp. Calmly, he set his feet and raised the compact, steel-armed crossbow. He sighted down a thick, broad-headed bolt.

Rhys moved to stand beside him but was paying more attention to the tree line behind the quickly approaching demon.

It shrieked at them loudly, sending a shiver down Ben's spine.

One hundred paces, fifty paces, thirty paces, and the creature kept coming closer. Ben started to get nervous and drew his longsword at twenty paces. Then the thrum of Grunt's crossbow filled the air.

The quarrel flew out and impacted the demon's chest, disappearing into the thick muscle.

The monster uttered a strangled wail and collapsed fifteen paces from Grunt's feet.

By now, the entire group was on their feet with hands on their weapons. The demon remained motionless.

Grunt, eyes staying on the creature, went back to retrieve his cup of kaf. "Always give it a few minutes before you approach the thing," he advised. "If they stop moving, they are almost always dead. But relying on 'almost always' is a good way of getting yourself dead out here. It's best to just wait a little bit if you can."

As they looked around the open field, nothing else stirred. "Looks like this one was alone," muttered Rhys.

"They usually are alone," agreed Grunt. "The swarms form when there is a shortage of food or when there is an arch-demon."

"An arch-demon?" asked Ben curiously.

"A big one." The hunter nodded. "It gives the little ones courage, I guess. They follow it, and all of a sudden, you have a swarm. As far as I know, no one is sure if they communicate or just follow the big ones out of fear. However it works, be ready to fight. It's not just the size and strength. As they mature and consume more life-blood, they get smarter. Maybe smarter isn't the right word." He scratched at his stomach. "Cunning is what I would call it."

"Stay away from the big ones," called Corinne. "Let Grunt and I handle those. They're not for the inexperienced or the faint of heart."

She was circling the fallen demon and examining it.

"See anything?" asked Towaal, ignoring the barb about experience.

Corinne shook her head. "Trying to tell if there is anything different about this one, but it looks like all of the others I've killed."

"How many have you killed?" asked Amelie innocently.

"Plenty," remarked Corinne.

Rhys cleared his throat then suggested to Ben and Amelie, "That does make some sense, about the arch-demon. If we face a swarm, stay away from the big one. Let the hunters or I deal with that."

Ben nodded and Amelie shrugged.

Corinne snorted at Rhys. "Have you faced an arch-demon? They are serious business, extremely dangerous."

Rhys raised an eyebrow at her and said, "Honey, don't worry about me."

Corinne coughed and her eyes opened wide. "Honey?"

Smiling sweetly back at her, Rhys responded, "I've been in a dangerous situation or two. I think I can take care of myself."

Corinne glared at the rogue, obviously unsure what to make of him.

Ben turned and walked to the fire to make breakfast. He was exasperated with the lack of trust in the group. They needed something to bond them together. Back in Farview, that would be a night of serious drinking at the Buckhorn. Out here, he wasn't sure what they could do to gain each other's confidence.

After eating breakfast, Grunt cut his quarrel out of the demon's body in a sickening demonstration of butchery and demon anatomy. Amelie looked on in disgust while he sawed his dagger through the heavy muscle in the demon's back and cut down to the head of the quarrel. Setting a foot on the body, he yanked the rest of the bolt through the corpse and pulled it out. It came loose with an unpleasant squelch.

"That is disgusting," stated Amelie, trying to not gag.

Ben chuckled.

Grunt turned to face her with a hurt expression.

"I only have so many of these things," he explained, shaking the gore-covered crossbow bolt. Tiny streamers of purple blood sailed through the air.

Corinne jumped backward and shouted, "Hey!"

Ben couldn't hold in his laughter. Soon Amelie, Corinne, and Rhys joined him. Towaal looked on, bemused. Grunt sighed and rinsed off the quarrel with his water skin. "Save the entire party from an attacking demon and this is the thanks I get," he muttered under his breath.

"We appreciate you killing the demon," Corinne said to mollify him, "but then you followed it up by spraying demon blood on me. And, well, I think Amelie said it best, that is disgusting."

"Sorry about that," muttered Grunt before kneeling again and digging his dagger into the demon's scalp to remove the small, stubby horns.

From camp, they followed a faint path through the field and toward the tree line. The fog burned off quickly and it was a clear, bright day. The air was chill, but with the thick, winter clothing, Ben found it quite pleasant.

The forest was filled with soaring birch trees. Their white trunks extended as far as Ben could see ahead of them. A narrow path wound its way through the thick trunks. Leaves crunched underfoot as they left the field. Ben pulled a strip of peeling bark from a nearby trunk when they passed and toyed with it as they walked.

Amelie, walking beside him, looked down at the thin sheet of tree bark and asked, "Is there something wrong with it to peel off like that?"

Ben shook his head. "No, that's just what some trees do. I'm not familiar with this variety, but," he shrugged. "I don't think anything is wrong with it."

Amelie continued walking and looked like she was going to ask another question but then stopped.

Ben smiled and added, "That seems like something a mage should know."

She chortled then shot a look at Grunt and Corinne ahead of them to see if they overheard. "Don't say that out loud," she whispered. "And, yes, I am sure many of the tree-focused mages know a lot about the fascinating subject of bark. I haven't gotten into that specialty yet."

Ben flipped the papery bark at her face and she swatted it away with a playful growl.

Their banter and the steady crunch of walking feet were the only sounds in the forest. Before long, it started to feel a bit creepy.

Ben spoke out to the group. "There are no animal sounds. Is that normal?"

Grunt shook his head. "It's normal deeper into the Wilds. A bit unusual this far south. Generally, that is a sign that a demon has been nearby. They feast on animals, just like they do people."

Ben reached for his sword.

Grunt waved his hand down.

"It doesn't mean there is a demon right here," he continued. "It just means one has been in the area. It could have been the one I killed this morning."

"How do we know when one is close? Should we be worried about a swarm of demons?" asked Ben.

"You'll hear it attack," responded Rhys.

Grunt agreed. "Aye, when you're hunting, how do you know a

deer or rabbit is nearby? You don't really know until you see them. Demons are easy, they will let you know when they charge."

Ben frowned. "When I'm hunting a deer or rabbit, I am the one who's trying to catch dinner."

Throughout the day, they continued down the faint path in the direction Ben saw smoke earlier in the morning.

"Who would live out here?" asked Amelie.

Corinne shrugged. "No one did last I passed through."

"It could be a campsite for hunters," added Grunt. "Not too many other people out here these days. Not too many hunters either, now that I think about it."

Faintly, Ben started to hear a new noise—chopping wood.

"Whoever it is," he remarked. "They sound like they are busy."

Half a bell later, they saw an opening through the trees and found the source of both the smoke and the chopping.

A log enclosure rose twice Ben's height in a field that was dotted with tree stumps. Fresh wood chips were scattered everywhere and they could see teams of men working at the far side bringing in more logs.

"This is awfully strange," muttered Grunt.

Rhys, pausing at the edge of the clearing, looked to Towaal. He asked, "Do we avoid it or go in?"

She adjusted her pack, scanning the enclosure then started forward. "One more night indoors and behind walls shouldn't hurt. We'll have plenty of time to rough it later. Keep your eyes open though. Something doesn't feel right about this."

As they approached the log structure, a small boy poked his head above the wall and watched them draw close. Ben guessed he'd seen no more than twelve summers.

"Ho the camp," called Grunt.

"Who are you?" asked the boy abruptly.

"Hunters passing through," answered Grunt. "I don't recall

seeing this here last time I passed by. We figured we'd investigate and see if we can find a place to stay this evening."

"Stay there," instructed the boy before disappearing behind the wall.

"Helpful fellow," grumbled Grunt.

They stood outside for several minutes that grew tense as the time passed. Finally, there was a bang on the other side of the wall and the gate cracked opened.

A rough-looking man stepped out and addressed them. "We haven't had a lot of visitors here, hardly any, really. How can we help you folks?"

Grunt and Corinne looked at each other. Then Grunt spoke up. "I passed through maybe four months ago. I don't recall there being anything to visit."

The man smirked and then jovially answered, "Right you are. And what were you doing here four months ago?"

Grunt frowned but went along. "I'm a hunter. I was returning from a trip north with a bag of demon horns to cash in at Northport."

The man set his hands on his hips and challenged, "We heard there would be hunters in this area, but I haven't seen any. Can you prove you're a hunter?"

Grunt dug the pair of demon horns he'd taken earlier out of his belt pouch and showed the man wordlessly.

"Very well," the man said, nodding. "We can shelter you for the night in exchange for those horns."

A pained look crossed Grunt's face but he handed them over.

"Welcome to Free State," said the man.

Ben blinked.

"Free State?" he asked their host, who was turning to reenter the compound.

"Aye," replied the man. "We're a community of people sick of living under the rule of lords and ladies." He gestured around the stump-filled clearing. "As you can see, there aren't any of those types around here."

Amelie harrumphed but Ben ignored her. They walked through the gates following the man.

Ben asked, "I'm guessing you have no official government here. It is all run by the community?"

The man looked out of the side of his eye at Ben. "Aye," he responded slowly.

"I've been to another place called Free State," expanded Ben. "Down near the City."

"The City." The man snorted incredulously. "That place is make believe, son. You might as well be talking about fairies and wyverns. Don't go saying things like that in front of people or they'll think you're kooky."

They walked past newly constructed buildings and stacks of fresh timber. On top of one, they saw a man perched high up, straddling one of the logs. He was shirtless, face turned upwards with closed eyes. A small stream of smoke was drifting out of a pipe he held in his hand.

"Of course," admitted the man, "maybe if they think you're kooky, you'll fit right in."

A woman and two children passed, leading a fat pig and litter of piglets. The pigs had stripes of orange mud hand-painted down their sides. The children stared unabashedly at the strangers.

"This place is weird," mumbled Grunt under his breath. Ben saw their host smile faintly but otherwise ignore the hunter.

Amelie looped a hand under Ben's arm and whispered, "What do you think about this?"

Ben replied, "I'm not sure what to think yet. Looking around, the place definitely reminds me of the first, but our host apparently doesn't know about that one."

They were being led to a large building near the center of the compound, well, not large compared to anything in the City or Northport. Relative to the rest of Free State, it was substantial.

"As Towaal said before we walked in," finished Ben, "let's keep our eyes open."

The large building was home to an older but still strong-looking woman named Mistress Albie. She greeted them warmly and showed them to several empty rooms in the back. The place smelled like freshly cut wood.

She apologized. "Sorry, sweeties. They just put the roof up a week ago and no one's had time to build me proper furniture."

"It's no concern. We'll be sleeping rough the next few weeks, so a roof over our heads is a luxury," reassured Towaal. "What is this place?"

"It's a hospital, dear," replied the woman.

"A hospital?" asked Corinne, confused.

"A concept from down south." The woman smiled congenially. "I will care for the sick and injured. Everyone here has to do something to earn their keep. That is how I will earn mine. I was a bit of a healer before," the woman paused. "Before I moved to Free State."

"And," Ben hesitated before asking, "why did you move to Free State?"

The woman smiled again, this time with a bitter twist in her lips. "That is a long story, young man. Maybe later we can talk about it."

They stored their gear in the rooms the woman provided and agreed to an offer of food later that night in exchange for work around the new hospital. The men moved a few heavy objects around for her and sealed up gaps in the log walls using a mortar she had mixed. The women helped her sort out an extensive-looking supply closet. With six of them helping, the work was done quickly. The woman seemed excited to have things straightened out.

"Now out of the kitchen," she called, "I'll have stew ready in a bell."

The six of them stepped out of the building and, after a quick conference, decided to split into two groups and explore Free State. Before they parted, Rhys looked at Ben and asked, "I've never heard of a place like this. Has anyone else?"

Ben met his eyes and nodded. Lady Towaal picked up on the exchange and motioned for them to keep it quiet. They'd shared very little of their backgrounds with the hunters, and on this, Ben agreed. Any more discussion about the Free State near the City would only lead to questions on why they were fleeing the City and hiking through the middle of nowhere in the first place.

Ben, Amelie, and Rhys went one way. The others went in the opposite direction. Quickly, Ben was reminded of the Free State they saw before. The people were moving about their daily tasks and eyeing the strangers out of the corner of their eyes. No one was unfriendly, but they were clearly not expecting company.

The difference in this place was that everything was new in the compound. The other Free State, despite being entirely mud and logs, was well established. Many of those structures looked to have been in place for years.

"There must be two hundred of them living here," muttered Rhys.

Ben nodded. It was a bit smaller than Farview, but not by a lot.

"What are they all doing here?" asked Amelie.

Rhys shrugged then suggested, "Let's ask them."

The first man they saw just happened to be struggling to roll a freshly bound barrel behind a hastily built wooden shed.

"Ho there," called Rhys.

The man paused and acknowledged them with a nod.

"That looks like a mighty heavy barrel," said Rhys.

The man stood and stretched. "You offering to help me with it?"

"We can help in exchange for," Rhys made a show of thinking. "For a little bit of what's inside of it?"

The man grinned. "I've got two more of these that I need to get onto racks. You get all three of them on the rack and there's a fourth inside I can open up for you."

Rhys slung an arm around Ben's shoulder. "Well, let's help the man out."

Half a bell later, dripping sweat and panting, Ben and Rhys followed the man inside where he tapped a small barrel a tenth the size of the huge ones they had just moved for him. The man produced four plain earthenware mugs and filled them to the top with a foamy, dark ale.

He raised his mug. "Thanks. I couldn't have done that myself. I'm going to ask the cooper for smaller barrels next time."

"You didn't brew this here," remarked Ben after taking a sip. It was a more pleasant draught than he expected. "Aged about two months in a fresh oak barrel?" he asked.

The man grinned. "You know your ale, boy."

"I've brewed a few myself," agreed Ben.

"Aye, me as well," responded the man. He stuck out a hand and introduced himself. "Peckins."

"Ben," replied Ben. The rest of the party introduced themselves. Ben asked, "Peckins, where did you brew this? Northport?"

"That I did," said the man amiably. "Had a little shop down there and made decent coin putting kegs on the guard houses' tap. That was before the changes started happening, of course."

"Changes?" asked Ben. Seeing the man's expression grow guarded, Ben added, "I'm not from around here. We just passed through Northport but only stayed two nights. It seemed like it was, ah, well armed when we were there."

Peckins spit on the freshly churned dirt floor and took a sip of his dark ale. "It's armed all right. If you ask me, they're preparing for war with the Coalition. Fat Lord Rhymer says it's demons, but I grew up in Northport, and let me tell you, there have always been demons."

"You don't believe there is a demon build up in the Wilds?" asked Rhys.

"Nah, they come and go," answered the man. "You think I'd move out here if I believed that load of crap they're telling people? You live here a few winters and you realize that some are worse than others. You get used to it. Be careful, don't go out alone at night, and don't go into the Wilds without proper protection. Don't get me wrong, you have to be smart, but it's nothing to raise an army over. Listen to me, that army is for the Coalition. Rhymer sees a war coming, and he means to get himself a piece of land further south. Sineook's charging more year after year, and Rhymer's always wanted farmland of his own that he doesn't have to protect from demons."

"And that's why you moved to Free State? Because you don't support a war?" asked Amelie.

"That's right, little lady," responded Peckins. "Lords and ladies try to force their system on you. They think you don't got any options. Believe me, you got one. You get up and you leave."

"Hmm," answered Amelie, glancing at Ben.

After finishing his mug and refilling it, Peckins continued, "About four months back, a group of folks from somewhere in the east came through Northport. They were talking about staking their own claim and getting out from under the boot of the lords. Sounded interesting to me. Well, Rhymer's men start looking at these folk hard, following them around and the like. Wasn't too long before the group decided they needed to go and offered to take some of us with them. Me and a couple score more took them up on it and here we are."

"And," Rhys inquired, "you're happy you left?"

Peckins gestured, sloshing the ale in his mug. "Aye, soon as that wall is finished, I think it'll be just fine here. We had a few encounters with demons, but nothing worse than they get in Skarston. They do okay."

Rhys, without asking, refilled his mug as well. Peckins didn't comment on it. The man was caught up in his story and kept talking, "I don't have anyone bothering me about taxes, no one telling me what I can or can't say, and no one acting like they are better than me just because their blood is high. Yeah, I think this place is going to be good for me."

When Ben and Amelie finished their mugs, and Peckins and Rhys finished two more, they left to continue exploring the compound. Like Peckins said, they saw the wall was almost completed, two man- heights tall and guarded with towers spaced at regular intervals. Ben hoped it would be enough to protect these people.

Shortly after, they returned to the hospital without speaking to anyone else. Aside from the wall, it all seemed domesticated and normal, what Ben would expect to see with a few hundred people starting a new community.

Towaal asked them what they found on their return. They related the story Peckins told them along with their other observations.

"We found the same," she stated. "We spoke to some of them about the demons, but they all seem more concerned with Rhymer's build up. They're afraid of war and oblivious to the dangers out here."

Grunt angrily stalked around the room. "These people are going to get killed," he muttered.

"We tried to warn them," said Corinne, placing a hand on his arm.

"That flimsy wooden wall won't do shit if a swarm comes," growled Grunt.

"As Corinne said," replied Towaal, "We tried to warn them. It is their decision to make."

That evening, Mistress Albie served them healthy portions of a thick vegetable stew. Noting some of the men's looks, she apologized. "Sorry. There isn't much meat. Until we get our walls up and breeding programs established, we'll all be on a tight ration around here."

"Have you had problems with demons taking the animals?" inquired Grunt.

Tight-lipped, Albie responded, "Some problems, but you have to expect that out in the Wilds. Unlike some of the folks around here, I came from the north and am fully aware of why this land is unoccupied."

"Aren't you worried about people being injured or taken by the demons? How will you earn a living if there are worse attacks?" pressed the hunter.

Albie smiled sadly and whispered, "That's why I chose to build a hospital."

"Oh," answered Grunt uncomfortably.

As the sun crested the horizon, the companions stepped out of the narrow opening of the gate and continued their journey north. None of them were eager to spend any longer than necessary in Free State.

"It's just so..." started Corinne.

"They don't understand the risk they are putting themselves into," finished Amelie.

"Exactly," agreed Corinne.

"Should we send word to Northport and see if they can somehow protect these people?" asked Grunt.

Towaal shook her head. "We don't have time to go back. Any delay would make our quest more difficult. Besides, they've been told about the risk, they just don't believe it. Armored soldiers showing up at the gate and evicting them won't make these people feel any better about living within Northport's walls. We just have to hope they see reason on their own. Before it's too late," she finished grimly.

Ben shuddered and tried not to think about the people in Free State. Their desire to flee from the coming conflict between the Alliance and the Coalition was too close to his own thoughts to be comfortable. As for choosing to locate at the edge of the Wilds, well, he wished them the best. That was all he could do.

They kept walking through the eerily quiet birch forest, making slow time through the untamed woods. In the distance, Ben could see snowcapped mountains peeking through the bare tree branches.

"Do we have to go all the way up there?" he asked, gesturing to the white-topped peaks.

"I don't think so," replied Towaal. "Based on what we learned from Long Axe, the richest hunting, as he called it, is near the base of that mountain range."

She slowed and pointed ahead. "Do you see that rounded peak?"

Ben nodded.

"Below there is a wide valley. In that valley is where Long Axe claims we should go," she stated. "It could be the place drawn on the map, two ridges branching out like arms. That is the same topography Long Axe drew from what he remembered."

"What he remembered?" interrupted Amelie. "I thought he was supposed to be the most knowledgeable hunter alive."

"He is," argued Corinne, defending him. "He's just, well, it's been a few years since he's been near that area, and he never actually went in, just looked down from the mountains above. Too dangerous to go into the valley, he told us."

"How many years?" asked Amelie flatly.

"A lot," responded Towaal, holding up a hand to silence Corinne. "He stopped going even within a few leagues of the place because it got too dangerous. Too many demons, and swarms he was getting too old to face, even with a company."

"Too many demons sounds like our place," remarked Rhys.

"Remind me again," objected Grunt, "why are we going to a place that is described as having 'too many demons'? It's the damned Wilds, there are demons everywhere."

"The Rift," reminded Towaal, "is likely the center of the highest concentration of demons in the Wilds. To narrow our search, we will follow the demons."

"Oh, right," groaned the hunter. "That sounds like a great plan."

~

THREE DAYS of marching up a steady slope and Ben was tiring. They had pushed harder during the flight from the Sanctuary, but they had fear to motivate them to move faster then. Now, fear was making it more difficult. The further they went the more likely demon encounters would be.

The terrain was getting difficult as well. Low ridges started cropping up and it was a decision each time to either walk around it or expend the energy to climb over.

After one particularly strenuous hump over a rocky ridge, Ben and Corinne dropped off a short ledge to level ground.

Ben asked Corinne, "So is this what it is like being a hunter?"

She winked at him. "Not to your liking?"

"Walking around in endless woods, climbing over rocks, waiting for a demon to pounce on me," he moaned. "No, not my favorite so far."

"Hunting demons, like any hunting, is basically setting a trap and waiting for your prey to approach so you can attack," she replied. "We are waiting to attack them, think of it that way. It's better than waiting on them to attack us."

"If we're setting a trap," he responded, "what is the bait?"

Ben paused when he saw her sly smile. "Never mind," he said

glumly. "I'm not sure how thinking about that is supposed to help."

Corinne grinned back at him.

Amelie slid down off the rocks and fell into the dirt beside them with an unladylike curse. Corinne laid down her bow and bent to help Amelie to her feet. While Corinne was pulling her up, a wild cry burst out from the woods. Ben spun to see a black shape charging through the white-barked birch trees.

Rhys had left to scout ahead and Towaal and Grunt were still descending the steep slope of the ridge. Ben yanked his longsword from his scabbard and he set his feet. Behind him, he heard Corinne scrambling for her bow and Amelie struggling to draw her rapier. He knew he would be the first to face the charge.

The demon crashed through a thin wall of undergrowth and was five paces from Ben, flying at him like one of Grunt's crossbow quarrels. Ben lunged forward, stabbing with his sword and twisting at the last second to duck under a powerful claw-tipped arm. It passed a hand length away from ripping across his throat. He felt the air swoosh by his head as the demon's swipe whistled by, catching nothing but air. His longsword was nearly jarred from his grip when the point impacted the demon's neck.

Hot, purple blood showered onto his hands and a heavy shoulder crashed into his chest, knocking Ben to his knees. He stumbled back to his feet as the demon collapsed and slid past him.

Corinne stepped up with an arrow drawn back to her ear, waiting for the creature to move. It twitched once then remained motionless.

Grunt jumped down from a rocky outcropping with his bastard sword drawn. He squatted, prepared to fight.

Rhys appeared as if out of nowhere, breathing heavily in the only sign that betrayed how rushed he was to get back.

Lady Towaal stood calmly above them on the outcropping and declared, "Nice work, Ben."

He stood still, stunned and surprised that the beast wasn't rising to continue the attack. His mind flashed back to his first encounter with a demon, back in Farview. He'd struck that one with his staff and it tore into Arthur. This time, his aim and his sword struck true. The demon was dead.

Corinne relaxed the tension on her bowstring and clapped him on the back. "Apparently you do know a thing or two."

Ben rubbed his chest where the demon's shoulder hammered him and murmured, "Like I said, this isn't the first time I've seen one of these things."

"You just got demon blood all over your tunic," remarked Rhys.

Ben looked down, saw the bloody purple smear his hand left, and groaned. "How do I clean that off?" he wondered.

Grunt, sheathed his heavy sword, and responded, "That my friend, is a question for someone else."

The rest of the party started moving again. Amelie paused to wait for Ben. "I've heard vinegar is good for bloodstains," she offered.

Ben looked at her. "Do you have any vinegar?" he asked.

She shrugged.

"Let's go." He sighed. They followed the others deeper into the forest.

SEVERAL MORE INDIVIDUAL demons attacked them during the next week, but all were quickly dispatched. It turned out Corinne had not exaggerated her skill with a bow. When given the opportunity, she peppered the creatures with arrows before they got close to any of the companions. When they did, the slow and weakened creatures were easily cut down by Rhys or Grunt.

Grunt seemed to relish hacking deeply into the beasts with his massive bastard sword. The huge blade cleaved big chunks out of them. On the third demon, Grunt nearly chopped the entire thing in two.

Ben and Rhys watched on as the hunter knelt to cut loose the horns.

"The stupid man is going to get himself killed," complained Rhys.

"What do you mean?" asked Ben curiously. From what he saw, the hunter knew what he was doing. It wasn't his first time in the Wilds, either.

"He's cutting too deep," explained Rhys. "These things are almost solid bone and muscle. While we're making it look easy so far, they don't go down easy. If he cuts one of them and doesn't kill it, he's going to have his blade stuck and a very angry demon at close proximity."

"Should we say something?"

Rhys shook his head no. "When a man carries a big sword like that, well, he's going to want to swing it in a certain way. No use talking to him. You'd probably just piss him off."

"Why does it matter what size sword he has?" asked Ben. "He's a professional hunter. I'm sure he's always looking to improve. You give me feedback on swordsmanship all of the time."

"You don't think it matters what size sword he has?" asked Rhys with a raised eyebrow.

Ben frowned.

"The man's traveling with a pretty girl half his age, he's named after a sound he makes, and he carries a sword nearly as tall as you…" Rhys shrugged. "Talk to him if you like, but I'm not going to bring that kind of thing up with a guy."

"Are we," Ben hesitated, "still talking about his sword?"

BEFORE DAWN THE NEXT MORNING, while Ben was standing watch, snow began to fall. Light flakes barely visible in the low firelight drifted down around his face. He kept walking through the swirling crystals. By first light, a dusting of white covered the surrounding forest and his sleeping companions. A narrow circle of clear ground showed where Ben was walking around the campsite to stay awake and keep warm.

Grunt sat up and brushed the snow out of his hair. "I need some kaf," he mumbled sleepily.

Rhys rose and stretched. He worked through a quick sequence of Ohms poses while Corrine stared at him strangely. Rhys smiled back at her. "It warms you up," he said.

"Really?" yawned Amelie from across the fire.

"Try it," suggested Rhys, and she did.

Corinne and Grunt both watched on, bemused. Ben silently noted that maybe he should be using the Ohms as well. The chill was stiffening his body and the Ohms would be a good way to loosen up.

Lady Towaal rose and shook out her bedroll, sending a cascade of half-melted snowflakes onto the ground. "Can you make two of those pots of kaf today?" she asked Grunt.

The man grunted and stuck two more branches into the fire. He blew gently at the embers. Ben watched as the flames flared up. Grunt settled his pot of water near the heat and then stacked a pile of wood they'd gathered last night just outside of the fire pit.

Ben moved to stand near him and held out his hands to the growing heat. "What is that for?" he asked, gesturing to the woodpile.

"I'm drying 'em out," replied Grunt. He dug a finger into the slushy snow next to him. "From now on, we'll have trouble finding dry wood. Best to set it by the fire the night before to cook out the moisture then pack it with you. It makes for a heavy load, but it's better than sleeping in the snow with no fire."

"We should also start setting up the tarps," said Rhys, who was hovering near the kaf pot. "Any more than this dusting and we'll wake up soaking wet and freezing."

The hunter nodded and dug through his pack to pull out a sack of oats. "Oatmeal?" he asked.

Rhys shrugged. "Why not."

Ben was eager to try out the snow shoes he had been carrying for the last week but he felt silly using them on the almost non-existent dusting of snow. After a bell, the sun had melted it all away anyway.

They found a trickle of water babbling through a wide and dry creek bed. They started following it north. It wound through the rocky hills and ridges they had been climbing. Even though it wasn't straight, it made for quicker travel. Ben guessed the creek bed would fill up in the spring when the snowmelt began to run off. In autumn, it was dry except for a little stream half a pace wide.

"How are we doing on direction?" asked Corinne as they looped in a wide arc around a prominent rock-studded hill.

"Good," answered Towaal. She looked like she would leave it at that but then continued, "At this rate of speed, we should have two more weeks of hiking to get there. Whether we can maintain our pace, we shall see."

Three weeks walk from the nearest civilization, thought Ben. That was a long way from home.

"And when we get there," asked the bow woman, "how long will it take to destroy this Rift?"

"That should be rather quick if we can get close enough," replied Towaal. She looked to Amelie. "We should be able to place the device and activate it in a few minutes."

"How do you, ah, activate it?" asked Corinne. "I'm not very familiar with magical devices. Have you used one of these before?"

"I do have some familiarity with magical devices," answered Towaal dryly.

Corinne glanced at her and frowned suspiciously.

Amelie caught up to the other women and asked Towaal, "Once the disc is activated, how far away do we need to be?"

Corinne's frown deepened.

Towaal's lips pursed. Then she replied, "Three or four hundred paces. Anything closer will carry a significant risk."

"Hold on," said Corinne. "What exactly does this thing do? I thought it would just shatter the stone. I've heard they use those in the mines."

"It will be a little bit more than that," responded Towaal.

"More?" asked Corinne.

"A bigger boom," explained Rhys.

They kept trudging up the creek bed. Corinne wore a pensive look. Over the last week, she had come to terms with the idea that the skills in the group might run deeper than they appeared on the surface. Ben suspected she finally accepted there was more to it than she understood.

Ahead in the creek bed, Ben noticed something sticking out of the dirt. He walked ahead to investigate.

Corinne joined him and they both peered down at a short stick with feather fletching sticking up at an angle. The feathers still looked fresh. Ben guessed it had been left outside for less than a day.

The rest of the party stopped with them. They all thought the same thing. Someone had recently fired this arrow.

Rhys pointed behind them at the rock-studded hill the creek looped around. "There."

They looked back and saw the angle and distance made sense.

"We don't have time to investigate every odd thing we come across," stated Towaal.

Rhys shook his head and argued, "We haven't come across much. This is recent. It's worth seeing if there is anything we can learn."

Towaal sighed. "Go ahead. Quickly. I will wait down here."

Rhys shook his head again. "I don't think we should split up."

Towaal grumbled and slung her pack down. "Well, I'm not climbing that thing with this pack on."

They all followed her lead and laid down their supplies. They headed toward the hill with only their weapons and a few water skins.

When they drew closer, Ben realized this was not just a simple hill. The rocks sticking out had a square shape, and the entire formation was a suspiciously perfect cylinder.

"Must be an old keep," remarked Grunt. "You find things like this from time to time in the Wilds. Ancient fortifications and signs of past civilization. Occasionally, you can even find old artifacts that are worth some coin."

"How old?" asked Amelie, trailing her hand across a waist-high block at the base of the structure. The stone was worn smooth around the edges and dirt and sediment had formed around it to incorporate it back into the landscape.

"This could be two or three thousand years old?" guessed Rhys. "There's no telling."

"So, possibly before the Rift was created," murmured Towaal. She was suddenly interested. She led the way, climbing up the steep, nearly vertical side.

From a distance, the climb looked intimidating, but once they started on it, Ben found plentiful handholds. The tumbled blocks provided high but easy steps to ascend to the top.

When they reached the top, they discovered where the arrow came from. Three men were lying sprawled in a grisly heap. Pale, they had been drained. The demons that killed them had consumed all of the life-blood in their bodies.

Crimson and purple splatters painted a space the width of a medium-sized house in Farview. A fierce battle had taken place. The men's weapons were stained from use, but there weren't any demon corpses to show their work.

A broken bow lay in the hand of one of the corpses. He must

have tried to hit a demon with it, thought Ben. The man's sword was still in his scabbard, untouched.

Grunt knelt by the bodies and rolled them all to be facing up.

"Nong," he said to Corinne, pointing to a short man whose chest had been torn open.

Corinne gasped and moved over to see. Confirming Grunt's assessment, she turned to the group. "Nong was one of the most experienced hunters in Northport. The man used his scimitar on demons like a butcher on a pig. He's fought and killed scores of demons. There was rumor he could be a blademaster if he chose to make a challenge.

Rhys knelt down and scooted the man's scimitar away from the body. It was free of the blademaster's glyph, but the wide blade was smeared in purple demon blood. Rhys looked around. "Well, it doesn't look like he killed one this time."

Grunt stood and started scouting the edge of the old keep. "Nong wouldn't have been brought down by a single demon. A swarm did this."

They quickly examined the rest of the space. There wasn't anything to see. Towaal acted like she wanted to explore the structure in more detail but Rhys confronted her. "We don't have time to investigate everything, remember?"

She set her hands on her hips, preparing to argue. Rhys held up a hand and overruled her. "If a swarm did this, then we really can't afford to stay here. If they are nearby, they'll sense us soon and we'll have no choice but to fight."

Towaal looked ready to continue the argument then deflated. She motioned for them to go. Rhys began the descent down the tower, followed by Corinne and Amelie. Ben stood at the top, waiting his turn. He looked out over the landscape around them. It was a higher view than they'd seen of the immediate area so far. He could see that for days they would be moving through the same terrain. Thick woods flowed like a river around rocky ridges and outcroppings. In the distance, he could see where the mountains started to rise.

He thought he could pick out two high, knife sharp spines of rock reaching out like grasping hands. Those hands were encircling the valley they believed contained the Rift. From a distance, it looked peaceful and calm. There were no telltale black masses of demons covering the hills, or any other sign of the danger he knew they would face.

Towaal started climbing down in front of him. He looked to see where the others were placing their hands and feet. He wasn't a natural climber and didn't enjoy heights, so seeing Rhys two thirds of the way down and progressing quickly made him feel a bit better...until behind him he heard Grunt utter a sharp curse. "Bloody hell," grumbled the man.

"What?" asked Ben, spinning around.

Grunt was staring out on the other side of the tower.

"Where are the others?" demanded the hunter.

"Still climbing," replied Ben, moving to join Grunt and looking in the same direction as the man. He held up one hand to shade his eyes then growled his own curse.

In the distance, maybe half a league away, there was a black mass moving down one of the bare rocky ridges. While Ben watched, it disappeared into the forest below.

"How many?" asked Ben.

Grunt grunted. "Enough. Call the others back up. We're better off with the elevation."

The party climbed back up to the top of the ancient tower and spread out, looking down into the forest and hills below.

"I don't see anything," complained Amelie to Ben.

"I saw it, just for a heartbeat, but they're out there," he responded.

Corinne had her bow in hand and Grunt was carrying his crossbow. None of the rest of them had ranged weapons.

Rhys briefly gave Ben and Amelie a tutorial about utilizing the upper ground to their advantage.

"Let me summarize," said Ben after Rhys walked them through some tactics. "When their heads come up, chop them off?"

Rhys grinned and nodded. "You've got it."

Amelie had both of her blades out and was swishing them restlessly back and forth.

"Those won't be much use against a large demon," mentioned Corinne.

Amelie looked to her questioningly.

"Stick to the skinny ones," advised the huntress. "A demon is a big pile of meat. It will be difficult to get in a killing blow with a light weapon like yours. And when fighting a demon, if you get close enough to hit them, you want it to be a kill."

Amelie breathed deep and replied, "Thanks for the advice."

Corinne nodded briefly. "When we get back to civilization," she said, tapping one of the hand axes that hung from her belt, "we should get you some of these. Less reach, but more penetration. Swing it hard enough and you can crack even the thickest demon skull."

Ben stalked the edge of his side of the tower. As the minutes passed, nothing happened. None of the companions questioned what he and Grunt saw, but he could feel them getting impatient.

Grunt, muttering under his breath, kept asking himself where they were.

After a bell, Amelie suggested, "Maybe they didn't see us."

"This close," replied the hunter, "they should have sensed us."

"Let's wait a bit longer," interjected Towaal. "They either sensed us or they didn't. If they did, we shouldn't have long to wait. If they didn't, and they've moved on, then it's worth waiting another bell to be safe."

Pacified, they all settled down. Ben sat on a flat block that could have been part of a wall circling the top of the tower long ago. His longsword was drawn and resting across his knees. Idly, he ran his fingers along the blade and looked down at the trees below. It was a windless day. Nothing moved.

Silently, they all looked out like spokes on a wheel.

After another bell, they started getting restless again.

"We could be up here all day waiting on nothing," complained Corinne.

"I know what I saw," barked Grunt in response.

Corinne stalked back to the edge of the tower and looked down. "Whatever you saw, it doesn't seem interested in climbing up here after us."

"We spent too much time up here," declared Towaal. "We shouldn't have taken the diversion and we've lost half a day of travel."

Rhys raised an eyebrow at her.

"I know," she grumbled. "It's my fault too."

Sulking, Grunt slung his crossbow back over his shoulder and stated, "Fine. We've waited long enough. I know what I saw, and it was a demon swarm, but you're right—they've had plenty of time to get here. If they aren't here, they must have not sensed us. Let's go."

The stocky hunter started down the tower and they followed behind him. On the ground, they quickly moved back into the creek bed and recovered their packs. Ben felt a slight breeze and a chill wind picked up.

Within half a bell, swirling flakes of snow danced around them as they marched onward.

That evening, Ben and Rhys strung up several tarps between three bare tree trunks to create an open shelter. They angled one of the tarps to prevent most of the wind and snow from blowing in on them. It wasn't perfect, but it was better than nothing.

After a simple dinner, Rhys produced one of his silver flasks and passed it around the group. Everyone took a sip, even Lady Towaal. They all knew that a large demon swarm could be too much for them to defend against. Seeing one in the distance was an unpleasant reminder that while the Wilds seemed peaceful on the surface, the deadly risk was real.

Towaal was the first to roll up tight in her bedroll. Everyone else followed quickly behind.

Amelie had the first watch. Ben met her gaze before he tried to get some rest. He was confident she was alert and would spot anything coming near them, but he still could not sleep for bells. By the time he finally did lose consciousness, it seemed like he was immediately shaken awake by Towaal.

"Your watch," she whispered.

He groaned and crawled out of the fleeting warmth of his bed roll. He stomped his feet into his boots to get them settled. Wrapping his cloak tightly around himself with one hand, he kept the other hand and the hilt of his longsword free.

The wind had continued to pick up through the night and now it was blowing steadily, bringing a cloud of snow with it. The ankle-deep accumulation crunched under his feet when he stepped out from under the tarps and began circling their camp.

Snow-heavy clouds obscured the moon and stars. The little light that got through illuminated the world in white and black. Flurries whipped up by the wind stung Ben's face and blinded him between rapid blinks of his eyes.

He traipsed around, straining to see more than a few paces in front of him. On one side of the camp, he saw a log with a clear patch on it. Where Towaal was sitting, he surmised. He couldn't imagine settling down in the cold and wet and waiting out the watch. Staying on his feet and moving were the only ways to stay alert and warm.

After three orbits of the campsite, he felt nature's tug and shuffled further away from his sleeping companions. He found a suitable tree and braced for the cold when he adjusted his pants to relieve himself.

Teeth chattering, he looked around and frowned when he

noticed something. Behind the tree, he saw a knee-high snow drift that accumulated next to a rock. Through the center of the drift was a gap slightly wider than his shoulders.

Finished, he shook quickly and then went to investigate.

Something had passed through the gap, he realized. He knelt down and tested with a hand and was surprised when he could feel indentions in the snow, like tracks where something had walked. He traced the size of the indention. It was too small to be even Lady Towaal's footprint.

Eyes wide, he bolted upright. The snow was falling, which meant any tracks were fresh. They hadn't seen any animals or living people since they left Free State. There was only one other being he knew of in the Wilds.

He rushed back to the camp and blurted, "Wake up!"

Towaal was the first to spring to her feet, still half-awake from her watch. The others were slower, but no one slept heavily due to fear of demons and the cold. Within heartbeats, all of the companions were standing and alert, weapons in hand.

"What is it?" demanded Towaal, looking around for signs of an attack.

"I found tracks," breathed Ben.

"Tracks?" asked Towaal, confused.

"There shouldn't be any tracks out here," protested Grunt.

Rhys pulled a stick of firewood from their pile then wrapped a rag around it that he pulled from his pack. He doused the rag with the contents of one of his flasks then stuck it in the fire. The makeshift torch burst into flame.

"You're drinking that stuff?" questioned Corinne.

Rhys smiled grimly. "I'll let you try some later. Ben, show us these tracks."

Ben led them out of the camp to where he had been standing.

He pointed toward the tree he was near and said, "I was standing here when I noticed them."

Rhys hovered his torch near the tree. He paused when he saw

a pale yellow stain on the snow. "You had better not be kidding," he grumbled menacingly.

"Uh, that's not the track," Ben hastily explained. "Over there." He redirected them to where he saw the disturbed snow drift.

This time, when Rhys moved the torch closer, they could all see something stout had brushed through the high snow. Leading away from the drift were barely visible tracks.

"Oh, damn," muttered Grunt.

They all pressed close, hands on weapons as they examined the finding.

"This will be gone by morning," mumbled Rhys, holding his free hand out to catch the steadily falling snowflakes.

Grunt, peered closely at the marks in the snow. "It could be demon. Hard to tell in the dark. A big one if it was a demon, mature. One thing for sure though, it's a fresh track.

"How fresh?" asked Towaal.

Grunt poked his finger to the bottom of one of the indentions. "About a knuckle and a half," he said, sitting back on his haunches and eyeing the snowfall. "Maybe a bell, bell and a half?" he speculated.

Towaal frowned. "I was on watch then, and wide awake," she added quickly.

She turned and pointed to the log Ben saw earlier, thirty paces away. "I was sitting there. I should have seen anything nearby."

"And anything passing here would have seen you," said Rhys.

Towaal looked at him sharply.

"But," Corinne said, "that makes no sense. I've never heard of a demon seeing a person and not attacking."

"Demons get smarter when they mature, right?" asked Ben.

Everyone nodded. Grunt asked, "What are you getting at?"

"How big was this one? I mean, how smart would it have been?" continued Ben.

Grunt shrugged.

Ben finished his thought. "Maybe if it was a smart demon, it saw Lady Towaal and didn't attack. Could it have been scared?"

"Scared!" exclaimed Corinne. "Of a woman with a belt knife?"

She shot an apologetic look at Towaal before continuing, "No offense meant. It's just, why would a demon be scared of an unarmed woman?"

Rhys looked at Towaal. "Is it possible?"

She frowned, deep in thought. "Maybe. I need to think."

No further answers came from Towaal, despite Corinne asking repeatedly. They all decided it was far too risky to try to track the demon in the dark, so they returned to camp. Rhys volunteered to finish out the watch. Trying to sleep, Ben and Amelie laid down next to each other.

"Do you think that's true?" asked Amelie. "That it was scared of Towaal?"

Ben rolled onto his side to face Amelie. "What else makes sense?"

She didn't reply. They both lay silently until finally falling into an exhausted sleep.

12

BITTER COLD

KNEE-DEEP SNOW and a bitter chill greeted them when they woke. Ben's breath puffed in front of his face in a white cloud. His cheeks and nose felt numb to the touch.

Rhys had already started stoking the fire. As soon as everyone was awake, he told them whatever tracks were there last night had disappeared under the freshly fallen snow.

Breakfast was quick and cold. They wanted to get moving as soon as possible.

Ben and Rhys untied the tarps and shook off the heavy snow. They were specially treated to repel water. They were sturdy, but Ben worried how much snow they could really take before leaking.

Rhys remarked, "We'll need to find better shelter from now on. We can't camp out in this every night and expect to stay healthy and rested."

Towaal overheard and Ben saw her grimace. He knew she wanted speed, but speed was pointless if they ended up frozen to death.

Again, Ben glanced around to see if anyone was taking out his or her snow boots. No one did. Instead, Grunt went in front and broke a trail through the knee-deep powder and they all followed closely behind in his footsteps. By mid-morning, they switched and Ben took the lead. They rotated throughout the day so the trailbreaker didn't get too exhausted.

At midday, a painful ache set into Ben's legs and his toes were burning.

"As long as you can feel them, you're okay," assured Grunt. "When you stop feeling them, shout out. That's when we need to do something about it."

Ben groaned and stomped his feet hard. A jolt of mild pain shot up from where his frozen foot impacted the ground and he figured he was still all right.

After an afternoon break, Corinne took the lead and they kept following the same creek they had been for days now. It wasn't straight. It meandered down from the north but had a wide bed. They made good time walking across the flat. Particularly now, walking through the trees would take twice as long because deep drifts of snow would form around the trunks.

Suddenly, Corinne held up her hand and stopped. The group watched her silently as she edged forward. Ben knew there was no immediate risk because she left her bow on her shoulder.

She waved them closer and they saw another set of tracks. This one was clearly from a wide, low-moving creature.

"That's no deer," joked Rhys grimly.

"Obviously," snorted Corinne. "My concern is what was it doing down here? The creek is small, but the water isn't completely frozen yet. Demons loathe water. It didn't come for a drink."

They all looked around but couldn't see anything other than white snow, steep, shoulder-high banks where the creek rose to during the season, and a thick forest of birch trees beyond that— nothing that explained a demon's movements.

Grunt muttered, "Who knows why it was down here. Who knows why demons do any of the things they do?"

Corinne turned to him. "Come on, Grunt. You've tracked more of these creatures than I have. How many times have you found signs of them near water? They just don't go near it."

Grunt shrugged.

"I'm worried this is something else, something new," said Corinne.

Rhys had wandered over to the creek bank and scrambled up it. He looked north and south then hopped back down onto the flat.

"It's not something else, it's definitely a demon," responded Rhys. "But it might be new."

He squatted down by the path in the snow and pointed. "You can't see where the feet have landed very well because the chest brushed a lot of the snow and obscured the path. Here and here, you can see where hands went down."

Ben walked forward and studied the marks Rhys pointed out. It all looked like holes in the snow to him.

"I've tracked them in the snow before, long ago, and this is what it looks like. This was a small demon. I estimate no more than waist-high standing up and maybe five stone in weight."

Corinne eyed Rhys. Ben waited for her to comment or argue with Rhys' assessment of the tracks, but she finally just nodded appreciatively.

Grunt interjected, "A demon that small is new, immature. They react in predictable ways. This..." He gestured at the water. "This isn't normal."

Rhys nodded. "That's what I mean. This is something new, different."

The rogue stood back up and adjusted his pack and weapons. "Up on the bank, the tracks are obvious. The demon has been following along this creek. It came down right where I did, circled in this creek bed, then climbed back up and continued on its way."

Ben frowned. "I don't get it."

"It's scouting," Rhys answered bluntly.

"Demons don't scout," objected Corinne.

"This one is," replied Rhys.

They stood silently for a moment, contemplating what Rhys was telling them.

"I believe Rhys is right," remarked Towaal.

"What do you know that you aren't telling us?" asked Grunt.

"What Rhys suspected last night is correct, I think," she said. "The demon scouted our camp but turned away."

"Why?" asked Corinne. Her curiosity was winning over her desire to argue.

"It saw me," answered Towaal.

"You think it could sense your power?" asked Amelie.

"I wasn't sure, but I believe this track supports the notion. We are better off assuming it's true," replied Towaal.

"You need to come clean with us, now!" growled Grunt.

"Do you remember the spark Amelie made when we first met in Northport?" asked Towaal.

Grunt nodded hesitantly.

Corinne remarked, "Handy little parlor trick, right?"

"It's not a parlor trick," responded Towaal. "And I can make a much, much bigger one."

Corinne frowned.

Grunt's eyes widened in surprise. "A mage!" he shouted.

Corinne looked at him then back at Towaal in shock.

Towaal simply nodded affirmation.

"Wait," realized Corinne. "If you are a mage, then what is she?" she asked, looking to Amelie.

"I'm still in training," answered Amelie with a smile.

"I thought that was just some gimmick," mumbled Corinne.

"Why didn't you tell us?" demanded Grunt.

"Would you have joined us if I did?" replied Towaal. "People are suspicious of mages. They are nervous about what we are capable of. I've found it's easier to only share that knowledge when it's needed. Up until now, you didn't need to know."

The man frowned but didn't answer.

Towaal continued, "You are right about one thing. An immature demon should not have the wisdom to be afraid of me or the foresight to scout our potential path. A demon that left tracks this size shouldn't be acting like it is."

"So, what is it?" asked Ben.

Rhys answered. "A swarm is led by an arch-demon. No one has been able to study the relationships closely, of course. There is speculation that the arch-demon is able to...direct the other creatures to some extent."

"Direct them on a scouting mission?" asked Grunt skeptically.

Rhys shrugged. "That is the only explanation I can think of for what we're seeing."

"What does it mean?" wondered Ben.

"It means," explained Lady Towaal, "that the demons are planning an ambush. They were smart enough to avoid our camp when I was awake on watch and they are smart enough to scout our potential path for a site to attack us."

"It was stupid enough to leave tracks we could find," pointed out Corinne.

Towaal smiled. "That is true. While they are displaying an unprecedented instinct for tactics, they are still beasts and not men. We need to turn it on them. If there is an arch-demon with sufficient maturity to think at this level, we should be very concerned. We need every advantage we can get."

THE REST of the day was filled with nervous tension. Grunt held his crossbow as they walked and Corinne kept an arrow nocked though not drawn. Ben and the others left the hilts of their weapons free, but there were no other tracks sighted and no incidents.

They stopped early that evening when they saw a concave rock wall beside the creek bed. It wasn't quite a cave, but it was deep enough to provide shelter and prevented anything coming from behind them or dropping down on top of them, snow or demon.

Going about the normal evening tasks of settling the camp was difficult. Towaal instructed everyone to try and appear normal.

"The risk isn't while the sun is out," said Rhys, laying out his bedroll on a cleared patch of ground.

"Try to get some sleep now," advised Grunt to Ben. "Rhys is right. Once the sun falls, we need to be on alert."

At the risk of not appearing normal, all but two of them laid down to rest while the light was still out. They anticipated a long night ahead where they would pretend to sleep while waiting for the demons to attack. Depending on how long that took, they could be up all night.

Ben found he had trouble sleeping. He couldn't stop thinking about a swarm of snarling demons descending on them.

They had made what preparations they could. With limited time and the frightening idea that demons may be watching them, they were limited in how ready they could be. Grunt and Corinne thought it would come down to an ugly, brutal fight— toe to toe, steel versus claw.

After several bells of clenched teeth and furtive glances into the darkness, it was Ben's watch. Rhys pretended to shake him awake and mumbled under his breath that it was all quiet so far.

Ben sat and made a show of stretching. Once he did, he realized that his muscles and joints were nearly frozen from lying still in the cold night. He stretched in earnest while Rhys flipped back his bedroll.

Rhys passed him a silver flask and offered, "Something to warm you up."

"Should I be drinking right now?" queried Ben.

"At any minute, a swarm of angry demons could be descending on this camp, trying to tear our throats out and drain the life-blood from our bodies. We don't know how many of them there are or when they might hit us." Rhys looked in Ben's eyes. "Have you ever had a better time for a drink?"

Ben shrugged and took a small sip from Rhys' flask. He coughed harshly and handed it back to the rogue. The fiery liquor reminded him of Myland's brew in the first Free State.

"Sorry," apologized Rhys. "I'm saving the good stuff for myself."

Rhys turned and crawled into his bed roll, keeping one side open and his longsword within reach.

Ben shook his head at his friend's antics and moved to sit by a large boulder that had been tumbled down the creek sometime in the past. Ben's role was to sit and keep watch for a few minutes then pretend to drift off to sleep on the boulder. He'd keep his eyes open just a slit and watch for any movement.

The rest of the party was lying down, pretending to sleep in their bed rolls. As soon as Ben shouted, they would be on their feet and prepared to fight. They didn't think the surprise to the demons would be an advantage, but they hoped to lure them in while everyone was prepared. If you're going to face a demon swarm, it's better to do it when you are expecting it, and not get surprised later.

Ben noticed Amelie's eyes reflecting the firelight and hoped that he was the only one who could see it. He couldn't blame her. It was almost impossible to lie still and wait, bell after bell.

He smiled and winked at her. He chuckled to himself when her eyes snapped shut and faint snoring sounds emitted from her direction.

Relaxing as much as he could on the hard, cold boulder, Ben

leaned back and rested his head against the rock that made up the shallow cave they were in. He put one hand on his longsword and tried to let the tension in his body dissipate. It wasn't really working, but maybe it would be enough to trick a demon.

Half a bell later, he almost jumped off the boulder when a slender, dark shape quietly floated down from the opposite creek bank.

Against the white show, the profile of a small, winged demon stood out clearly in the moonlight.

Ben's hand tightened on the hilt of his sword. He fought hard to not make any sudden movements. They wanted to be sure an attack was happening before showing they were ready.

Completely silent, the small demon darted forward and stopped on the far side of the creek. It stayed there briefly, then retreated and swiftly ascended the bank, disappearing from Ben's sight.

Getting its friends, he thought.

He didn't have to wait long. Two minutes later, several dark shapes plummeted off the creek bank, landing with soft thumps in the powdery snow. They charged across the flat.

"Now!" shouted Ben, leaping to his feet.

Piles of firewood burst into flame at the same time the demons hurtled over the creek, jumping wildly to avoid the narrow stream of water.

Grunt's crossbow thumped and Corinne's bow twanged. There was no time for multiple shots before the demons got to them, but Ben saw at least one crash to the ground, shrieking a pained cry.

The light from the firewood piles illuminated the creatures as they made it across the creek. Towaal had lit them using her magic and heat from the campfire.

Unfortunately, cold, which they had in abundance, wouldn't damage the naturally resistant demons. The icicle trick she used on Lady Ingrid would also be useless. Towaal explained it took too long to form the frozen material and direct it. Ingrid had been stationary and the demons were moving as fast as a prime race horse.

Ben tried counting their attackers but didn't have time. A small wave of demons was on them within heartbeats of his companions rising to their feet.

Rhys rushed forward and met them first. Grunt flanked him on the right and Ben on the left. They hoped to keep a space to allow Corinne to continue firing arrows. Towaal and Amelie were behind her and away from direct contact. Amelie's rapier and defensive fighting style would be ineffective against the brutes. Towaal didn't need to be close for what she had planned.

Rhys slashed back and forth neatly, carving into two of the things and pushing them back, gaining the women valuable space to work behind them.

An arrow flew over Ben's shoulder and caught one of the dark shapes in the shoulder. It kept coming.

Ben stepped up and squared off with one of the thin varieties. Just like the one in Snowmar, it reached out and tried to catch his longsword. He let it wrap its hand around his blade. Then he twisted and yanked, slicing off fingers. This time, he continued his movement and drew his blade across the demon's neck, cutting almost to the bone.

A gurgling scream penetrated his ears, and the thing fell backward, clawing at the fountain of purple blood pumping out onto its shoulder.

Ben turned and took a wild swing at the back of a demon facing Rhys, catching a meaty piece of its shoulder, spinning it around. Rhys darted over and thrust his blade deep into its back.

Grunt was alone, facing the last two standing demons. He was holding them at bay with his heavy bastard sword. An eviscerated body of a third demon showed why the other two were reluctant to get too close.

Ben took a step to help him but was startled when Corinne shouted, "Ben, down!"

He turned to see her loose an arrow right at him. A heartbeat later, he realized it was going high, right above his head. He heard it impact a body and another thin demon crashed down on top of him, flailing violently. Claws dug painfully into his back, gouging flesh and forcing him to the ground.

Ben shoved it away and rolled in the snow, trying to gain distance to use his sword.

Behind him and across the narrow creek, a deep voiced roar split the night and shook his bones.

The small demon paused momentarily and Ben took advantage, leaping forward off his knees and cutting it down.

Several more booming roars followed and his blood ran cold. From the other creek bank, seven ox-sized creatures sprinted toward them. They were bigger than the one in Snowmar, and they moved like wolves on the hunt. They were the largest demons he had seen. At least until he saw what loomed behind them—a massive shape he struggled to comprehend. Standing twice as tall as him and with wings extending the width of a small house, it started moving forward.

"Oh, shit," muttered Rhys.

It was an arch-demon. Ben swallowed hard. The thing was huge. He glanced over and saw Rhys was standing near a heavily panting Grunt. The demons Grunt had been facing now lay dead on the ground.

Both men's swords rose and they set themselves, prepared to meet the next wave. Ben struggled to force down a surge of terror as the huge black shapes easily cleared the small creek.

"Aim for the neck!" yelled Rhys.

A crackle and pop split the air. The hairs on the back of Ben's neck stood on end. Lady Towaal joined the fight.

A brilliant blaze of ball lightning burst around the men and rolled forward into the charging demons. Earsplitting howls of pain stabbed into Ben's head.

The first demon in the charge cartwheeled backward, flames bursting from its chest where the lightning impacted it. The iridescent bolt of energy traveled back and jumped from demon to demon, cascading through the first seven and making them dance like marionettes on a string.

The lightning leapt from the first wave and imploded in on the arch-demon coming behind the others. It was still on the far side of the creek and was enveloped in a brilliant web of exploding, hissing light.

An incredible roar tore out of the demon's throat. The sound and vibration was enough to send Ben stumbling back several steps.

For several sustained heartbeats, the lightning continued to pound the massive creature. All energy focused on blasting into its body, again and again.

Then suddenly, it stopped. Ben heard Lady Towaal thump to the ground behind him.

All was silent but for the crackling pop of small fires dancing on the bodies of the demons. The air was filled with the awful, acrid stench of burning flesh.

In the fading bonfires they had set, Ben could see smoke rising off of the bodies. Nothing moved out in the creek bed.

"What in the..." started Grunt. He stepped forward to examine the bodies, visibly stunned he was still alive.

A bestial roar exploded from the arch-demon, loud enough to shake showers of snow out of the trees behind it. It staggered to its feet, flames licking its wings where Towaal's lightning had torched it. One then two shuddering steps forward, and the creature hurtled into the sky, its tattered wings flapped to propel it toward the companions.

Grunt, in front of the others, raised his bastard sword, but then jumped backward when the huge demon landed right where he had been standing.

The ground shook under Ben's boots with the impact of the landing.

Grunt yelled an unintelligible battle cry and stepped forward, swinging his huge sword at the beast. One swing was brushed aside by a heavy-clawed hand, but then the next sunk deep into the demon's side.

Purple blood flowed out. Grunt snarled, yanking hard to clear his blade, but the demon caught it with one hand. The creature reached forward with its other hand and gripped Grunt's arm.

Rhys flew at it. Swinging to avoid Grunt, he slashed and cut deeply into one of the demon's arms, springing loose the hand that was on Grunt's sword. It still had Grunt's arm though. It rose to its full height, taking Grunt with it. Dangling in the demon's powerful grip, his legs kicked helplessly in the cold air. The creature grabbed his other arm. Roaring in the hunter's face, it slowly tore him apart.

Guts, gore, and the remains of what had once been a strong, powerful man, rained down onto the trampled snow.

Rhys, unable to reach high enough on the demon or around Grunt's body to deliver a killing blow, chopped into the demon's other side. Now, twin rivers of purple blood flowed down its ribcage and legs. It didn't seem to slow it.

The demon swung at Rhys, half of Grunt's body still in its clawed hands. The rogue ducked low to avoid the decapitating blow.

Ben stepped forward, unsure how to attack the monster.

"Stay back," warned Rhys, calling over his shoulder at Ben. "Guard for other demons while I'm out," he instructed.

Ben, unsure what Rhys meant, felt a thump in his chest and saw Rhys' longsword ignite with a glowing white light. Over Rhys' shoulder, Ben could see the sigils on the blade were blazing forth with the light of a small moon.

The demon, dropping the remains of Grunt's body, covered its eyes and stepped back.

Rhys surged forward and, with one mighty blow, cut through the towering creature's leg, severing it at the knee.

Squealing in an unexpectedly high pitch, the demon dropped down. Rhys spun in a full circle and with incredible speed. He hacked the demon's massive head from its body. Almost a pace wide and with horns extending the length of Ben's arm, the head landed heavily on the ground.

Smoke trailed from Rhys' longsword and Ben was startled to see the demon's purple blood burning off the weapon, leaving it as clean as when Rhys pulled it from his scabbard.

Recovering from the wind up and swing, Rhys stumbled a few steps to the side like a drunk after a long night in the tavern. He dropped his blade, the light extinguishing immediately, and fell full-length, face first in the snow.

THE PUTRID SCENT of burned demons filled Ben's nostrils. He nearly vomited at the unpleasant aroma. Instead, he choked back the wave of bile in his throat and crawled out of his bedroll.

Corinne, sitting on the same boulder Ben was when the attack started, looked his way. Her eyes had a far-off look, like someone who spent the last couple of bells realizing there was a lot more to the world than they thought. Ben understood that look.

"Anything?" asked Ben.

She shook her head silently. Of course not, thought Ben. If there had been other demons or another attack, she would have woken them.

In front of him, the carnage of the night before was splayed out in a visceral tableau. While Corinne continued to stare sightlessly, Ben walked forward and observed in the light of day what he had only seen by firelight the night before. Nineteen demons and one hunter lay dead. Ben didn't even remember facing all of the creatures, but there they were. He avoided the red splatter where Grunt had gone down and walked amongst the demons instead. Most had wounds from Rhys' and Grunt's swords. A few had arrows sticking out of their bodies. The biggest ones had burns from Lady Towaal's lightning.

The arch-demon was charred nearly head to toe, impossible to see the night before. It had gapping wounds where both Rhys and Grunt had cut it deeply. Its head, lying propped on one side by its long curving horns, came up to Ben's waist. He shuddered and stayed back, certain it was dead, but still unwilling to go near those incredible fangs.

Uncomfortable after examining the head, he walked back to Corinne.

"I didn't even shoot," she said morosely.

"What do you mean?" asked Ben. Her arrows were jutting out of several of the monsters behind him.

"That thing." She pointed to the arch-demon. "It literally tore my friend in two. I didn't even shoot it. I just sat there, too scared to act. How can I call myself a hunter if I'm too scared to face a demon?"

Ben sighed. "I didn't do anything either. That…" He paused. "That was a bloody big demon. I don't think you know how you will react to something like that until you see it."

"Well," replied Corinne, "I know now. I don't think I can do this," she finished with a grimace.

Ben frowned.

"A couple of months ago," he started, "I lost a friend, too, a man named Mathias. I felt awful about it. I thought if only I had done more I could have saved him. I thought long and hard about what I had to do next. Let me tell you what I thought, and maybe it will help you too."

Ben sat next to Corinne on the boulder and continued, "The world is a hard place. And this journey we're on, it's only going to get harder. If we stop trying, if we stop moving, we're as good as dead. If we're not committed to doing anything necessary to get through this, then we're dead. Before last night was the easy part. That part is over now. Until we get back to Northport, we have to be ready. We have to be prepared for anything."

Corinne stared at the arch-demon.

"I know it will take some time to get over Grunt's passing. I know it won't be easy," consoled Ben, "but here we are, and going back isn't any easier. We're over a week from Free State and even further from what I would consider safe. We need you. We have to keep going and complete our mission. We have to make sure Grunt didn't give his life for nothing. Are you still with us?"

"What other choice do I have?" responded Corinne, her eyes glistening with unshed tears.

Ben wrapped a comforting arm around her shoulder.

"Did you just quote me, extensively?" asked Amelie from her bedroll. "I seem to recall telling you something very similar to that."

Ben put his arm back down at his side. "I…uh…"

Amelie stood up, smirking at him. "It's okay. You respect my advice enough to use it as your own. As long as we are clear on that, you can feel free to share my wisdom with others. I suppose I should be flattered."

She rolled her eyes at Ben then turned to look at the sleeping bodies of Lady Towaal and Rhys. Ben coughed discreetly and stood, shaking his arms and stomping his feet, trying to get some warmth. They'd used all of their firewood on the bonfires.

"How long do you think they'll sleep?" asked Amelie.

Ben shrugged. "Towaal was out for two days last time she did that. As for Rhys, I'm not even sure what he did."

Rhys' eyes popped open. "I killed that big demon, right?"

Ben frowned down at him. "How long have you been awake?"

Rhys sat up, stretching, and yawned. "I figured when I woke up alive that you all had it handled, so I went back to sleep."

"What did you do last night with the sword?" asked Corinne.

Rhys rose to his feet and looked over at the dead arch-demon. "I chopped its head off. I think that's what finally stopped it."

"Seriously," said Ben. "It looked like your sword was... Well, I don't really know what it looked like. Like magic, I guess."

Rhys looked around and saw his longsword resting in its scabbard by his bedroll.

"It's mage-wrought," he offered.

"Yeah," replied Ben, "but you said it didn't have any special properties."

"Oh," conceded Rhys. "I may have lied about that."

"What?" exclaimed Ben. "Why would you lie to us?"

"Sorry. For what it's worth, I've done way worse things."

Ben stared at his friend.

Rhys sighed and added, "Friends or no friends, some things are not meant to be discussed. The properties of that blade, well, that's something I wasn't ready to discuss at the time. It is a difficult topic." He bent and picked up the weapon. "It's something I'm not prepared to go into detail about now, either."

Amelie interrupted the discussion. "However you did it, you cut down that demon and saved our lives."

"Prolonged, maybe," responded Rhys glumly. "Last night, we learned an important lesson about what we're facing and what Northport is going to be up against even if we are successful. The level of coordination and planning that went into that attack was amateur by human standards, but unheard of by demons. Since the aftermath of the Blood Bay War, I don't recall anything like that."

"What lesson did we learn?" asked Corinne somberly.

Rhys walked to Grunt's pack and nudged it with a foot. "Think he'll mind?" he asked Corinne, not answering her question yet.

"He's not in position to complain," she snapped.

Rhys squatted down and began rummaging through the pack.

He pulled out the kaf pots. Finally, he answered, "That swarm was small compared to what Rhymer was telling us about. We had a mage with us and still had to pull out all of the stops to survive. Well, most of us survived. We can't risk facing a larger swarm. Maybe we'd all make it through, maybe we wouldn't."

"How do we avoid the swarms?" asked Ben.

"First," said Rhys, ticking off items on his fingers, "we make some kaf. Second, we get the hell away from here. This may draw others." He gestured to the litter of demon corpses surrounding the campsite. "And third, we get somewhere Towaal can rest, and we tell her to come up with a plan."

Two bells later, Ben stomped a trail through the knee-deep snow. Amelie and Corinne followed behind him, and Rhys brought up the rear, stumbling and staggering along with Lady Towaal in his arms. Ben knew even Rhys with his seemingly boundless energy would quickly tire carrying the mage. Ben offered to take turns, but instead, he ended up with Rhys' pack, which was shockingly heavy.

When he asked what was in it, Rhys winked and said, "Liquid weighs a lot. Maybe we should drink some to lighten the load?"

"Not yet," replied Ben. "Later tonight. Definitely later tonight."

Ben sighed and shoved through a waist-deep snow drift that had accumulated between several boulders strewn across the creek bed. His pants and boots were treated to be water resistant, but he could already feel the damp cold seeping through the leather. By the end of today, the lower half of his body would be sopping wet, if it didn't freeze. His feet and toes tingled painfully.

"How are you doing up there?" called Amelie.

"Okay," he huffed. "I don't think we'll make it far today."

"We've got to keep going," she reminded him. "There's a pile of dead demons behind us that I don't think we can stay near safely. Besides, the quicker we move, the sooner we get done with this."

Ben waved a hand behind him without looking back.

Shortly after that, he heard a groan. He looked back and saw Amelie walking with one palm held upturned in front of her.

"What?" he asked.

"Snow," she replied with a grimace.

He looked up and saw she was right. High above, a swirl of light flakes was floating down to them.

"Let's keep moving," called Rhys from the rear. "It looks like heavy clouds, but it's light so far. The further we get, the better."

Ben nodded and started up again, raising his legs up and pushing them back down to pack the snow. He kicked and shuffled through it to blaze a path for the others.

Half a bell later, the snow started coming heavier and faster. Thick flakes landed on his cloak and leathers and stuck. Others blew into his face and melted on his skin, stinging his cheeks and coating his eyelashes. Within minutes, his front was coated in white powder.

"Climb up the bank and head for the trees," shouted Rhys.

"We'll move at half the speed in the trees," argued Ben.

"It's getting heavier," responded Rhys. "Pretty soon we're not going to be able to move at all."

"Shouldn't we find shelter then?" asked Ben. "There could be another cave if we keep on the creek bed."

"We don't have time," responded Rhys, shifting Lady Towaal in his arms. "Find us a way to climb out of here and get into that forest. I'll show you something."

Ben shrugged and moved over to the creek bank. It was shoulder high and not too steep, so he started to climb it. Halfway up, he tried to pull himself over the top using a thin bush. Suddenly, he was tumbling backward down the bank. A pile of snow followed in a mini avalanche. He thumped softly into the cold below and he felt two paces worth of snow come sliding down on top of him.

His feet were sticking up and he waved them wildly, trying to get his bearings. They were the only thing he could move and he realized the rest of him was packed under the snow.

A strong pair of hands gripped his legs and he was yanked out of the drift.

"Are you kidding?" muttered Rhys. The rogue went back and lifted Towaal off the ground where he had laid her.

"That bush came loose!" explained Ben.

Rhys stomped by, shaking his head, and easily ascended the bank, which was now almost completely cleared of snow. Amelie and Corinne followed him up and Ben scrambled after.

Up top, the snow was piled deeply between the birch trees. The white bark of the trees and the snow combined to make it seem like the entire world had lost color.

Rhys nodded ahead. "Let's try that way."

Ben started breaking a new path. The snow was nearly mid-thigh now and he struggled to keep pushing forward.

One hundred paces further, and Rhys called a halt. "This is silly. Let's stop here. It's as good as any other place."

Ben glanced around. They stood in a small circle of trees. They were leafless and the thick snow fell heavy and silent on top of them. There was no sign of shelter.

"Uh, Rhys…" started Ben.

"I said I would show you something. Here." He handed Lady Towaal to Ben. The mage was dead weight in his arms. He knew carrying her in this weather would wear him out in minutes. He couldn't believe Rhys had lasted as long as he did.

Ben looked on with Amelie and Corinne as Rhys quickly pulled all of the tarps out of their packs and started stomping around the small clearing, packing the snow down tight. In minutes, he'd covered the entire area and started stringing the tarps tightly together over the packed area. He laid one down on the ground. After the tarps were tied, he began feverishly piling snow against them.

Ben looked at the girls and raised an eyebrow, wondering

what Rhys was doing. Corinne's eyes lit up in understanding.

"A snow hut!" she exclaimed and rushed forward to join Rhys, dropping her pack and weapons. Together, they tossed handful after handful of snow onto the tarp structure then packed it down tight.

They kept going until the entire thing was covered in hard pressed snow. In nearly half a bell, they'd accumulated a pile that was even with Ben's head.

"You'd be warmer if you helped," called Corinne.

Ben shifted slightly, lifting Towaal up. The mage was breathing softly in his arms.

"Right," said Corinne. She looked at Rhys and asked, "Think it's good?"

"Only one way to find out," he answered.

She dove into the snow and wiggled underneath. She was burrowing a hole below the tarps.

Ben frowned at Rhys, but the man just kept circling the snow hut, as Corinne called it. Rhys continued to put on and pack more snow.

Soon, Corinne called from within and said, "I think we're good."

Amelie sighed and dropped down, following Corinne into the structure and dragging her pack behind her.

When Ben came in dragging Towaal, he saw Corinne had pulled down the tarps and they were sitting in a cone of snow. She was moving around the interior, pressing up against the cold mass to shore up any weak spots. Holes were poked near the top but only a few flakes made their way within.

It was cold inside, but away from the light wind and falling flakes, it felt better. Ben laid Lady Towaal down on one side and checked her breathing. Slow but steady.

"It will warm up soon," said Corinne.

"This," Amelie asked, gesturing to the snow surrounding them, "will warm up?"

Corinne nodded. "Our body heat will warm it. Some of the snow may melt, but it should refreeze and create a barrier between us and the outside. It's not going to be hot, but it will be a damn sight better than out there."

Rhys poked his head in and instructed, "Ben, you come with me. We're going to collect fire wood. Corinne and Amelie, let's make this as comfortable as we can. The snow is coming down faster and faster out here. I suspect we may have to hole up for a day or two."

The ladies nodded and Ben crawled out of the snow hut after Rhys.

Ben stood up and brushed the snow off of him. Heartbeats later, he realized it was futile. Fat flakes landed on him faster than he could brush them away. Looking around, he complained, "Rhys, I don't think we're going to find dry firewood in this. We won't be able to get anything lit."

Rhys grinned. "I have a plan for that, too."

Quickly, they dug through the powdery snow and eventually came up with two big armfuls of damp wood.

"A fire will help warm that thing up, if you can get it started" said Ben doubtfully.

Rhys shook his head. "No, can't have smoke from the fire in there. We won't be able to breathe."

Ben looked at his friend blankly. "You think you're going to get a fire started with damp wood outside in a snow storm?"

"I've got a plan," responded Rhys calmly. "Make a fire pit and I'll be back."

"If it's not for warmth, do we even need a fire?" argued Ben.

Rhys grew serious and nodded. "Towaal has some herbs in her pack that make a tea. We need to boil it." He said no more, but Ben understood. If it would help the mage get on her feet quicker, then it was necessary.

Rhys crawled into the hut. Ben grumbled, digging down to the hard dirt and clearing an area of snow. He was going to wait to see what Rhys had in mind before he started trying to dig into the cold, frozen dirt.

"Perfect," said Rhys when he reemerged. Amelie followed behind him. She was pulling her cloak on still. A sour look painted her face.

"I'm not sure I can do this," she complained.

"Sure you can," encouraged Rhys.

Ben looked on silently.

Amelie squatted down near Ben's makeshift fire pit and studied the stack of wood. She turned and gestured to Rhys and Ben. "Come close. This isn't going to be pleasant."

"I know," murmured Rhys.

"Are you ready?" asked Amelie.

Rhys nodded.

Ben asked, "Ready for what?"

Amelie placed a hand on his leg. Suddenly, a chill swept through his body. It was like a cold ache that started in his feet and crept up to the top of his head. He felt like his body heat was being drained out.

He started to stumble backward, but his muscles locked up, freezing both figuratively and literally.

"Too much," groaned Rhys through gritted teeth.

Amelie clenched her jaw and remained focused on the stack of kindling.

Ben, unable to move, saw a tendril of steam break loose from the wood. Soon, more steam was boiling off. Before his eyes, the stack ignited in a burst of flame.

Amelie fell backward away from the sudden heat.

Rhys, moving slowly and stiffly, edged toward the rest of the wood. "Quick. Before that burns out, add more," he instructed.

Amelie, getting control of herself, stuck thicker sticks into the quickly diminishing blaze. More steam billowed up and the wet wood popped and hissed.

Ben watched in amazement as the new pieces slowly caught

fire and the original wood burned to ash.

Rhys rocked forward and expertly added more fuel, setting the newer, wetter sticks on the perimeter where the moisture could cook out and arranging the burning pieces into a neat, efficient fire.

"Did you just use magic on me?" demanded Ben, stunned.

Amelie sighed. "I think it's more accurate to say I used you for magic. I drew heat from your body to warm up the firewood. I'm surprised it worked."

"That's not right," complained Ben. "You shouldn't be able to just do that without asking people."

"She couldn't do it if you stopped her," pointed out Rhys. "Remember what Lady Towaal taught you at the farmhouse? If you hardened your will, you could easily prevent Amelie from drawing your heat. Hopefully, in addition to getting a fire started, this serves as a good lesson. Always keep your will hardened."

Rhys boiled water for Towaal's tea and Ben cooked a simple meal for dinner before letting the fire die down. As he cooked, the snow continued to dump, and he was ready to crawl into the snow hut as soon as he could.

It wasn't warm, but it felt downright hot compared to the bitter cold outside. Even next to the fire, shivers had wracked his body.

He stripped off his wet outer layers and reclined with the others while they ate. Their only light was a small candle Rhys found in Towaal's pack.

"Who brings a candle into the Wilds?" asked Corinne.

"Someone who plans to read," responded Rhys. He dug out the book Lady Towaal had brought with her from Northport, one of the four they'd borrowed from the Librarian.

He flipped through it idly before coming to the map page.

"I think this is why she brought it, but for the life of me I can't see why."

They all took turns looking over the map, but no one was

struck with any brilliant insights on how it could help their situation. The map depicted two ridges extending out from the base of the mountain. They formed a bowl that was open at the bottom. That's where they planned to enter. Ben thought maybe they could make it over the ridges, but to be sure, they would have to see them in person. Other than that, they assumed any geography drawn on the map was guesswork at best. It had been centuries or maybe millennia since the map was made.

Before long, the low light and exhaustion from hiking in the deep snow overtook them. The snow hut had warmed with their body heat, and despite the cramped quarters, they felt more comfortable than they had in days. One by one, they fell asleep where they lay.

Ben took the first watch and moved into a sitting position. The ceiling of the hut cleared his head by two hands. He knew if he lay down, there was no way he'd remain awake.

Outside of their hut, he could see through the small vent holes that it was near total dark. Heavy clouds obscured any moon or stars. The only sound was the steady breathing of his sleeping companions. He wondered if the snow was still falling. He couldn't hear a thing, of course, and in the darkness, he couldn't see either.

Briefly, he considered crawling outside to hold his watch there. A demon attacking them while they were in the hut would be a messy affair. He thought about the thigh-deep snow and bitter cold compared to the relative warmth of the hut. He decided they would have to risk it.

Alone with his thoughts, he practiced hardening his will. It was difficult to know if he was doing it well, since neither Towaal nor Amelie was awake to test him, but the way a half-trained initiate was able to pull heat from his body scared him. A fully trained mage would easily defeat him. He resolved to keep practicing every moment he got—sitting quietly at night or while they were walking.

Eventually, he thought enough time passed that his watch was done. He scooted over to wake Corinne.

In the black of the hut, she yawned and patted his hand in acknowledgement before sitting up. He crawled back to his bedroll and was instantly asleep.

He woke to the sound of Rhys grunting and swearing.

His friend's legs were hanging inside the snow hut but the rest of his body was in the hole going out the entrance. Bright morning sunlight spilled in from the vent holes.

The girls were already awake and watching Rhys' legs.

"What is it?" asked Ben.

Amelie grinned. "Apparently it snowed quite a bit last night." She pointed to Rhys. "We're blocked in, so he's digging his way out."

Rhys' legs thrashed around one more time then wiggled out of sight.

Ben smirked, pulled on his treated leathers, and followed his friend into the morning. The entire world was bathed in brilliant white light. He had to cover his eyes with one hand. After the dimly lit snow hut, the daylight stabbed into his eyes.

The snow was now waist-high all around them.

"Now this," declared Rhys, "is snowshoe worthy."

Ben nodded.

"But first," said Rhys, "we need to get Towaal up and moving. That means another fire and more tea. We should also take the time to find any edibles that we can and supplement our food supply. At this pace, we're going to be running thin by the time we get back."

Corinne wiggled out while he was finishing and offered to look for food or game. Ben collected firewood and teamed up with Amelie to heat and light it again.

This time, he concentrated, and just like the farmhouse, he was able to sense what she was doing. After earning one hard scowl when he hardened his will and stopped her, he let her draw his heat. She did it slower and smoother this time, lighting the fire without chilling him near to death.

Rhys made tea and gently tipped it into the still-sleeping Towaal's mouth.

The bright light lifted everyone's mood, but they still had no solid plan. By evening, it was apparent they wouldn't have much more food. Corinne came back empty-handed.

"Tight rations while we're resting. We'll save as much as we can to eat when we're moving and need the energy."

One more night in the snow hut kept them warm and out of the cold at least.

THE NEXT DAY, Towaal finally woke.

"How long?" she asked groggily, blinking and examining the interior of the hut.

"Two days," replied Rhys.

"Where are we?" she asked, poking a finger experimentally into the snow and ice wall.

"A snow hut about two bells walk north of the demon attack," said Rhys. "A blizzard swept through the next day and we couldn't make much progress carrying you."

She nodded, looking around. "Grunt?"

Corinne's eyes fell down and Rhys quietly answered, "The arch-demon was injured by your lightning but wasn't killed. It rose unexpectedly. Grunt faced it first."

"Did you finish it?" probed Towaal.

Rhys nodded.

"We need to talk about our plan," he said. "We wouldn't have survived much more than that swarm. If we face that again, we might not finish this mission."

"Let me think," she answered.

Outside of the hut, they stoked another fire into life and

tamped the snow around it to form chairs to sit on. Ben came up with the idea and was rather proud of it, but no one else seemed impressed.

Towaal sat down with the map page in the book. She studied the map and flipped to other pages before going back, muttering under her breath as she read.

They fixed a simple breakfast then Ben and Amelie practiced walking in their snowshoes. The light powdery snow still sank under their feet, but with the wide shoes, they stayed above most of it. Ben found it much easier to walk in the shoes than trying to break a path.

The air was freezing cold, but the light exercise of walking and the bright sun kept them reasonably warm.

Finally, after a bell of reading, Towaal announced she had an idea. She called them close and traced a finger along the map.

"You see this?" she asked, showing the ring of mountain range that surrounded the valley the Rift was located in.

They all nodded.

"It appears to have the same geological characteristics as some islands in the south sea," she said. "We might be able to use that."

"Islands in the south sea?" asked Rhys skeptically.

She nodded.

"As in volcanic islands?" pressed Rhys.

"Exactly," replied Towaal.

"If you are thinking what I am, isn't that rather dangerous?" he worried.

"Yes," agreed Towaal. "Extremely dangerous you might say, but I would attempt a controlled release."

"What are you talking about?" demanded Corinne. "Something that is more dangerous than what we were already planning on doing?"

"A volcano," explained Towaal, "is a rupture in the crust of the world. When these ruptures happen, extremely hot gases and a substance called magma are released. Sometimes, the release is in the form of a violent explosion, which naturally few have survived to describe. The release can also be slow and steady, which is observable and is documented in the Sanctuary's library."

"And how does this help us?" challenged Corinne.

Towaal pursed her lips. "If my suspicion is correct, then this valley we are traveling to is actually a dormant volcano. If we can activate it from a distance, we could direct the magma to the Rift and destroy it from afar. Assuming the release is controlled, it might be safer than facing the demon swarms we think will be populating the valley."

"Might be?" inquired Ben.

Rhys tapped his finger on the map. "Here," he said. "It looks like a tall hill from the drawing, just a few days walk outside of the valley. You might be able to far-see from it."

Towaal glanced at the map. "It's not too far out of the way. Let's give it a try."

Walking north again, Ben felt comfortable with their plan. It wasn't perfect, and he didn't like the risk Towaal implied about the volcano release, but it was better than nothing.

One snowshoed step at a time, he mused, picking up one foot and placing it in front of the other.

"Not too bad, once you get used to it," remarked Amelie, who was walking beside him.

"Yeah, it's a little awkward at first, but I think I'm getting the hang of it," he responded.

Amelie was about to reply when an angry shriek filled the forest. Ben's breath caught and held for several heartbeats.

Rhys commented, "Just one of them."

In the distance, they saw a black shape leaping through the high snow, disappearing then reappearing as it struggled forward.

Corinne slung her bow off her shoulder and smoothly nocked

an arrow. When the creature popped up again, she timed it and loosed a shot, hitting it near the center.

A pained howl burst out, but it kept coming.

She fired off two more arrows before it crashed down into the snow and didn't come back up.

They all listened for a tense minute, but no other sounds intruded on the quiet, snow-shrouded woods.

"Nice shooting," complimented Ben.

"One good thing about the snow," answered Corinne, "it slows them down. Easy targets."

"At least there's one good thing," said Ben, kicking loose a clump of powder, which had become lodged on top of his boot.

A WEEK PASSED and they encountered several more demons, but nothing that they weren't able to deal with quickly and reasonably safely. The constant cold and effort required to hike through the snow were taking a toll on them, though. Ben felt the entire group was wearing thin.

"Just two or three more days," grumbled Rhys one morning. They were out of kaf and he had to be stingy with his liquor before that ran out as well.

Ben felt his friend's pain. They were all grumpy and on edge. In the last two days, they had started seeing more and more tracks that signified demons were in the area. Mostly, it was one at a time, but late in the afternoon yesterday, they stumbled across what could only be a swarm. Rhys and Corinne both studied the path broken in the snow. Neither could tell exactly how many demons were in the pack. Enough, figured Ben.

The trees started to thin out and were replaced by rocky outcrops and ridges. It was a broken land they traveled over. Fewer trees made it more obvious how devoid of life the rest of the terrain was. Anything that took a breath and had a heartbeat had been consumed by the demons. Ben ached to see a rabbit hop through the snow or hear a bird chirp.

"There," pointed Amelie.

Far in the distance was a high stone butte. It could be the one on the map.

Rhys squinted at the butte and guessed, "Two days walk, maybe a day and a half if we push it."

"It will take half a day to climb that," remarked Towaal. "Let's push it."

The short northern winter nights didn't leave much daylight for hiking, but after seeing the butte, Towaal suggested they walk through part of the night. The moon was high above and the snow-covered landscape provided plenty of light to go by. Worst case, if they tripped, they would land in a cold but soft pile of snow.

The wind picked up at night and sent a chill down Ben's spine. He shivered as it whipped his cloak around his body and sent a blast of loose snow swirling around his legs.

Finally, a day and a half later, they made it to the base of the tall rock tower. It rose half the height of Whitehall, Ben estimated. Out in the desolate Wilds, it stuck up above anything else near them.

They circled the butte until they found a section where a loose scree had collapsed, giving them an easy ramp halfway up to the top. It was steep, but with the thick snow covering it, they were able to climb up with little problem.

At the top of the scree, they found a seam of rock angling toward the top. They would try to climb it.

"Anyone bring any rope?" wondered Ben.

No one brought any. Each of them would have to brave the climb on their own.

Rhys went first, removing his snowshoes and scampering up the seam. It was as wide as his foot. Ben's heart caught in his throat as he watched his friend climb higher.

"Scared of heights?" asked Corinne, noticing Ben's nervousness.

"Climbing ice-covered rock three weeks away from the nearest physic and surrounded by swarms of demons? Why would I be scared?" he joked back, barely concealing the quaking in his knees.

Amelie came up behind him and placed a comforting arm on his. She smiled at him but remained silent as Corinne placed a confident foot in the seam and started up after Rhys.

Ben studied where she placed each hand and foot, hoping he could repeat her motions when he made the climb.

Near the top now, Rhys paused and leaned back, gripping an invisible piece of rock as he looked up at the remaining three paces. Ben watched in amazement as he scaled, spiderlike, up a flat-seeming section of rock.

Shortly, Rhys disappeared over the top lip of the butte. Corinne, following close behind, paused at the last section. Rhys reappeared and hung halfway over, one hand vanishing above the lip to, Ben hoped, hold onto something. He motioned to Corinne, who passed her pack to him. Rhys hauled it up. Corinne, unencumbered now, followed him up and out of sight.

Towaal went next. Despite her scholarly appearance, she made good time. She scaled the last section quicker than Rhys or Corinne. Ben watched in amazement.

"She's magically holding herself to the rock." Amelie scoffed. "It has to do with gravity and amplifying the force from the butte."

"Huh?" asked Ben.

"Never mind," said Amelie. "Just don't feel bad. She cheated."

With that, Amelie started up.

Ben was impressed with how easy she made it look. Just like Corinne, Rhys materialized to take her pack at the top and pointed out where she could place her hands.

Ben sighed and placed a booted foot on the seam near the

base. He looked down and saw a layer of ice was coating the rock. If he was going to fall and die, might as well climb quickly, he thought. The higher the fall, the quicker the end.

The hard ice was slick beneath his feet but there was enough rock to support him. He was able to find crevices with his fingers and pull himself upward. Halfway to the last section, a breeze picked up.

His arms and legs shaking, he made the mistake of looking down and realized his assessment was right, the butte was roughly half the height of Whitehall, and he was now three-fourths of the way to the top. He closed his eyes and pressed his cheek against the rock, immediately regretting it. It was ice cold. Having his fingers wedged in there was bad enough.

Vowing not to look down again and calculate the time it would take his body to impact the rocks below, he continued upward.

As he edged along the narrowing seam, a piece of rotten rock hived off under his foot and went clattering down the side of the butte. His foot slid down with it, but he gripped hard with his fingers and quickly regained a solid position.

Rhys poked his head over and remarked, "You still coming?"

Ben looked up and whimpered, "Yeah, almost there."

Closer, Ben was able to shrug out of his pack and Rhys leaned down and lifted it effortlessly away. Ben swallowed and felt along the rock face above him, feeling for any nook or cranny he could wedge his fingers in.

Rhys came back and frowned down at him. "What are you doing? Just go up the same way I did. Look, right there." He pointed to a crack in the rock that would be a perfect finger hold. Ben hadn't seen it.

"Oh, right," said Ben. He scooted over to take advantage of Rhys' suggestion. He pulled himself up and kicked below, trying to find a foothold. Slowly, he started scaling the flat part of the rock face.

One more time, Rhys came back and groaned. "Still climbing?"

Rhys reached down with one hand and gripped the back of Ben's tunic. He dragged Ben over the lip of the butte. Ben's body scrapped across the rough rock.

"We don't have all day," muttered Rhys.

"Well," Towaal remarked from across the flat surface at the top of the butte, "we actually do have all day, and probably two or three days after."

Rhys raised an eyebrow.

Towaal explained, "It will take a few bells to far-see and scout the valley. After that, I'm not sure how long it will take to create a rupture."

"Anything we can do to help?" asked Rhys.

"No," replied Towaal. "Amelie can observe and I will likely need the power in the disc she is carrying. The rest of you are free to do as you please."

"Let's explore," said Rhys to Ben and Corinne. He pointed to a gaping hole in the center of the butte.

Ben walked over and looked down. He couldn't see far in the dark, but saw enough to know it went deep. The hole had a rough square shape. It made no sense that something like this would exist in the middle of the butte. "This can't be natural," he guessed.

"My thoughts exactly," agreed Rhys.

Ben and Rhys dumped their gear and Rhys started work on fashioning a torch. Ben watched him. Out of the corner of his eye, he also observed what Towaal and Amelie were doing. Towaal pulled out one of their cooking pans and laid it flat on the top of the rock. She poured half a skin of water into it and then moved to look north, toward the valley.

It was there, in the distance. The two sharp ridgelines they had seen on the map. From the top of the butte, they looked just like Ben would have pictured them. He could see the narrow gap

between the two ridges they had planned to pass through. He saw
what looked like a frozen river creeping out of it. Beyond that, he
couldn't see anything.

Rhys, igniting his torch, gestured to Ben and Corinne.
"Come on."

Rhys stuck his torch in the hole and they peered down. About
two man-heights below was a landing with rough-hewn stairs
descending from it.

"Now that's awfully strange," remarked Rhys.

"Who built stairs inside of there?" wondered Corinne.

"Only one way to find out," replied Rhys. He then dropped his
torch and smoothly slid into the hole, hanging onto the edge with
his hands then dropping the rest of the way down.

"Are you sure you'll be able to get back out of there?"
called Ben.

"Hope so," answered Rhys. "You coming?"

Ben and Corinne shared a look. Then she, too, dropped down
into the hole. Ben sighed and followed.

The landing was small for the three of them but Rhys moved
down onto the steps, giving them room to look around.

There wasn't much to see. It appeared both nature and man
had created then enlarged the hole. There were no signs
about why.

"Let's move down," suggested Rhys.

He started down the rock steps, which curved gently as they
went. Ben estimated they made two rotations before they
reached the bottom.

They found themselves in a large, open room. It was filled
with debris that had mostly turned to dust or rust.

On one side of the room, there was an indention for a fireplace. A narrow chute led up from it, but the fireplace itself only
held lumps of red brown dirt.

Along the walls, there were knee-high piles that Ben imagined were tables and chairs at one time. Now they were unrecognizable.

In the center of the room was one of the few things that had not decayed into non-existence. It was a large black-onyx table. Ben brushed aside a layer of dust and saw it still retained a glossy sheen.

"Don't touch that," hissed Rhys.

"Why?" asked Ben.

Rhys waved around the room. "It's been ages since anyone has been in here. Furniture, iron in the hearth, it's all disintegrated. Why do you think that table still stands, fresh as the day it was made?"

"I wouldn't call it fresh," complained Ben.

"It's mage-wrought," explained Rhys.

"A table?" questioned Ben, looking down at the glossy surface.

Rhys shrugged. "I imagine it was created with a larger purpose in mind than eating dinner on. We'll bring Towaal down to examine it later."

Suddenly, a warm glow filled the room. Corinne stumbled backward, cursing. In front of her on the wall a yellow stone was emitting a steady glow.

"I said no touching!" barked Rhys.

"I barely nudged it," exclaimed Corinne, staring fixated at the stone.

Rhys sighed and walked over to it. It hung at eye level and was embedded in the wall. "I've seen these before," he said. He quickly walked around the room and tapped three more of the stones. The room filled with a warm light.

"The skill and power it took to fashion these to work for hundreds of years," Rhys said to himself. "Unbelievable."

"Hundreds of years?" asked Ben.

"If not thousands," responded Rhys. "Look around here. Anything that isn't mage-wrought has completely turned to dust.

How long do you think it would take iron to rust into nothingness in a dry chamber?"

Ben shrugged. He had no idea how long it took iron to rust.

"A long time," declared Rhys.

From what Ben could tell, his friend was right. It had been a long, long time since whoever occupied this chamber had done so.

"Look over there," said Corinne, pointing to a far corner of the room that had been obscured in darkness. Now that the wall lights were functioning, they could see a narrow hallway and stairs leading deeper into the rock.

A quick circuit of the first room showed there was nothing else to see. They headed down the stairs.

The stairs twisted down in a spiral and at the bottom they found a dark hallway. Ben guessed it was directly beneath the room above.

Six doorways lined the hall in front of them, five gaped open. Whatever door guarded them had long since rotted away. The sixth door, at the end of the hallway, appeared brand new.

"Look at the floor," said Corinne.

Rhys held his torch low and they could see a thick layer of undisturbed dust.

"Nothing has been in here for ages," she continued.

"So, why is that door new?" asked Ben.

"It's not," explained Rhys. "At least, I don't think so." He marched down the hall, glancing into the other rooms before he got to the end and stood in front of the door. He paused, examining it closely before tracing a hand along its surface. Soft glowing green sigils appeared when Rhys brushed over them. They quickly faded away when his hand moved.

"Preservation magic," he mumbled.

"Should we get Towaal?" asked Ben.

"Yes," answered Rhys. "I think she'll want to see this."

Towaal, it turned out, did want to see what they found. She

stopped her far-seeing preparations and immediately followed them back down.

In the first chamber, she quickly examined the table and in an awed tone remarked, "Unbelievable."

"What is it?" asked Amelie.

"A far-seeing device," answered Towaal. "We're wasting our time up top with that pan of water."

Ben remembered in Fabrizo a merchant had tried to sell him such a device, but that one was the size of his palm. This was a table large enough to seat a dozen big men.

"How does it work?" he asked.

"Sight is simply our perception of light," replied Towaal. "When we see an object, we are really seeing the light reflecting off of it. This device captures and displays that light. A skilled practitioner can use their will to move the source of the light, which will then be visible here," she finished, tapping the table.

Ben frowned, not understanding.

"It lets you see stuff far away," added Amelie helpfully.

Ben rolled his eyes at her.

"I will examine this in more detail later. Now, I am even more curious to see the door you found," said Towaal.

They led her down the stairs and she cautiously approached the door at the end of the hall. Just like Rhys, she waved her hand over the door and read the sigils.

Satisfied, she grabbed the doorknob and turned. Silently, it twisted in her hand without a squeak or a hint of disrepair.

Corinne shuffled to stand nervously behind Ben as Towaal swung the door open. Towaal looked back at them then walked into the room without speaking.

They all rushed forward to peer into the doorway behind her.

Inside, they found a surprisingly large sitting room with an open door to a bedchamber.

Filing in, Ben gazed around in wonderment. Unlike everything else they had seen, there was no sign of age or wear in this room. It was perfectly preserved, like someone had just walked out moments before. It smelled nice.

"Amazing," breathed Towaal.

"Have you not seen a spell like this before?" questioned Rhys. "I did not think they were uncommon."

"Not to this extent, no," replied Towaal. "You are right, they are not exactly uncommon. They are frequently used on important legal documents or declarations like Argren's Alliance, if he trusted mages that is. I have never seen one that was able to sustain itself for a thousand years without needing to be refreshed, and covering two entire rooms. Whoever set this was quite powerful."

"I saw some preservation magic worked in the Sanctuary," remarked Amelie, "but nothing like this. How is it done?"

"It's the same concept as the long-lived," continued Towaal. "An element of control is established which can arrest the natural process of decay. You were never shown because initiates don't typically have anything that needs to be preserved. Frankly, I find the spell's use rather silly. Why not just recopy an important document?"

"Long-lived?" asked Corinne derisively. "Are we talking fairy tales now? I can accept a lot about magic, but I never really liked that one."

Rhys grinned broadly at her. "If you don't like that fairy tale, how about a handsome prince charming coming to the rescue of a damsel in distress?"

Corinne snorted. "I am not in distress, and you are certainly not handsome. I think you'll have better luck claiming to be a long-lived."

"Maybe I'll try that," responded Rhys, his smile growing.

Towaal ignored the banter and continued to examine the room. Ben followed with his eyes, seeing a well-appointed room buried deep in the mountain.

In the sitting room, a simple writing desk and chair sat

against one wall. Towaal sifted through the few items on the desk. A small notebook made its way into her hand, but the rest of the items were basic and she left them. A quill for writing, blank pages of parchment, and what appeared to be a poor attempt to carve a wooden pipe.

On the other wall were two comfortable-looking chairs with a stack of books between them. A crystal decanter of some amber liquid rested on a short table.

A thick rug covered the floor. Ben paused when he saw hanging against one wall a simple, solid purple flag.

"The Purple?" he asked, looking at it.

Towaal frowned and bent close to examine it. "Nothing special about it and no markings," she said. "But who knows? I am not aware of any other significance to the color."

The notebook and books would take further examination by Towaal and the decanter by Rhys. Other than that, the room was bare.

They moved back to the bedroom and Ben's breath caught. A shimmering suite of armor stood in one corner, and beside it was a weapons rack. The rack held a massive mace and an elegant longsword. The armor was heavy plate. It looked like it had just been polished. The gleam of the metal reflected the room. Ben saw the companions moving in it as they approached.

A helmet with a purple plume hung above the armor. Rhys leaned close to see it. He slid a visor down to cover the face and Ben frowned. There were no eye slits in the visor. It completely covered where a person's face would be.

"Mage-wrought," whispered Rhys. "There must be some mechanism to see through the metal."

"Mage-wrought armor?" asked Towaal curiously. She moved to look closer. Lightly, she touched the helmet and the plate. Faint sigils followed in the wake of her touch. None of them meant anything to Ben.

"That's got to be worth a king's ransom," breathed Corinne.

"More like the entire kingdom," responded Rhys frankly. "I have seen a lot, but I have never seen an entire suit of mage-wrought armor. Mage-wrought armor would be almost impossible to break or penetrate. A man could be near invincible in this."

Ben moved over to the weapons rack and looked at the mace and the sword. The mace was a huge, oversized weapon. He couldn't imagine the strength it would take to wield it. Sharp spikes sprouted out of the end of it and the shaft was as thick as his forearm. It had to weigh half as much as he did.

The longsword though was a normal-sized weapon. It had a brilliant silver blade and a finely forged cross guard shaped like the spreading branches of a tree. The hilt was wire-wrapped and on the pommel where a lord might keep a gem, was a round, smoothly polished sphere of a strange wood.

Towaal joined Ben and suggested, "Take it."

"What?" he asked, shocked.

"The longsword. Take it," she replied.

"I-I'm not sure..." he stuttered.

"It is also mage-wrought. It will take further research to determine its properties, but at the least, it is a finer blade than what you have now. Take it," she said again.

"What about Rhys? He's a better swordsman than I am. He should use it," argued Ben.

Rhys tapped the hilt of his own longsword and said, "I already have a mage-wrought blade. That one is yours."

The companions watched quietly as Ben reached out and wrapped his hand around the hilt. He lifted the sword off the rack. He wasn't sure what to expect, but nothing extraordinary happened. It was a little lighter than his own blade but near the same size. The wire hilt felt cool to the touch.

Rhys pulled a simple leather scabbard from behind the armor stand and handed it to Ben. It was inscribed with a glyph, different from the blademaster one. Ben had never seen its like before.

He stepped back and whirled the sword through the air in a gentle figure eight. Maybe it was just his imagination, but it seemed a light breeze stirred the still air of the room.

Lady Towaal nodded appreciatively and remarked, "I must study that further when we've reached safety. I believe we have found something very special."

"What about the rest of it?" asked Corinne, pacing in front of the armor and the weapons rack.

"I don't think this will fit any of us," said Rhys, gesturing to the armor. "Whoever wore that is at least a hand taller than I am, and even bigger than the rest of you. That would be more of a hindrance than anything else."

"That is too bad," murmured Towaal. "If I am interpreting the sigils correctly, I believe that armor would imbue a prodigious amount of strength into the wearer. Someone in that armor would be capable of doing amazing things."

"That makes sense," grumbled Rhys, looking wistfully at the armor then at the mace. He moved over to the heavy weapon and lifted it, barely. He let it thump back down onto the rack. "I don't think any of us wants to lug that thing back to Northport, even if it is mage-wrought."

"So, nothing for the rest of us?" complained Corinne.

"It doesn't look like it," said Rhys.

Amelie, after realizing none of the weaponry was appropriate for her, had moved over to a wardrobe and opened it up. It held clothes that seemed to match the wearer of the armor. She rifled through but came up with nothing of interest.

They walked back out into the sitting room and Towaal collected the assortment of books by the chair. Rhys unstopped the decanter and sniffed at it. A sly smile crawled across his face and he tucked the crystal container under one arm.

"Come on," chided Towaal, pursing her lips in frustration at the rogue. "I want to look at the far-seeing table. Gather our packs up top and bring them down before you do any further research on that mysterious liquid."

Rhys affected a hurt look, which drew no sympathy from anyone.

"Fine." He sighed.

Back in the main room, the ladies cleared the dust off the onyx table. Ben and Rhys climbed up to collect the packs. Up top, Ben could see another storm was forming above the mountains. Dark, angry clouds spilled over the peaks and down into the Rift valley.

"How far do you think it is to the Rift?" asked Ben.

Rhys squinted, gauging the distance. "Four or five days, depending on the weather and how often you have to walk around those hills."

"Do you think we would have made it?" asked Ben.

Rhys' expression grew grim. "Do you think Towaal will be able to open up a volcano under the Rift from five days walk away?"

"I..." Ben didn't know.

"Hopefully she can," Rhys responded. "I'm just saying don't cross it out that we might still have to walk a little farther north."

Ben swallowed. "Let's get back inside. I'm done with snow for a little while."

The men cleared out the hearth and raided the preserved bedchamber for furniture. Borrowing Corinne's hand axes, they hacked the writing desk and chair into kindling. The dry wood would burn quickly. Rhys suggested they cut up the bed too. The thick logs of the bedposts would last for a while.

"Why don't you use those fancy mage-wrought longswords to cut up the wood?" asked Corinne when they handed back her axes. "I'm not an expert, never seen one actually, but I've heard they never need to be sharpened."

"Every tool has a purpose and every purpose has a tool," answered Rhys solemnly.

"My axes are for cutting through a demon's skull," remarked Corinne.

Just then, a cool light filled the room from behind them. The far-seeing table flared into life.

The group clustered around while Lady Towaal danced her fingers over the glass smooth surface, explaining to Amelie what she was doing.

"The device is setup like a bird's eye looking down," she said. "This one appears to be roughly the same height as the top of the butte we're housed in. It's likely we could adjust that, but I need to understand better how the makers created this."

Amelie leaned over the table and looked down. It showed rock and forest, just like the terrain around them.

Ben watched, open mouthed. He'd never seen anything like this.

Towaal slowly moved a hand over the table and the image moved with it, showing more rocks and trees.

"See. When I exert my will, I can alter the location we are seeing. These here," she said, tapping a glowing set of glyphs near the bottom, "are the focus for my will. They signify direction and...likely some other things I am not sure of."

"How do," Corinne asked hesitatingly, "how do you make it work? Could I do it?"

Towaal smiled at the huntress. "With training, yes. Small far-seeing devices are relatively common. They are used by all manner of adventurers and seafarers. The larger the surface and the greater the distance, the more difficult it is to manipulate. Without sufficient training and practice in how to extend your will, I do not believe you would be able to control this device."

Adjusting the display on the table with growing confidence, Lady Towaal kept speaking. "That being said, this table serves as a focal point, which makes this much easier and clearer than what I originally intended. I believe it will also extend the range of what I can see. My method would have required more effort and time to get it right. It's obvious that whoever created this table did it with the purpose of a scouting device for the area."

"But why?" asked Ben.

"If this outpost, or whatever it is, was for the Purple..." started Amelie.

"Then maybe they were using it to monitor the Rift," finished Rhys.

They all looked back at the far-seeing table silently. Everyone shared the same thought. It made sense that the chamber was a monitoring station for the Rift. The obvious question was, what happened?

The soft, consistent yellow glow of the wall lights and the flicker of light from the table as Towaal searched the area began to get tiresome after a while. Ben couldn't help but think what happened to the original occupants of the room. With the armor and equipment they found in the bed chamber, paired with the magical talents of the people who built the devices, they were prepared to defend themselves. Did they just fade away, or were they attacked?

While the ladies worked on locating a point of reference for the far-seeing table, Ben picked up Rhys' torch from earlier and wandered back down the stairs to the lower level.

He walked to the preserved room and looked through it again aimlessly. The clothing held his interest briefly. It was an unfamiliar style. He wasn't sure if that was because it was ancient or because it was just a different culture.

In the room, the only decoration was the purple banner hanging on one wall. The only sign of the occupant's interests had been the stack of books and the decanter of liquor. He didn't count the amateurish attempt at carving a pipe. To him, that looked like someone trying desperately to relieve boredom.

He walked back out into the hall and ducked his head into the other rooms.

They were similar to the preserved one with the notable exception that they were not at all preserved. The contents of the rooms had crumbled into dust. In the fourth room, he heard someone come in behind him. He turned to see Corinne in the doorway.

"Find anything?" she asked.

"No," he replied. "Dust and...just dust."

"Strange, isn't it," she said.

"It is strange," he agreed.

"No, I mean, specifically it is strange there is nothing left in any of these rooms. Why was that one room preserved, and how come nothing is left in these?"

"Maybe no one had time to cast a spell on these?" he guessed. "They could have left in a hurry or didn't have that kind of skill. Over time, anything in here would disintegrate."

"Not the devices the mages created," she challenged. "The lights and table not only stayed intact, they still work! That is craftsmanship. The preserved room had mage-wrought stuff inside. Even without the spell or whatever it was they did, that stuff could have survived. If these people left in a hurry, how come none of these rooms have anything remaining?"

Ben looked around the room they were standing in. Ankle-deep piles of dust covered large portions of the floor where neither weather nor wind had blown through.

"We never really looked in these rooms," he admitted.

Corinne strode in the door and kicked through one of the dust piles, covering her mouth as the ages-old debris floated into the air.

Ben waded after her. Soon, the entire room was filled with a cloud of dust. They walked back out, coughing and grinning at each other.

"Let's do another," she suggested.

They stormed through two more rooms, kicking the dust around, coughing and laughing. Ben's clothes were coated in pale grey dust, but after three weeks in the Wilds, he thought it might be an improvement. In the third room, Ben heard a clink when Corinne's boot swept through a particularly deep pile.

"Hold on," he said. "What was that?"

"What was what?" she said, breathing heavily with her hand over her mouth.

Ben shuffled slowly through the area he thought he heard the sound and was rewarded when his foot touched on a small lump.

He kneeled down and brushed the dust aside with his hand to reveal two wooden ovals. They were the size of his palm, hollow in the middle, and inscribed with runes.

Corinne kneeled beside him and asked, "What is that?"

"They look like wood," he said, "but they sounded like metal, and, well, they're still here."

Corinne reached a hand forward.

Ben cautioned, "Should you—"

He didn't finish before her fingers closed around the objects.

On closer examination, they learned nothing. They were smooth like polished wood and heavy like metal. They had a similar look to the disc Amelie carried and the one they found in the woods used for a ward. Maybe all magical devices looked like that, thought Ben.

"Let's show Towaal," he suggested.

"Sure," answered Corinne. "But these are mine."

"Whatever," agreed Ben. Not that he could complain. The mage-wrought longsword was strapped to his side.

They cleaned out the other dust-filled rooms, finding nothing, and then went back upstairs where the rest of the party was huddled around the far-seeing table.

Towaal took a look at the small objects but couldn't identify their purpose. She rapped one against the table, listening to the metallic clink. She handed it back to Corinne with a shrug.

"Let's put it with everything else we need to research when we find time," advised the mage. "They're clearly mage-wrought, of course. There seems to be some sort of linking between them, but I don't have time to look into that now."

Corinne nodded, obviously disappointed.

"Let me look," offered Amelie.

Corinne handed over the two wooden ovals and Amelie knelt down, placing them on the floor, and peering close to examine them.

Ben wasn't sure what she could tell that Towaal couldn't.

Amelie traced her fingers over the objects and moved them closer then further apart on the floor. She frowned at them, presumably trying to exert some will on the intractable wood. Finally, she clinked one on the floor, just like Towaal did.

Muttering quietly under her breath, she sat back on her haunches.

Corinne stepped close, peering down at the artifacts.

"Here," said Amelie.

She handed Corinne one of the ovals.

"Go over to the far side of the room and rap it against the floor, just like I did."

Corinne took it and did as she was instructed. Walking back to Amelie, she asked, "Anything?"

"I believe so," replied Amelie. "These are indeed linked and I think they are transferring sound. I'm not sure how…"

"Amelie!" exclaimed Towaal. She waved the initiate over. "Come look, I've found the valley."

Amelie stood and tried to hand back the wooden oval, but Corinne stopped her.

"You keep that one and I'll keep this one," said the huntress. "If they are linked, maybe by keeping them separate, we can figure out how to use them."

Amelie nodded then moved to Towaal's side.

13

THE RIFT

THE NEXT MORNING, they continued to examine the rift valley through the far-seeing device.

Clustering around the table, the companions all watched as Towaal manipulated the display to scan across the valley. Unlike the rugged terrain leading up to it, the floor of the valley was smooth and steady. It was crowded with thick trees, and at the height they were observing from, they had little visibility into what might be moving in the area.

Sweeping back and forth, a clear picture began to emerge. The valley formed a shallow bowl with a river running through the middle. There were no features Ben could see until they got to what would have been the center of the valley.

In that area, on a hill that was clear of vegetation, stood an ancient stone structure.

From above, it looked to be the same level as a four-story building and was formed in a perfect circle. It stood balanced on its side, like an open gateway. Around it, they could see a few dark shapes moving.

"Demons," observed Rhys.

Towaal nodded. "I'm not sure we would have survived going in there."

Suddenly, there was a flicker of light near the rift and a new shape emerged near the stones. Other black shapes rapidly converged on it but their view was too far away to see exactly what was happening. Moments later, the shapes scattered.

"What was that?" asked Corinne.

"I'm not sure," murmured Towaal. "Recruiting a newly arrived demon into the swarm?"

"Well," said Rhys, "one thing is clear. We just witnessed a demon arrive through that thing. We might be the only people alive who have seen that. The suspicion about the Rift existing and being a source of demons is confirmed. The question is, what can we do about it?"

It was all very strange. The same creatures that tried to rend his flesh and consume his life-blood every time he saw them looked rather peaceful. Of course, they were a four-day walk from where these demons were and none of them could sense Ben's party. Still, he started to grow uncomfortable looking down at the monsters.

Towaal left the view hovering over the Rift structure for several minutes but they did not see anything new.

Next, she moved over to the river that flowed through the valley and traced its source. Then she scanned along the rim of the ridges, which formed the bowl. She was moving quickly now, barely pausing before moving onto the next scene.

"What are you thinking?" asked Rhys quietly.

"This valley appears to be consistent with what we know about volcanoes," she answered. "Clearly, it is not active, but we may be able to delve deep and uncover the original source of the geological structure."

"And then?" asked Rhys.

"Then we try to open it up and destroy the Rift," she replied.

By midday, Towaal had viewed whatever she needed to on the

far-seeing device. She was ready to start delving the ground for sources of heat.

She moved up top with Amelie and the others followed. They had nothing better to do than wait. Ben shivered in the cold, but he had no interest in sitting in the chamber below by himself.

"This will be difficult due to the distance," explained Towaal to Amelie. "Generally, you want to be as close as possible to what you are delving. Proximity improves your sense."

"And what are we sensing?" asked Amelie.

"Heat," replied Towaal. "It is challenging to extend outside of yourself even a short distance. This far away, it will be very difficult. At best, we will be able to detect basic sensations like heat or light. For our purposes, I hope to find an extreme source of heat. This far away it could be impossible but I am hoping the magma is so hot I can overcome the distance barrier."

Towaal and Amelie both settled down on the rock of the butte, looking north toward the Rift valley. Ben and the others wandered around, looking over the edge and generally wasting time.

The mage and initiate had gone silent, focused leagues away.

As Ben watched, Amelie's eyes flicked open and she glanced sideways at Towaal. He smiled at her. She caught his look in the corner of her eye then frowned and closed her eyes again, clearly not sensing anything that she was supposed to be.

For a bell, Ben paced nervously, waiting on Towaal to say something. She just sat quietly, though.

Corinne began walking next to Ben and whispered, "Do you think she's really doing anything?"

He shrugged. "I hope so. After seeing the demons around the Rift, I don't want to try to go in there."

Corinne nodded. "I don't have any experience with mages. She seems very, uh, domineering. Is that the right word?"

Ben snorted. "Yeah, I think that's right. And if you think she's bad, you should meet Mistress Eldred."

Finally, Towaal's eyes snapped open and she stood. She stretched to work out the kinks from sitting on the hard rock.

"Well?" asked Rhys impatiently. He was a man of action and sitting and watching Towaal 'sense' was quickly fraying his nerves.

Towaal answered brusquely, "I located a source of enormous heat and I believe it will be sufficient for our purposes. We are lucky, it's already near the surface. I believe in a few decades, there would have been a natural rupture."

"Decades?" asked Corrine

"That is a short period in geological terms," explained Towaal.

"Will you be able to do it from this far away?" inquired Amelie.

Towaal pursed her lips then shrugged. "It will be difficult, but anything in this world is possible if you have the will to do it."

"How—" asked Amelie.

"Beneath the ground," said Towaal, "there are plates that cover this world. The plates are floating on hot, liquid rock. They shift and move over the course of tens of thousands of years. We need to move one of these plates a little quicker than that. When it shifts, I hope to open a rupture beneath the Rift."

"Wait, do what?" asked Corinne.

Towaal looked at her stoically. "I'm going to try and make a bunch of extremely hot liquid come bursting up beneath the Rift."

"Oh," responded Corinne.

"But first, I must rest," said Towaal. "We need to create a small nudge and speed up something that was going to happen in a few years anyway, but still, I'm not sure I will be able to do this. I want to be as prepared as I can be." She started toward the hole going down into the butte then turned to Amelie. "I will need the disc you are carrying. The repository of power."

Amelie nodded and followed Towaal down into the mountain.

Rhys sighed. "One more day on this rock."

Ben nodded.

"Draw your sword," said Rhys, sliding out his own weapon and backing up to clear space. "Let's see what you can do with a mage-wrought blade."

That evening, Towaal reclined in the corner of the room and thumbed through the notebook she had taken off the writing table in the bedchamber. Earlier, she'd glanced at the books she'd collected by the chair. She left those for later and perused the notebook.

Puffing on his pipe and fiddling with the crystal decanter they'd found, Rhys asked her, "Find anything interesting?"

"Maybe," she replied. "I believe we were right. This room and the rooms below were created for the purpose of observing activity around the Rift. It could have been this Purple we heard about or someone else. The writing in here describes observations about the Rift. From what I gather, this log was started shortly after the Rift was created and continues for years, if not longer. It is short notes describing the Rift, but there are no dates and few points of reference. It seems to have been for personal use."

Rhys set the decanter down and meandered closer to look over her shoulder.

"What did they observe?" he asked.

"This section here," said Towaal, touching the page, "discusses demons staying clustered in the Rift valley. The author speaks about how they expected the demons to disperse once the food sources vanished—animals presumably—but they didn't. It speculates that the demons are getting sustenance from another source, possibly the Rift itself."

"How would that work?" asked Rhys.

"I'm not sure," admitted Towaal. "From what we saw in the far-seeing table, the Rift is by far the largest magical device I have ever heard of. Who knows what energies it bleeds off and what effect that might have on those near it. I'm not sure how something so large could remain powered for so long. There is a lot we don't know, but according to this writing, we are fortunate to not have tried entering the valley. The writer describes swarms of demons living within it."

Rhys frowned and puffed harder on his pipe. He wandered off, letting Towaal get back to reading the notebook.

~

IT STARTED SLOWLY. Towaal sat quietly again in the same place, looking north. The early morning sun kissed the peaks of the mountains in the distance and spread across the forest floor below.

The bitter cold of the night before faded with the coming of the sun, though the air still carried a painful chill. Ben kept his hands tucked within his cloak as they watched. What they watched for, he wasn't sure.

The repository, the wooden disc, was resting in Towaal's lap and she had one hand placed on it. Nothing happened visibly, but at one point, Amelie's eyes widened, and her breath caught. Ben assumed Towaal was starting to exert her will.

Below in the mountain, the far-seeing table was set on the Rift, but so far, there was nothing to see. They were milling about up top, waiting on Towaal. Beads of sweat formed on her forehead and froze in the cold air. She paid it no mind.

As Ben watched her, a smile played across her lips. He thought he heard something—a grating crack and boom from far off in the distance. It was muffled though, like something underground.

Rhys strode to the side of the butte, looking north. Minutes passed and nothing happened.

Finally, Towaal opened her eyes and declared, "I've done what I can."

Casually, she tossed the repository over the side of the butte. It had crumbled into pieces. "It's useless now."

Ben blinked and looked at the vista in front of them. He'd expected something more dramatic. As far as he could tell, nothing changed.

"Did you, ah, do anything?" he asked.

"Watch," said Towaal, pointing north.

Ben looked but saw nothing.

"Was that magic?" asked Corrine. "I thought it would be more exciting, like the lightning."

Towaal shrugged. "Sorry to disappoint. Sometimes exertion of will is obvious, sometimes it is subtle."

Another faint crack echoed across the open air.

"Something is happening," said Corinne. She stepped on top of a knee high rock and shaded her eyes to get a better look.

Suddenly, another boom shook the air and seconds later, the ground. Corinne stumbled off her rock. Ben caught her arm. She looked at him, frightened.

"There," shouted Amelie, pointing. A thin plume of smoke was rising into the sky.

Another boom and the butte shook again. Small rocks tumbled down the sides and the entire rock formation shuddered, causing them all to stumble.

"Is it safe up here?" worried Ben.

"It's safer than climbing down right now," asserted Rhys.

"Let's go look at the far-seeing table," suggested Towaal. "From there, we can see what is happening."

They all agreed. The smoke was rising into towering black plume. It had already tripled in size from just a minute before. Ben eyed it nervously as they all clustered around and climbed down into the hole.

Loud cracks and bangs filled the air as they descended into the butte. Stomach-turning shudders shook the structure. Ben tried to ignore them and moved into the dark of the rock.

In the chamber, the far-seeing table was lit up with a vision of the area surrounding the Rift. At first glance, nothing appeared to have changed. Then Ben saw a shadow in one corner of the table and pointed it out.

Towaal shifted the view and a third of a league away from the Rift, they found smoke pouring out of the trees. They watched as more and more smoke billowed up from an unseen source. Then a tree burst into flame and they all gasped. Ben involuntarily took a step backward. Tree after tree ignited like lantern wicks.

Now in addition to the smoke, steam from the snow-covered ground wafted into the air. Their view was obscured until a gust of wind whipped away the steam and smoke. They saw an orange red glow creeping across the ground.

"It's working," breathed Towaal.

"You weren't sure?" asked Corinne.

"The theory was sound," muttered Towaal, "but theory is just that—theory. I knew we didn't have another choice."

The perimeter of the steam was expanding rapidly. Towaal adjusted the view again, trying to circle the area. It was difficult to see what was happening underneath the cloud.

Finally, she gave up and shifted to the edge which was closest to the Rift.

"What's that?" asked Corinne, pointing to one section which hadn't yet been obscured. Between the trees, they could see motion.

Unable to bring the view closer, Towaal centered on the area Corinne had pointed out.

"Something is moving under the trees," she said.

"Demons," answered Rhys. "They're running from what you unleashed."

"But that can't be demons!" objected Corinne. "Look, the movement is almost constant. For that to be demons, there would have to be..." she trailed off. For it to be demons, there would have to be hundreds of them.

"Look at the Rift," suggested Ben. "It was clear of trees there. We should be able to get a better view."

Nodding, Towaal swiped her hands over the table and they were observing the Rift again.

Now, there was nothing they could see in the clearing except the stone circle.

Tension filled the room. Black shapes poured into the clearing and Corinne let out a hiss. The creatures streamed around the Rift like water bursting from a dam.

"We expected there were a lot of demons in that valley," said Ben anxiously.

"Yes, but…" Towaal didn't need to finish. As they watched, a constant flood of darkness swelled out of the forest and moved past the Rift into the trees on the other side. Hundreds then thousands. They kept coming.

They watched for half a bell until the smoke and steam started intruding on the view. Flickering light from burning trees peeked out between the swirls of smoke. Towaal moved her hands around rapidly, hovering from side to side. She was looking to see if the magma flow was making its way toward the Rift.

Finally, the last line of trees surrounding the Rift clearing burst into flame and the tail end of the black shapes vanished into the opposite tree line.

With less smoke from the burning trees, they could see the creeping line of magma flow into the clearing. All activity in the room stopped as they watched in silence. The bright orange and red wave of heat approached the Rift.

"Hopefully this works," mumbled Rhys.

Ben shot him a look to see if he was joking, but his friend kept his eyes on the far-seeing table.

Minutes passed before the slow-moving mass of liquid reached the base of stone. The magma, as Towaal called it, flowed around the structure like honey pouring into a pan. Ben leaned forward, looking for any visible change in the Rift.

"I don't think..." started Corinne.

Then they all jumped back from the table.

A brilliant blue web of lightning arced across the Rift. It was odd watching it, since no sound transferred through the far-seeing table. Ben imagined it sounded like a violent thunderstorm.

Silver-flecked smoke started to boil off the stone and the blue lightning became intense. They all watched as a subtle lean became more pronounced. The stone started to sink into the magma below it. Through the far-seeing table, the vision didn't seem real to Ben.

Lower and lower, the stones dropped. The silent lightning grew increasingly violent. Soon, Ben could no longer see the stone and only saw crackling blue energy surrounding it.

"What will happen when it gets completely melted?" wondered Ben.

Before anyone had time to answer, the far-seeing table cracked across the middle and flickered into blackness. The stone lights in the room exploded, showering them with hot shards of rock. A razor sharp spike of pain raced through Ben's body. His eyes watered with the sudden, unexpected blast of discomfort. Heartbeats later, a loud snap sounded through the butte and Ben stumbled back from the table to his knees.

He was frozen on the floor as excruciating waves of pain raced across his body. It radiated from his head and pounded through him in rapid pulses. Minutes or hours passed, he couldn't tell. The only thing that existed was the excruciating blanket of pain.

But finally, with each heartbeat, the pain slowly faded. He took a gasping breath and kept his forehead pressed against the stone floor, waiting for the agony to subside. When he was finally able to open his eyes, he saw Corinne was sitting next to him, gripping her head with both hands. She was lit by the meager fire left in the hearth. All of the other lights in the room had gone out.

Across from them, he saw Lady Towaal's boots and legs prone on the floor. He stumbled up and staggered around the table to find her lying on her back, eyes open staring sightlessly at the ceiling. A trickle of blood oozed out of her nose.

Amelie crawled over to the mage, wet streaks coursing down her cheeks.

"What happened?" croaked Ben.

"The spell around the Rift broke," mumbled Amelie, pain lacing her voice.

"Her senses must have still been extended," rumbled Rhys, shuffling over to tend to the mage.

"Is she okay?" worried Ben.

Rhys stared back at him.

Ben looked down at Lady Towaal's body. Her chest rose and fell with shallow breaths, but other than that, she was completely motionless.

"Never mind," mumbled Ben apologetically.

"Maybe with rest she'll be okay. Like before," suggested Corinne.

"We don't have time for that," remarked Rhys. "We need to leave. Now. Get your things."

"What?" exclaimed Ben.

"The demons," choked Amelie.

Rhys nodded. "We just saw what had to be thousands of demons fleeing that magma. Towaal thought they were in the valley because they somehow fed on the Rift. Their source of sustenance is gone now." Rhys paused. "Thousands of them. What do you think they'll do?"

"Oh, shit," Ben cringed.

Getting Towaal's unconscious body to the top of the butte proved easy, but once they got there, they had to pause. They didn't have rope and needed to scale down a wall that was twenty-man heights above the ground.

After a brief consideration, Rhys used his and Towaal's cloaks to rig a sling for her that he hung off his back. Ben was given Rhys' pack to carry down. He tried to think a way out of it, nervous about carrying both from such a height, but asking one of the girls to do it was too big a blow to his pride.

"You go first, Ben," suggested Rhys.

"Wait," interjected Corinne. "What about the magic armor and mace? I was promised a fortune by Rhymer when I get back, but that stuff is worth...I don't know how much it's worth," she said with her hands on her hips. "A lot of fortunes."

"You want to go down and get it, carry it up here to the top, then climb down this mountain holding it?" asked Rhys with one eyebrow raised. "Not to mention the three-week hike back to Northport carrying twenty stones of extra metal with a few thousand demons on your heels?"

Corinne frowned.

"You know where it is now. If we survive this," suggested Rhys, "you can come back at your leisure."

"You won't take it?" asked Corinne.

"All yours," assured Rhys. "Now, I personally do not want to be climbing down when a thousand-strong demon swarm gets here. I'm ready to go."

Ben swallowed a lump in his throat then made his way to the edge of the butte. He tried to ignore the towering plume of black smoke and the continuing booms, cracks, and shudders that echoed down from the north. The rock was just barely moving, he tried to tell himself.

He glanced down and immediately wished he hadn't. Both his and Rhys' packs weighed heavily against his back. He turned and scooted his boots to edge. He knelt down and started slowly working his way back.

Rhys looked at him and rolled his eyes. Amelie gave him an encouraging smile. Corinne ignored him, her eyes were locked on the still growing cloud of smoke.

One foot over, and his boot hung unsupported in the open air.

Shaking, he laid down on his stomach and scooted back further, testing with his foot to find the bumps and cracks he'd used on the climb up.

Amelie knelt beside him and looked over the precipice. "Move your right foot about a hand to the left," she suggested.

He did and sighed with relief when his foot was able to slip into a firm crack in the rock. Resting his weight on that foot, he slid the rest of his body off the top. He was hanging on the side of the cliff.

"Left foot straight down four hands," encouraged Amelie.

Slowly but surely, he descended toward the narrow seam they used to climb up. Amelie guided him on where to place his hands and feet the entire way.

He would have to take her dish-washing shifts he thought ruefully as he finally reached the relative safety of the icy seam. His body was shaking. His fingers were already numb from the cold and strain of gripping the rock.

Amelie started down after him and the rest followed. Ben kept edging his way down until he was a man-height above the loose snow-covered scree that reached half the height of the butte. There, his foot found a slick patch of ice. His boot slide across it and he lurched, trying to maintain his balance. Arms flailing, he felt himself leaning backward.

"Ben!" shouted Amelie, watching him helplessly get pulled away from the rock by the two heavy packs on his back.

Each heartbeat seemed to take a minute. His body left the rock, and he fell.

He landed almost instantly, cushioned by the packs and the waist-deep snow covering the slope.

Staring up at the others, lying in an upside down snow angel, he groaned in embarrassment.

"You're not hurt, are you?" called Amelie, just two man-heights above him.

"You look ridiculous," added Corinne from higher up.

Grumbling, he thrashed around in the snow while the others reached the bottom. He was trying to get his snowshoes on but he was already half buried from the fall. Flailing wildly, he was finally able to somersault back and get settled atop firmer snow where he could strap the bindings onto his feet.

Panting from the effort, he collected the packs and rose to see the rest of his companions with snowshoes already on, waiting for him.

"Right," he said. "Let's go."

Letting him keep the little remaining dignity he had left, they followed without comment.

After two days sitting inside the warm chamber in the mountain, the brutal cold of the Wilds hit hard.

They stumbled and slid down the loose snow and rock slope, several of them flopping over and having to be pulled out by their friends. By the time they reached the bottom, everyone had cold snow in uncomfortable places. Ben drew ragged breaths as they stepped onto the flatter area surrounding the butte. Walking in the snowshoes was easier than breaking a path through deep powder, but that didn't mean it was easy.

At the bottom, Rhys took charge. "Let's keep moving," he said. "The days are getting shorter. The more distance we make during the available light, the better."

They all agreed and started moving, heading toward the creek bed they followed on the way in. It wasn't perfect, and Ben was nervous about passing the site of the battle with the demon swarm, but it would be the quickest route back to Northport.

Slogging through the snow with both his and Rhys' pack on his back, Ben realized that despite the discomfort, they were exceptionally lucky. Had they walked into the valley as they originally intended, surely they would have been found and overwhelmed by the demon swarms. Instead, they were able to accomplish their quest and were on the way home.

"You know," he said to Amelie who was striding beside him, "This could have been worse."

She nodded in agreement. "It could have been much worse." She glanced back at Rhys who was following with Towaal still in the sling.

"When we get back to Northport, do you think Rhymer will help you and send troops to Issen?" asked Ben.

Amelie adjusted her pack, buying time before responding. "With what we saw in the far-seeing device, he can't leave Northport unprotected. Besides, it might already be too late. If the Coalition was just waiting on Lord Jason to arrive, then he's had plenty of time to get there now."

"What will we do then," Ben wondered, "if Rhymer can't help?"

Amelie smiled at Ben. "I'm glad you're not giving up. I don't want to either, but..." She sighed. "I really don't know what we can do next."

"We'll think of something," encouraged Ben.

Smiling at Amelie, he stumbled and nearly fell when a large clump of snow fell from above and landed directly on his head.

Corinne barked out a laugh.

Ben brushed the snow out of his hair and looked up at where it fell from. Descending right at him was a slender demon with wings spread wide.

"Demon!" he shouted.

In a smooth motion, he shrugged out of the two packs and reached for his longsword. His hand closed around the wire-wrapped hilt, and he swept it out, cutting above his head. He met the falling demon with his mage-wrought steel.

The blade cleaved through the demon like a hot knife cutting butter.

A spray of rank purple blood splashed onto the white snow. The demon's body crashed through the top layer and disappeared from sight.

Looking to where it fell, Ben saw several dark shapes racing through the trees.

Corinne saw them too. "More of them!" she called. She nocked an arrow on her bow.

"Form a circle, backs together," instructed Rhys.

All around them now, Ben could see dark shapes circling. How many were there? Ten? Fifteen?

"Amelie, look above us," shouted Rhys. "Corinne, shoot some of the damn things!"

An arrow sprung from her bow and a howl of pain followed.

"I can't get a good shot because of the trees," she snarled through gritted teeth.

"It doesn't matter," challenged Rhys. "Slow them down, or we're going to be neck deep in claws and teeth. They're waiting on something, let's not let them do that."

More arrows flew and most of them hit a mark. Ben couldn't tell if she felled any of the demons, but she caused enough damage that suddenly their tactics changed. From all directions, the creatures surged forward, charging at the companions.

Ben felt his friends around him, all focused outward on the oncoming attack. Rhys had his longsword out. Corinne scrambled to drop her bow and raise her two hand axes. Amelie held her rapier and dagger defiantly in front of her.

"Step high to avoid getting tripped up in the snow," advised Rhys. He dumped Towaal in the middle of the group.

Ben kicked his feet, knocking the accumulated snow off his flat snowshoes.

Sensing that this could be the end, he lost himself in a battle haze. Just like when he'd taken the charge of the first demon in Farview, his instincts took over. His mind forgot everything Saala and Rhys had taught him. Muscle memory from practice and repetition took over. Without thinking, he stepped forward, shielding Amelie and instructing her, "Watch my back."

Shining silver mage-wrought steel spinning in front of him,

Ben stepped carefully forward to meet the first wave of attackers. He lashed out at the incoming demons. Body parts and blood flew freely in the wake of his blade.

The first demon that came near him didn't have a chance. Ben simply stepped forward and lopped off its head, brushing aside its body as the momentum carried it into him.

The next wave came in a pair. They were two thick-armed squat demons. Ben shuffled to the side to throw off their charge, reminiscent of what he'd seen Saala do at Snowmar. The demons turned toward him but not quick enough to prevent him stabbing into the chest of one, using its body to block the other. He then slid out his sword and flicked it over the dead demon's body to cut across the eyes and into the brain of the second.

His blade cut cleanly through muscle and bone. He marveled at the ease he was able to use the light weapon with great effect.

Glancing back, he saw Corinne expertly dancing around one of the creatures. It was struggling after her, fouled by the deep snow. She hacked at it with her axes, chopping deep lacerations in its skin. While Ben watched, the demon left an opening. She darted in, burying one of the axes in its skull. The body joined one just like it at her feet.

Ben didn't bother looking toward Rhys, he knew his friend would hold his own. Amelie, though, was being pressed back by one of the thin ones. She was efficiently defending with her rapier and dagger, but couldn't get in a lethal counter attack.

Ben stepped up behind her opponent and thrust his sword deep into its back, the tip of the silver steel sliding out the creature's front.

"Thanks," breathed Amelie, then pointed over Ben's shoulder.

He turned and met the charge of a large, shoulder-height attacker. He ducked under a set of razor sharp claws that slashed toward his throat. Then he drew his blade along the thing's abdomen, spilling its tangled white guts onto the snow.

Seeing nothing in front of him, Ben turned to check on his

companions. Amelie was standing wild-eyed, looking around for more threats, but she seemed fine. Rhys was delicately picking his way out from a pile of dead creatures and body parts scattered and him. Corinne was wincing with a hand pressed against her side. Crimson blood leaked down her fur-lined leathers.

Ben hurried to her but she waved him off.

"Just a bad cut. I've had worse," she said. "I'll need to get stitched up eventually, but I can move."

"Move?" asked Ben, confused.

"There's an arch-demon out there somewhere," warned Rhys. "That must be what they were waiting for."

A piercing howl sliced through the air. Ben turned to see the arch-demon staking toward them. Wings tucked in behind its back, it still brushed against the trees as it came forward. The stark contrast of the white snow and the black nightmare approaching them was jarring.

Not as big as the one from the creek, saw Ben, but still half again as tall as a man. Not as big as a house wasn't very reassuring.

It howled again, enraged at what they'd done to its swarm.

"Where are...What is happening?" mumbled a confused voice.

Lady Towaal was weakly pushing against the thick cloaks that bound her in the sling.

"Don't worry," said Rhys. "We've got this."

He glanced at Ben and then down at Ben's new longsword. "Ready?"

Ben turned toward the arch-demon. It was twenty paces away but approaching rapidly. "Right behind you," he said nervously.

"I thought we'd trained you to be a hero," chided Rhys as he stepped forward.

Ben came beside him, on his weak-hand side.

"I'll go high. You go low," said Rhys.

"What do you mean high?" asked Ben.

Rhys was already charging forward, stepping high so his

snowshoed feet danced lightly across the top of the snow. The roaring arch-demon sped up to meet his attack. Its thick legs churned through the deep snow, slowing it down.

Ben groaned then followed his friend. He was stunned when Rhys leapt into the air, jumping higher than Ben would have thought possible.

The arch-demon reacted by swinging a powerful, claw tipped hand at Rhys. The rogue was ready and lashed out with foot, kicking the hand. The force of the blow sent him spinning into the snow.

It left the demon open for Ben, though. He came in right behind his friend and slashed a deep cut into the demon's thigh and a second, shallower laceration across its thickly muscled stomach.

Ben jumped back barely in time as the demon reacted. He felt a sharp breeze sweep by his face as long claws passed less than a finger length away from ripping his head off.

The demon attacked again, slowed by the injury to its leg. Ben scrambled backward, without a thought of counterattack, only survival.

Rhys came to his rescue, swooping in from behind and severing the hamstring on the demon's good leg. It crashed down in the snow and tried to swivel toward him. He scrambled backward, escaping safely.

Both legs wounded, the huge creature struggled toward Rhys on its knees.

Both of Corinne's hand axes flashed into Ben's view and smacked into the arch-demon. One sank deeply into the creature's ribcage and the other bounced off its horned head.

Roaring, the creature turned to see the new threat. Rhys took the opportunity. He surged forward and stabbed his longsword up through the beast's neck and into its skull.

Instantly, it stopped moving and toppled forward. Rhys

jumped free with his blade before the heavy body crashed down into the snow.

"That was close," said Corinne with a sigh of relief.

THAT EVENING, they stopped as soon as the sun began to set. It was early, but Corinne's injury was steadily leaking blood. Rhys insisted they tend to it. Lady Towaal had fallen back to sleep after briefly and wildly looking around.

Behind a large boulder, they found an area relatively clear of snow. Rhys brushed away what was there and Ben strung up the tarps for additional shelter. They both collected firewood. Ben allowed Amelie to tap him for heat to generate a fire. When she did it, he practiced hardening his will and shutting her off. She punched him in the shoulder harder than he thought was necessary.

After the fire was started, handfuls of snow were added to the tea kettle to melt and make water.

Amelie pulled out a needle and thread and gestured to Corinne to pull up her shirt and show her injury.

"Have you done this before?" Corinne asked Amelie skeptically. "I wouldn't think stitching people is something they teach at mage school."

"She did it for me," said Ben, defending his friend. He pulled down one sleeve of his leathers to show the scars he'd gotten climbing over the wall and getting cut by the glass shards.

"I remember those scars. Pretty nasty looking," remarked Corinne dryly.

"I didn't say she did it well," joked Ben.

"Shut up, both of you," instructed Amelie. "Someone's got to do it. So, it's me or one of those two."

Both girls looked at the men.

Rhys was standing by the tent, stealing a sip from one of his flasks. Ben was struggling to retie one of the tarp strings that had come loose. They both looked back at the girls, grinning.

Amelie continued, "I haven't had much reason to practice, but I was taught to sew by my nursemaid."

"Your nursemaid taught you to sew? Very well." Corinne sighed. "Do your worst, Amelie."

Amelie pushed up Corinne's leathers to reveal three hand-length cuts along her ribcage. They ran deep, nearly to the bone. Amelie whistled between her teeth and frowned at the amount of thread she had.

"That isn't a good look," cringed Corinne.

"This may take a while," murmured Amelie, placing a tender hand on Corinne's pale skin.

"Here," said Rhys, handing over his flask.

"What's in it?" asked Corinne.

"Don't worry. It will get the job done," assured the rogue.

"That's what I'm worried about," she snapped back, but she tilted it up and took a big swig anyway. She then splashed some down on her wounded side. She cringed as the alcohol poured over the open wounds.

Amelie went to work. After a few false starts and unnecessary pokes, she finished up some rough stitches in reasonably efficient order. She took out a rag and bathed Corinne's side to clean the wound. Gently, she wiped the blood away.

Corinne caught her hand and met her eyes. "Thank you," said the huntress. "I owe you."

"Hopefully, you don't need to do this for me," replied Amelie with a smile.

THEY TRAVELED QUICKLY after that and pushed themselves to the point of complete exhaustion. The risk of stumbling into a demon was real, but they knew what was behind them. They couldn't allow themselves to be caught by the swarm from the Rift valley.

Anytime they needed a reminder, they could look back and see the black tower of smoke still rising from where Towaal released the magma.

A soft layer of ash joined the snow, giving the world a sickly grey tinge. Ben wanted nothing more than a bath.

After two weeks of nothing but hiking and sleeping, he was mindlessly putting one foot in front of the other. The occasional demon broke the monotony, but luckily, it was individuals and not a swarm. Ben had no regard to which direction they were heading. He hoped Rhys or Corinne knew.

Towaal and Amelie were in worse shape than Ben. The night before, both the mage and the initiate slumped down in their bedrolls and were snoring before dinner was served. Rhys shook them awake and insisted they eat. If they didn't, they'd lose the remaining energy they had.

The only thing that kept them going was the haunting specter they'd seen in the far-seeing table. Thousands of demons fleeing the valley were now out in the Wilds. They would be looking for food. The only place that could sustain a swarm that size was Northport. They had to get there. They had to warn Rhymer.

That night, as Ben sat by the fire, he estimated that the next morning they would arrive in Free State. They weren't close enough to hear the chopping yet, but he could sense it was close. After Free State, it was a day and a half to Skarston. Pulling his cloak tightly around him, Ben watched the flames flicker lower.

The last time they'd passed through this area, it hadn't been so cold. A month had passed. A month since he'd had a hot bath or decent mug of ale. Free State wasn't exactly ideal, but the place did have roofs and beds. If they could find Perkins again, it had ale. He could use a tall one.

The next morning, blue sky filled the horizon above the trees and a brilliant yellow sun warmed their backs as they set out again. The air was cold, and the ankle-deep snow made hiking a bit more difficult, but compared to where they had been, it felt good. Ben breathed in deeply and felt the chill air fill his lungs.

Exhaling, he asked, "Should we stop in Free State?"

They would arrive midmorning, if what they recalled from the surrounding landscape was correct. A lot had happened since then.

"No," replied Towaal, shaking her head.

"We're almost at the point of collapse," argued Corinne tiredly. "And, not to be rude, but you are worse than the rest of us. You can barely keep your head up."

"We keep moving," stated Towaal. "If we stop, that will delay us another night to Skarston and another night to Northport. We can't afford any delays."

"Remember what's behind us," added Rhys.

Corinne grimaced but remained silent. She knew what was coming.

Stomping forward, Ben stole a glance at the mage. Dark bags hung below her eyes and her booted feet shuffled through the snow listlessly. The way she looked, he wasn't entirely sure she'd make it to Northport at this pace. She hadn't recovered from whatever happened when the Rift was destroyed. She needed rest.

"Will power," whispered Amelie, walking next to Ben.

He looked at her questioningly.

"It's good for more than casting spells," explained Amelie. "Lady Towaal has spent decades, maybe centuries for all I know, refining her will power. I know what you're thinking, that she looks like she could collapse dead any minute. That's the thing, she will keep going until she gets to Northport, or she does collapse dead. She's determined we get there and she won't bend."

"That's crazy," grumbled Ben.

"It's a good lesson," remarked Amelie. "One we should keep in mind."

"What do you mean?" he asked.

"The Sanctuary is filled with people like Lady Towaal," answered Amelie. "People who are determined. I've been thinking about that as we've gotten closer to what we think is safety."

Ben frowned.

Amelie continued, "The Sanctuary isn't going to give up on us. The war between the Alliance and the Coalition is just getting started. We still know that the Sanctuary betrayed the Alliance, we still killed their people. They won't let us live our lives unmolested. They are going to come for us, Ben."

"It's been months," he argued. "If they haven't found us yet, it's because they don't know where to look. In Northport, just Rhymer, Franklin, and the Librarian really know who we are, and they aren't going to talk. The Sanctuary is publicly telling people you are dead. If that is out there, they can't keep hunters and soldiers looking for us. I'm not saying we're in the clear, but I think we're kind of in the clear. As long as we stay smart."

She looked ahead into the trees. "Maybe. Maybe the soldiers won't be guarding the roads, maybe the hunters won't be scouring the woods, but the mages are whom I am worried about. If Lady Towaal was looking for us..." Amelie gestured to the mage who was marching ahead of them. "Would she ever stop?"

"You're right," replied Ben ruefully. "We may always need to be careful, but we still have the advantage that they don't know where to find us."

"Mistress Eldred might be able to find us," remarked Amelie. "Remember the blood magic? If she can feel some affinity for us, she could track us down."

Walking through the woods, Ben felt sickening discomfort thinking about Eldred. The rest of the flight from the Sanctuary was a blur now, but he distinctly recalled the moment when Amelie smashed the glass on the mage's face. Her terrible scream, the awful visage of her skin melting away…that was burned into his memory forever.

He wondered if it had killed her. They asked Towaal earlier, but she didn't know.

The Sanctuary had the best healers in Alcott. If Eldred hadn't died immediately, it's likely someone could have saved her. If they did save her, Amelie was right, the woman would never stop hunting them.

Nothing they could do about that now but keep going.

Ben ducked under a low-hanging branch and pushed it up for Amelie to duck under as well. As he did, he realized there was another source for his discomfort. By now, they should be close to Free State. They heard none of the chopping and other sounds from their first visit.

"Rhys," he called.

His friend was walking at the front of the group and looked back.

"I don't hear anything," remarked Ben. "No chopping, no blacksmith, nothing."

Rhys nodded. "You're learning."

"What does that mean?"

"It means we need to proceed with caution," answered Rhys. "It means the discussion about stopping in Free State might be moot."

"You think they were overrun?" interjected Corinne.

Rhys shrugged. "It's possible. Only one way to know for sure."

They adjusted weapons and tried to shake off their weariness. The closer they got without hearing anything, the more obvious it became something was wrong.

Two bells later, none of them were surprised when they entered the clearing around Free State and saw broad sections of the log palisade torn down. Bodies were scattered near the openings where the townspeople must have rushed to defend the breaches. Thankfully, they were far enough away to be spared the gory details.

In the field before the broken wall, a few dark lumps marked demons that had been felled by arrows from the town. The silence spoke to the number who got inside successfully.

"Do we investigate?" Rhys asked Towaal.

"No," she responded remorsefully. "No one is alive in there. We keep going."

Ben looked back as they passed the freshly built town and felt a tinge of regret they didn't do more to warn the inhabitants. Peckins and Mistress Albie were kind people.

He understood their desire to get away. The Alliance, the Coalition, and the Sanctuary...none of it made sense to him. The leaders had no interest in the wellbeing of the people, so the people left. Unfortunately for these folk, they picked the wrong place to start over.

A DAY AND A HALF LATER, as the sun was sinking beneath the skeletal branches of the birch trees, they approached Skarston. Free State was overrun, all of its occupants dead. The same swarm could have moved further to the larger town of Skarston. Bigger walls, watchtowers, and professional armed soldiers would all make a difference, but would it be enough?

The wind changed direction, and minutes later, they got their first clue. An acrid, greasy smell floated toward them.

"Burning demons," muttered Corinne.

"Someone must be alive to burn them," said Rhys hopefully. They all knew a swarm big enough to overrun Free State would inflict serious damage in Skarston. A swarm like that couldn't be defended against bloodlessly.

With twilight falling on the forest, they finally saw the flickering fires of the burning demon pile. Thick, black smoke billowed up into the night air. Ben coughed as the wind moved a noxious whiff of the stuff in their direction.

On the walls of the town, braziers burned. By the flickering light, they saw men moving around.

Closer though, they were able to pick out other details, like where the stone wall had been pulled down in one section and the heavy gates left open and hanging at an odd angle.

Corinne started walking faster, obviously eager to see what happened inside. She'd grown up in Skarston and still had friends living behind those walls. The rest of them kept pace.

At the broken gate, a weary soldier rose to greet them. He was standing atop a tipped over wagon, which blocked the entrance.

"Ho travelers!" he called.

"Ho Skarston," replied Corinne, still fifty strides from the gate.

He spoke to someone inside then turned to face them again, holding a crossbow. "State your business before you get too close."

"Hunters returning from the Wilds," replied Corinne with a snarl. "Since when do I need to explain my business to you before entering my hometown?"

"Corinne?" asked the guard. "Is that you?"

Drawing closer, the huntress responded, "We grew up three blocks away from each other, Efrain. You don't recognize me?"

The soldier clambered down from the wagon and strode forward to greet them. Behind him, two more faces appeared from behind the barrier. The man embraced her, crushing her against the hard steel of his chainmail.

"Oof, careful, Efrain," she complained.

"Sorry," he choked. "We've lost so many. I...It's good to see you."

"What happened?" asked Rhys quietly.

The guard turned to him. "A swarm like I've never seen before. No one has. Last I heard, we counted forty seven of the bastards. All corpses now, but they took a toll. Come on." The guard waved for them to follow and he started back toward the gate.

"We'll have to climb over," he said apologetically, looking at the women. "We weren't prepared for anyone to come in from the north, so we didn't leave a way in."

"We can manage," responded Corinne. She then looked at Ben and smirked. "You're okay with that, right?"

Ben rolled his eyes and, looking at the chest high wagon, remarked, "I think I can handle it."

They scrambled over the wagon, following Efrain into Skarston. Ben's breath caught when he reached the top of the wagon and he got his first look inside the town.

Damage and destruction littered the streets. Grim streaks of dark reddish brown led from several of the nearby buildings.

"Sorry," mumbled Efrain when he saw their faces. "We started cleaning up, but, well, people didn't see much point in it."

"What do you mean?" asked Corinne.

"Evacuation," declared another man who had just arrived. He wore a badge of rank hanging from around his neck, but it was his air of quiet authority that gave him away as a leader.

"Captain Ander," said Corinne.

He nodded to her and growled, "Glad you're alive. We can use your skills more than ever back in Northport. We're falling back to there," he declared.

"Makes sense," nodded Rhys.

Ander glanced at him then continued talking to Corinne. "Now, little lady, I'd like to hear what you were doing out there and what you saw."

She looked to Towaal, who quietly advised, "We tell Rhymer and Franklin. No one else."

Ander set his hands on his hips and prepared to argue, but Corinne silenced him with a look. "You know me, Captain. You know who my father is. We are headed straight to Lord Rhymer. We'll rest here tonight. We leave at first light for Northport."

Mouth opening to respond, Ander was cut off by Lady Towaal. "Captain, retreating is the right decision. One thing we can tell you is to not waste time. Demons are coming, Captain. Many, many more than you faced here. As Corinne said, we leave at first light. I recommend you and everyone else still breathing in this town comes right behind us. You won't survive the next wave."

She then pushed past the captain and shuffled down the battle-scarred and bloodstained street.

"I..." started the captain, but the rest of the companions followed Towaal, too tired to discuss it further with the man.

The inn they stayed in last time was abandoned, but the beds and a few items in the larder remained. They helped themselves and quickly retired. After over a month in the Wilds, they could taste the comforts offered in Northport.

14

PREPARE FOR THE WORST

THE TRIP from Skarston to Northport went by in a blur. Exhausted, they were determined to finish the journey with no more delays.

They passed the town of Kapinpak but didn't stop. The gates of the small town were shut tight. Ben didn't see any people. He hoped they fled.

When they finally arrived outside of Northport, he was glad to see the gates of the walled city remained open. As they drew closer, he felt the sense of grim realization that had settled over the place since the last time they were there.

Northport was getting ready. The people in the streets were armed to the teeth. Every man, woman, and child had some weapon on their body. Most were utilitarian swords, but some of the poor residents had meat cleavers, wood axes, and other repurposed tools.

The first wave of survivors arriving from Skarston was the last sign people needed that this was more than just a temporary swell in the demon population. Everyone in Northport was now convinced that the threat was serious.

As they drew near the center of the city, they saw the wide-open square in front of Lord Rhymer's keep was decorated with a variety of colorful numbered flags.

Ben frowned at them, unsure what the significance was.

Rhys cursed under his breath.

"What?" asked Ben.

"They'll use those flags for marshalling Rhymer's army," responded Rhys. "Each flag represents a company. He's planning to march."

"March where?" queried Ben.

"Does it matter?" answered Rhys. "His men are needed behind these walls protecting his people."

They walked straight up to the front gate of the keep, not bothering with the complicated deception they used to gain entry last time. On this visit, they let Corinne lead the way. As a hunter, she had a pretext for entering the keep. The guards waved her through as soon as they saw her.

Once inside, they moved again to the big audience chamber still filled with costumed and perfumed courtiers. It was the one place that wasn't on a war footing. Many of the people inside seemed completely oblivious to what was happening outside in the city. The wheels of bureaucracy rolled on.

Catching one harried-looking page by the arm, Corinne demanded, "Where is Seneschal Franklin?"

The page eyed Corinne's dirty, unkempt look and scoffed, "I don't think the seneschal has time for you. Maybe you should try the baths first."

Corinne's small fist pounded into the page's stomach. Doubled over wheezing for breath, he collapsed to the floor. Gasps of disbelief echoed around them and a space cleared around the companions.

"My way was subtler," muttered Rhys under his breath.

Ben glanced at him.

"Sort of subtler," admitted Rhys.

Waiting for the page to recover, Corinne stood above him. She looked up when several guards appeared.

"What is the meaning of this?" demanded a guard, looking over Ben and his companions.

The coughs and squirms of the page were ignored.

Corinne stared back at the guards with one eyebrow raised. "We need to see Seneschal Franklin, immediately, and alert Rhymer that I have returned."

"Oh," said the man, meeting the Corinne's gaze and ignoring the page. The guard turned on one heel and waved them to follow. "This way, Lady Corinne."

"Lady?" grumbled Amelie.

Corinne glanced at her. "You didn't tell me you were an initiate, and I didn't tell you that I had, ah, esteemed patronage. Now we both know everything."

"Almost everything," Ben corrected.

Both ladies looked back at him and he winced. He was saved from explaining, though, as they quickly reached a small, wood-paneled room where Seneschal Franklin sat, pouring over a ledger filled with neat handwriting.

He rose and nodded to them with a relieved look. "You made it back."

"Most of us," murmured Corinne softly.

To the guard, Franklin instructed, "Please ask Rhymer to come see me. Tell him it's urgent."

"And bring ale. Plenty of cold ale," added Rhys.

The guard looked at Rhys askance, but Franklin conceded. "Go ahead and get him the ale, after you've spoken to Rhymer."

Shortly, they were ensconced in a small private dining room with the seneschal, Lord Rhymer, two of Rhymer's generals, and the watch commander.

Franklin had already quizzed them on the success of their mission and he succinctly relayed the news to Rhymer and his men. The generals and watch commander looked skeptical, but the trust the seneschal and Rhymer had in Ben and his companion's story prevented them from speaking up.

At least until Franklin reached the part about the huge demon swarm they saw in the valley. One of the gruff men couldn't contain his disbelief anymore and objected.

"Hold on now," barked the general. "You're expecting me to believe this fairy tale? Some ancient Rift we've never heard about, magic powers, volcanoes? I don't buy it," he declared, staring down the company.

"General," rebutted Franklin, "I'm sure you have heard rumors about the Rift. It wasn't common knowledge, but I can't believe someone in your position hasn't heard rumblings. Don't be naïve."

The man snorted and sat back. "I don't believe this and don't know what it changes. So what if they saw a big demon swarm? We knew it was out there. Doesn't change a damn thing about what we need to do."

Rhys interrupted brusquely. "General, if your plan is to go out and meet the demons, you'll get annihilated."

"What do you know, hunter?" snarled the general.

"I know a lot more than you think," responded Rhys coolly. "There are thousands of demons and they are likely coming this way!"

"There's nothing in the histories about a swarm that big," challenged the second general. "If a swarm that big is even possible, then surely there would be some record of it happening before. There isn't even a mention of a swarm one hundred strong, from what I understand."

"I didn't write the histories," retorted Rhys. "I can only tell you what we saw."

"Well, I can only tell you that you're full of shit!" shouted the first general.

Rhymer pounded his fist on the table and stood up. "Enough of this," he barked. Looking between Rhys, Towaal, and Corinne, he asked, "You are absolutely certain of this, that you saw over one thousand demons?"

"We didn't stop and count them," grumbled Rhys.

"Yes, we saw them," declared Corinne. "I personally witnessed it. I assure you there are over one thousand of them. I believe it could be a great deal more."

"If Corinne says she saw it, then she saw it. I propose we treat this as the fact it is and move on," remarked Franklin. The old man glared at the generals, challenging them to respond.

Ben recalled that Corinne was specifically chosen for this mission and that the guards had called her a lady. What else was there?

The generals, not quite mollified, sat back and held their objections. Franklin's, and apparently Corinne's, opinion carried a lot of weight with Lord Rhymer. The generals were fighting men first, but their tactical instinct worked on the battlefield or in the lord's keep. They knew when to retreat.

"So, now that we have that settled," said Rhymer, "what does that mean for our plans?"

"If," the first general leaned forward and looked around the group, "we assume that this, ah, historically sized demon swarm is coming, then we should adjust."

The second general nodded. "We cannot meet a force like that in the open. The hunter is right, that many would defeat us in the field. The protection of our walls is worth keeping...but if we stay behind the walls, you must know one thing." He paused. "We will be sacrificing the countryside. Our original plan to march out and meet the demons is based on the premise that we are unwilling to give up the towns around us. We cannot stay within the walls and protect people outside of them. One thousand demons in the swarm or one hundred, anyone who is outside of these walls and does not flee will die. I know you say it's settled, but..." The man shifted uncomfortably in his chair. "Despite your warnings, some of the outlying towns have not evacuated. We will lose all of those people. Thousands will be slaughtered if we do not venture out."

Rhymer looked unsure but Corinne spoke up. "It's not a choice, sir. I'm not sure you have the men to defeat what we saw in any situation. If you fight without the protection of the walls, Northport is already fallen."

Following the meeting, Rhymer and his generals closed the doors and began to work on a plan to protect Northport. Franklin started sending messages to all of the surrounding towns again and urging retreat.

Ben and his companions, for the first time in over a month, had nothing productive to do. Exhausted, they washed up and retired to an early dinner of a hearty mutton shank and ale.

Poking at the potatoes and carrots on his plate, Ben glanced at his friends. They were all a bit worse for wear, but they were also all alive. Unbelievable almost, that only Grunt fell in the Wilds.

Seeming to read his thoughts, Rhys advised, "Sometimes it's best to acknowledge you were lucky and move on. However it happened, we lived to fight another day."

"We were lucky, weren't we," replied Ben morosely. "One more encounter, one more demon in the swarm, there are a lot of ways we could have failed."

"What's wrong with being lucky?" asked Rhys.

Ben pushed his potatoes around some more. "I've learned a lot in the last year. I was able to hold my own against some of those demons, but it isn't enough. One of those arch-demons could have taken me down easily if I didn't have you with me. If training with a blademaster like Saala, and with you, if that's not enough, then what is?"

"All success has a little luck to it," responded Rhys. "You have to accept that. No matter how good you are, any fight can go more than one way. A blademaster can lose to a farm boy if he's unlucky. Doesn't matter how long he spent training."

"So, we should just trust in luck?" Ben retorted.

"You know better than that," drawled Rhys. "It is a mix. Luck plays a role, certainly, but so does preparation and skill. Think about it this way. Maybe you don't have the skill to face an arch-demon on your own, but if you hadn't been training, any one of those demons you cut down could have killed you. Back in Farview, that's what almost happened before we arrived, right? Instead, this time, you killed them. That's your preparation and skill. The luck is that you didn't have to face more than you could handle."

Ben sighed and sipped his ale.

"Every living swordsman is lucky," added Rhys. "Think about it. Somewhere, there is one person who is the best in the world. All the rest of us are just lucky we haven't had to face him."

"Or her," interjected Amelie.

"Or her," coughed Rhys, covering his mouth with one hand.

"Are you saying it's better to be lucky than good?" asked Ben.

"No," said Rhys, shaking his head. "I'm saying it's better to be both."

The preparations to fortify Northport began the next morning. Everything they had seen previously was a fall back option with the intent that the army would meet and defeat the demons in the field. Now, they knew the battlefield would be on the city walls.

Ben nearly slept through it. The scent of a warm breakfast and fresh kaf drew him out of his slumber, though.

In the common room outside his sleeping chamber, he emerged to find Rhys and Amelie clustered around a set of trays.

Rhys turned with a piece of bacon hanging from his mouth, a mug of kaf in one hand and a freshly baked biscuit in the other. "Come gef fome fekfst," he mumbled around the bacon.

Ben saw the trays were piled with fresh food. He dug in. The day before, they ate what was available in the kitchen in the middle of the afternoon. It was better than camp food, but day-old mutton had nothing on a hot, fresh breakfast.

Ben devoured the bacon, eggs, biscuits, and jam. None of his companions paused to speak. After over a month in the Wilds, food was their one and only concern.

Finally, feeling stuffed to the point of explosion, Ben sat back and sipped on his half mug of cooling kaf.

"We've got to talk about it," Ben said.

"What's that?" asked Rhys.

"What to do next," replied Amelie on behalf of Ben.

Ben nodded. "Exactly. Do we stay, or do we find help elsewhere for Issen? Try Whitehall maybe?" Ben leaned forward in his chair. "This isn't over."

Rhys took another bite of bacon and chewed slowly. Ben and Amelie were both waiting for his leadership.

"That's up to you two," he finally responded.

"Us?" they both asked at the same time.

"Towaal and I are here for the same reason," Rhys responded. "We came because you did."

"Me too," said Ben. He turned to Amelie. "I came to help you and Issen. I still want to do that."

She sighed. "I'm not sure we can help Issen now."

Ben frowned at her.

Amelie continued, "Whatever we do next, we should consider that Issen may be beyond our reach."

Rhys nodded. "I think we can all agree there is no chance Rhymer will release forces to support your father, at least until after he's dealt with the demons. After that, we can only hope he still has men remaining."

"Just because we can't help Issen right now," Amelie replied, "does not mean we can't help anyone. There are other people who could use our assistance."

"You mean, stay and fight?" inquired Ben.

"Yes," murmured Amelie. "I think they'll need all of the swords they can get. But...I can't ask any of you to stay with me. This isn't my fight, but I am willing to be a part of it. It's not yours, either. There's no reason for you to stay if you don't want to."

"No, Amelie," said Ben, "I am with you. I can't turn my back on this. Maybe I can make a big difference, or maybe a little one. They will have my sword on the wall. Whatever happens."

"What about you?" Amelie asked Rhys, who was silently observing them.

"If you both stay, then Towaal and I will stay with you," he said. "Northport will have my sword and her magic."

"I appreciate that," responded Amelie. She sat up straight. "Do you think we should talk to Towaal before you commit for her? Staying and fighting is going to be dangerous. It will be a battle like none other."

Rhys snorted. "You don't think Towaal knows what is dangerous and what is not? Girl, she's seen things you would not believe and she's survived more battles than you've even heard about."

Amelie sat back and crossed her arms, frowning at Rhys.

"Sorry I called you girl." He sighed, reaching to refill his kaf mug. "I'm just saying she knows what she's getting into."

"She's sleeping!" objected Ben.

Rhys chuckled. "That's true. I mean she knows that following you two will be dangerous."

"Following us. What do you mean?" asked Ben.

Rhys grumbled, "Towaal and I decided to hitch our wagon to your horse, so to speak."

Ben and Amelie both looked at the rogue, waiting for more.

"I wish she was here to explain this," he mumbled, shifting uncomfortably in his seat. "Over the years, we've both done things—some bad, some good, some bad in the pursuit of trying to do good. We gained skill, gained power, and when I wasn't drinking it all, I gained a decent pile of gold. But so what? We didn't change anything. The world keeps going on like it always has, and there's nothing I can point to in my life and tell you it made me proud."

Ben sipped his kaf and watched his friend. He didn't think he'd ever seen Rhys so uncomfortable. It was kind of funny.

"It's been a long time coming," continued Rhys. "Towaal and I have been working together for years now. We've both realized that in all of our years, and there have been a lot of them, that we haven't done much good, certainly not enough to outweigh the bad."

Amelie looked at Ben, clearly not understanding where Rhys was going. Ben shrugged and waited for his friend to finish.

Rhys, seeing the look, sucked on his teeth. "I'm saying this all wrong." He placed both hands flat on the table and met Amelie then Ben's eyes. "Towaal and I will follow you, whatever you decide to do. You're familiar with this process, Amelie, but, Ben, maybe not. We're swearing fealty to you two."

Amelie gasped and Ben's jaw fell open.

Rhys sat back, seemingly satisfied that his message was conveyed.

"What are you talking about?" exclaimed Amelie.

At the same time Ben asked, "What does fealty mean?"

Rhys frowned. "Maybe I said that wrong." Scratching one ear, he added, "Karina and I talked, a lot, on the way to find you. We talked about how we've been trying to do the right thing in the last couple years, but we've failed. We've failed a lot. You can see what's happening with the Alliance, Coalition, and Sanctuary. What have we done about it? We realized that maybe there is a better way. We can be a resource for someone who knows how to use our skills, someone who is going to try to do the right thing, for you two."

"I'm just a brewer!" shouted Ben.

Rhys shook his head. "If you were just a brewer, you'd be back in Farview now, brewing. You're a warrior, Ben, a warrior for what you believe in."

"He's right about that," conceded Amelie. "Since we left Farview, you haven't had to do any of this. You've been with me, with us, because you wanted to. Because you saw a problem you could help fix and because you thought it was the right thing to do."

Ben sat back, unsure of what to say.

They all turned when Towaal's bedroom door opened. The mage walked slowly into the common room. The bags under her eyes had receded, but she still looked worse for wear.

"What are you talking about? I heard shouting," she asked.

"Rhys said you were pledging fealty to us," replied Amelie flatly.

Towaal looked at Rhys. "I'm not sure I'd put it exactly like that..." she mumbled. "But we will follow your lead. This world needs people like you, leaders like you. We will go wherever you take us."

"They're going to stay and fight the demons," remarked Rhys.

"That's a good start." Towaal nodded. She then sat down and started devouring breakfast.

Ben and Amelie met each other's eyes. They had a lot to talk about.

The rest of the day, the group recovered from their travels. Towaal went back to sleep after breakfast. Rhys suggested they practice the Ohms. They hadn't been able to do it in the snow, so Ben felt a little rusty. Once they got into it, he quickly fell into the rhythm of the movements. Amelie didn't know as much of the series as Ben, so she did what she could. Then she sat back and watched while Ben and Rhys continued.

By the end, Ben felt centered and relaxed. Well, as relaxed as someone could be, knowing an army of demons was descending upon them.

"Shall we go look at the fortifications?" suggested Rhys.

"Sure," replied Ben. Despite all of the time he'd spent with the guards in Whitehall, Ben had never actually been on a battlement. He was curious to find out what was up there.

They all strapped on their weapons and left to explore.

"Will we be assigned a post?" inquired Amelie. "I've never been in a battle before."

Rhys shook his head. "We're not assigned to a company, so no one is going to come looking for us. The military the world over is organized in rigid bureaucracies. If we aren't on someone's list, we won't be assigned."

"Where do we go to fight then?" asked Ben.

"Wherever we are needed," responded Rhys. "We can check with some of the hunters in the city and see what they are doing. They are likely serving in a flying squad or something similar. We might also see something we can help with when we are on the walls. Where the fighting is the hottest, that's where we want to be."

"Where it's hottest?" asked Amelie, nervously fingering the hilt of her rapier.

"You wanted to fight in defense of Northport, right?" Rhys grinned.

They were nearing the tall outer walls of Northport and Ben saw a familiar mop of red hair bobbing ahead.

"Corinne!" he called.

The huntress turned and waved to them. Just like on the quest to the Rift, she was dressed in tight-fitting leathers and had her bow and axes strapped on.

She was walking with Seneschal Franklin.

"Hello," said the elderly courtier as they approached. "I heard you are intending to stay and fight with us. I am glad. Your swords are each worth a couple dozen of our soldiers if what Corinne tells me is true."

"I'm not sure about that," muttered Amelie under her breath.

"We're going to look at the battlement," added Ben.

"That's where we are headed," said Corinne. "Come with us."

She turned and they started down the street again. "Have you been assigned a company?"

"No," replied Ben. "We were just talking about that. Where will you be fighting?"

Franklin snorted.

Corinne shot him a look. "We were just talking about that too."

Ben raised an eyebrow.

"My da wants me to stay behind and help protect the keep," she continued. "Like we will have anything left to fight for if the demons reach there."

"Your da?" asked Ben.

"Remember? I told you about him when we first met," reminded Corinne. "I told you he used to be a good shot with a bow, back in his day."

"Still is a good shot," grumbled Franklin.

"You're her father!" exclaimed Amelie.

The elderly seneschal shrugged. "That's what her mom tells me."

Corinne gently shoved her father's shoulder. "He doesn't like to take ownership of me. He thinks I'm too wild. Instead of hunting demons, he wants me to settle down and have a hundred grandbabies for him to play with."

Franklin shook his head. "She exaggerates," he complained. "Every father has a right to be protective of his daughter."

"There is protective, and there is over-protective," challenged Corinne. "I have skills that will be useful in the fight ahead. You can't always keep me away from danger, Da."

"He sent you with us, didn't he?" asked Ben.

Corinne looked at her father. "You're right. He did do that."

"You should only fight when you need to," remarked Franklin. "And I'll be the first to admit, she does know how to do it, but I want her to fight for something worthwhile, instead of just fighting!"

They walked on toward the wall.

Franklin added with a sly twinkle in his eye, "Also, her mom keeps pestering me to find a suitable husband so she can start on those grandbabies."

Corinne stumbled and coughed. The rest of the group chuckled.

For a seneschal to a powerful lord, Franklin sounded just like any father.

"Here we are," said Rhys, bringing them all back to business.

They stood near the base of the outer wall. Ben looked up to see a steep stone staircase crawling to the top.

"I'm touring the defenses for a report to Lord Rhymer," said Franklin. "You are all welcome to come with me. Maybe along the way we can find a good spot for you."

Atop the wall, they found a wide walkway populated with a throng of soldiers scurrying about preparing for war. Spears and quivers full of arrows were being set at regular intervals. Rocks, massive bolts, and heavy iron balls were placed conveniently for catapults and trebuchets. Kettles of thick black liquid were stored far away from braziers of hot coals.

Outside of the wall, brightly covered stakes were placed in the ground to help archers gauge distance. Workers were digging holes and pounding in forests of freshly sharpened stakes. Other men were digging trenches and filling them with water. Ben realized they were doing anything they could to slow the charge of the demons. Unlike traditional war, none of this would scare the creatures off, but any delay in the attack would give the ranged weapons more time to thin out the horde.

Behind the wall, the first blocks of buildings were evacuated then boarded up. Temporary watch towers had been erected on the roofs. Ben could see they would be used as archery platforms. Narrow walkways were placed between some of the rooftops where men could retreat if the walls fell. The sound of hammering filled the air as men scrambled across the hastily erected structures, making last-minute adjustments and extending the fortifications deeper into the city.

On the streets below, wagons, barrels, furniture, and other heavy debris were cobbled together to block off avenues. They would funnel the demons into dead ends where men from above could rain death down on them.

It was all cleverly designed to create confusion in the simple creatures and lead them into situations where men wouldn't have to engage hand to hand.

Ben saw hunters with tightly packed groups of soldiers clustered around them. Discussing tactics, he surmised.

"Demons are common in the Wilds," explained Franklin, "but most of our soldiers serve around Northport or to the south. Some have faced demons, some have not. We asked the hunters to give them any insight they can." He shrugged. "You folks know, fighting a demon isn't like fighting a man."

As they walked, Franklin started to fidget nervously. They began looking at him strangely. Finally, he asked, "Will Lady Towaal fight with us? We heard she has been ill since you returned."

"Our quest took a lot out of her," acknowledged Rhys. "She is resting now and has no intention of leaving before the attack. Honestly, I am not sure what she will be capable of in the next few days, if anything. If she is able, she will assist."

Franklin nodded, not entirely pleased with the answer, but obviously glad to have it in the open.

Every two hundred paces, they passed an open platform holding artillery. A heavy guard stood around each of the massive weapons and a bristle of polearms leaned against the battlement, making them look like wild hedgehogs.

Amelie peered closely at baskets of ammunition set behind the artillery.

"Expecting intense fighting around these?" asked Rhys, gesturing to a looming catapult.

"A human opponent would focus on these weapons as soon as they got close," answered Franklin, "but a typical demon isn't tactically minded. We are not sure they will understand the significance of the artillery."

"I think we should assume they will," advised Rhys. "The swarms we faced had limited tactical knowledge, but it was more than I have ever witnessed. If there is an arch-demon mature enough to lead thousands of its brethren, it's likely to be very intelligent. Plan for the worst."

Franklin nodded. "Based on your report of the ambush, we've tried to account for more than just animal instincts. If they are smart enough and a large enough number…" The seneschal left the rest unsaid. They all knew that if the demons displayed the intelligence of a human commander, Northport might not win the battle.

Near the end of the tour, Rhys turned to Ben and Amelie. "I think we have two choices. We could join a flying company and respond to whatever threat is most urgent, or we could protect one of these artillery weapons."

Amelie responded, "Let's protect the artillery." Quietly she added, "I have some things I want to try. It will require a great deal of concentration and I want to be stationary."

Ben nodded. "That sounds good to me."

"All right then," replied Rhys, clapping his hands together. "We'll figure out which one is closest then wait for the bells to ring."

15

A RINGING BELL

BEN WAS NERVOUS. Two days after the tour of the wall, the preparations around Northport continued with no sign of the demons. That morning though, he learned there was also no sign of Captain Ander or the remaining soldiers from Skarston. The assumption was they didn't make it out in time.

"Do you think they will really attack in one large swarm?" asked Ben.

He was doing some light sword practice with Amelie. He wanted to spend more time adjusting to the weight and feel of his mage-wrought blade, and she could use all the practice she could get with her two blades. They kept the exertion minimal to not wear themselves down. It was more about staying sharp than developing anything new.

"I don't know," she answered, breathing heavily. "Each swarm we faced in the Wilds had an arch-demon, but the one at Snowmar didn't. I don't know what that means. Is it even possible for that many demons to work together?"

"I don't think they have before," answered Ben. "But who knows."

"Maybe Towaal will find something out," responded Amelie.

"Maybe," replied Ben doubtfully.

Days earlier, Towaal had ensconced herself in the library. They heard she was making the Librarian's life a hell. Supposedly, Lord Rhymer himself had to go down and instruct the man to continue assisting her. The Librarian had been outraged when they returned from the Wilds and related their story. When Towaal demanded more access to his stacks, he became apoplectic. He was rather fussy when it came to his books and seemed to take it personally they had destroyed the Rift without consulting him further.

"Has Rhys said anything?" inquired Amelie. "He's rather old, isn't he? And he lived in Northport for a time. I would think that he knows something. Anything could help."

Ben shrugged. "He's been closed in with Corinne. I'm not sure if they're discussing battle plans or, uh, something else...but he hasn't told me anything. I get the impression when he lived here, he spent most of his time carousing."

"Well, that doesn't surprise me," muttered Amelie.

The sun fell behind the walls of Rhymer's keep. The courtyard they were practicing in fell under a shroud of twilight. The keep was built of dark stone. As soon as the sun vanished, it turned into a rather creepy, gloomy place. Ben thought that if he lived there too long, he'd grow depressed. Maybe that was why Rhymer was such a lush. The thought of being home and sober was too much to take.

"Deep thoughts?" asked Amelie.

Ben smiled and shook his head. "No, just thinking that I'm ready to get out of this place."

"Me too," agreed Amelie. "Come on. Let's find something to eat."

The mess hall was near the center of the keep and Ben found it more pleasant than the formal dining room where most of the courtiers ate. In the mess hall, it was guards, maids, masons, blacksmiths, and other craftsmen who kept the keep running.

Ben appreciated being around the people who got their hands dirty. In the courtiers' dining room, he always felt like he was being watched. Amelie had not publicly announced herself, so speculation was running high on who they were and why they seemed to have Rhymer and Franklin's ears.

Ben led Amelie to the mess hall. She smiled at him but stayed silent. She was perfectly comfortable in the dining room and didn't mind the stares. She'd grown up in that environment.

They walked to the front of the room to collect trays, plates, a mug of ale, and an overflowing ladle of soup. Soups and stews were common in the mess. It was easy for the cooks to make a large batch and keep it going throughout the day. The dining room had finer fare that was cooked to order. Ben did miss that.

Sitting down to eat, Ben spooned up his first bite then dropped it when an incessant clanging started.

Amelie's startled eyes met his and they both stood up.

"That's the signal," he declared needlessly.

All around them, guards and soldiers were getting to their feet. Other staff were quickly scooping up what remained on their plates before leaving to their stations. Chambermaids and farriers would become nurses and stretcher-bearers once the fighting started.

Amelie grabbed a loaf of bread and Ben chugged down half a mug of ale before they scrambled to follow the soldiers out the door.

The keep was organized chaos. Everyone had an assigned role, but the eve of a battle was still frantic. They passed several people who seemed to have lost their nerve.

One young soldier was getting sick out a window. A maid stood beside him, encouraging him to get it together, to be brave. Young lovers, thought Ben. He hoped the man made it back to see his girl.

Outside the keep, they rushed down the main thoroughfare, joining a host of soldiers headed in that direction. Coming the other way were townspeople who had not yet evacuated their residences. Their faces were painted with nervous panic. Many of them were carrying armfuls of valuables and supplies.

"They should have left earlier," remarked Amelie, observing one woman struggling to keep her two crying children with her and not drop a cloth-wrapped armful of candlesticks and food.

Ben nodded in agreement.

Torches flared into light ahead of them. Men rushed through the flickering flame lit streets to ignite more of them. Ben could see atop the city walls that the bonfires were burning high in the giant braziers as well. In darkness, the demons had the advantage.

Rushing up the steep stone stairs to the top of the wall, Ben almost forgot to be nervous about the height. A shout from below drew his gaze down. He quickly leaned against the cold stones of the wall as they made it the rest of the way up.

On top of the wall, the pace of the soldiers was slower. The men who'd made it there were in place and ready. Soldiers checked over bow strings and adjusted armor. For them, it was now a waiting game.

"Hurry up and wait," remarked Rhys when they found him already stationed near the catapult.

Two dozen soldiers and half a dozen artillery men also stood on the platform. Ben walked to the battlement and looked out through a crenellation into the quickly darkening fields below. The last slivers of sunlight were falling away as the sun ducked below the city behind him.

Huge bonfires were placed in the killing field. They lit the archer's stakes but not much else. As far as Ben could see, there was nothing to see.

"Are we sure the demons are coming?" he inquired.

A man bearing the rank of a sergeant rested his forearms on the battlement beside Ben. "Aye, they're out there."

"I don't see anything," remarked Ben.

"Cords were placed throughout the forest," explained the man. "Long, thin cords tied to flags at the tree line. Half a bell ago, those flags started getting pulled down, like a big force was moving out there and knocking down all of the cords."

Ben stared hard at the dark forest, still not seeing anything, but confident the man's explanation was correct.

Amelie was sitting near the back of the wall. She was cross-legged on her cloak and had her eyes closed.

Rhys caught Ben's look and shrugged. She was trying to do something magical, Ben guessed. Given her skill, maybe she didn't want to over-promise. Anything would help. They still weren't sure if Towaal was rested enough to fight. She hadn't left the library even for food in over a day.

Bells passed. The men rustled about nervously. On the platform, every few minutes, someone would go look out into the darkness. Then they would turn and shake their heads to their companions. Nothing to see.

Some of the men told dirty jokes under their breath, so Amelie couldn't hear. Others pleaded with their fellows to relay messages to loved ones if they didn't make it. Rhys lay down with his head on his cloak and took a nap.

The soldiers stared at him. Ben shook his head ruefully. He wasn't sure if his friend was trying to show off, be calm and reassure the soldiers, or if he really was napping. It was hard to tell with Rhys.

Further down the wall, watchtowers poked upward. They would be the first to spot anything. Some of them even had far-seeing devices. Those would be nearly useless, he knew. It was a cloudy night and the light was low.

Amelie remained silent with her eyes closed, focused on whatever she was doing.

To pass the time, Ben wandered over to inspect the catapult they were guarding. It was a massive thing, nearly the size of a house. Twisted ropes pulled back the lever arm, storing tension that, when released, would fling the arm forward and launch rocks or heavy iron balls out into the field in front of them. A team of a half dozen men was standing ready to winch back the arm and reload it.

Firing as quickly as possible would be critical because the weapon was difficult to aim. Once the demons passed through its range, it would be rather ineffective. After that, they had a rack of crossbows leaning against the wall. The artillery men would switch to those when their catapult no longer served its purpose.

"How far does it shoot?" Ben asked of one of the men.

"About four hundred paces," answered the man proudly. He laid a hand on the weapon. "We haven't gotten to use her in real combat, but she works great in practice."

The man went back and hefted one of the head-sized iron balls. "These things'll break limbs, crush heads, and can blow a hole right through you if it's a direct hit." He pointed to a separate pile of rubble. "We got rocks, too, if we run out of proper ammunition."

Ben walked over and lifted one of the balls. He nearly dropped it on his toes. The thing was heavy!

"They keep rolling," said the man, smiling. "That's why we like them more than the rocks. Hit the first line and roll back into the second, breaking legs, making 'em trip over the balls. It's nasty but effective."

Ben stumbled forward and dropped the ball back into a basket full of them. Who in the hell carried those up the stairs, he wondered.

Late in the night, the moon was passing overhead. Fatigue was starting to creep in. Well past when they would normally be in bed, the men were getting agitated at standing and waiting for something they could not see. The commanders would not risk opening the gates and sending scouts to confirm the demon presence. They would not release any of the men, either.

Ben heard mutters and grumbling, but the threat of demons

was enough to keep everyone on watch. So far, no one near him had tried to sneak away.

Suddenly, a shout rang out from one of the watchtowers.

Ben and most of the other men rushed to the battlement to see what was happening.

At first, he couldn't see anything. Then a flash of darkness swept through the light of one of the bonfires. The shape crashed into the fire, scattering the big pile of logs and sending them toppling over.

The fire flickered out on some logs as they rolled across the ground. The little light they had in the field got a bit smaller.

A score of arrows flew into the air. The captains called for the archers to halt. The dark shape had pulled back, and the arrows fell harmlessly around the burning logs.

Down the line, another bonfire was hit and its logs also scattered.

"Making it harder to see them," grumbled the sergeant standing again at Ben's side. The gruff soldier looked back at his squad. There was nothing for them to do. Launching the catapults at an individual demon would be a waste of ammunition.

A quarter bell later, all of the bonfires were knocked over. Many of the logs still burned, but the light they threw off was lower, less concentrated.

"Smart." Rhys sighed, surveying the darkened battlefield. He'd finally risen from his nap when the shout had gone out from the watchtower.

Further down the wall, a shout pierced the night. It startled Ben and the men around him. He turned but couldn't see what happened. The soldiers shifted nervously. Then behind him in the other direction, another yell tore into the air.

Nothing was moving in the field below them. He couldn't see what was attacking the men.

"Flying demons!" bellowed Rhys. "Look out above!"

Ben swept his sword out and stepped away from the battlement.

Heartbeats later, a shape swooped in silently out of the night. It violently crashed into a man ten paces away. The man flailed backward and flipped over the back wall with the force of the blow. The creature sailed away into the darkness. The man shrieked on his way to the hard cobblestones below. His yell ended in a crunch. Ben winced and cowered down, looking into the black sky.

All of the torches and braziers the men had on the artillery platform were lit, but in the middle of the night, they couldn't see anything above them that was outside of the firelight. Ben realized that by the time one of the flying demons entered their circle of light, it would be too late to react.

Looking around wildly, he saw the polearms sticking out from the crenellations of the platform. They were there to prevent the creatures from scaling the wall.

"Raise the polearms!" he called.

The sergeant broke his scan of the blackness above and looked at Ben uncomprehending. Ben grunted in frustration and ran to one of the nearly six-pace-long weapons. He pulled it up and set the butt of the weapon on the stone floor. Angling it up and out, he positioned it so any flying demon coming in from outside of the wall would run straight into it.

"That's right," said the sergeant, looking on, finally understanding. He turned to his squad and shouted, "Treat it like a cavalry charge. Set polearms."

All down the wall, other men heard, saw what was happening, and started raising their own weapons. The walls of Northport grew spines like an angry porcupine.

Near Ben, a winged demon came swooping in and slammed into one man's polearm. The momentum of its flight snapped the thick wood in two and the creature crashed onto the walkway atop the wall. A yard of sharp steel and broken wood stuck out of its torso. The man holding half of a broken polearm stared at the creature in shock.

Other men scrambled forward and thrust swords into the demon's twitching body. The beast made one last attempt to move, but two more swords stabbed into it, pinning it to the ground where it quickly fell still.

A cheer went up from the nearby men before their officers admonished them to remain vigilant and keep the polearms up.

Crashes and howls spread down the line as more of the flying demons smacked into the wall of steel.

Another one hit nearby and landed wounded on their platform. Ben and Rhys darted forward, swords raised to finish it.

Shaking the purple blood off his longsword, Rhys clapped Ben on the back. "Good suggestion with the polearms."

The sounds of battle filled the air but not enough to cover the creak and heavy thump of a catapult firing. Two more sounded from different parts of the wall.

The sergeant ran forward to peer between two merlons.

"Damn," he called back to his artillery team. "Fire!"

The sergeant started back to help his men, but a black shape flew down and landed on his back. Long claws wrapped around his neck and tore into his throat while the demon rode his falling body to the stone floor.

Crimson blood sprayed out across the platform. Rhys was there before the creature could turn to anyone else. His longsword plunged into its chest.

The rogue glanced where the sergeant had been looking then yelled at the men around him, "You! Get your polearms up, they're still coming in." Addressing the catapult crew, he barked, "Fire freely. The flying ones are just a distraction. They're coming!"

Ben lunged to the edge and looked below. Across the plain, a black swarm was approaching in the flickering light of the failing bonfires. In the dark, he couldn't hope to count them. The little light that was left down there started to go out. Black shapes trampled over the fires and extinguished them.

At the gate, flaming bales were pushed over the side of the wall just in time to see a monster the size of four oxen come charging in to pound against the iron barrier. The entire wall shook with the impact. Two more followed right behind it. The three creatures vanished back into the night. The gate still held. Ben knew it wouldn't hold much longer. It was designed to withstand whatever a human army could throw at it. This was something out of a nightmare.

The catapult thumped behind Ben and the heavy iron balls went flying into the darkness. They couldn't see where they landed or what the damage was, but Ben knew they would hit something. The entire field was crawling.

Time for watching the attack below vanished when three more man-sized flying demons came hurtling at their platform.

One collided with the small forest of steel-tipped polearms, knocking them to the side. That cleared space for the other two demons to land in the midst of the men.

Still gripping the tall wooden hafts of the polearms, men were ripped to shreds before Ben, Rhys, and half a dozen other swordsmen arrived.

Slipping to a stop on the blood-soaked stone, Ben lashed out at one of the creatures along with another man. Both of them cut into its flesh, but in the twisted tangle of man and beast, they couldn't get a clean strike. The demon pivoted, reaching for the other man. That gave Ben an opening. He thrust his mage-wrought longsword home. The blade plunged easily into the demon's heart. Twisting his weapon as he brought it out, Ben jumped back from the purple fountain of blood that splashed down to mingle with that of the dead men.

The soldier nodded his thanks to Ben then turned back to scanning the sky.

Stretcher-bearers rushed forward for the wounded men and corpses.

Rhys took charge of the platform. With the sergeant dead, no one thought to challenge the rogue's right to command them. They saw the silver glow of the glyphs on his longsword and knew not to argue.

He set half the men to hold the unbroken polearms they had left. The others he put on sword duty to handle any demons that landed. He admonished the catapult crew to fire faster, demanding that they fling more heavy iron over the walls.

"Every demon you hit is one less we have to fight hand to hand," he yelled.

Ben looked around for Amelie and found her standing now, bent over one of the baskets of iron balls.

"This one," she instructed the catapult crew. "Fire from this basket."

"What did you do?" asked Ben. He moved to stand beside her but kept his gaze upward. In the black night, they would only have a heartbeat to react if a demon got in past the polearms.

"Wait and see," she said, breathing heavily. She pulled her rapier and dagger, but they both knew the light weapons would be a last resort and only used if the soldiers got overwhelmed.

The catapult crew loaded the arm again, pulling iron balls from Amelie's basket. Out of the corner of his eye, Ben caught her wince when a man dropped one of the balls into the catapult's hand.

As soon as the last ball was loaded, the men yanked a lever and the arm snapped forward. The scattering of iron soared out into the fields beyond the wall. Ben kept his eyes toward the sky, but his concentration broke when a violent eruption happened out in the field.

One after another, bursts of flame flashed like fireworks. They illuminated a scrambling horde of demons trying to get away from the explosions. In the sharp light, Ben saw pieces of iron fly out from each blast and shred the nearby demons into tatters of ugly meat. Ten paces around each explosion was a carpet of dead demons.

Rhys looked at Amelie, wild-eyed. "Can you do that again?" he shouted.

She pointed to the pile of balls the catapult crew was now very gingerly loading. "This entire basket is primed. I think I can do more. It should be faster now that I know what I'm doing."

"What are you waiting for?" demanded Rhys.

She frowned then scurried around the rest of the ammunition, briefly laying a hand on top of each pile and concentrating.

Loud cracks and explosions in the field after each time the catapult launched signified her work wasn't going in vain.

Rhys looked around then waved to her. "Come on. Let's get to another catapult and see what you can do there."

He left instructions with the men and sent a runner for reinforcements. That catapult was now the most destructive weapon in Northport's arsenal. It was critical to keep it firing.

Ben rushed after Rhys and Amelie as they darted between soldiers to the next catapult. The wall shook beneath his feet. He knew the huge demons were again charging the gate. Too bad they couldn't hit one of them with Amelie's exploding iron.

At the next catapult, confusion reigned.

The stones were slick from blood and half the defenders were missing. Rhys gestured to Amelie and she crouched by the waiting ammunition stores.

Ben grimaced when he saw none of the men were raising polearms. There were no officers left alive that he could see.

He and Rhys strode forward, but before Rhys could bark out orders, a black shape crashed into the back of one of the men. The fallen soldier went sprawling forward and his companions rushed to defend against the new attacker.

Rhys and Ben started to help as well, but out of the corner of his eye, Ben caught something coming between the merlons of the battlement.

He turned to find a lithe, long-limbed creature pulling itself onto the wall.

"Behind you!" shouted Ben.

Rhys turned just in time to see the beast gain its footing and charge forward.

One of the soldiers stepped between Rhys and the demon only to have his head torn off by a brawny black arm.

Rhys jumped forward, slashing his sword and severing one of the long arms. He then ducked the other as the demon swung at his head. Rhys rose from his crouch, slicing his glowing silver longsword across the creature's stomach. It fell backward to tangle with two more like it.

Ben charged, hurtling over the fallen body of the soldier and stabbing into one of the demons before it gained its footing. His mage-wrought blade slid in easily, and the demon screamed, falling backward into the darkness.

"Let's go!" cried Amelie from near the ammunition cache.

From the way the catapult crew was loading the iron, Ben could tell she'd told them what would happen. The men could see the brilliant explosions from the first catapult.

With a last, quick instruction to the remaining men on the wall, Rhys started off toward another catapult platform with Ben and Amelie in tow.

They heard a thump and series of loud explosions behind them as the catapult arm launched a wave of death out into the field. Ben thought he could hear screams of pain and terror out there, but they were drowned out by the ones close by.

The wall shuddered again, followed by a painful screech of torn metal. Rhys paused halfway to the next catapult platform.

"If they break through that gate…" He snarled.

"Go," demanded Amelie. "I can get to these catapults on my own. They need your sword."

"Amelie," Ben started to protest.

She cut him off.

"If the demons break through those gates, the fighting will be focused in the streets, not up here. Go!" She pushed past them, jogging to the next platform.

Grim-faced, Rhys turned and waved for Ben to follow. "You ready for this?" he asked.

Running after him, Ben panted, "For what?"

Rhys pointed ahead, down below the wall. Ben saw a huge demon forcing its way through the broken gate. Sharp, torn metal scored its side, leaving deep purple gashes. A broken log jutted out from one shoulder. The huge beast surged forward despite its injuries, clearing the gate and stumbling into the streets of Northport.

A wave of arrows and crossbow bolts flew down into it, but the one big creature was a small problem compared to the horde that flowed around it. Smaller demons flooded the streets.

"Here," said Rhys, stepping off the wall and onto a flight of stairs leading down. They would get to ground level two blocks away from where the demons were racing in.

Makeshift barriers and walls had been erected to steer the demons into cul-de-sacs, which would be used for killing grounds, but the big demons that had attacked the gate could smash through those barriers easily.

Ben realized the battle plan was falling apart.

In the streets, confused, panicked men rushed by in both directions. No one thought the attackers would so easily penetrate the walls. The idea had been to keep them outside and whittle down their numbers with the artillery and arrows. Close quarters battle with so many demons could be catastrophic.

Ben stayed close on his friend's heels as they weaved closer to the fighting. Ahead, he could see a temporary wall silhouetted by firelight.

The wall burst inward with explosive force. A shower of broken timber and bodies rained onto the street in front of them.

A huge demon stood square in the middle of where the wall once stood. It took one slow step forward and men turned in a flock and fled. The demon was larger than the arch-demons they'd faced in the Wilds, but it moved sluggishly, like it was moving through honey. It was strong though, strong enough to smash through the wall Rhymer's men had built.

Rhys squared his feet and in a booming yell screamed, "Behind me! Hold your ground."

His longsword flared to light, filling the street with a soft white glow.

Ben stepped up beside him, eyes focused ahead on the massive demon.

He could hear the clatter of armor as men arrested their flight and started to form up behind them.

The demon bellowed a deep cry, which shook Ben's bones, and then started forward. He could feel the heavy steps through the stone street.

Rhys charged ahead, running straight at the demon. Ben cringed. The creature had to be three times as tall and five times as wide as a man.

Ben groaned and followed Rhys, unwilling to let his friend do this alone.

The beast rose to its full height, roaring at the men filling the street in front of it. Rhys kept going, heading directly beneath the creature and scampering between its legs. Ben hoped the chaos around them was as distracting to the demons as it was to him.

The demon leaned down to catch them, but they were faster.

Rhys veered to the right, so Ben lurched left. Both of them swung hard with their mage-wrought blades and cut deeply into the demon's legs. Ben felt his weapon connect with the tough tendon at the back of the leg. He yanked violently to clear the blade.

With a satisfying twang, the tendon snapped. Above him, the creature howled in shock and pain. Slow, like a tree falling in the forest, it toppled forward.

In the rapidly closing space between its legs, Ben could see the soldiers. They were scrambling backward so the giant wouldn't fall on them.

Wasting no time, Rhys spun and leapt onto its back. The demon rolled on the ground, trying to dislodge the man, but he was too quick. He flung himself up toward its neck and, with both hands, raised his longsword above his head. The silver glyphs sparkled along the length of his blade. He plunged it deep into the beast's neck, shoving the sharp steel until the hilt met flesh.

A muffled squeal crept from the creature, hampered by the sword sticking through its neck. On the other side of it, Ben could hear the frantic cheers of the soldiers.

Ben smiled, amazed at his friend's bravery and skill.

The moment was over quickly when Rhys drew his longsword from the demon. He looked to Ben. Grim-faced, the rogue pointed over Ben's shoulder.

A chill tingled down Ben's spine.

He turned to see a swarm of upward of forty demons starting toward him. They had been prepared to follow the large one when it cleared the breach in the wall. Now that its body was blocking the narrow street behind him, Ben was the only human in the street.

He set his feet and brought up his sword. Calm washed over him. The waiting, the mad rush along the wall, the unseen demons swooping in from the night...that was over. Now the threat was clear, the solution obvious. Kill as many demons as he could. If he didn't kill enough, he would be dead. That didn't matter. There was only one path to take.

The demons arrived in a tangled wave of teeth and claws. If they worked together, there would be no way for Ben to defend against them, but they didn't work together. Pushing and shoving, they struggled to get to their target.

He sidestepped the first claw, which slashed toward his head. He neatly severed the arm. A second demon, clambering over the back of the injured first one, caught the point of Ben's blade in its right eye. A third lost its head when he yanked his sword free and continued the motion, swiping through muscle and bone.

The sound of a powerful wind grew in the back of Ben's head but he ignored it, focused on the howls and bellowed challenges in front of him.

He danced around the first three demons, using their bodies to keep the bulk of the attack away from him.

Dropping to one knee, he eviscerated another that drew too close and felt a painful tug and tear on his left shoulder as one clawed hand got to him.

Hot blood spilled down his arm. The demon paid for it when Ben spun, pulled by the momentum of the claw on his shoulder, and slammed his longsword deep into the demon's chest.

He turned with his blade still in the demon's body, attempting to use it as a shield to block another pack before they swarmed over him. The creatures surged into the back of the dead demon.

The force knocked Ben back to the ground. He barely kept a hand on his weapon, pulling it free and rolling to his feet in one motion.

Spinning, he slashed in a circle around him, separating hands and clawed fingers from their owners. The spin took just a heartbeat, but he knew the end of the fight was near. He was surrounded by the creatures. There was no way he could defend all sides.

Suddenly, Rhys dropped from above, jumping off the body of the huge demon he'd killed, to land at Ben's side. Grinning maniacally, the rogue lashed out with a blazingly fast attack, cutting and hacking a clear space in front of him.

Ben tried to mirror his friend's movements. He stood back-to-back with Rhys. They were surrounded by a growing number of snarling demons. More and more of the creatures turned down the street as they poured in from the busted city gates.

"Keep them back!" shouted Rhys between heavy breaths. "If they get close enough to foul your blade, we're done."

Ben didn't have the concentration or breath to spare a response. He was furiously slashing through meat and bone. His mage-wrought sword cut better than any traditionally forged steel, but the effort was draining. The gnashing teeth just beyond his reach pressed closer and closer. The demons coming in now were pushing the ones in front of them, ambivalent to the fact they were shoving their fellows into the path of Ben's razor sharp blade.

Demons were pushed into his reach, and he killed them, but he couldn't reach the live ones that were doing the pushing. They were getting closer, a flailing, purple blood soaked pile of teeth, claws, and hunger.

He had to push them back.

Without thinking, he acted on instinct. He pulled back his left hand and swept it in front of him, like he was swatting a fly out of the air.

An enormously powerful wind gusted forward, blasting the demons in front of him and blowing them down the street. Tumbling demons scattered in front of him like leaves in a storm.

Ben stumbled forward into the suddenly clear area, and Rhys fell back, barely keeping his feet without Ben's support behind him. Rhys spared a quick, startled look over his shoulder. His eyes fell down to Ben's mage-wrought sword. Then he turned to face the creatures in front of him. None of them had been blown away.

Spinning, Ben took his friend's side. The two of them furiously defended against the surging tide of demons.

There was no thought of defeating the howling mass attacking them. It was only defense and survival.

Behind them, howls of rage alerted Ben that the creatures blown away by the wind were coming back. Within heartbeats, they'd be on him.

Distracted by the threat behind him, Ben shoved his sword into the stomach of a squat, thickly muscled attacker and was pulled to his knees when it twisted, falling to the ground. The demon's heavy body lay on the hilt of his sword. He couldn't get an angle to pull it free.

His left hand dropped to the hunting knife Serrot had given him. After all of this time, it was still hanging off his belt. Ben knew the knife wasn't sufficient for this task.

A thin winged demon appeared over the back of the dead one Ben's sword was trapped in. Ben glanced to Rhys, but the man was being pushed back, swinging frantically to keep three of them away from him.

With a determined scowl, Ben drew his knife. He may fall, but he wouldn't make it easy for them.

Then an arrow bloomed in the head of the demon and two more sprouted right behind it.

Flight after flight of arrows rained down on the swarm of demons. They flinched back momentarily, giving Ben time to kick at the demon body in front of him, turning it enough he could pull his sword free.

A battle cry broke out. Ben saw the soldiers who had been blocked by the huge demon crawling over it. They were jumping down into the street to join the fight. Pushing past Ben and Rhys, they charged forward with a wall of polearms and spears leading the way. Stabbing and pinning demons, the next wave rushed in with swords and axes.

Above them, arrow after arrow continued to fall into the flailing swarm.

Ben looked up and saw Corinne's brilliant red hair framed in the light of fires that were now burning throughout the city.

She had a team of archers with her. She met Ben's eyes before waving to her crew and directing them to move down to another rooftop and rain death on another swarm of demons. The soldiers were mopping up what was left of this one.

Panting, Ben turned to Rhys, who was gingerly touching a bloody gash across his stomach.

"You okay?" asked Ben.

"I'll live," grumbled Rhys. He looked at Ben's injured shoulder. "You?"

Ben glanced down at his blood-covered left arm. Seeing it, he felt the sharp sting of pain. He clenched his teeth. "I'll live."

"Good," replied his friend. "We're not done yet."

The captain of the men in the street was shouting orders and organizing his company. They had cleared the street and were falling back to behind the huge, dead demon. Men were instructed to collapse materials that had been left for that purpose to re-block the wall. Two squads were holding the street with a bristling wall of weaponry. As demons peeled off the main thoroughfare and came their way, men pounced on them, pinning them with polearms then finishing them with swords.

Seeing the effectiveness of the organization, Ben's heart rose. Maybe they would make it through this.

Rhys though, was visibly growing worried.

"They're being driven," he growled.

"What do you mean?" asked Ben

"Look. Hardly any of the demons are coming this way," said the rogue. "Something is directing them elsewhere."

Ben frowned. Rhys was right. Two blocks down the street, they could see a constant stream of demons pouring in through the gates. Some of the demons turned toward them, but the majority kept going straight. In his experience, a normal demon wasn't strategic enough to focus on another objective when a source of life-blood was near it.

"Where are they going?" wondered Ben.

"Let's find out," answered Rhys. Setting off at a limping run, he turned to the back streets and deeper into the city.

Ben followed, his longsword bobbing in front of him. He hefted the blade and thought about that powerful wind which saved his life.

Dodging through the nearly empty cobblestone streets of Northport, Ben and Rhys made their way toward the center of the city.

The people they saw were mostly women and children. The occasional man scurried by also, drawing a disparaging glare from Rhys. Those people were trying to figure a way out. Ben didn't know if there was one, but uniformly, they were heading away from the main gates. Maybe the city wasn't surrounded and they could escape out the back. Seeing some of the frightened children clutching their mother's hands with tears pouring down their faces, he hoped they did find their way to safety.

Travelling roughly parallel to the main thoroughfare, they hoped to get ahead of the massive swarm of demons that had breached the gates.

They could track the progress of the swarm by the sounds of battle. It was becoming clearer each block. The demons were headed toward the keep. Ben knew there were barriers, traps, and diversions set up along the way, but with the speed the demons were moving, he didn't think they'd be slowed long.

Huffing and puffing after his limping friend, Ben called, "What's the plan? Get to the square in front of the keep and make a stand?"

"The two of us against a thousand demons?" responded Rhys. One bloodstained hand was holding the wound on his stomach, the other was carrying his longsword. "That's a death sentence, for sure. I, at least, am not ready to die."

"What do you think we should do? Run?" challenged Ben.

"I'm not ready to give up yet, either," replied Rhys. "It's your call. I was serious about it when I said I was ready to follow you, but if you want my advice, we get ahead of these things and see where they are going. Maybe we'll see an opportunity that doesn't involve getting eaten."

Ben nodded and kept jogging. His shoulder was throbbing now, each step sending a jolt of fresh pain down his arm and into his body. He wasn't used to the deference from Rhys, and he wasn't entirely convinced the rogue meant what he said, but for now, his friend was right. They could get ahead of the swarm and see what their objective was. The two of them standing in front of an unstoppable army of darkness didn't have any appeal, but maybe there was something they could do.

The sounds of fighting faded behind them. They'd gotten ahead of the creatures but not by a lot. Cutting over from the back streets to the main ones, they made quick time and before long came into the open square.

Ragged companies of men were arrayed in formations, prepared for the advancing demon horde. They were arrayed around a solid core of serious looking hunters. Those men and women had faced demons and knew what it meant that thousands were currently headed their way.

Rhys looked them over and declared, "Mostly stragglers and the injured. It looks like they're pulling men from the back walls too. They'll be fresh at least. The generals must have adjusted the plans and are funneling the demons into the square. I'm not sure they realize that is what the demons want."

"Should we say something?" asked Ben.

Rhys shook his head. "Rhymer knows he has to make a stand. If they fight street by street, the people are going to get slaughtered. The demons got inside too quickly."

Ben grimaced. The men standing in front of them didn't seem sufficient to stop what he saw coming through the gates.

As they approached, a tall man draped in light chainmail and carrying a heavy broad sword walked toward them. It was Franklin.

"She's back there," the seneschal said, hooking a thumb over his shoulder.

"Who?" asked Rhys.

"Lady Towaal," responded Franklin. "Didn't you come to help her?"

"Why not?" Rhys shrugged.

The seneschal looked over the two of them, eyeing their injuries. "Looks like you got some action."

"We were near the gate," replied Ben. "We saw your daughter."

The man's face paled. "Corinne was supposed to stay here with me."

"She was well when we saw her," assured Ben. "She was on the rooftops and had a squad of men with her. She's going to have a lot of new notches to make in that bow of hers."

Franklin nodded proudly. "Good. Now, you better get to Lady Towaal and see what she wants. She took a company of my men and won't tell me a damn thing. Hopefully she's got a plan. I've got preparations to do here. We lost contact with both of our generals."

The man stomped off toward the arrayed soldiers, muttering under his breath.

Ben and Rhys rushed toward the library to find Lady Towaal standing imperiously in front of it. She was surrounded by a company of heavily armed soldiers. The men looked fresh and ready.

Without saying anything, Rhys raised an eyebrow when they approached.

"Good. You're here," she stated.

"Do you have a plan?" asked the rogue.

"Of a sort," replied Towaal sharply. "I believe the demons will come here." She gestured back to the library. "When they do, we shall try to stop them."

"How will we do that?" challenged Rhys. "From what we saw

at the gate, there are well over a thousand of them in the city, maybe two thousand."

Ben saw the blood drain from the faces of several soldiers near them. The men turned to their companions and started whispering furiously. Their captain quickly tamped it down. He instructed them to focus ahead then turned to glare at Rhys and Towaal.

"With this," answered the mage. She drew a polished wooden rod from behind her belt. It was covered in tiny, intricate carvings and was the length of three hands. "It is a repository that contains a rather large amount of power."

"You've had this the entire time?" griped Rhys.

"No," answered Towaal, shaking her head. "I found it in the library. There was a cache of rather unique items and documents. That is why I believe the demons are coming here. They have no thought of human strategic warfare. They couldn't care less about taking the keep itself. To them, the valuable thing about Northport is the life-blood in our bodies, but if the documents are correct, they will also want what is inside of here."

"What is inside there?" asked Ben, looking at the non-descript building.

"The answer to the Rift and the organization meant to police it. The Purple," answered Towaal. "That group has been around a long time, and I believe we will soon find they aren't quite as dead as we thought. I'm counting on it, actually."

The guards were shifting nervously. Screams, demonic howls, and the sounds of combat were drawing closer.

Ben looked to where the street emptied into the square. Nothing was there yet.

"And…" prodded Rhys. "We don't have much time."

"The Rift was a door to another realm, as we suspected, but more importantly, that door has two keys." Towaal paused briefly. "One of the keys was here in the library, and one is stored somewhere in the Coalition city of Irrefort. With the keys, enough knowledge about how the doorway between the realms works, and with sufficient will, another Rift could be opened."

Ben frowned in confusion.

"Seeing the observation room in the Wilds got me thinking," said Towaal. "What if, instead of watching the Rift, they were watching the demons? Studying them, learning from them? The documents I found in the library support that. In fact, it seems they were focusing on one particular demon, a demon so powerful they abandoned their outpost in the Wilds and retreated to Northport. They were worried this supreme arch-demon was beginning to sense the rift key."

"What are you saying?" growled Rhys. He was nervously holding his longsword and kept his focus on the street where any minute a horde of demons could appear.

Towaal answered, "There is a demon coming down that street that can sense the rift key. It may have the knowledge and the power to utilize it and open another Rift, a Rift uncontrolled by man but by demon."

Rhys grunted like he had been punched in the stomach.

Towaal added, "An incredibly powerful demon that has been feeding on the power of the Rift for millennia. Think about how strong a demon can be after months of feeding. Multiply that by a thousand."

"That thing is coming here?" exclaimed the captain of the soldiers. He had drawn close to overhear the conversation.

"I believe so," answered Towaal flatly.

"And what? W-We're supposed to fight it?" sputtered the captain nervously. Ben hoped the captain's men weren't paying attention to him.

"I will take care of it," said Towaal, rubbing a hand over the wooden rod she held. "With a little help, I hope. Just keep its minions away from me."

Rhys nodded brusquely. "We can do that."

"Captain!" called one of the men, pointing across the square.

Several thin-bodied and long-limbed demons streaked into the open space and were met with a hail of arrows. They quickly fell under the onslaught. Ben knew more would be right behind them. He gripped the hilt of his longsword and waited.

Soon, another wave of demons burst out of the street and raced across the open square. Flight after flight of arrows soared into the sky and came crashing down into the demons with deadly effect. The stream of darkness did not stop or even slow. More and more of the creatures poured into the open.

A line of soldiers advanced with pikes and spears lowered. They crouched on one knee and set their weapons like they were meeting a wave of heavy horse.

Ben winced as the sound of the impact rolled across the square. He could see the silver-grey armor of the men disappear under a crush of demons. A company of men wielding swords and axes rushed to defend their companions. From two hundred paces away, the details were obscured, but the screams and death cries told them all they needed to know.

Behind Ben, a man was getting noisily sick while his squad sergeant admonished him to get back in line.

"Should we…" the captain asked Towaal.

"No," she replied calmly. "This is just the beginning. We wait."

Ben shifted nervously. He hated seeing the soldiers fight while he stayed back. With his training and mage-wrought blade, he could make a difference. He knew it.

Rhys placed an assuring hand on his arm. "It's just as important knowing when to fight as how to fight."

"They're getting slaughtered," Ben groaned.

"Look," said Rhys. "I believe Franklin has a plan."

More companies of soldiers were pouring into the square directly opposite of Ben and his companions, flanking the demons. A brilliant tactical move, if they had been facing a human opponent.

Another wave of shouts and crunching armor sounded. Ben

looked to see the guard pouring out of the keep. Atop, Lord Rhymer was sheathed in heavy plate mail and was observing his household troops rush out to join the fight.

"The keep is unprotected," remarked Ben.

"Rhymer means to finish the fight in the square. After how easily the demons got through the main gate, I don't blame him for not wanting to hide behind that one. Besides, if Towaal is right, that's not where the demons want to go," answered Rhys. "They want to go here."

The ferocity of the fight intensified as more soldiers charged into the battle and demons continued to storm out of the streets leading to the square.

The men around them began to get antsy. Their friends and neighbors were fighting and they just sat back and watched.

They didn't have to just watch for long. On one side of the battle, the line of men bulged and a swarm of twenty demons broke free. They headed straight for the library.

"Here we go," called Rhys.

Ben looked to Towaal, but she was still staring intently toward the street where the demons poured from. Whatever she was waiting on, this wasn't it.

Ben, Rhys, and the company of soldiers stepped forward to deal with the charging demons. Ben and Rhys took the lead. The soldiers, noticing the mage-wrought blades, fell in behind them. No one else volunteered to be in the front, facing a demon swarm.

Charging forward, the two friends cleaved through the first wave of demons in a swirl of flashing steel. Purple blood and the bodies of demons spilled in their wake.

The soldiers pounced on what was left, swords rising and falling as they took out their frustration on the remaining creatures.

A few men went tumbling backward, clutching ugly wounds,

but the fight was short and brutal. Twenty dead demons lay scattered on the cobblestones.

"You're getting good at this," remarked Rhys. "Another year or two, and you could add a blademaster sigil to that scabbard."

"I don't think so," said Ben, ruefully shaking his head. "I'm just learning how to fight these things."

"Learning how to fight is learning how to fight," replied Rhys sardonically.

"Demons are different," said Ben, wiping purple demon blood from his blade. "They have no cunning, no strategy. A good human opponent will think about your weaknesses and try to exploit them. A demon just comes right at you. That's the only thing they know how to do. There is no fear, no caution. Once you understand that, it gets rather easy."

"Recognizing that and incorporating it into how you fight is a skill," responded Rhys. "And anytime you think fighting a demon is easy, you have skill. What you're talking about, that is you thinking through their weakness and altering your attack to take advantage, just like a good opponent should."

Ben shrugged, wincing as his injured shoulder moved. He supposed Rhys was right.

"Behind us!" yelled one of the soldiers.

They all spun in time to see several winged demons dropping off the roof of the library and landing in their midst. The demons were right next to Towaal.

The mage crouched in alarm. Ben and Rhys rushed to defend her.

Two soldiers went down, landing near her feet. She staggered backward. Then Ben and Rhys arrived, chopping down a demon from behind. The soldiers took care of the rest of them, but several human bodies joined the fallen demons on the ground.

Rhys barked out orders to the men to circle up and keep eyes in all directions. The captain of the soldiers stood by, stunned. A tenth of his command was already dead and his sword was still spotless. The pace of the battle was too much for the man.

"Why didn't you," Ben waved a hand in front of Towaal, "Do something?"

She winced. "I'm still weak from the Wilds. I have to conserve everything I have to face what is coming."

He frowned. It had been weeks since she fell unconscious in the Wilds. Certainly she had recovered by now.

A new roar drew his attention away from Towaal. Ben turned to see a dozen arch-demons enter the square. They stood twice Ben's height. Even from a distance, he could see the claws extending from powerful hands. They had thick muscle-covered chests and shoulders which spanned the width of a wagon. They looked bigger and stronger than anything they'd faced in the Wilds.

"Get ready," murmured Towaal. "The leader will be close behind these."

"T-That isn't the..." stuttered Ben. He was cut short when another wave of normal-sized demons began racing their way.

The soldiers in the square were starting to break with the arrival of the arch-demons. Ben saw several men turn to flee. Their captains exhorted them to stay in the lines, but a pack of creatures standing twice the height of a man was enough to turn anyone's spine to jelly.

Ben left Towaal's side to join the soldiers and Rhys. He saw one of the arch-demons scoop up a wagon and launch it high into the air. It crashed into a squad of solders, sending them flying like lawn bowling pins.

"Shit," muttered the captain under his breath. The men behind him weren't quite as polite about it.

Ben met Rhys' eyes.

Towaal called up to them, her voice barely audible above the screams and fighting in the square. "I will not be able to assist with these."

"Whatever you did with that blade before, it's time to do it again," said Rhys. His longsword was steadily glowing brighter and brighter. It might have been Ben's imagination, but silver smoke appeared to drift off and away from the blade. In the dark of the night, it would have been impossible to see without the glowing runes lighting the faint tendrils.

The soldiers took a step back from Rhys. The rogue ignored them. He was focused on the swarming demons in front of them and the larger arch-demons who were quickly catching up. They were all headed directly toward the library.

"I don't know how I did that," admitted Ben.

"You used your instinct," responded Rhys. "Remember, anything in this world is possible if you have the will to do it."

Slowly, Ben followed his instinct and took a tentative step forward.

"There we go," encouraged Rhys, taking a step to match Ben.

Ben felt himself sliding into the sense of calm he'd felt earlier in the fight near the gates. There was no time to turn, no time to run. Fighting the evil creatures charging across the square was the only choice. It was simple.

He took another step then broke into a jog. Delay was pointless. The sound of the wind filled his head again.

It wasn't the soft, subtle breeze that stirred the leaves on a sunny spring day. This was the sound of a storm howling through the bare branches of winter's trees, a screaming gale blasting down the mountainous ravines and valleys that surrounded Farview. It was the sound of home, the sound of a place that had no ruler but its own, it was the sound of defiance.

Rhys followed in Ben's wake. Behind them, Ben heard the clatter of armor as the company protecting the library fell in. Despite themselves, Ben suspected. But they also had to know that there was only one way to live through this battle. Kill or die. The demons would give no quarter.

Towaal yelled something, but Ben did not hear. He was

entirely focused on the closing wave of demons. Squat, muscular shapes that reached the height of his shoulder were leaping and bounding forward. They were closing quickly, only fifty paces away.

At twenty-five paces, the two sides were rushing forward at full speed, eager to engage and finish it.

Ben drew his hand back. Still running, he violently swept it across his body, pushing with all of his might at the air in front of him.

A blast of thunderous wind raced ahead of the charging men and blew into the line of demons like an avalanche. Bodies twisted wildly as they were picked up and scattered backward. They fell on their backs and sides and slid across the cobble-stones, pushed by the powerful wind.

Men surged into the wake of the gale and fell on the fallen and stunned demons. Scores of demons were slaughtered where they lay, too confused to understand what happened to them.

The arch-demons were the first to recover. They hadn't been thrown as violently as their smaller fellows, and they quickly rose. They bellowed challenges that shook the foundations of the buildings ringing the square.

Berserk madness filled Ben's veins. He ran right at them, his mage-wrought blade drawn back for the first swing.

Beside him, Rhys ran as well, his longsword now clearly trailing a brilliant streamer of silver smoke.

Briefly, Ben thought the towering creatures cringed at the sight of the two men. It could have been his imagination. Before he could be sure, he was amongst them.

He slashed neatly into the first demon's thigh and kept moving to avoid its sweeping claws. Another spun, trying to catch him, missing with its grasping hands, but fouling his path with extended wings.

Ben cut at the leathery appendage then jumped to the side,

barely avoiding a huge taloned foot, which slammed down where he had been headed.

Between the legs and wings, he saw Rhys spinning and cutting like a mad dervish. His blazing glyph-covered blade passed through the flesh and bone of the demons with the ease of slicing through cold air.

Howls and confusion filled the square. Within heartbeats, the massive creatures were stumbling away from Rhys. All of their attention was on the rogue. He and his blade were a blur.

Ben took advantage and plunged his sword into the spine of an easy target. Twisting, he yanked the weapon free and endeavored to make contact with the crowd around him. The things were so tall it was near impossible to get a killing blow, but the mage-wrought steel cut clean and deep.

Ducking and spinning, he wasn't able to avoid the back of one clawed hand whipping down, trying to catch him. It struck him squarely in the face, just above his right eye. The force of the blow sent him flying.

He ricocheted off the leg of another demon and fell to the ground, stunned. Blood poured into his right eye. Blinking furiously, he scrambled to his feet. Out of his one good eye, he could see a third of the monsters had been felled. One by him and the rest by Rhys. The others surrounded him.

Abandoning his attack, Ben jumped away from one huge beast. He was engulfed from behind by another's wing. The leathery skin tumbled him forward and he was rolling across the cobblestones. Animal instinct took over. He twisted away as a massive foot stomped down a hand's length away from him.

Ben was on his back, staring up at a demon twice his height. It was directly over him, legs spread on either side. Its huge head was tilted down and he looked into its soulless eyes. A human would have sneered at him. The demon just raised its foot, ready to crush out his life.

A spear punched into its abdomen and the creature howled.

Ben shoved himself back, pushing with his heels and elbows.

Armored men swarmed around him, thrusting polearms into the arch-demon then getting clobbered by its heavy arm. Half a dozen of the men were swept away like crumbs brushed off a table. More men surged forward behind them. Through the blood staining his vision, Ben recognized the captain. He'd finally gotten into the fight.

Ben lurched to his feet and stumbled away from the fighting. His vision was swirling and brilliant flashes of color pulsated in front of him. He tried to wipe the blood out of his eye and ignore the ringing bell that filled his head.

Originating from where the demon had struck his skull, waves of nausea roiled his body. He hung his head and dropped to one knee.

As he was going down, a sharp and painful tug caught the back of his tunic and spun him around. He crashed onto his back in time to see a squat, muscular demon leaping forward to land on him. It wasn't one of the massive arch-demons, but it was big enough.

A heavy foot slammed onto his sword arm. Ben quickly realized struggling to free the arm was useless. The demon weighed twice what he did, and from his back, he had no leverage.

The creature opened its maw wide and descended to tear out Ben's throat. He could feel its awful breath on his face.

With his left hand, he yanked out his hunting knife and whipped it up into the demon's jaw. He shoved as hard as he could to punch through the tough flesh.

A hand's length from his face, he saw his steel slide through the bottom to the top of the demon's open mouth, ending with three fingers of the knife buried in its brain.

A shower of foul, purple blood dripped down onto his face. The heavy creature's body collapsed on him.

Struggling weakly, Ben tried to wiggle out from under the weight. He was trapped. His sword arm was now free, but the other hand was pinned underneath the demon, still gripping his hunting knife. He managed to push its head off to one side so its blood was no longer drenching his face, but he couldn't get out from under it.

His breath was coming short and fast, his ribcage unable to expand with the weight on top of him.

Ben felt a thump through the cobblestones and turned to look. One of the arch-demons was walking toward him. Broken spearheads and wounds from the soldiers' swords marred its body, but none of those soldiers were in Ben's field of vision now. The demon had an unobstructed route to him, and he couldn't move. Pinned beneath the creature on top of him, he had no way to defend himself. He panicked, knowing that death was just moments away.

With a reserve of strength he didn't know existed, he made a final, determined effort to pull loose. Bit by bit, he exerted everything he had and was able to pull his left hand free. With both hands in the open, he shoved down on the dead creature and slid himself out from under it.

He scrambled across the cobblestones, searching for his sword. The approaching arch-demon was just a long stride away when Ben turned to face it. He saw his longsword now, behind the approaching monster, too far to reach. His knife was still buried in the dead demon at his feet.

The wind he felt earlier wasn't in his head. He realized it was tied to the sword. Without the weapon in his hand, he couldn't pull the same trick.

Scrambling backward, he looked for anything he could try to defend himself with, but he knew it was too late. The massive demon roared, and Ben cringed, imagining the pain when those arm-length teeth ripped his body apart.

Suddenly, a spear of silver light burst through the front of the demon's chest then drew back. Surprised, the creature dropped to its knees, right in front of Ben.

Ben jumped away, knowing that if he got trapped under that one there was no way he could get out from under it.

Slowly, the demon toppled forward.

Ben smiled when he saw Rhys standing behind it, blazing silver longsword held shakily in front of him.

"You look like shit," muttered Rhys, sinking down to his knees, clearly exhausted.

Around them, a score of the remaining soldiers all watched silently. A dozen arch-demons, each twice the height of a man, were dead. Limbs the thickness of Ben's torso lay neatly severed next to bodies that had razor clean stab wounds and lacerations. Thin tendrils of silver smoke curled away from many of the brutal injuries.

The fighting continued in the square around them, but in the immediate area, it was clear. The smaller demons were either scared of the arch-demons or scared of Rhys. The other soldiers made for easier targets.

"Did you do all of that?" panted Ben, glancing at the carnage.

Rhys, shoulders and body slumped, shivers running violently through him, didn't answer.

Ben sat down, the sting of his injuries nearly overwhelming him. He could feel blood leaking from his body. His head, shoulder, back, and arms all had open, freely bleeding wounds. Without medical care, he knew he wouldn't make it very long.

Sitting on the ground, he looked up. The cobblestones were still shuddering with the stomp of heavy feet. In the square, nothing seemed to have changed. Men and demons fought, but the biggest of the creatures were lying dead, felled by Rhys.

Soon, the remaining soldiers around him noticed the thumps as well and turned. Swords and spears were raised in preparation. For what, Ben couldn't see.

Then he did.

Above the heads of the nearby soldiers, he saw a massive monster of a demon enter the square. It towered above the buildings around it, standing at least five or six stories tall. When it entered the square, it spread its wings. In the darkness of the night, Ben couldn't tell where they ended.

He sat calmly, watching it. His head may reach the top of its foot, he thought. The soldiers had two reactions. Half of them stood staring, too frightened to move. The other half turned and fled. Ben didn't blame them. There was nothing they could do to face this opponent. Swords and spears would be useless against a monster like that.

Towaal, though, she was ready.

An arc of brilliant white lightning shot across the square and impacted the demon's chest, four stories above Ben's head.

The creature roared with fury. Ben felt his hair stir with the force of the sound. He winced, covering his ears with blood-sticky hands.

Flexing, the creature seemed to pull into itself. Then it burst outward, the lightning blasting back and leaping uncontrolled across the square. Men and demon alike burst into flame as it danced among them. Almost as soon as it started, the lightning flickered out. It left a colorful afterimage burned into Ben's eyes.

The demon strode forward and casually scooped up a squad of men in two powerful hands. It tore off their heads and sucked in their life-blood as easily as Ben would bite an apple.

From the firelight in the square, Ben could see a smoking wound the size of a large man's shield burned into its chest. If the injury bothered the demon, it didn't show a sign of it.

Next, one of the huge braziers placed in the square blazed higher and higher. The flames whipped up into the sky. The burning brands within the brazier flared with an unnatural intensity. From over one hundred paces away, the heat of the fire was uncomfortably close to singeing Ben's skin. He raised an arm, trying to block the heat radiating toward him.

The towering inferno soared higher and higher until it collapsed, a wave of fire crashing down onto the arch-demon.

The creature howled and drew its wings around itself, crouching under the blistering heat. The red and orange flames obscured it for several heartbeats until they vanished in a puff of hot air.

The stench of burning flesh filled the square, but Ben was dismayed to see the demon rise from its crouch, stretching to its full height and flapping its wings.

Undeterred by the fire, it started forward.

Silver smoke, just like what Ben saw coming off of Rhys' sword, swirled across the ground. It raced at knee-height, like a flood coming down a mountainside. Narrow slices split off and cracked upward at the demon, lashing at it like whips. From all directions, over and over again, the silvery tails struck upward. The demon stumbled back, unsure of where the sudden pain was coming from.

Men and demons fled away from the smoke. It drifted around where Ben sat, but he felt nothing from it. The whips were causing damage to the huge demon, though. Thin lines of purple blood bloomed along its arms, legs, and sides.

The big demon's wings folded around it again, but the constant whipping from the silver smoke continued. The demon roared and Ben felt like his eardrums may burst. The sound was like metal tearing, amplified one hundred fold.

Ben looked back toward the library. He couldn't see Towaal. A curtain of the silver smoke and more mundane black smoke from fires throughout the city blocked his view. He knew she was back there somewhere, directing the smoke whips to strike.

The demon stomped its foot and the ground shuddered. The silver smoke fell back then rushed forward again, lashing the creature faster and faster, but as Ben watched, he saw the strikes were getting weaker and falling lower on the demon's body.

One whip stiffened, thickening until it was a good two paces across. It thrust upward, racing toward the demon's heart, but the huge creature waved a massive hand and scattered the lance of smoke. It dissipated in the night air, falling down into the smoke swirling around below.

In heartbeats, the attack stopped, and the demon cautiously shook its tattered wings. It was visibly injured, but as it started to stride forward again, Ben saw none of the slashes had cut deep enough to be fatal. Superficial wounds wouldn't be enough to stop the monster. He hoped Towaal had more up her sleeve than that.

The demon scanned the square, looking for the source of the attacks. It stopped halfway across. It was staring toward the library, where Ben knew Towaal would be standing.

He struggled to his feet to get a better look. He saw the diminutive woman standing proudly, facing the demon while the rest of the square looked on or fled.

She held a broken wooden rod in her hand. She wasn't doing anything.

The arch-demon snarled, drawing Ben's attention.

It strode forward, the ground shaking with each powerful step. In heartbeats, it would be on Towaal.

Ben rushed to his sword, unsure what he could do to help. Raising the weapon, he knew the huge demon was moving far faster on its long legs than he could. The blasts of wind he'd used earlier wouldn't reach that far.

Then, behind Towaal, a frenzy of sparkling lights exploded out of the library and rushed toward the demon. They looked like fireflies, or sparks from fireworks, but they moved faster than a crossbow bolt.

Wave after wave of the things flew out from the library door and slammed into the demon. It paused, darting to the side, trying to avoid the stream of lights. They followed right after it. The creature waved a massive hand and sent the cloud flying away. The lights turned and came back. Each light sunk into the demon like a tiny pinprick. There were thousands of them, and they kept coming. Prick after prick.

The demon staggered backward, snarling in rage. Smaller demons rushed forward, swarming around its feet, but the lights ignored them. They kept lancing into the arch-demon. It fell another staggering step backward. A cheer went up from the men in the square.

A flight of arrows flashed into the sky. Ben turned to see a company of archers on a rooftop at the edge of the square. They were firing down on the arch-demon and the swarm around it. Arrow after arrow. The cascade of tiny, stabbing lights from the library continued unabated.

Emboldened, the men who had been fighting a losing battle against the rest of the demons felt the tide turn. They fell on the creatures near them. The spell of the battle between the huge arch-demon and the mage was broken. Fighting intensified everywhere.

The big arch-demon didn't participate. It couldn't. The lights hit it again and again, still blasting out of the library door like sparks out of a blacksmith's forge. The creature was covering its eyes and staggering backward. It was now almost to the edge of the square. The lights showed no sign of stopping.

Then an explosion hit it in the back. It lurched forward like it had been punched.

It was one of Amelie's iron balls, realized Ben. A smaller explosion than they'd seen at the walls, but enough to do damage to the demon. A cluster of brave men stood nearby on a rooftop, hurtling the ammunition from a makeshift sling. They launched another one.

Another explosion followed and the demon crashed into one of the buildings lining the square. Its huge arm punched through the wall. The structure teetered and leaned alarmingly against the building next to it. The swarming lights picked up in intensity, prick after prick.

A third explosion lit the square, this time hitting the arch-demon in the front. Ben could see an ugly chunk of meat had been blown out of its shoulder. He knew from before, sharp pieces of iron would be embedded into its flesh.

A ball of white lightning danced across the space and crashed into the huge creature. It wasn't as big a blast as the first one, but it sizzled and hissed when it struck the demon, burning and shocking.

It was too much. An anguished cry spilt the night, stabbing into Ben's head like a spear. He fell to one knee, gripping his head, but the impact on the smaller demons was bigger. As one, they turned and fled, rushing down the city streets and toward the exterior walls. The huge arch-demon careened after them, arrows, lightning, and the firefly sparks chasing it, unrelenting.

From the library, Ben heard a whoosh, like a fire flaring to light. A thick cloud of the sparks blasted out the door. The dense cloud bathed the square in a bright glow. Flying across the square, the sparks smashed into the back of the huge arch-demon, penetrating through its wings and sinking into its flesh.

Standing at the entrance to the square, blocking the main thoroughfare, the massive creature turned. It leaned back as if to howl, but instead of sound, a stream of the sparks billowed out of its mouth and eyes. The sparks poured out as the arch-demon twisted in silent agony. Its life was draining out with each tiny spark. It seemed to deflate in front of Ben's eyes. Omnipotent power leaked into the air, heartbeat by heartbeat.

Two more staggering steps then the huge creature crashed into a nearby building, smashing through the mortar walls like they were parchment.

With a boom that shook the entire city, the demon fell flat. It lay motionless as the rest of the building collapsed down on top of it. Only its feet were visible, the rest it obscured by rubble.

The sparks swirled higher into the sky, high above Northport, and then blinked out one by one, until none remained.

Dust and smoke drifted across the suddenly quiet square.

Slowly, Ben could hear cheers growing throughout the city as more people realized the demons were on the run. The terrified cries of the creatures grew faint and the wild celebrations of men rolled across Northport like a wave.

Frantic captains and sergeants rushed out of the square and toward where the demons had fled. Ben was sure they were extolling their men to remain on guard. The demons were running now, but they were still a threat. They were still demons. The officers had to ensure the celebrations didn't get out of hand.

Ben smiled. They had done it. They had driven off the demons. His smile faded though as he surveyed the area around him. Armored bodies lay like a thick carpet.

Northport still lived, but many of its defenders did not.

16

IN THE RUBBLE

BEN SAT. Blood dribbled down his sides and dripped steadily to the cold cobblestones below. All around him lay the dead—men and demons. A sour charnel scent filled his nostrils. He was too tired to be sick.

Several paces away, Rhys knelt with his chin lying on his chest. Ben could see he was breathing, but he didn't seem to have moved since before the huge demon entered the square. Whatever he did with his sword drained him.

Ben felt weak and cold. He knew it was the loss of blood. He couldn't bring himself to move and find help.

He watched as soldiers and eventually women and children entered the square. The men stared about dumbfounded, looking at the carnage and death. The women searched frantically, trying to find husbands, lovers, or sons. The children stared uncomprehending and blank faced. It was surreal. They couldn't process what had happened. Like Ben.

"You alive?" asked a sweet voice behind him.

Ben shifted to see Corinne, flanked by a pair of serious-looking archers.

"Yeah, for now," he rasped.

"You look like shit," she mentioned.

"So I've been told," Ben groaned.

"Take him to the triage tent," she instructed the men beside her. "We'll get you patched back up," she said to Ben.

"Him too?" asked Ben, tilting his chin toward Rhys.

"What happened to him?" asked Corinne, rushing toward the rogue. She knelt and wrapped her arms around the man, but he didn't react.

"He killed a dozen of those big demons," answered Ben. "It drained him."

"By himself?" exclaimed Corinne.

Ben nodded.

She tersely demanded to one of the archers, "Take him to the keep. Send for Oliver, Rhymer's physic. He's the most likely to be able to deal with something like this. Do it now!"

The archer and Corinne lifted Rhys, looping his arm over the man's shoulder. The man staggered under the weight of Ben's friend. A determined look on his face gave Ben confidence he would make it to the keep. The other archer bowed to Rhys in respect. Rhys didn't see it, which maybe was for the best. He didn't need anything more to inflate his ego.

"We have more wounded than physics," murmured Corinne, watching the archer limp away with Rhys.

"I don't need..." started Ben.

Corinne interrupted him and barked an order at the second archer beside her, "Take him to the tent. Don't listen if he says anything different. I'll be checking."

The man dragged Ben to his feet. Ben's injuries stretched painfully. He gritted his teeth as he felt a fresh stream of blood leak from the open wounds.

With the man's assistance, they left to find help. Every couple of paces, they stepped over the body of a man or a beast.

∾

BEN WOKE up to see Amelie staring down at him.

"You look like shit," she remarked.

"Still?" he asked jokingly. He shifted to sit up and winced at the pain. He'd forgotten how cut up he was.

She shrugged. "I don't know what you looked like earlier. I'm just saying you look like shit right now."

"What time is it?" he asked with a groan.

"Almost evening," she responded.

His body ached. He could still feel the sharp sting where the demons had torn his flesh. He finally sat up with a grunt and his head swam.

"Here," said Amelie, passing him a cup of water. "If you can, you need to eat to get your strength up. They told me you lost a lot of blood."

He swung his legs off the bed onto the floor and cringed as the motion pulled the hasty stitches the field physic had sewn into him. He slowed down. Ben didn't want the stitches to tear loose and have to go back to the triage tent. The harried physic put about as much attention into his stitching as Ben did into lacing his boots.

They were in Ben's room in the keep. He was shirtless, too tired the night before to change his attire. He still wore the same pants he'd fought in. They smelled awful.

"A bath also. As soon as you've finished eating," added Amelie, pulling a face.

She placed a hand on his shoulder, looking at the rough stitches there. "I think I could have done a better job than this."

A warm tingle crept into his arm where she touched him. She was trying to heal him. He didn't comment, but gently moved her hand and tried to stand. Ben's stomach rumbled when he rose unsteadily to his feet.

"I think the physic was in a bit of a hurry," muttered Ben. "There was a long line."

"Can you change your pants on your own?" asked Amelie.

"They smell horrific, and I think you have demon blood in your hair." She shook her head, frowning at him. "I changed my mind. You need to wash up now. I can't sit next to you and eat food until you smell a little bit more like soap and a lot less like dead animal."

Ben smiled ruefully. "I'll manage."

"Good. I'll wait for you outside," she said. "We have a lot to discuss."

Ben changed as quickly as he could, grimacing at every movement. Amelie waited patiently for him in the hallway. They went to the mess hall. The dining room was closed, there was no one to staff it, explained Amelie.

"Rhys and Towaal?" asked Ben as they sat down.

Two-day-old bread, cold meat, and hard cheese. Not a feast, but his stomach rumbled as he realized it had been a full day since he'd eaten.

"Towaal is in the library. She went in after the battle and hasn't come out since. I saw some things during the fight, things I can't really explain..." She shrugged. "Something happened in that library, but it has been so hectic I haven't had time to talk to her. I ducked my head in to see if she was okay and she ignored me. Back to normal for her."

Ben swallowed a bite of the stale bread. "And Rhys?"

"His wounds will heal," she said with a frown. "I checked on him earlier and he's...different. You need to see him. He was asleep when I looked in, but maybe he's awake now."

Ben looked at her curiously. What did she mean?

Amelie continued without giving more details, "The city is a shambles. I don't think anyone has any real idea yet how many people were killed. Entire neighborhoods were flattened in the fighting and companies of soldiers have gone missing. Bodies of demons and people are everywhere. I heard Rhymer is giving instructions to have it cleaned up, but last I was outside, there was hardly anyone moving about."

"They were up all night fighting," mumbled Ben around a tough piece of sliced mutton.

"That's true." Amelie sighed. "Someone will have to do something about the bodies soon though, or else there will be pestilence. After war, that many corpses have been known to kill more than the battle itself."

"I saw Corinne at the end," said Ben. "She made it."

Amelie looked down. "I heard Seneschal Franklin didn't."

Ben grimaced and took another bite of mutton.

Amelie sat silently then asked, "After we finish eating, do you need to rest?"

Ben shook his head. "I don't think I could. I'm tired but not sleepy, if that makes any sense. How about you?"

"I slept enough earlier."

"Let's check on Rhys then find Lady Towaal," suggested Ben.

"Just what I was thinking," agreed Amelie.

Outside of Rhys' room, they could hear heavy snoring and moved on without looking in. He'd done enough and they didn't want to disturb him.

As they walked through the keep, it felt like nothing happened. There were fewer guards and maids shuffling about on their errands, but the place hadn't felt the impact of the battle. Everything was neat and tidy, just like the first time he had walked through these halls. The lords and courtiers of Northport remained safe and secure within the keep.

Once they passed out of the gates, it was a different story.

Heaps of corpses littered the square. Ben's stomach clenched. He paused, worried he might get sick.

"Awful," murmured Amelie. "Why isn't Rhymer doing something about this? Where are the soldiers?"

There were a few scattered teams of men with rags wrapped around their faces slowly loading wagons full of dead demons. With the number of dead, it would take them at least a week just to clear the square.

"The walls?" wondered Ben. "If it was me, I'd have men on the walls."

They picked their way carefully through the muck and carnage, heading toward the untouched library.

Ben looked to where the dozen arch-demons had fallen. Their bodies still lay there. Probably too big for any of the wagon crews to lift, he thought. He glanced over and saw the biggest one still lay buried in rubble, only the huge feet showing where it fell. He realized uncomfortably that someone was going to have to cut the creatures up and cart them out in pieces.

"You were very impressive last night," mentioned Amelie. "When we were on the wall, you held your own and did just as much as Rhys."

"I don't know about that," protested Ben. "Look at those arch-demons there." He turned back and pointed to the massive creatures. "That is what Rhys did. If it wasn't for him, I'm not sure we would have won the fight."

Amelie whistled. "That is impressive. Maybe next time you will do the same."

"Next time," Ben snorted. "Let's hope there isn't a next time."

"They're still out there," she reminded him. "Hundreds, maybe thousands of them fled. Someone has to face them."

"You weren't so bad yourself," responded Ben, changing the subject. He knew she was right, but he didn't want to talk about it. "Those artillery balls were amazing."

Amelie blushed. "I realized something when we were in the Wilds. I don't have the training Towaal has, and I certainly don't have the power, but proper preparation can make up for that. I can be smart. Every force has an equal and opposite reaction. I used that with the balls and just redirected the force when they impacted. Instead of following a natural vector, it expanded outward from the core of the iron. Amplify it, add a little heat to the mix, and you've got a pretty effective weapon. It only worked because the velocity of the flight was so great."

"You lost me after equal and opposite," responded Ben.

"Well," said Amelie, "That's the theory–law, really. Every force has an equal and opposite reaction."

They stepped into the unguarded door of the library and blinked in the darkness. Ben found a candle near the entrance and lit it with a striker kept there for the purpose. No one was around, so they continued deeper into the stacks.

"Like the Alliance and Coalition?" asked Ben after a pause.

Amelie frowned. "I'm talking physics."

Ben shrugged. "I don't know much about that, or politics really, but from what I've observed, that is what's happening. The Coalition raised a force and the Alliance responded. Equal and opposite. Maybe it's not a theory in a book, but if you see it, that means something, right? I think there's a word for that..."

"Information gathered through observation is empirical evidence," mumbled Amelie, lost in thought.

"Empire what?" asked Ben, confused.

"Never mind," she replied quietly. "In pure physics, the opposite forces are reactions. They don't have an aspect."

"I'm not following," replied Ben.

"They're not good or evil, right or wrong," explained Amelie. "They are natural forces."

They were in the open room in the center of the building now but couldn't see anyone or any light. They crept around tall shelves, looking for a sign of Lady Towaal.

"So, you're saying it's not the same," asked Ben in a whisper, "because the Coalition is evil?"

"I'm not sure," answered Amelie.

Ben looked at her out of the corner of his eye.

"When Argren formed the Alliance, he said it was for the good of the people," she continued. "He said we would stand together to fight evil, and I believed him. But earlier, when Lord Jason visited Issen, he also claimed the Coalition was for the good of the people. He said it in almost the same words. Myland in Free

State didn't think there was any difference between the two. What if…" Amelie paused, gathering her thoughts. "What if Argren and Jason both believe what they say. What if they both think they are doing good?"

Ben frowned. He hadn't thought of it like that. "Well, I wouldn't say that what either group is doing is good right now. Lord Jason tried to capture you and is attacking Issen. Lord Argren hasn't lifted a finger to help and seems to only be interested in protecting his own interests."

"Exactly," responded Amelie.

Ben rubbed his hand over his face. He was still exhausted from the battle the day before and wasn't prepared for this type of thinking.

"Deep discussions," echoed a tired voice behind them.

Ben and Amelie both jumped in surprise. They spun and nearly dropped the candle into a pile of dry, loose leafed books.

"Be careful with that," scolded Towaal, looking at the candle. "Every time I think I teach you something…" She waved for them to follow her into the darkness. Muttering quietly, she kept talking to herself, "Nearly burning down the most important library left in Alcott. Unbelievable."

Ben and Amelie exchanged a sheepish glance then followed her to a back corner where she ducked through a curtain.

Brushing it aside, Ben saw a narrow stone hallway lit by a single wall sconce. The hallway appeared to lead beyond where he thought the wall of the library should have been. At the end of it was a warmly lit doorway that Towaal disappeared into. They scampered after her.

Through the doorway was a small room, roughly the size of Ben's apartment in Farview. It contained only a short wooden shelf, a tall cabinet, and a well-worn reading chair.

The doors of the cabinet hung open to reveal a set of shelves holding a scattering of miscellany. Ben couldn't tell the purpose of any of it, but given its place in the library, he assumed Towaal stumbled across something important.

"We came to check on you," said Amelie, peering around the room.

"Of course," murmured Towaal. Dark shadows hung below her eyes and she had a rumpled, distracted look about her. Compared to her usual, professional demeanor, it was shocking. She reminded Ben of when he'd seen Amelie and Meghan just after big exams at the Sanctuary.

"Are you okay?" asked Amelie.

Towaal nodded. "I have been learning a lot over the last two days."

Ben waited for her to continue.

"The Purple has not entirely disappeared," remarked Towaal.

"They were here?" asked Ben, looking around the room with renewed interest.

"Yes," answered Towaal. "The Librarian was more than he seemed."

"The Librarian is part of the Purple!" exclaimed Amelie. "Does Rhymer know?"

Towaal replied brusquely, "I am certain Rhymer knows more than he's told so far. I want to find out what I can in this place, and then I will confront him. This is too serious to keep secret. And the Librarian was part of the Purple, not is."

"What do you mean?" queried Ben. "Is he dead?"

"After the battle, the Librarian is no more," she answered. "He..." She frowned, visibly searching for the right word. "Disintegrated."

Ben stared at her.

"I believe he utilized more will than he was capable of commanding," she explained. "Whether on purpose or on accident, he somehow converted himself into pure energy. It was expended attacking the arch-demon."

"The lights!" guessed Ben.

Towaal nodded. "Yes, that was him. I was at my limit and had used all of the power stored in the rod. Without him, the arch-demon would have run rampant. As I suspected he would, the Librarian stepped in and defended Northport."

"As you suspected?" asked Amelie.

"Yes," replied Towaal. "I knew that if the arch-demon had truly been alive for millennia, even with the repository, I would be insufficient. I counted on the Purple resurfacing. They had to prevent the slaughter and harvesting of the life-blood in Northport as well as protect the rift key."

"How did you know they would be able to, uh, resurface?" asked Ben. "How could you be sure?"

Towaal replied, "When I found the rift key and the documents relating to it, there were clues. The Librarian was extremely upset I found what I did, and after that, he refused to answer questions. It was enough for me to put some pieces together. For example, there is only one Librarian listed anywhere in relation to this library. How no one else seems to have noticed that, I do not know. The mind believes what it wants to believe, I suppose. Certainly no one expected there to be a male mage. The man we met was long-lived."

"What about his assistant?" asked Amelie.

Towaal shrugged. "He is missing. Whether he had something to do with the Purple, whether he is also a male mage, I do not know."

Ben frowned. "And you think the Librarian was here to protect this rift key?"

"I can only assume, yes," answered Towaal.

"Are there others? Other members of the Purple in Northport?" asked Amelie.

Towaal did not answer. Most likely, she didn't have an answer.

"So, it's over then," declared Ben. "You have the rift key, and the arch-demon was defeated. Now we can focus on our other problems, like Issen."

Towaal coughed. "Not exactly."

Ben frowned, dreading what was next.

"We have a rift key here, which, of course, must be protected at all costs," continued Towaal. "If you remember, right before the fight, I mentioned there is another key. These documents lead me to believe it is located in Irrefort."

"The capital of the Coalition?" Ben groaned.

Towaal nodded.

"What does that have to do with us?" griped Amelie.

Towaal sat down in the lone reading chair in the room and slumped back, silent.

Amelie stared at her. "You want us to go to Irrefort?"

Towaal didn't deny the accusation.

Ben paced back and forth across the small room. "What do you expect us to do in Irrefort? Go ask Lord Jason if he has any magical keys to create a new Rift?"

"I'm not sure what you should do," answered Towaal quietly. "I wish I had the answer. Helping Issen would be an honorable thing to do if you can figure out how to do it, and I worry the demon problem is not yet finished here. Hundreds of demons fled after the battle. Maybe we could help with that somehow."

She sat in the chair listlessly, not meeting their eyes. "I cannot help you by giving you the answer. I am trying to help by sharing information that is contained in these documents." She waved to a sheaf of parchment stacked on a small writing table. "As you've been told, I am willing to follow your lead. It's up to you what you want to do."

"And if we did go get this rift key..." started Ben.

"It would need to be protected or maybe even used," finished Towaal. "Remember, we do not know what the consequences of destroying the first rift will be. If I could go back, I would have spent more time interviewing the Librarian. At the time, of course, we did not know his role, and he did not have a chance to confront us before we made our final decision. He was rather angry at us afterward. I can only hope we did not make a mistake."

"This is not enough information," protested Ben. "You're asking us to make decisions about things we know nothing about. We need to know more."

"I agree," nodded Towaal sagely, "but I do not have the information you want."

"Who does?" exclaimed Ben.

"The Purple," replied Towaal calmly.

"But," complained Ben, frustrated at Towaal's reticence, "we are back at square one. Where do we even find one of these Purple?"

"The Librarian was located in the same place as a rift key," remarked Towaal. "Maybe the rift key in Irrefort also has a guardian?"

"Well, that is just…" Amelie started then paused. "I'm too tired for this," she finished helplessly.

After breakfast the next morning, Ben went to check on Rhys.

In his friend's room, a chambermaid directed him outside to a small, bare courtyard. Rhys was sitting, wrapped in a heavy cloak, and sipping a cup of kaf.

Ben stepped into the courtyard and Rhys began speaking without looking over. "Funny, isn't it. It is cold when you think about it, but after the Wilds, I find it quite comfortable outside."

Ben grunted. It felt pretty cold to him.

He walked toward his friend then slowed as he got close. Something was different about Rhys.

His friend finally looked over and gave a wan smile.

Ben stared, confused. Shallow laugh lines webbed out from Rhys' eyes, his cheeks looked gaunt, and two wings of snow white graced his hair at the temples. Rhys was older.

"You look…different," said Ben hesitantly.

"That I do," agreed Rhys.

Ben sat next to his friend on the iron bench and almost immediately regretted it. Despite Rhys' opinion, the bench was damn cold. The chill crept through Ben's thick wool britches.

He looked at Rhys again. He didn't know where to start. How do you ask a friend why he suddenly appears fifteen years older than he did the day before?

Rhys brushed back his cloak and laid a hand on his longsword leaning against the bench.

"When Towaal explained mage craft to you, she discussed how anything was possible with enough will and knowledge," he murmured. "For the most part, that is true. To be complete, there is a third ingredient to performing magic. Energy. Will and knowledge are the tools to manipulate the world around us. The material you are actually manipulating is energy. The electricity she raised, the heat Amelie used to start a fire, it is all energy. If there is no energy in the environment, a mage, or someone using a magical device, can draw that energy from within themselves."

Ben nodded. Towaal hadn't said it this way, but that was similar to what she described.

Rhys kept talking after a sip of his kaf. "You've seen Towaal draw from her own reserves. She gets tired and sleeps. There are other, more permanent sources of energy that can be drawn from."

Rhys' sword lay between them, the wire-wrapped hilt sticking up. Ben edged his elbow away from it.

"I don't understand," responded Ben.

"Demons feed on our life forces as a source of energy, for example."

"Oh," said Ben, a sickening feeling growing in his stomach.

"That type of thing," remarked Rhys, "you can't just get a good night sleep and recover from."

"You mean, there is a slower recovery, or no recovery?" asked Ben hesitantly.

Rhys finished his kaf and shrugged. "I've been alive a very long time. I've seen a lot of things I didn't believe were possible and a lot of things I didn't expect to see. So, who knows? Anything is possible with enough will."

"Is there," Ben paused, "anything I can do?"

"Like make me a casserole?" snorted Rhys.

"I, uh, I guess I don't know," replied Ben sheepishly. "If I can help…"

"No, Ben, there's nothing you can do," answered Rhys. He raised his empty mug. "Come on. I need a refill."

Rhys stood slowly and grimaced. He placed a steadying hand on the arm of the bench as he rose. "This will take a bit of getting used to. I think it must be similar to what you feel like when you try to drink with me."

Ben snorted. "Faker."

The rogue chuckled then headed back inside the keep. Ben followed behind. His friend didn't move like the creaky grandfather he pretended to be when he stood, but he also didn't move like the buoyant raconteur he had been a few days before.

THE CLEANUP of Northport progressed slowly. After a few days, Rhymer devoted more resources and the city started to look like a livable place again. One by one, markets reopened and kids came out from hiding to play in the streets. The scars of the battle would last for years though, maybe generations.

Ben and Amelie briefly pitched in, but Ben quickly found he had no interest in carting off several-day-old dead bodies. He didn't even know where to begin on rebuilding. They'd fought for Northport, and that was enough.

Rhymer was a whirl of activity, the polar opposite of Ben's impression of the man when they were in Whitehall. He supposed losing his crutch of a seneschal and nearly losing the entire city was a wake-up call for the man.

Towaal remained buried in the library, trying to learn anything else she could about the Purple and their purpose with the Rift.

Rhys drank, heavily.

In and of itself, that wasn't unusual for the rogue, but he carried a darkness around him now. He'd lost some of his jovial, joking nature. Corinne spent a lot of time with him. Mostly, she stayed silent by his side. Ben hoped that, in time, his friend would come out of himself and see her there. She had lost her father. They both could use someone to lean on.

Ben prodded Rhys about it, trying to cheer him up.

Rhys responded sharply, "I'll be fine. She'll be fine. We both just need to move on, to go in a new direction. How is that going, by the way?"

Ben sighed. That was the problem. He and Amelie didn't know what direction they should take. She was worried about her father and family in Issen. There were the rift keys to consider in Irrefort. Expeditionary parties would be formed in the coming weeks to scout the demons' movements, and there was the ever-present threat from the Sanctuary. If they knew where to go, they would leave that day.

Instead, they delayed in Northport. They spent their days resting, practicing the sword, the Ohms, and hardening their wills. Amelie practiced some minor healing on Ben's wounds, and while he would always have scars from the fight, the sharp stab of pain faded away. It was tender, but he could live with that. For sword practice, he was able to move about without fear of tearing open his stitches.

Word came that the siege had begun in Issen. The messenger said Amelie's father was putting up a stout defense. The Coalition was reported to have four times as many men, but Lord Gregor had his walls. A siege could last for months.

When she first heard, Amelie wanted to rush immediately to her father's side. After discussing it with Ben and Rhys, she realized that without an army at her back, there wasn't much she could do. It was unlikely they'd even reach Issen with the Coalition completely encircling it. Getting captured outside of the city walls would just make it worse for her father and everyone inside.

She needed an army, and Lord Rhymer was in no position to provide one. They didn't know who else to turn to.

~

A WEEK AFTER THE BATTLE, Ben and Amelie were returning across the square from another fruitless discussion with Lady Towaal. The woman was buried in ancient paper and artifacts. She had no advice she was willing to give the two young folk. She just turned it back on them, asking them what they wanted to do.

The square had a scattering of people rushing about trying to finish their chores before they lost the last light of day. It was growing colder and a light dusting of snow had fallen the night before. It still clung to the cobblestones and coated the eaves of the rooftops like a light froth on a freshly poured ale.

Ben imagined in better times the square would be filled with young people escaping from their parents' clutches and congregating with their friends. The sounds of laughter and children getting into innocent trouble should be filling the space. Now, no one had time for that.

Ben meandered along, lost in his thoughts, until Amelie clutched his arm.

"Ben," she hissed, "is that..."

He followed her look and saw a slight figure darting ahead of them and vanishing down a narrow side street. He knew that brisk, determined stride.

"Meghan," he muttered.

"Should we get Towaal?" asked Amelie.

"We'll lose her if we do," replied Ben anxiously. He started toward the street Meghan went down, pulling Amelie behind him.

"Is this a good idea?" worried Amelie. "She betrayed us, Ben."

"She did, but she's my sister and was your friend," he responded. "Maybe it wasn't her, maybe some other way they found out. Maybe she had a change of heart."

"She could have men with her, or worse, a mage," argued Amelie, jogging along behind Ben as they hurried to catch sight of Meghan.

Ben felt Amelie's sense of foreboding. Meghan showing up here was unexpected. He doubted she could have found them without help, but he had to know. He had to know why she betrayed them.

"You should get Towaal. Tell her we saw Meghan," suggested Ben.

"If this is a trap, you can't go in alone," snapped Amelie.

They reached the street Meghan went down and Ben peered ahead into the shadows. The sun was setting, and the narrow streets of Northport would quickly be plunged into darkness.

"If this is a trap, we need Towaal," rejoined Ben.

"I'm going with you," demanded Amelie.

"Fine." He sighed.

"There!" exclaimed Amelie, pointing. They saw Meghan just in time to see her turn down another street, crimson cloak fluttering behind her as she walked.

"She's not being very circumspect," mentioned Amelie.

Ben nodded. Meghan wasn't trying to hide from them with that cloak, he was sure of that.

Several more blocks and they were trailing half a block behind her. Ben slowed their pace to follow from a distance.

Half a bell, they followed Meghan's cloak through the thin

crowds. She never once looked back, which eventually made Ben doubt she knew she was being followed.

"What if this isn't a trap," he wondered.

"Then I'm going to knock her head for tattling on us at the Sanctuary," grumbled Amelie.

"And if it is a trap?" Ben smirked.

"Then I'm still going to knock her head," snapped Amelie.

Meghan turned and entered a long building. They stopped. They were in the warehouse district of Northport and the streets were nearly empty.

"If I was going to set a trap for someone, I'd do it here," stated Amelie. She fidgeted, looking up and down the rough street.

Ben agreed.

"Let's move around back," he suggested. "No sense in walking right in and making it easy on them."

They dodged through a narrow alleyway cluttered with crates, barrels and other debris. Near the back of the warehouse, Ben spied windows high up, under the eaves of the roof. They'd be opened in the summer to get a cross breeze through the big structure, he guessed.

Silently, he pointed at them. Amelie looked around then waved him forward. A stack of broken and rotting crates leaned against the wall at the end of the alley. They appeared to have been there for years, sitting out in the weather.

Ben walked up to the boxes and shook them gently. The pile barely moved under his hand. He glanced back at Amelie and shrugged. They would either be able to climb up the pile and access the window above, or they would come crashing down with a huge amount of noise then land in a pile of broken wood. Either way, there was no chance he was going to walk in the front door of the warehouse. The pile was the only other option.

He knelt down to boost Amelie up, and she started scaling the stack, grabbing loose planks and hauling herself up and over each crate.

Ben followed slowly. Amelie was smaller than him. Just because the structure didn't collapse under her weight didn't mean he would make it. Concentrating on listening for any ominous sounding creaks, he crawled up the pile. Watching Amelie above him, he wasn't paying close enough attention to where he was putting his hands and earned himself a nasty splinter from a broken piece of crate.

Muttering under his breath, he sucked on his hand, trying to draw out the sharp spear of wood. A bit more carefully, he continued upward.

At the top of the pile, the crates shifted dangerously under their weight. Ben and Amelie moved slowly to not jostle the stack and send it all crashing to the ground.

They found the windows under the eave were shut. Ben examined them and saw they were loosely fit. He could see a simple catch through a gap and drew his hunting knife. Wedging it into the gap, he jimmied it along to push against the catch, springing it free. Then he pulled the window open.

"You learn that from Renfro or Rhys?" whispered Amelie.

"Heard about it in a story," he explained.

Peering into the dark warehouse, he couldn't see much, but saw there was a second floor to the place.

He sheathed his knife then wiggled into the open window. He promptly fell half a man height down to a dusty wooden floor. He froze, worried the thump of his fall would alert someone.

Nothing happened.

Amelie came in after him and he helped her down more gracefully.

They were in between two head-high rows of nondescript ceramic jars. Ahead of them, Ben could see the second floor ended in a loft. Down below, on the main floor, there was the flicker of light.

He met Amelie's eyes and held a finger to his lips. She nodded then followed Ben as he crawled forward, inching along the dusty board floor, and prioritizing silence over speed.

Glancing over the ledge of the loft, he saw Meghan in the middle of the floor. She was still in her crimson cloak and was facing an armed man. The man had three more companions seated at a table behind him. It looked like they had all been playing cards and drinking. The men wore no identifying marks, but Ben was certain who they were, Sanctuary men.

"What do you mean you haven't seen them!" demanded the man.

Ben pulled back so he could no longer see the people below. He could still hear.

"I think I was clear. I haven't seen them," retorted Meghan angrily. "I've checked every inn in this damn town. They aren't staying at any of them. They must be staying in the keep. It's the only other option. We can't take them in that place, so the best chance is to draw them here. I'm not sure how else I can explain that to you, captain."

Ben and Amelie looked at each other. They'd been certain it was her, but hearing her voice after so long brought everything that happened in the Sanctuary crashing back. The last time they heard that voice was minutes before she betrayed them.

"I'm sick of this waiting," snarled the man. "How can you have not seen them! How can they have not seen you!" His heavy boots thumped on the stone floor of the warehouse. He sounded like he was pacing back and forth. "If you were in the square all day like you said, then I am absolutely sure you would have seen them, or they would have seen you. I'm starting to doubt your loyalty."

"No one would have even known they left if it wasn't for me, captain," retorted Meghan sharply. "And don't think you can threaten me by casting dispersions about my loyalty. The mages know what I did and where my allegiance lies. I don't really give a damn about what you think. Until a mage tells me differently to my face, we're doing this my way. I don't want Initiate Amelie, I want all of them. We do it my way, we take them all at once. You heard the same orders I did. I've had just about enough of your shit."

Ben lay on his back, listening. Involuntarily, his hand gripped his longsword. Hearing his sister say in her own words that she betrayed him was almost too much.

The captain snorted. "Whatever. I'm done playing these games. If you are as loyal as you say you are, then I can only assume you are incompetent. Either way, I'll let the mage deal with you."

"There's no mage here..." Meghan stopped.

Ben and Amelie exchanged a silent look. Both, curious, rose up slowly to peer back down over the edge.

A new woman was standing in the torchlight. She was dressed finely and had a jewel-pommeled belt knife hanging on her side. She had to be the mage.

"I-I..." Meghan stuttered. "What are you doing here?"

"How do you think we knew to come to Northport?" chided the guard captain. "Ignorant girl. You think we just happened to choose this city? We've been following the mage's instructions this entire time. We brought you to help finish this without having to expend her. She is not pleased with your ineffectiveness."

"But my plan will work!" objected Meghan. "We heard there was magic used during the battle. Certainly they are here. I just need more time to find them."

The woman, the mage, stared back at Meghan then tilted her head. Ben's breath caught. The woman's face was brilliant white, porcelain white. Her lips were painted blood red, her cheeks blushed, and perfect black eyebrows arched over stark, dark holes. She was wearing a mask, he realized, a porcelain mask. The rest of her head was covered by a dark hood.

Unspeaking, the woman circled Meghan, tracing a finger across the back of her bright crimson cloak.

"I thought you were…" Meghan swallowed visibly. The taint of fear laced her voice. "I thought you were going to Whitehall when you recovered."

The woman didn't answer. She gripped Meghan's chin and turned her head to look into her eyes. Briefly, she held the look then released Meghan. Meghan's hand shot up and rubbed where the woman's fingers had pressed into her flesh.

The porcelain-faced woman nodded to the captain. The man grimaced and yanked out his belt knife.

Meghan's eyes popped wide open. She shouted, "No!"

It was too late. The captain took two quick strides forward and plunged his dagger into Meghan's side. Again and again, he punched his knife into her. Blood soaked her dress. Ben watched in horror as his sister slumped in the captain's arms. His feelings toward Meghan were complicated with her betrayal, but some part of him always hoped they had been mistaken.

Whatever her crimes, he certainly didn't want to see her stabbed to death in front of him. He remembered when he was just a little boy and she was the one person in Alistair's house who was kind to him. A sick feeling coursed through his body. He shut his eyes.

Amelie elicited a tiny whimper and the porcelain-faced woman turned upward. She stared into the darkness where Ben and Amelie lay motionless. They were frozen, scared to breathe.

The soldiers, noticing the mage's look, stood at the table and gripped their weapons while the captain dropped Meghan's body to the stone floor. He stepped delicately back from the growing pool of blood that surrounded her.

He looked at the woman.

She returned his look and made a sharp gesture with her hand.

To his men, the captain barked, "Prepare the bowl for a seeking. We should have enough material for one more. The mage will confirm where exactly Initiate Amelie is and we will go and finish this."

He paused, also scanning the darkness above. "Before we leave, search this place from top to bottom. Make sure we don't have any lurking rats."

The porcelain-faced woman sat at the soldier's table while they bustled about. She stared silently at the scattered food and drink they'd left beside their cards.

While the men were banging and rustling around pulling out supplies, Ben and Amelie slithered backward very carefully. Ben hoped the sounds the soldiers made would cover any inadvertent scuffs. Staying still wasn't an option. If the men searched upstairs, there was nowhere to hide. If the mage could magically locate them, Ben wanted to make damn sure they weren't sitting in the same building.

After a nervous minute, they were standing back at the window. Ben hoisted Amelie out then crawled after. Every fiber in his body was screaming at him to hurry.

On the boxes outside, he looked back at the slatted-wooden window and thought about closing it. Surely the soldiers would suspect someone had been there if he did not, but the risk of a squeak or creak was too great. The soldiers would know someone had been there, but they wouldn't know who.

Scampering down the boxes, Ben winced at each little sound they made. Luckily, the men inside didn't hear anything.

Once on the ground, he and Amelie set out at a fast jog.

Between breaths, he asked, "What is a seeking?"

"I don't know, but I can guess," she replied.

He picked up the pace and they sped around startled strangers who, still nervous from the demons, watched them pass into the darkness.

It was full night and the streets were sparsely lit. Ben knew they were leaving an easy to follow trail for anyone who had the inclination, but if this mage could seek them out somehow, it was pointless to try hiding. Both of them knew without needing to say it—they had to find Towaal. Quickly.

∼

DARTING ACROSS THE SQUARE, they headed to the darkened library building.

At Towaal's request, new guards had finally been posted there. The two men tried to move to block the door. Ben and Amelie flashed past them.

"Thanks. We know where we're going," he shouted as they blew by.

The men stood, startled.

Careening through the stacks and bashing into walls in the pitch-black building, Ben and Amelie burst down the narrow hall into the Librarian's private room. The Librarian's former room, Towaal had claimed it as her own.

She owlishly glanced up at them from a notebook, a single lamp lighting the small space.

Panting, Ben and Amelie both started talking at once.

Towaal held up a hand and frowned, clearly sensing their panic but obviously not understanding a thing they said.

Ben glanced at Amelie and nodded for her to tell it.

"We found Meghan, or maybe she found us," she began, "but she's dead. Killed by Sanctuary soldiers and...and a mage. A woman wearing a white porcelain mask."

"You're certain she's a mage?" asked Towaal, jumping to her feet.

"She must be," assured Amelie. "They spoke about her doing a seeking. The captain said she would be able to find me. Do you know what a seeking is?"

"I have not heard of a seeking," said Towaal, shaking her head, "but we should assume what you heard is correct, they will be able to find you. We've known this day would come."

Amelie nodded, still catching her breath.

Towaal darted around the room, gathering up documents and books.

While she worked, she barked out, "Why did they kill Meghan?"

"Meghan was supposed to be bait in a trap for us, I think," answered Ben. "They were upset she hadn't found us yet."

"Describe this woman's mask?" she asked next.

Ben did, detailing the creepiness of it. He then asked Towaal, "Who is she?"

The mage shrugged. "I am not aware of any mages at the Sanctuary who wear a mask of any type, much less the porcelain one you describe."

Snatching up a final book, she queried, "You said the soldiers were getting supplies for this seeking. What did they get?"

"We were sneaking away," said Amelie, "but before we lost sight, I saw a bowl, a small wooden box, a golden dagger..."

"And a red-colored vial," finished Ben, frowning.

"Oh, shit," muttered Amelie.

"What?" demanded Towaal.

"The vial," Amelie quaked. "It could have been blood."

"And?" replied Towaal curtly.

"Mistress Eldred had my blood. Could she have tracked me here with it?" asked Amelie.

"It's possible," allowed Towaal, a grim expression stealing across her face. "There is a theory that has floated around through the years...It doesn't matter. They tracked you somehow. We need to go. We need to get Rhys."

"Rhys—" started Ben.

"I know what his sword did to him," interrupted Towaal brusquely. "That is unfortunate, but the man must fight. On one hand, I can count the number of men in Alcott better than him with a blade. That's not counting his other abilities. If Eldred is here, we need him."

Ben gulped.

Towaal was finished packing and bustled out of the door. Ben and Amelie followed closely behind.

The guards had moved into the building, following Ben and Amelie. They stared in surprise as the trio rushed back out. The guards made no move to stop them.

Barreling across the square, Amelie asked Towaal, "Is Eldred dangerous? Can the two of us not face her?"

Towaal shouted over her shoulder, "She is very dangerous. She is very strong. Her knowledge of battle magic is undisputed. She has an, ah, affinity for causing pain and damage. I think that's why she spent so much time with the initiates. I do not care to face her."

Fifty strides from the keep, a raspy voice sounded in Ben's head, "Where are you running to, Karina?"

Towaal froze. She then pivoted on one heel to face the porcelain-faced mage.

Ben struggled to determine if he'd heard the voice or thought it.

"Eldred," Towaal stated flatly. It wasn't a question, but the porcelain mask bobbed in acknowledgement.

Eldred's voice, like a snake moving across a dry rock, sounded again. It was like a hollow echo inside Ben's skull. "Tsk, tsk. You know the Veil is looking for these two."

Ben watched warily. Behind Eldred, a dozen armed Sanctuary guards fanned out. He worried more about the mage. Something wasn't right with the masked woman, and after watching Meghan get murdered, he didn't think she had any intention of taking them alive.

Towaal didn't answer Eldred. Instead, she slipped a hand inside her pack and drew out an ancient, palm-sized copper disc and a black book with a purple emblem embossed on the cover.

Eldred's head turned to follow the motion as Towaal passed

Amelie the book and showed her the copper disc. "You see this. You understand why I am showing you?"

Amelie nodded.

"What is that?" sounded the voice in Ben's head. "What have you found? It feels foreign to me, old. Did you find something special up here near the Wilds? It doesn't feel like a weapon or a repository of power," declared the voice with a note of triumph. "What do you hope to do with it?"

Obviously sensing something was off, the pedestrians in the square were starting to disappear. They didn't know who the two women were or why the armed men were intently gripping their weapons. After the demon attack, no one needed to know. They didn't want trouble.

Ben eyed the walls of the keep. This far away, he wasn't sure if Rhymer's soldiers could tell what was happening.

Towaal responded, "You are correct, this is very old. It was created long before our time, before the Veil's time."

Eldred titled her head, listening. The porcelain mask stared at them, giving away no hint of what she was thinking.

Towaal took a deep breath then asked, "Would you like me to show you what it does?"

A flash and an awful ripping sound split the night air and a shimmering light flashed into view. A bestial shriek filled the square.

A dark shape shot out and one of Sanctuary guards went down, screaming.

Without looking back at them, Towaal shouted, "Run!"

Ben swept out his longsword and Amelie's gaze bored into her former teacher.

Eldred stared confused at the fallen guard and the black shape that was attacking him.

"Do not be stupid. There is something wrong here. I am sensing an unnatural power in that woman. Something dark and terrible. I can try to delay her and I have an idea to save myself, but not if I am protecting you as well," growled Towaal. "Run, and do not look back!"

Two more small creatures materialized in the square and leapt forward. The Sanctuary guards slashed and hacked at the little demons. Red and purple blood sprayed from torn flesh as the melee raged.

"What have you done! How did you do that?" demanded Eldred, the painful scrape of her voice screeched across Ben's conscious like nails on slate.

He and Amelie ran.

An explosion ripped behind them but neither spared a glance back. At a full sprint, they charged down a street and Ben steered them toward the southern gate, exactly where Eldred would expect them to go. With the ruckus in the square, he didn't think she'd be following immediately.

Cracks and booms rocked the city as the battle escalated. They could hear the roar of the demons. It sounded like a lot of them. Within heartbeats, shouts and alarm bells went off as Rhymer's worn-down military was called to action once again.

At the gate, the guards were milling about in confusion, clearly unsure if they should be keeping demons out or keeping people in.

Ben helped them.

"Demons in the square," he yelled as they approached. "Dozens of them. All swords to the square!"

The sergeant in command listened for a heartbeat. The sounds of battle confirmed what Ben told him. With a wave of his hand, his men left their posts and ran to face the threat.

Unmolested, Ben and Amelie slipped out the gate and raced into the darkness. A thin sliver of moonlight lit the way.

They made it to the forest surrounding Northport. Trees enveloped them like a comforting blanket. Ben didn't fear what was in the dark, he feared the white porcelain face behind them.

They kept running until a quarter league into the forest a

razor sharp pain stabbed into his skull. He stumbled forward onto his hands and knees. It pulsated down his body in waves, wracking him with violent shudders.

Slowly, the pain subsided. He saw Amelie lying beside him panting and gripping her head. Her eyes were squeezed tightly shut.

"The Rift," he mumbled. "It's like when we destroyed the Rift, but smaller."

Amelie scrunched up on her elbows and knees, whimpering softly.

"Maybe that means Eldred is dead. Maybe that means…" she choked, her thought left unfinished.

A thunderous boom shook the ground. Ben looked back and saw a violent plume of fire light the sky from Northport.

"She's not dead yet," he responded.

Amelie staggered to her feet. Through gritted teeth, she groaned, "We need to keep moving."

Motivated by terror, Ben and Amelie ran through the night. The thin, winter bare branches soared above their heads, letting in the cool light of the moon.

They had their weapons, two water skins, and the clothes on their backs. That was it. There was no food, but even if they had some, they wouldn't have taken time to stop and eat it.

"Do you think Towaal…" started Ben.

"I don't know," gasped Amelie. "Maybe."

Alive or dead, Ben didn't know which one he was asking.

By the time the sun peeked above the horizon, they were stumbling forward, exhausted. Ben could barely keep one foot in front of the other. No matter how frightened they were by Eldred, he knew they would have to rest.

In the pre-dawn light, he spied a thick stand of bushes fifty paces off the road. He dragged Amelie toward it. He hoped it was far enough away that casual passersby wouldn't notice two people sleeping underneath. He was so tired he didn't really care.

17

THE ROAD II

BEN JOLTED awake and looked about in a panic.

Slowly, his drumming heart slowed. Around him, the bright winter sun shone down on a quiet forest. The bush they were tucked under appeared undisturbed. Amelie still slumbered beside him. It was cold, early winter, but he'd been snug in his thick woolen cloak. Lying pressed next to Amelie, he'd retained enough heat to sleep, just like their first night outside of the City. As he sat up, the chill snuck in. He shivered, and his stomach rumbled to express its discomfort. It had been a day since he'd eaten. The excitement and panicked flight the night before took a lot out of him.

Amelie, stirred by his movement, opened her eyes. Her cheeks were rose kissed from the cold. Aside from a lone leaf sticking out of one side, her hair was delightfully mussed. He smiled down at her and she smiled back.

"Back on the road, no food, no direction," she mumbled sleepily. "We're starting to make a bad habit of this."

He nodded then scrambled out from under the bush to see what their surroundings looked like in the midday sun. He noticed immediately, there was no conveniently located tavern with keg full of ale and a hearty soup on the fire. He shook his head ruefully. Amelie was right, this was beginning to be a habit.

She crawled out and stood beside him.

"Do you think Towaal and Rhys are okay?" she asked.

"Towaal said she had a plan to escape," he responded. "I trust her. But the fire and explosions last night..."

Ben didn't continue. What was there to say? Hopefully their friends were all right, but there was nothing he or Amelie could do about it now.

He stretched and watched a bird flap away from a nearby nest. Ambling over to peek in, he saw half a dozen small eggs.

"I'm going to feel guilty about this all day," he grumbled before scooping the eggs out and splitting them with Amelie.

Cracking the small things open, they sucked out the raw yolk. He preferred his eggs fried with an ample shake of salt and a side of hot bacon, but you take what you can get.

Tossing the broken eggshells to the ground, Amelie asked, "Where to now?"

Ben sighed. "We don't know what happened last night in Northport. There is no way we can go back there. Issen is under siege and getting captured outside the walls wouldn't help your father. With it encircled, I don't think our odds of getting inside would be good. I'm sorry, Amelie, but I'm not sure what we can do right now to help your family."

Amelie nodded. She didn't want to say it out loud, but Ben was right, they didn't have the resources to assist Issen.

Ben continued, "The Sanctuary is likely to follow us anywhere we go, and most importantly, they now know we were in Northport. Even if Towaal defeated Eldred, they will know. They will be looking for us in Whitehall also, that is too obvious, maybe even Farview, for all I know. We have to do something unexpected, something they would never guess we will do."

Amelie moaned, "I was worried you would suggest this."

Ben grimaced apologetically. "We know there could be consequences to us destroying the Rift and we saw how easily Towaal opened a new one. There is only one group of people who may know how these things work. We have to understand what we unleashed by destroying the first one. We have to tell them about it. The demon threat is real. Someone has to confront it," he insisted.

Amelie adjusted her sword belt, wiggling her two scabbards so the rapier and dagger rested easily on her hips.

"Lead the way then," she said. "I don't know how to get to Irrefort."

18

REVIEWS, ACKNOWLEDGEMENTS, AND NEWSLETTER

I STARTED WRITING AS A HERMIT, squirreled away in my office during the dark hours when my family was sleeping. For three years, only my wife was aware that I was working on a book. She was suspicious. My previous hobby, painting, ended with one still-blank canvas. My mom was the second person to know. I told her I wrote a book about a week before Benjamin Ashwood was published.

Since then, as you know, I've gone public. The encouragement, positive reviews, and comments I've gotten have been amazing. I'm not sure I would have gotten around to writing the second book without that. So, thank you early readers for keeping this alive.

And thank you to my wife and family for giving me the space to keep going. I wrote Endless Flight in six months, which was six times faster than Benjamin Ashwood. What I did on my time for the first book, I did on their time for the second. My wife has been remarkably understanding. She only occasionally gives me The Look. The kids though, are responsible for almost all of my interruptions. Wait, why am I thanking those guys? Let's move on. Outside of the family, I need to thank James Z for his feedback on Book 1 and his input on Book 2. In a few quick e-mails, he saved you all from reading some ridiculous and physically implausible sword fighting scenes.

I had the same professional team involved with Endless Flight as I did with Benjamin Ashwood. My cover and social media package were designed by Milos from Deranged Doctor Design (www.derangeddoctordesign.com). Milos did a great job of creating a cover that matches the feel of the book. And inside the cover, Nicole Zoltack did great work proof-reading (www.nicolezoltack.com). She's proven that I know almost nothing about the English language. Tantor Media is my audiobook publisher. After reading this, I'm certain you'll need an audiobook too. They can be found on all major online outlets. Finally, Eric Michael Summerer is the narrator for the audiobooks and he did truly amazing work.

Thank you for reading my book,
AC

To stay updated and find out when the next book is due, or to receive **FREE Benjamin Ashwood short stories**, I suggest signing up for my Newsletter. In addition to the short stories, I stick in author interviews, news & events, and whatever else I think may be of interest. One e-mail a month, no SPAM, that's a promise. Website and Newsletter Sign up: https://www.accobble.com/newsletter/

Of course I'm on **Facebook** too: https://www.facebook.com/ACCobble/

If you want the really exclusive, behind the scenes stuff, then

Patreon is the place to be. There are a variety of ways you can support me, and corresponding rewards where I give back! Find me on **Patreon**: https://www.patreon.com/accobble

DARK TERRITORY: Benjamin Ashwood Book 3 is available now! You can find it at nearly any online book retailer.

Made in United States
Orlando, FL
28 April 2022

17303998R10240